ALL THE STARS
IN THE
HEAVENS

ALL THE STARS IN THE HEAVENS

★ *A Novel* ★

ADRIANA
TRIGIANI

HARPER

An Imprint of HarperCollins*Publishers*

All the Stars in the Heavens is a work of fiction. While many of the characters herein lived and worked during the Golden Age of Hollywood in and around the movie studios in Los Angeles, California, and some, like Loretta Young and Clark Gable, appeared in films, the scenes, events, moments, and leaps of storytelling exist only in the imagination of the author. Accordingly, *All the Stars in the Heavens* should be read solely as a work of fiction, not as a history or biographical account of the lives of any of the artisans who made movies, including the actors, their agents, bosses, secretaries, or family members. The author's intent was to create a world to enchant and entertain, much like the fictional stories dramatized by the stars on the silver screen in the early days of Hollywood.

HarperCollins books may be purchased for educational, business, or sales promotional use. For information, please e-mail the Special Markets Department at SPsales@harpercollins.com.

Endpaper image © John Springer Collection/CORBIS
Photograph of John Clark Gable courtesy of Sister Agnes Eugenia S. J. and author's private collection.

FIRST EDITION

Designed by Jaime Putorti

Library of Congress Cataloging-in-Publication Data has been applied for.

ISBN: 978-0-06-231919-7
ISBN: 978-0-06-06243085-4 (International edition)
ISBN: 978-0-06-244072-3 (Signed edition)

15 16 17 18 19   OV/RRD   10 9 8 7 6 5 4 3 2 1

IN MEMORY OF MARY J. FARINO

ALL THE STARS
IN THE
HEAVENS

PROLOGUE

⁂

OCTOBER 2000

A cold gust of wind sounded like a faraway train whistle as it blew through South Bend that morning. Winter had arrived early in Indiana, in the middle of October beneath a cloudless sky.

There was proof of it everywhere.

The mighty Saint Joe River had frost on its banks as it twisted past Saint Mary's College in hungry green torrents. Overhead the sun was centered in the sky like a yellow diamond on blue satin. The farm fields surrounding the school were flat and fallow, faded to a dull gold that would soon turn white with the first snow. A tall heap of cornhusks burned in a nearby field; by the time the smoke reached Saint Mary's, its scent was sweet.

Roxanne Chetta hung her head out of a window in the art studio in Moreau Hall and took a slow, final drag off her sunrise cigarette. As she exhaled, the smoke burst into small blue curls before disappearing into the cold air. She put the cigarette out on the windowsill, snapped the window shut, and shivered. She pulled the hot pink bandana out of her hair and retied it, anchoring her bounty of wild curls off her face so she could see.

Roxanne stood back and squinted at her senior arts project, an ambitious painting, twelve feet high and fifteen feet wide. She had painted it over the course of a year, stealing late nights alone in the studio between the janitor's final rounds and the first class of the morning to make perfect what she knew could never be.

At twenty-one, she was a young artist, but she was a practical one. As the sun shifted in the skylight, the studio was drenched in color, a sort of woolly pink. Roxanne saw something new in the painting, or in this instance, something to refine. She patted the pockets of her overalls, searching for the palette knife.

Sister Agnes Eugenia, around eighty years old, observed the art from the open door. She wore the traditional habit of the order of Saint Joseph, a billowing dark blue tunic with a wimple attached to a blue veil, and a silver crucifix around her neck. She placed her hands in the deep habit pockets. "What is it?"

"It's a blizzard," Roxanne said as she found the knife in her back pocket.

"I can see that. But where?"

"Bellingham, Washington." Roxanne stepped close to the painting and, using the the blade, followed an edge of a wide brushstroke, lifting off a thin layer, refining a line. She wiped the knife on her pant leg, leaving a white smear of paint.

The painting, depicting the woods of Mount Baker in snow, was blanched and textured, speckled with painterly shadows of gray. The trees were layered in line, form, and depth in shades of white from milk to chalk. Roxanne had painted diamond dust, snow that does not cling but blows through in a haze of glitter, with tiny pointillist dots of silver, barely discernible on the field of white. The painting was an expanse of stillness. There was a purity to the image, a grace that comes when a place is rendered sacred upon discovery.

"You're from the Northwest?"

"Nope, never been there," Roxanne admitted.

"Then how do you know how to paint it?"

"Well, that's the point. The *how*. The painting is an interpretation of a story I heard as a child that I've been told is true, but to me it's just a dream. I tried to paint the past, if anybody can actually do that."

"So you made it up."

"I guess I really wanted to prove Einstein's theory that imagination is more important than knowledge."

"Is it?"

"I think so. Don't you? You've never seen heaven, but you believe in it. And from the looks of your habit, you've staked your life on it."

"You're blunt."

"I'm from Brooklyn. Blunt was invented in Red Hook."

"Yes, well, here at Saint Mary's in 1962, when I was dean of students, that attitude would have put you in detention."

"Thank God it's not 1962," Roxanne said without taking her eyes off the painting. "I do not like to be confined."

"That's obvious."

"What are you doing up so early, Sister?"

Sister Agnes folded her arms into her sleeves. "If you must know, I'm having a spiritual crisis."

"Oh, Sister, if you're having one of those, come sit by me." Roxanne sat on a work stool and pulled up a folding chair for the nun. "I love a lapse of any kind."

"Something tells me you're the wrong person to confide in," Sister said as she sat down.

"Probably. But right now, I'm all you've got. Father Krauss is doing laps over at the Regina pool, and he won't be finished for an hour. Talk to me."

Sister Agnes Eugenia shifted in the chair. She patted her crucifix, and took a deep breath. "I spent my whole life in anticipation of everlasting life, the eternal, heaven, whatever you want to call it. I've lived in service to the idea of it, and guess what? Now I can't see it. I thought when I got closer to dying, I would be able to see it."

"Aren't nuns supposed to have blind faith?"

"Supposedly."

Roxanne picked up a can of turpentine and a rag. She dabbed a corner of the painting where a drop of paint had dripped. "If you don't mind me prying, why are you having a crisis?"

"I went to the doctor. Evidently, I have a bad heart."

"A nun with a bad heart. That sounds like a logline on a poster for a potboiler from Warner Brothers in the forties."

"You know about old movies?"

"It's a family thing. I'm the great-niece of Luca Chetta. He was a scenic artist in the movies, back in the day—they called him a scene painter. He got his start during the golden age of Hollywood."

"The best movies were made during that era."

"I think so. My uncle Luca knew all the stars. They acted, and he painted."

"So art is in your veins."

"I like to think so."

"So why Bellingham, and why a blizzard?"

"*The Call of the Wild.*"

"Clark Gable and Loretta Young," the nun mused.

"Uncle Luca painted the cabin and the saloon. And while he was painting, he fell in love. He told my mom the story behind the movie so many times when she was growing up that she passed it along to me. It's a love story."

"How grand." Sister leaned back in the chair. For years she had been the nun who chose the films the order watched on Friday nights. Sister Agnes liked movies made before 1950, and very few thereafter. "So what's the story?"

"Oh, Sister, it's a doozy. It's right here on the canvas." Roxanne stood and pointed at the artwork. "You see the snow."

"I do."

"And I see snow. But I also see adventure. Risk. Mayhem. Mirth. Romance. And sex."

"Sounds like an epic."

"With a secret. A secret hatched in a blizzard."

Roxanne had painted smatterings of Tiepolo blue on the frosted roots of the trees, revealing something hidden deep in the earth like rare truffles. The meaning of Roxanne's painting was in the blue.

Just as a blank page is eventually filled with letters in blue ink, those letters become words, which become sentences, which become the scene, which becomes the story that carries the truth.

The truth is where the story begins.

The story isn't the art, nor its players, nor the paint, the technique, or the interpretation. The feelings are the art. The rest is just the way in.

1

1917

Vine Street looked like a painting that morning.

The sun blinked behind a roll of fog over the Hollywood Hills, turning the world into a watercolor still life. A row of pepper trees on either side of the wide street shimmered in the light, their mossy leaves tinged in yellow spun like coins as a breeze blew through their branches.

The delivery boy took a deep breath, inhaling the scents of tuberose and gardenia from the flower arrangement he carried. The spray was almost as tall as he was, and certainly wider. Long stems of white delphinium framed the bouquet, their blossoms shaking like bells as he walked.

The boy noticed a lemon grove next to the studio and thought about picking a few later to take home to his mother, who would surely peel the skin into curls, soak them in boiling water, then roll them in sugar until they were candy sweet. Oranges, lemons, and limes were ripe for the picking; between the sunshine and the citrus fruit, even the poorest children looked robust.

California was a dreamscape in 1917, the emerald Pacific lapping at its jagged coast with crests of white foam. The land was rocky, the air dry, the foliage green, and the sky blue.

There was ongoing speculation about undiscovered gold mines and untapped veins of silver ore deep in the earth. On the surface, railways connected the west to everyone else, zigzagging across the state like zippers. As far as the eye could see, the landscape was filled with potential.

Show business was exploding. No longer were live theater, burlesque, and vaudeville the backbone of American entertainment; pennies weren't dropped at the arcades or buckets of silver in the nickelodeon. Now there were moving pictures, and audiences could not get enough of them.

Barns were raised, not to house cattle and horses but to host actors, cameras, sets, and lights. California's clement weather meant round-the-clock production, and producers reveled in the possibilities for profit.

If you were beautiful, young, and lucky, you might make it big in pictures, but if you couldn't catch a break, you could serve the anointed whose dreams *had* come true. You might cook and clean for the stars, drive them to the studio, sew their costumes, paint scenery, style their hair, or write their scenarios. You could be useful here. There were many stories to tell, and many hands needed to bring them to life.

The barn doors of the Jesse L. Lasky Feature Play Company rolled open to reveal a movie sound stage in full production.

The clatter of making a silent picture was deafening. Orders were shouted over the clang of metal, the drone of machines, and the screech of a rip saw. As the orchestra warmed up, the haphazard sound of scales, the pluck of violin strings, the low bellows of a trumpet, and the bright tinkle of piano keys underscored the din.

The air was thick with the scents of sawdust, tobacco, and fresh paint.

The boy observed the mayhem. It was as if he were peering into the gears of a Swiss watch, its workings synchronized on a vast concrete floor cluttered with equipment. The crew, in a perpetual hurry, rushed past him carrying all elements of spectacle, from costumes to props.

His boss at the flower shop had said, "Time is money," but here, they really meant it.

Overhead, electricians atop the steel flyspace sorted cables and manned the rigs to operate the lights. The crew dropped wires through the open mesh like marionette strings. A gaffer scaled a ladder to flip the metal barn doors on a light.

Painted backdrops hung neatly from the ceiling like decks of cards, ready to descend with the hoist and release of a pulley. The soles of the carpenters' workboots on the open metal grid above looked like brown tiles to him. Below them, a stage manager hollered as the crew hoisted mattresses into the air with military precision and dropped them in place on wooden boards that faked box springs as set decorators moved in to dress the beds.

Where there had been nothing, there now was a world.

Two men rolled a flat on wheels into position. It was painted with trompe l'oeil bricks and a sign that read CHILDREN'S WARD. A scene painter followed, dabbing at the lettering until it was just right.

The movie camera, a black box with a thick glass lens, was centered on long black sticks in the middle of a platform on wheels. Under a sheath of midnight-blue velvet, the operators removed large wheels of film from tin canisters and snapped them into place. A cameraman stepped onto the lift and repositioned the camera. Slowly, like a barge, the rig and the cameraman floated into place in front of the hospital set.

Nearby a young actor, dressed as a patient, sat in front of a mirror as a makeup artist dipped his thumbs in gray powder and filled in the sockets under the boy's eyes to make him look ill.

An extra dressed as a doctor buttoned his lab coat, while a gaggle of young actresses, one more stunning and white-hot blond than the next, stood in their satin slips, smoothing their stockings and pulling nurses' uniforms over their creamy shoulders. The delivery boy watched them through the flowers, knowing he shouldn't. A pretty nurse winked at him as she snapped the garter of her stocking. "Are those for me, squirt?"

The ladies laughed as the boy backed away in fear. A rolling rack of costumes careened through like a runaway train car, just missing him.

The director, Robert Z. Leonard, redwood tall with the face of a bulldog, paced, studying the scenario typed on yellow paper as though it were a bad headline on the front page of the *Los Angeles Tribune*. He was thirty-five years old but had the wizened countenance of a much older man, a man with too much responsibility and not enough time.

Behind the camera, musicians took their seats. They wore casual open-collared shirts and gabardine trousers. The trombonist wore a natty panama hat tilted back on his head so the brim wouldn't interfere with the slide bow of his horn. They chatted about upcoming gigs as the conductor flipped through his sheet music.

"Hey, mister, is this where they're filming *The Primrose Ring*?" the boy asked.

"In all its glory," the conductor replied.

The delivery boy looked around. Everyone on the sound stage had a purpose; remembering his own, he hollered, "Flowers for Miss Murray." Louder still, "Flowers for Miss Murray."

Off in a corner, the actress Mae Murray took a long, slow drag off her cigarette, exhaling puffs of white smoke into the air that formed a pompadour cloud over her platinum blond hair, tucked neatly under a nurse's cap.

"Over here, kid." She waved and relaxed into the rest chair, a contraption that actors could lean against without wrinkling their costumes. The slant board had a pillow behind her neck covered in satin, another at her waist. Two flat arm boards kept the sleeves neat.

Mae wore a crisp white nurse's uniform, and her face was covered with a thick paste of pale makeup to match. Her blue eyes were rimmed in black kohl, like sapphires set in onyx. Petite, with lovely legs and delicate hands, Mae knew how to smoke without disturbing her carefully drawn bee-stung lips, which had become her signature. It isn't many things that make a movie star memorable, it's usually one thing; for Mae Murray, it was her lips.

"From Mr. Lasky, ma'am," the boy said as he wedged the flowers onto a nearby table filled with similar arrangements. He wanted to tell Miss Murray that he loved her in the movies, but he was overwhelmed. This was the first time he had ever delivered flowers to a star, and he was awestruck. Perched on the slant board, she looked almost as big as she did on the movie screen.

"You tell Mr. Lasky he's a peach." Mae handed the boy a dollar, which was more than his weekly pay.

"Thank you, Miss Murray!" The boy tipped his hat and ran for daylight as a dresser lifted the white shoes off Mae's feet.

"That's better." Mae wriggled her toes in the thick white stockings. "I've got big feet."

"I've seen bigger," the dresser lied.

"Not on a frame this small. They're freaks of nature. Look at 'em." Mae twirled her foot in a full circle. "Canoes."

"These shoes are too small," the dresser admitted. "But they're all we've got."

"You don't see the shoes." Robert Leonard handed Mae her script.

"If I wasn't married to the director, I'd demand shoes that fit," Mae teased.

"Darling, you know about budgets."

"Yeah, yeah. Kiss me, Bobby." She puckered her lips. Her husband kissed her. Mae flipped through the script. "Lot of weeping and wailing here."

"Mr. Leonard? We need you to choose the background." Ernie Traxler, the assistant director, an energetic young man of twenty-four, eager to impress the boss, handed the director a list of names.

Robert scanned the list and handed it back to Ernie. "You choose them for me. You did well with the town-hall scene."

"Thank you, Mr. Leonard. I'll take care of it." Ernie smiled.

"See you on the set, hon," Robert said to his wife.

"Miss Murray. Your lunch." A runner approached with a tray.

"What've we got today?"

"Ham sandwich and lemonade," the boy said as he hooked a tray onto the arm of the slant board. The costumer draped a large, starched linen napkin over Mae's costume to catch any crumbs.

"I should be eating a rare steak and raw tomato. That's how Mary Pickford stays slim."

"B-but you ordered . . . ," the boy stammered.

"Teasing ya. Ham for the ham, honey." Mae smiled as she lifted the bread and removed the meat. She ate half a slice of the bread sparingly buttered.

The crew dropped a row of leather harnesses covered in beige velvet and attached to long ropes secured with iron bocklebee clasps from the overhead grid. Ernie Traxler led a group of extras dressed as fairies onto the set. The men wore thick green leotards with chest armor made of silk leaves; the women, pale green tulle skirts with satin vests.

Four little girls dressed in taupe undershirts and leotards, with a flounce of green tulle tied at the waist, were led to the dangling yokes. One girl began to whimper fearfully, and two cowered away from the harnesses. But the fourth girl raised her arms eagerly.

"Uncle Ernie!" She smiled. "Up!"

"You're a good girl, Gretch."

Ernie helped hoist his four-year-old niece into her harness. Gretchen grinned, extending her legs behind her and her arms to her sides, as though she were in flight. Gretchen began to swing in the harness as the crew loaded the rest of the girls into theirs. Two of her fellow fairies began to cry, the first rumbles of a revolt.

"Look at Gretchen, girls. She doesn't cry."

Gretchen was a few feet off the ground. "Higher!" she commanded. The stagehand guided the rope on the pulley heavenward as Gretchen made her ascent. The higher the girl went, the happier she was.

Gretchen's cousin Carlene, emboldened by her cousin's courage, raised her arms. Ernie hoisted his daughter into the harness. She did not smile, nor did she extend her arms; instead she kept her eyes on Gretchen, gripping the straps with her hands as though she were under a parachute.

Mae Murray looked up at the children as they hovered over the crowd. Mae's highest dream was to become a mother, but it hadn't happened. Doctors had advised her to adopt, believing that she could not have a child, but she was only in her early thirties, and she held out hope that there would be at least one baby for Robert and for her.

Gently the crew raised the children in the harnesses to meet Gretchen, who was now about ten feet in the air. The first assistant director placed the extras beneath the fairies as the cameras pushed in to film the dream scene.

Gretchen dropped from the sky in a flourish. She had blond ring-lets and pink cheeks. Her costume sparkled with flecks of diamond dust, and woven through her hair was a garland of tiny stars, a crown fit for a princess. She extended her arms and smiled, looking in the direction of the camera, but not into the lens. Mae shook her head. "Who's the blondie?"

"That's my niece," Ernie Traxler said. "Gretchen Young."

"She'll have my job one day," Mae said as she stepped off the rest chair and entered the scene.

2

Alda Ducci gently bathed a newborn baby girl with a soft cotton cloth. She dipped the fabric into the clean, warm water, wringing it in one hand while keeping a firm hold on the infant.

"*Che bella*," she whispered.

A nun helped the new mother into a fresh gown and rolled up the sheets, replacing them with clean white ones. She folded the old gown, rolled the sheets into a tight bundle, and turned to go, closing the door gently behind her.

All evidence of the birth had been removed quickly and neatly.

"How is she, Sister?" the baby's mother asked.

"She's perfect," Alda assured her. Alda wasn't a nun yet but a novice in training, but to the unwed girls who gave birth at Saint Elizabeth's, they all looked alike. The nuns and novices wore the same black work dresses, with a gray apron tied tightly over the top, their hair pinned back by a black veil.

At twenty-five, Alda was ten years older than the mother of the baby.

Saint Elizabeth's Infant Hospital was a home for unwed mothers with a floor that served as a hospital where the girls delivered their babies. The home was run by the Daughters of Charity of Saint Vincent de Paul, a Roman Catholic order of nuns with deep roots in

Italy, devoted to the service of the poor. Their convent, chapel, ward, and hospital were contained in a large red brick building, situated in the heart of San Francisco. The operation blended into the city block without notice. Inside, there was rarely an empty bed.

The light from the window threw a golden glow on the infant. Outside, the tap of car horns at the corner of Masonic Avenue seemed to herald the arrival of the girl.

"May I hold her?"

"It's better if you don't," Alda said softly as she swaddled the infant.

"Please." The young girl's brown eyes filled with tears, her cheeks flushed with defiance. She straightened her dressing gown and pushed herself up in the bed. She sat up straight, to show Alda that she was up to the task of holding her own baby.

Alda had helped deliver over a hundred babies at Saint Elizabeth's. She was well schooled in the rules of the birthing ward and her religious order. She was never to hand the infant over to the mother, only to the nursery, where the baby had already been legally adopted through an outside service. In fact, at this moment, the baby's new parents were waiting behind the wall to claim her.

But in Alda's experience as a midwife, not one young mother had ever asked to hold her baby. Most of the girls didn't want to see their babies, or learn the sex. Some would quietly ask if the infant was "all right," which was usually the extent of their curiosity.

Alda believed their indifference masked a deeper pain, one that she prayed would lessen in the years to come. Most of the girls were eager to be done with the ordeal of childbirth and return to life as it had been before the baby. Their deepest hope was to forget their stay at Saint Elizabeth's altogether.

The nuns tried to make the girls' stay in the home pleasant. They also did their best to encourage the girls to pray and develop a spiritual life. Every day, the girls were required to take in some sun, walk, and pray in the garden behind Saint Elizabeth's.

The meditation garden was enclosed by a tall wooden fence. The nuns had planted trumpet vines and morning glories that climbed up the walls in thick clusters of orange and purple. You could not see in or out, and the cascading water of the fountains helped drown out the street sounds. The novices grew roses that bloomed bountifully in shades of blood red, the exact color of the leather that bound their missals.

A statue of the Blessed Mother Mary was positioned in the center of the garden, surrounded by benches. In a corner, a fountain of Saint Elizabeth carved from Italian marble attracted birds and penitents who knelt and prayed at a wrought iron kneeler.

Serious contemplation, daily mass, the celebration of feast days, and holy days of obligation took place inside in the chapel on the main floor. Votive candles made by the nuns from fresh sheets of beeswax were replenished at the shrine daily, as the girls burned through them, petitioning God and the saints to grant them forgiveness for the act that had brought them here, or a reprieve for what lay ahead. A gold vase at the foot of the altar was filled with fresh roses from the garden.

There was order to life inside Saint Elizabeth's, and a certain serene beauty.

As much as the nuns attempted to make the place warm and inviting, this was a home for unwed mothers. It wasn't a place to be young and socialize, nor was it meant to live on in their memories. This was a place to hide.

Over time, Alda observed that there were ultimately two kinds of girls at Saint Elizabeth's: those who were eager to please, and the rest, who were already jaded, turned hard-hearted by fate. The latter carried their stories in their souls, of their innocence lost or taken without their consent. They handled the long nine months like a prison sentence, knowing there was nothing to look forward to once they were free to go. Others, despite their predicament, remained cheerful, completing their schoolwork and reading the latest pulp novels, which were passed around the ward until the bindings fell away from use.

Many girls had been abandoned in the outside world, shunned by their families, so they found Saint Elizabeth's on their own. Mother Superior had a soft spot for desperate girls who knocked on the door, and would find a way to take them in. Other girls had been sent by their parents, who were forced to remove their daughters from their homes lest they taint the family name. The girls wrestled with the loss of their reputations, their dreams, and their babies. At night, the self-recrimination would find a voice, and the wailing from the beds became so loud and mournful that Alda would escape to the garden to collect herself.

While they had months to think about what brought them here, the girls dared not think too much about what would happen after the birth of their babies. They had been treated well at this halfway house, and if that was any indication of the way the order handled the adoptions, they trusted that their babies were going to good homes. However, once they signed in for their stay at Saint Elizabeth's, they had no choice in their babies' future.

The girls had each other, and while there were moments of camaraderie and seeds of true friendship, there was nothing carefree about their days in the home. The mood was generally somber. Once the girls went into labor and delivered, they left soon after, without goodbyes or a celebration or an exchange of addresses to keep in touch.

Before lights-out, the novices handed out tall glasses of fresh milk to the girls. Despite the want of the Great Depression, the girls were well fed. Much of the food was donated, some left in baskets on the stoop of the convent. Local farmers delivered fresh eggs, cheese, and milk. The nuns made bread. There was plenty of fresh fruit and vegetables. The nuns served fish from the local wharf, and sometimes on Sundays, there was a beef stew or a pork roast.

At night Alda sat with the girls and read aloud to them. A few would turn away, wishing for a radio instead, but Alda persisted. She read from *Jane Eyre*, *Pride and Prejudice*, and even Edna Ferber's popular novel *Showboat*, so the girls might feel that they were still part of the outside world.

Alda tried to lift their spirits, to make them laugh. She fretted about their physical well-being and worried about their souls, knowing that shame might turn them inward and bitter, leading them to make worse choices than the ones that had brought them here.

Some girls were so naive, they weren't even sure how their pregnancies had happened, while others wanted to erase the memory of how they had. Their shame bound them together, and Alda shared it. She had a role in what seemed to be an impossible situation for the mothers and their babies. There was no relief at Saint Elizabeth's, only adoption as an alternative to the deep sorrow and regret of the mother. There were stories of stillborn babies, lost and mourned, and the occasional father of a baby showing up to steal his girlfriend away and marry her, but they were the rare exceptions. Mostly, these healthy young women gave birth to robust babies who were delivered to their overjoyed adoptive parents.

"Please, Sister. My baby," the girl implored her.

Alda lifted the newborn, shiny and pink, swaddled in a white cotton blanket, and held her close. The scent of the baby's skin was sweet and clean, like the petals of an orchid. Instead of placing the baby in a bassinette and walking out of the room to deliver the baby to the nursery, as was the standard protocol, Alda turned and brought the infant to her mother. Alda's conscience told her that it was wrong to keep the infant from her mother, no matter the rules.

The girl cradled her newborn baby in her arms. "Thank you, Sister."

The girl had long black hair; the baby had a shock of the same. The girl smiled and tenderly kissed her daughter.

"What's today?" the girl asked. "The date?"

"March 17, 1934."

"Saint Patrick's Day!"

"A feast day."

"I've always loved the name Patricia. I'm going to call her Patricia."

Alda stood by the side of the bed, every muscle in her body feeling depleted, as if she had experienced the labor pains herself. Alda had wiped the girl's brow, held her hand, encouraged her, and rubbed her feet through the long labor. She had indulged the girl's dream of keeping the baby, and let her ruminate aloud as to how this goal could be achieved.

As Alda coached the girl through childbirth, she never mentioned the worthy couple waiting outside to adopt her baby and take her to their home, nor did she share that the couple had impressed the adoption service who assigned the babies to their new families. Alda's job was to help deliver a healthy baby to her adopted parents. Alda had seen the file, with a handwritten note attached. It said:

Preference: girl
Status: urgent

Alda was never to show emotion, but this morning she couldn't help it. Something was different about this baby. Every birth is magical, but this one had *intent*. This baby was wanted. She had a name.

Mother Mary Justine, the superior of the convent, pushed through the door. A tugboat of a woman, dressed in gray, she moved through the hospital like a spinning tire.

"Oh dear," she said when she saw the girl holding her baby.

Mother Mary was a lifer. She had joined the order at the age of twelve. Now in her sixties, she moved at a clip and ran the home with authority and precision. It was as if keeping the place on schedule and moving forward would somehow make up for the despair that brought the girls to her office in the first place.

"Sister Alda, what is going on here?" Mother demanded.

"She insisted, Mother."

"I want to keep my baby, Mother Superior. I've named her Patricia."

Mother Mary placed the file on the nightstand, buried her hands deep into her sleeves, and went to the foot of the bed. "You know this isn't up to me. Your mother wants you at home. You have four younger brothers and sisters, and your mother tells me another is on the way. She needs your help."

"Please." The girl began to weep.

"Your father wants you to come home and put all of this behind you."

The girl clutched her baby and looked at Alda. "Will you help me?"

The girl's plea seared Alda's heart like a silver arrow. Surely there was one small room with one crib somewhere where this girl could live and work and raise her daughter.

Alda turned and faced her superior. "Mother, is there something we can do? Can we send her to the Carmelites in San Paolo? Or even to the Mother House in Los Angeles?"

The girl's face opened up with beatific hope. "Please! I can take care of her. I've done a good job with my brothers and sisters. I'll go anywhere you say, as long as you let her stay with me. There isn't anything I wouldn't do for her. She's *mine*."

Mother touched Alda on the shoulder. Alda moved off to stand by the windows. She had violated every aspect of her training, and she knew it. She had indulged the girl; she had not discouraged her from keeping her baby.

Alda tried to get control of her feelings, but couldn't. She began to weep as though the loss was her own. She had spent her youth with the Daughters of Charity, and she was feeling little of it. She lifted her apron and tried to dry her tears with the hem of it.

"There's a lovely family who will take good care of your baby," Mother Mary said gently.

"I won't give her up!" The girl pulled her baby close.

Mother kept her voice low and even. "Someday, when the time is right and you are older, you will meet a good man, marry him, and have many children. You are healthy and strong, and you will have everything you dream of."

Dreams seem so beside the point in this moment, Alda thought.

"I won't have *her*." The girl looked at Alda again in desperation. "She'll never find me."

Alda turned and faced the Mother Superior. "Please, Mother. Isn't there something we can do?"

"Sister Alda. Go," Mother Mary ordered.

"Don't let them take her away from me!" The girl wept.

Alda bowed her head obediently and went out into the hallway. She leaned against the cold tile wall, too exhausted to move and too disappointed to pray.

A nun pushed a bassinette with another newborn from a different birthing room to the nursery. The hallway was still. All that could be heard was the soft sweep of the nun's skirts as she passed, and the cooing of the baby, who sounded like a bird.

———

The ruby-red roses, their petals clustered tight, tilted up toward the sun. Alda clipped the long stems at the base and laid them gently in the cutting basket, just as her mother had done when Alda was a girl in Italy.

Mother Superior took a deep breath from the bench across the garden. She tucked her rosary beads into her pocket and made her way to Alda.

"Need a hand?" she asked.

"I'm almost done, Mother."

"You have enough for the chapel."

"Yes, Mother. And enough for the table in the foyer."

"Sister, come and sit with me."

Alda took a place on the bench next to the Mother Superior.

Mother Superior looked Alda directly in the eyes and held her gaze. "After much prayer, I'm going to ask you to leave us."

Alda's mind raced. Yes, she had thoughts of leaving St. Elizabeth's, and occasionally doubts, but after a good night's rest, she always changed her mind and decided to renew her commitment to the unwed mothers and their babies. She had prayed, and the answer had come. She was to serve others as a nun. The message had been clear. "Mother, I don't want to go."

"It isn't your decision."

"You've asked me to be obedient. I honored God's will. I'm doing the work I was born to do."

"Sister." Mother sighed. "You can't plead your way into staying. My decision is final," the nun said wearily.

Alda felt a fury rise in her, one that she had kept buried deep whenever the work in the convent frustrated her. "What have I done?"

"You have served us well."

"So why am I being punished?"

"This isn't the right path for you."

"I believe it is." Alda raised her voice. "If the Daughters of Charity don't want me, I'll join another order. "

"And eventually you will come to the same conclusion I have, and so will they."

"Mother, you must reconsider."

"You're not being punished, Alda." This was the first time that Mother had referred to her by her birth name. "This work isn't for you."

"I've worked hard."

"It's not the work, it's you. You imagine a happy ending to every story. We can't encourage that here. This is a place of misery—"

Alda tried to interrupt the nun, but Mother Superior stopped her.

"—though there are cheery moments. I know. I've witnessed them. You want the girls to be happy, but it isn't to be. No matter what we do, we can only get their minds off their troubles for a short while. We can fix them up and send them back out into the world to try again, but we can't make them happy."

"Then what is our purpose?"

"To get them through this time." Mother Superior leaned forward. "Look, Alda. I'm old. I've got white hair under this wimple, but a couple years ago it was as red as your roses. I tell myself that our work is God's work, but I'm not so sure. I have my own doubts. Do you think I wanted to take that baby away from her mother? It's a horrible thing to do. I tell myself it's for the best, but I don't always believe it. I want you to get out while you're young. You have a chance to build a life that has meaning. You're joyful. So go and be happy."

"I don't have your doubts."

"Not yet. If you stayed here long enough, you would have them too. I was like you. I thought I could fix it all by becoming a nun and devoting my life to this work. But I couldn't, and you can't, and the little girl jumping rope on DeSales Street as we sit here who is about to get the calling to be a nun can't fix it either. All we can do is hold a girl's hand and get her through the pain. That's our role."

"Why did you wait until now to tell me?"

"I was hoping that things would change. That you would change. But six years in and you're still trying to change people. I used to have hope too. I don't want you to lose yours. And the truth is, I thought you might transform over time, and toughen up."

"I've worked hard to keep my heart open because so many of the girls we serve have already given up. Sometimes my belief in them is all they have."

The Mother Superior looked off in the distance. It appeared she might change her mind, but as quickly as a cloud moved across the sun, she strengthened her resolve to release Alda from the novitiate.

"Something came across my desk, and I thought of you." Mother reached into her pocket and removed a letter from the envelope. "There's a job. A good job. Father McNally from the Church of the Good Shepherd in Los Angeles wrote to me. He's looking for a young lady who is good with a needle and thread, and who can write. You have excellent penmanship, and you're a crack seamstress—every baby leaves Saint Elizabeth's with an embroidered blanket."

"If I'm going to work for a priest, I'd rather be a nun."

"You won't be working for the church, but for a family. I'm told this is a fine Catholic family, very devout. You would be a secretary to one of the daughters. She works in pictures. Her name is Loretta Young."

In the recesses of her memory, Alda remembered the name. Perhaps she had seen her on the cover of one of the fan magazines that the girls passed around.

"I'm sending you to the family today."

Alda thought about her fellow novices who had left the order before her, dismissed in secret, banished at night. It was always the same. There were hushed conversations behind closed doors, followed by lonely footsteps, and the creak of the doors as the novices who remained looked out to see who was let go. The novice's room would be empty, save a blanket folded on her cot and an empty washbasin. There was never a meeting, a discussion, or a proper farewell. The novices who remained were left to fret about the transgression that led to dismissal and agonize over their own shortcomings.

A convent runs on two kinds of fear: fear of failing God and fear of dismissal.

Alda would join the novices who failed, those who would never take final vows, young women who had broken the long line of the gray habit. There was mystery in the divine, but none in real life. If Alda had worried about how the rejected would fend for themselves beyond this convent in the world outside, she was about to find out.

Alda noted that the sun was shining brightly on her dismissal day. Maybe this was a sign. She wasn't leaving in darkness, but in the warmth of the morning sun. She fought hard not to cry, and knew better than to plead with Mother Mary Justine any further. It did little good for the girl who wanted to keep her baby, and Alda knew it would do even less for her.

Alda stood and bowed to Mother Superior. She kissed her hand and thanked her. Mother walked Alda back to her office in silence.

Alda entered the same small room next to Mother Superior's office, where she had changed out of her traveling clothes and put on the work habit of the Daughters of Charity years before. This time, a satchel had been packed with a cotton slip, one set of undergarments, one pair of stockings, and a nightgown.

A simple navy-blue cotton shirtwaist dress hung on the back of the door.

Alda removed her habit, the veil, the wimple, the apron, the long tunic, and the petticoat. She rolled down her black wool stockings and folded them neatly. She pulled on pale gray stockings instead and slipped back into her shoes. She was allowed to keep her brown work shoes, as another pair had not been provided.

Alda pulled the cotton slip over her head. She stepped into the blue dress. It felt flimsy after the layers of wool and work apron. She shivered.

There was no pocket in the dress, so there was no place to put her train ticket. She looked at her work habit hanging on the wall and wept.

There were many pockets in the habit, pockets under the apron, sewn into the bias of the tunic, to keep rosaries, thermometers, handkerchiefs, and a small missal to read while the girls slept. And now she wore a garment that didn't have a single pocket.

The sisters had taught Alda how to read, write, and speak English, care for expectant mothers and coach them through the birth of their babies. She had developed skills, but wondered if they had any value in the place she was going. For the first time since she could remember, Alda did not have a purpose.

Alda dried her tears. Without saying good-bye to the novices, the nuns, or the girls in the ward she had read to the night before, Alda left Saint Elizabeth's through the same door she had entered six years earlier.

Alda had entered the convent to hide, hoping that a life of contemplation, prayer, and service would give her a fresh start after what she had endured in Italy. Now she was on her own again, to invent a new life once more. She had been afraid of the unknown when she arrived, but the terror she felt as she departed Saint Elizabeth's was worse.

Alda carried the satchel in one hand and a train ticket in the other. As she pushed through the door of Saint Elizabeth's, she turned to take in the foyer one last time. The nuns had filled the gold vase with the flowers Alda had cut that morning; the red petals looked like flames.

The sweet scent of the roses was the last thing she remembered as she walked out of the convent and into her new life.

———

Gladys Belzer stood before the stately colonial-style home she shared with her daughters and shielded her eyes from the sun.

Perched high on a cliff in Bel Air, this was the grandeur she had imagined for her family, an imposing white brick mansion that honored her ancestral roots in the south and her family's rising prominence in the film industry.

Sunset House was the perfect calling card for Mrs. Belzer, one of the most popular interior decorators in Beverly Hills. Gladys had graduated from running a respectable boardinghouse on Green Street to decorating the homes of some of the biggest stars in the movies. She built the business on referrals, some through her popular daughters. Gladys was known for her excellent taste, instinctive use of color, and respect for history and architecture, all of which were wrapped up in an elegant European sensibility that proved to be in hot demand.

Gladys believed that the exterior of the home was the prelude to the decoration within, so the driveway, lawns, gardens, and even the mailbox outside must be as stunning as the rooms inside.

A set of white brick stairs, with banisters made of frilly white wrought iron, crisscrossed the steep hill like icing on a wedding cake. The stairs weren't used much, but from Sunset Boulevard, they added architectural interest and a fairy-tale ascent to the castle.

A movie star's home required a grand entrance in order for her to make one.

The entry portico, an imposing two stories high, was anchored by four majestic columns that could be seen the length of Sunset Boulevard. The wide circular drive was paved in brick and could accommodate the longest Duesenbergs and Packards Detroit had made.

Grand old magnolia trees with white flowers nestled in waxy green leaves were staggered along the property line. Clusters of vivid pink blossoms in the branches of silk-floss trees framed the sides of the house. The hill tumbled down to the street in splashes of color, purple bougainvillea and yellow jasmine twisting through cascades of green ivy like party streamers.

A house painter stood by dipping a brush into a metal sleeve of white paint, leaving a bold stripe on one of the columns.

"How's this one, Mrs. B?"

"It's still too antiseptic. Hospital white. Can you bring it down with a touch of gray?"

"Yes ma'am."

Gladys Belzer, at forty-five, had recently separated from her second husband, George Belzer, nicknamed Mutt (and evidently thrown out because he had behaved as one). Instead of wallowing in the failure of the marriage, she let the disappointment fuel her ambition to build her business to new heights to take better care of her family. The more personal challenges Gladys faced, the better the results in her career. It had always been the case.

Gladys worried about her children. The failure of her second marriage was particularly painful. Her husband had given her Georgiana, her fourth daughter, the baby, and he had been an excellent accountant, getting the finances of her business in order. She credited him with encouraging her to buy property as an investment.

But he had been unfaithful, and for Gladys, this was untenable. She worried that she had set a terrible example for her children in this regard, which was one of the reasons she cleaved so closely to the teachings of her adopted Catholic Church. She felt that the church, with its empirical authority and dogma, might make up for the loss of a man at the head of her household, or at least she hoped it would.

Gladys was a stage mother to her daughters, all of whom had

found their way into acting in motion pictures. Even her son Jackie had appeared in a couple of movies as an extra before losing interest. The girls had also begun as extras, but eventually earned speaking parts. However, only one, her Gretchen, who went by the stage name Loretta Young, was devoted to the craft, and therefore was the most successful.

Jackie had entered law school. He had grown up as a ward to their wealthy neighbors, the Lindley family, who had unofficially adopted him. For most of the years of his childhood, before Mutt Belzer courted Gladys, Jackie came and went between the two houses in what became a natural and mutually beneficial arrangement. Gladys allowed it because her son was happy and enjoyed the attention of Mr. Lindley, his surrogate father, a role Gladys could not provide since his own father, John Earle Young, had left her and their children and, true to his word, never returned.

Gladys left the painter to his work and went inside.

She surveyed the grand foyer, with its luxurious carpeted staircase shaped like a corkscrew. A chandelier dripping with sparkling crystal daggers threw shards of light on the marble floor, as though diamonds had been scattered across it. Inspired by Italian frescoes, which she had seen in books, Gladys commissioned an artist to paint a mural with a scene set in the old South. The pastoral setting, using a palette of moss green, midnight blue, and dusty pink, featured her daughters as antebellum characters in hoop skirts and picture hats.

If Gladys wanted to sell something as an interior decorator, all she need do was display the item in her own home. Hand-painted murals became the rage in Beverly Hills.

A similar rationale helped Gladys sell her customers French antiques, English chintz, Italian damasks, and French toile along with custom-dyed wool rugs. Sunset House became a venue for chic garden parties and proper teas that introduced guests to her largesse, her daughters, and most importantly her keen eye, which led to lucrative commissions.

Just as Gladys created idyllic homes and gardens, her daughters were creating images for the public, on film and in magazines, of the glorious power and potential of youth. The girls took their popularity seriously. It was not enough for an actress to deliver a great performance on a sound stage; the girls also had a responsibility to their fans, and to the public, to be examples of moral purity. The veneer was lacquered to a high polish, so dazzling you could skate on it. The Young sisters were popular with the studio bosses because of their talent, but even without it, they would have been welcome in the front office as well-raised young ladies with lovely manners.

Gladys sat down at her desk and pinned swatches of gold chenille to a collage she had created for a client. Gladys had sketched the rooms, painted the scene, and pinned paint samples, wood chips, and swatches of fabric to a corkboard.

Often the clients kept the collage when a project was completed, as the design board itself was a work of art. Without a traditional education, Gladys devised her own approach to interior decorating, which had its roots in gracious living and homemaking. She expanded her acumen as she learned about architecture, studying the work of her contemporaries James Dolena and Wallace Neff. Gladys designed from the bones out, keeping within the style of the architecture. She used the best materials, went for opulence, and insisted upon comfort, outfitting the home for gracious living, down to the silverware.

While Gladys learned about floor plans from architects and techniques from contractors, she learned about scope and drama from the great set designers in cinema. Gladys observed the work of Cedric Gibbons, who encouraged her to use her imagination and take risks with color and historical authenticity. Like William Haines, a popular matinee idol turned interior decorator, Gladys kept an inventory of fascinating objets d'art in a warehouse full of antique furniture, chandeliers, and fine art. She shopped for her clients in her own warehouse. The collection grew as she worked with buyers, who traveled abroad and brought treasures from around the world, which eventually wound up in the most stylish homes in southern California.

"Miss Gladys? There's a young lady here to see you." The housekeeper showed Alda into the study.

"Father McNally sent me." Alda handed Gladys a letter.

"Alda, we've been waiting for you. I'm Mrs. Belzer." She hit a button on the telephone. "Honey, come downstairs and meet your new secretary."

She smiled at Alda. "We have an intercom in the house, so we can find each other. It's a busy household."

———

The intercom at Saint Elizabeth's was only used in emergencies. Alda could not imagine why a private home would need one. She looked around. How many rooms were in this house, anyway?

"How was your trip?"

"Very fast." Alda couldn't believe that she was in Los Angeles in a matter of hours. San Francisco and Saint Elizabeth's already seemed like a faraway dream.

A glamorous young woman skipped down the staircase and into her mother's study, wearing a peacock-blue satin housecoat and matching slippers. She took a final puff off her cigarette and put it out in an ashtray on a side table. "Hi, I'm Gretchen."

"Not dressed yet?" Gladys chided her.

"Not getting dressed. I have the day off before we start tomorrow. I'm going to do everything from my room." Gretchen winked at Alda.

"This is your new secretary, Alda Ducci."

"I think there's been a mistake," Alda said softly. "Mother Superior told me I would be working for Loretta Young."

Gretchen laughed. "That's my stage name. I'm also not a blonde— this is just for a role. I'm a standard brownette."

Regardless of hair color, Alda was taken in by her new boss's arresting beauty. Loretta's coloring reminded her of the doves of Padua, with her gray eyes, black lashes, soft blond hair, and golden skin. Loretta's lips were naturally full without the enhancement of lipstick. She was very slim, long-legged, not too tall. If Gretchen had a physical flaw, Alda could not find it.

Alda stared. Loretta didn't mind, used to it.

"You may call me Gretchen."

"Loretta is an Italian name. It's from ancient Latin," Alda offered.

"Really? I didn't choose it. At first, I hated it, now it's all right."

It was obvious to Loretta and to Gladys that Alda had just come from the convent. Her black hair was pulled back in a tight braid, her dress was secondhand, and she was wearing work shoes. Alda wasn't wearing a proper hat or gloves, and her traveling satchel was made of boiled wool. She was thin and about Loretta's height, but she was as plain as Loretta was glamorous.

"Your room is ready for you, Alda. I hope you like it."

"Thank you, Mrs. Belzer."

Alda followed Loretta to the staircase. "You'll like it. Mama decorated it herself. Don't get attached to anything, because you'll leave in the morning and come home to a room you don't recognize. My mother changes paint colors like nail polish." Loretta took Alda's suitcase. "You're Italian?"

"Yes."

"Father McNally didn't mention that."

"It's not something I can change."

Loretta stopped and looked at her. "Why on earth would you?"

Alda laughed. "I wouldn't."

"Good for you. You say what's on your mind, don't you?"

"Shouldn't I?"

"Feel free. You're honest. That's something you don't find much in Hollywood."

"I admit I don't know anything about your work. I haven't seen a movie since I went into the convent."

"How long were you in?"

"Since 1925."

"You missed *The Sheik*."

"I'm afraid so."

"And everything in between. Not to worry, we have some prints here—you can catch up. It'll be fun."

Alda followed Loretta down a long hallway on the second floor, contemplating a family that could show movies in the same place they lived. Everything about this house and the people in it was fascinating. They lived like royalty, and unlike the entitled, they had worked for it. This scale of opulence earned and shared could only happen in America. Every aspect of the decor was bold. The wallpaper was a print of large white hydrangea blossoms. The doors to the rooms were each painted a variation of green. The rugs were soft and thick like grass, the furniture covered in feminine watermarked silks. This was a house full of women. If it wasn't apparent in the decor, it was obvious in the scent of rose and vanilla that filled the air.

"Why did you change your name?"

"Colleen Moore didn't like it. She was an actress I worked with," Loretta said as she stopped in the doorway of her sister's room.

"We call her Gretch the Wretch. When she acts like one." Polly Ann smiled.

"This is Polly. She's the oldest."

"And the wisest," Polly said.

"And the shortest," Loretta joked.

Polly had the coloring of a mink, dark brown eyes and black hair. She too was a beauty. Alda wondered where they kept the sisters who weren't.

"If you need anything, just knock on my door. My sister isn't the most organized person you'll ever meet," Polly teased.

"Don't scare my new secretary."

"She's never had a secretary." Polly winked at Alda.

"And I've never been one," Alda admitted.

"Great. We're all even." Alda followed Loretta down the hall to her new room. Alda had never seen such a lovely room. It was painted lilac with gray trim. There was a twin bed with a satin coverlet, a rocking chair, a dresser and vanity. A set of French doors led to a small balcony. The doors were open, and a gentle breeze fluttered the sheers.

"It's small," Loretta apologized.

"I'm afraid it's too much." Alda looked around.

Loretta placed Alda's satchel in the closet and closed the door.

"What kind of room did you have at Saint Elizabeth's?"

"It was a cell. Just a bed and a washbasin. If you don't mind, where is the washbasin?"

"You don't have one." Loretta pushed a door open to a small bathroom with an enamel tub on four legs. "You have a sink. This is your bathroom."

"Mine alone?"

"Yes. Every bedroom has a bathroom. This tub is special; it's the only thing Mama brought from the Green Street boardinghouse. Come on. I'll show you my room. Do you get up early?"

"I used to be up before dawn."

"I'd like you to come with me to the studio every morning. I leave here at four a.m. Sharp. I drive myself."

"Is the studio far?"

"We could walk it, but why would we?" Loretta led Alda down the hall into her own room, a grand suite that extended across the back of the house. The room was light and airy, and gave Alda the feeling of being in a treehouse.

A series of windows opened out over the garden, with a view of the swimming pool. The long rectangle was filled with turquoise water, which was replenished by a fountain shaped like a Greek urn. Alda had never seen anything so lovely.

Loretta's room was decorated in shades of palest pink. Her four-poster double bed, dressed with organdy satin ruffles, was in an alcove. There was a fireplace with a crystal vase of peonies spilling over the white marble mantel. A sofa and two comfortable reading chairs were covered in flowery chintz. A coffee table was stacked neatly with scripts bound in leather. Loretta used ashtrays for paperweights. A ceramic cup, shaped like a palm tree, was full of sharpened pencils.

"I'm a lucky girl," Loretta admitted, seeing her room through Alda's eyes.

"And I'm Sally." Loretta's sister stood in the doorway with her arms folded. Sally, another Young sister, had light blond hair, brown eyes, a trim figure, and an attitude.

"Sally was in *The Sheik*."

"I don't remember it." Sally shrugged. "Gretch, can I borrow your gold lace dress tonight?"

"No, you may not. Beat it."

"Why not?"

"Because I'm wearing it."

"Mama said you were staying in."

"I'm wearing it in."

"Ugh. What else have you got?"

"There's a blue velvet in there."

"I don't feel blue."

"That's all you're getting. Either borrow that one or wear your old chiffon."

Sally went to the closet and opened it.

"The shoes?"

"Take them." Loretta sighed. "I have work to do."

"You sure about the gold dress?"

Loretta surrendered. "Just take it, Sal."

"And the gold shoes?"

"You can't very well wear blue shoes with a gold dress."

"Thank you!" Sally left with the gold ensemble.

Loretta offered Alda a cigarette. "Sorry. Nuns don't smoke."

"I didn't take my final vows. I only made it as far as novice. But my Mother Superior smoked. When I'd catch her smoking in the kitchen, she had an expression of pure bliss on her face."

"I'm with Sister." Loretta lit her cigarette.

"Told me she'd have to answer to God someday for her vice."

Loretta looked at Alda.

Alda blushed. "I don't mean you. You can do whatever you wish."

"I've been smoking since I was nine years old. Mama caught me at thirteen. But I was on a movie set. I wanted to look older. And it helped my voice. I used to squeak—this gave me some timber."

"How long have you been working in pictures?"

"Longer than I've been smoking." Loretta sat down and showed Alda a chair. "This little table is where I do all the heavy lifting before I go to the studio. I learn my lines and I make notes."

"How can I help?"

"We'll have to figure it out as we go along. Is that all right with you?"

Alda nodded.

"Now, you've had a long trip, and I bet you could use a good soak and a nap."

"I'm not tired."

"I insist. I'll get you up in time for dinner. It ought to be good. I saw Ruby making dumplings."

"How many more people live here?"

Loretta laughed. "You've met everyone but the baby. She's in school. Her name is Georgie."

"So there aren't as many children as there are doors?"

"My brother Jackie is in law school. When he comes home for breaks, he stays with another family."

"Why?"

Loretta shrugged. "He likes them. I used to play at Mae Murray's house. Met her on a set. She was a big star in the silents. She didn't have children of her own, so Mama loaned us out. My cousin Carlene and I loved it. We took dance classes, went to parties. We played in Mae's closet. Our house is nothing compared to Mae Murray's."

"How is that possible?" Alda wondered.

"I became a serious actress because of Mae. You see, I wanted her closet. Mae's big life stoked my ambition. I've yammered on enough. You need to unpack. If you need anything, just knock on my door." Loretta smiled.

———

Alda sat in the rocking chair in her new room. She had been anxious on the train, and now she was plain worried. Alda had nothing in common with these girls. She had no idea how to be a secretary, and it seemed as though Loretta knew even less. Alda was frustrated that Mother Superior had dismissed her so casually. How dare the Mother Superior pawn her off on a family she didn't know, in a city she had never seen, in a country she had not yet claimed as home?

When Alda entered the convent, she had offered up her long hours at work and her homesickness for Italy to God, but here in Beverly Hills, where the Young sisters lived in luxury, she felt disconnected from the world she knew and the life she had built. Her faith did her little good in this moment; in fact, she questioned how she had ended up here, when all she ever wanted to do was serve her church, her God, and the unwed mothers of Saint Elizabeth's. If this was her fate, and it surely seemed to be, she wondered if she would ever find any meaning in it. What kind of a woman was she supposed to be in this castle, where every object, piece of furniture, and inhabitant was dazzling beyond measure?

Alda decided she must return home to Italy. It seemed like the only option. She had to start over and figure out a way to go back to the beginning. She had no idea how much the ticket cost, or how she would get to New York City to board a transatlantic liner. Perhaps she could convince Mrs. Belzer to loan her the money for a return passage. The thought of asking such a thing of someone who before a few hours ago had been a stranger made her feel helpless. Alda began to cry, and soon she was sobbing.

A girl of nine with a high ponytail and wide-set hazel eyes, wearing coveralls, pushed the door open. She observed Alda in tears. "Don't you like your room?"

Alda sat up straight and dried her tears. "No, it's very nice."

"I'm Georgiana."

"I'm Alda."

"Where are you from?"

"San Francisco."

"Why do you sound like Dolores del Río?"

"Who's that?"

"She has an accent like you."

"I'm Italian."

"I don't know where Dolores is from. She's in pictures."

"Is everybody in Los Angeles in pictures?"

"Practically all."

"You too?"

"Yep."

"Do you like it?"

"Somebody brings you lunch. And you get to play on the grid."

"What's a grid?"

"It's on the ceiling. Some people call it a catwalk. But I never saw a cat up there. That's where the wires are for the electricity."

"That doesn't sound safe."

"It isn't. If you get caught, they call your mother."

"So why do you do it?"

"Because it's fun."

"Well, I guess that's as good a reason as any."

"Are you going to stay here forever?"

"I don't know."

"You should. Mama has a good cook. Her name is Ruby."

"I heard."

"And we have a big yard. Did you see the pool?"

"It's very nice."

"Do you know how to swim?"

"Oh yes, I used to swim when I was a girl."

"So put your suit on and we'll go swimming."

"I don't have a suit."

"Borrow one from Gretchen. Everybody else does."

———————

Alda dove into the swimming pool. The warm water enveloped her, clear and blue, reminding her of the water of the Adriatic off the coast of Rimini, where her parents took the family to visit their cousins every summer.

Georgie jumped in and swam over to her. "Nobody ever swims with me."

"Why not?"

"Gretchen hates the pool. She likes to look at it, but she doesn't want to get in it. Polly and Sally never want to ruin their hair. They're busy trying to get boyfriends."

"How do you know?"

"The guys come over here. Sometimes they stay for supper. I hate it. Mama makes them come to dinner so she can give them the once-over."

"How does your father feel about that?"

A look of pain flashed across Georgie's face. She dove underwater and swam to the end of the pool. She surfaced and gripped the wall, her back to Alda.

Alda swam to her. "Georgiana. Did I say something wrong?"

"You're mean."

"I am?"

"My dad left us. He doesn't live here anymore."

"I'm sorry."

"He doesn't like the movies. Says that Hollywood ruined his life. He doesn't like me."

"That's not true."

"How do you know?"

"Because every father loves his daughter. How could he not? You're so much fun."

"I know."

"And you're a good swimmer."

"I'm the best swimmer in the family."

"I'm sure your father knows that."

"He taught me how to swim."

Georgie demonstrated her backstroke all the way to the deep end. Alda followed her, extending her arms over her head.

"You're too slow!" Georgie laughed.

"I'm rusty!" Alda called back to her. As Alda floated on the surface, the sky overhead reminded her of the deep blue the artist Giotto used on the ceiling of the Scrovegni Chapel in Padua. Staying with a family in their home reminded her of her own, whom she missed terribly.

———————

Loretta and Polly watched Alda swim with Georgie from the balcony off Loretta's bedroom.

"What do you think of her?" Loretta asked.

"I'm not sure. What do you think?" Polly sat on the window seat.

"Alda got baby sister off our backs, so that's already a plus."

"Don't you wonder why she got kicked out?"

"She didn't fit in. That's what Father McNally told Ma." Loretta sat next to her sister, pulling her knees close to her chest.

"But why? What did she do?"

"I've been fired from jobs. They never really tell you."

"That's true," Polly reasoned. "But why did she leave Italy in the first place?"

"Who knows?"

"Shouldn't you ask her?"

"Why do people ever leave home? They have to. Come on. She seems nice. So she's timid. It's her first day," Loretta reasoned.

"She's awfully backward. How is she going to survive at the studio?"

"She's smart. Evidently. She worked in a hospital."

"She only has one dress."

"How do you know?" Loretta asked.

"I looked in her closet."

"Polly!"

"I know. Terrible of me."

Loretta watched as Alda swam the length of the pool at a clip as she raced Georgie. "She can swim like a fish."

"Yeah, but we're in show business. Not the Olympics. We're going to have to help her, you know."

"I know." Loretta went to her closet, opening both doors. She surveyed the contents like a librarian looking through the stacks.

"This is what you get when you go through the church instead of an employment agency." Polly sighed. "Can you send her back if it doesn't work out?"

"I don't think so." Loretta emerged from her closet carrying three dresses, a pair of shoes, and a set of pajamas. "Father McNally sent her. When has he ever steered us wrong?"

"Priests don't know everything."

Loretta went down the hallway to Alda's room. She wasn't about to get in an argument with Polly. Loretta was a lot like Gladys Belzer in that way; she did not like to fight. Gladys never raised her voice, and Loretta didn't either.

"Where are you going?" Polly followed her sister down the hallway into Alda's room. Loretta opened Alda's closet door.

"Alda needs clothes. What have you got?"

"Don't drag me into your charity projects."

"And don't give me any guff. Go and see what you have, and check Sally's closet too. I've loaned her enough clothes; she can give something to Alda."

Loretta hung the dresses in Alda's closet neatly, put the shoes on the shelf, and lay the pajamas on the bed. Polly came in with new stockings in a box, and a linen bag of new underpants.

Loretta looked in the bag. "I gave you these for your birthday."

"I didn't like them."

"Good to know."

"At least they're new."

"When you give, it's supposed to hurt." Loretta placed Polly's donations in the dresser drawer. "When you give something you didn't want anyway, it doesn't count."

"Nobody likes a martyr, Gretch."

———————

Alda turned the spigot on the tub and placed the stopper in the drain. She turned and looked at herself in the mirror. Polly's wool bathing suit, a black tank, hung loose against her frame. Perhaps Georgie was right; one of Loretta's might have fit better.

As Alda slipped out of the fabric, she thought about the warm water in the lake in Padua, and how she would lead her brothers there on hot summer days. The lake was Alda's refuge; whenever she had time, she went there to swim, or sit on the banks and dream. It was there that she met Enrico, who had come from Trieste to work for his uncle's farm one summer. She had fallen in love with him, and he with her. Her family approved of him. She was eighteen, old enough to marry. Perhaps he would ask her; she certainly had hoped he would.

On the shelf over the vanity was a series of crystal decanters filled with bubble bath, lavender, orange blossom, and verbena. She drizzled verbena into the bath, and soon the room had the scent of a lemon grove in full bloom. As she slipped into the bubbles, she let go, the muscles in her body relaxing. She floated in the grand tub, almost on the surface, like a gardenia in the shell of a fountain. She had not soaked in a bathtub since she left Italy.

The nuns made their own soap, thick lard-based blocks sweetened with leaves of juniper, but not much else. Bathing had been perfunctory. Alda would scrub hard, rinse with the hottest water she could stand, and quickly dry herself to get into her habit and back to work. Bathing in the convent was about cleanliness, not indulgence. For seven years, Alda had almost forgotten she had a body. Only when it ached was she reminded of its existence.

As Alda emerged from the bath, she reached for the towel on the rack next to the tub. The towel unfurled, she dried herself with the luscious thick cotton. She inhaled its scent—it reminded her of a newborn's skin. Alda wrapped the towel around her.

She went into the bedroom and opened her closet to put on her blue dress. It was gone; instead she found new clothes. There were dresses. A navy blue coat. Two pairs of shoes. She opened the drawers of the dresser. Cotton undergarments, new. Underpants with tiny pin bows at the waist. Simple matching brassieres with matching pink satin bows at the base of the straps. Alda began to feel dizzy. She sat down at the foot of the bed, confused by the array of clothing, by the variety and by their beauty.

She may have been overwhelmed by the kindness of the Young sisters, but she was also apprehensive. She had made the transition to a new life in a matter of hours. Was her destiny this subjective? The particularity of her circumstances was the stuff of the books she had read aloud to the girls at Saint Elizabeth's. Was she worthy of this life? Who was she now, the young woman wearing other girls' clothing, living in another family's house, in a new job for which she had not one whit of experience? She hadn't chosen this path, but perhaps it had chosen her.

Alda stood at the closet, determined to make a selection, but she didn't know how to choose something to wear. The Saint Vincent habit had been her uniform; she never had to make a decision. It should have been a simple choice, Alda thought as she shuffled through the garments on the hangers, but she had no idea what appealed to her. She wasn't sure if she liked burgundy more than soft yellow, dotted swiss more than gingham. She had no idea if a puffy sleeve was better than none at all. She didn't know who she was dressing for, and why. She only knew that she needed to pick something.

Alda closed her eyes and decided to wear the first dress her hand landed on. She laid the burgundy shirtwaist dress on the bed and went to the dresser, pulling on the undergarments carefully, so as not to undo the bows. She pulled on the stockings, smoothing them as she went. Whether silk or wool, all stockings pulled on the same. She pulled a silk slip over her head and straightened it over her body, careful to line up the seams with the curve of her hips. She stepped into the dress, buttoning the front.

Alda looked in the mirror and brushed her hair. It was so long, it hung to her waist in glossy black ropes. The only girl in this house with long hair was Georgie, and she was not yet ten.

Alda went to the desk and opened the drawer, finding a letter opener and a set of large scissors. She took the scissors, went to the mirror, and in two whacks bobbed her hair to ear length. Dropping the coils into the wastebasket, she brushed her new short hair, feeling instantly lighter and, for reasons she could not name, happier.

Loretta rapped on the door.

"Come in!" Alda called out.

As Loretta and Polly came into the room, Polly gave a wolf whistle, long and low.

"Polly! That's rude," Loretta scolded. She looked at Alda. "You cut your own hair!"

"Nice," Polly marveled. "Alda, you look good."

"Thank you."

"So the clothes fit?"

"They do. I can't thank you enough."

"We couldn't let you wear that old convent stuff. You'd show up at the studio tomorrow, and they'd mistake you for a background extra on the bread lines."

"Don't insult her," Loretta snapped. "She was a novice in the convent. She served the poor."

"I'm sorry. I feel terrible," Polly said, half meaning it. "Gretchen is a saint."

"Knock it off, Pol."

"Kindness shown is always appreciated," Alda said. "You have been very kind to me."

"Wait till Mama sees you! I hope you're hungry."

Sally entered, dressed head to foot in gold. "How do I look?"

"Like a pie server at Chasen's," Polly said.

"If nobody asks me to dance, I'll serve dessert." Looking at herself in the mirror, Sally caught Alda in the reflection. "Is that Alda?"

"It's me."

"You look swell."

Alda followed the girls down to dinner. This time last night she had been serving the girls of Saint Elizabeth's vegetables in hearty broth, baked eggs and bread. They'd worn their regulation night-gowns, powder blue, with thick white wool socks.

The distance between the haves and the have-nots is a train ride.

————

Loretta popped her retainer into her mouth, wiggling it into place on her top teeth. "I have buck teeth, and this is supposed to straighten them."

"But your teeth *are* straight."

"Because I wear this contraption. Do they have braces in Italy?"

Alda shook her head.

"Usually you get braces when you're a teenager. But I never had time to get the full-on permanent kind, because I was working, so the orthodontist made me a retainer. I hate it, so I'm always losing it. I leave it anywhere and everywhere. The dashboard of the car. In my pockets. Restaurants, even. They're expensive, and Mama hollers when I lose them. So if you don't mind, can you remember to look out for it?"

"I will."

Loretta sat down on the sofa next to Alda and opened her script.

"Let's begin with the basics. This is a script. The story of the movie."

"I read books, so I understand."

"They're different. A book describes everything. The script is just the story and the dialogue. I have to memorize everything that's underlined."

Alda looked at the pages. Most every line was Loretta's. "How do you do that?"

"I just go over it and over it and over it. Here's how you can help me. You'll read me the line before—the final word of that line is called the cue. And then I'll say my line." Loretta used a wooden ruler to show Alda.

"What do these marks mean?"

Alda pointed to a series of small slashes, inverted letters, and letters removed by a black square marked above with a different letter.

"Ignore those. They are for me. I have trouble when I read. The letters jump, and sometimes they're out of order. It takes me forever to read anything. So the first thing I do when I get a script is write my lines so I can read them."

"You have to work very hard to read."

"Oh, it's almost impossible. And you know, the only thing that an actress can do is read books to find parts."

"Would you like me to read for you?"

"That's a splendid idea."

"I will be happy to—"

"A keen intellect is a weapon in your arsenal as an actress. At least that's what Father McNally says. I'm not terribly keen. And I still get butterflies."

"It's frightening to get up in front of people and perform."

"But I've made fifty pictures. You think I'd be Miss Confidence. But it's always like this before I start a new picture. I live in fear of getting fired."

"I know about that."

"Did they kick you out of the convent?"

Alda nodded.

"Well, that's their loss." Loretta smiled at Alda to reassure her.

"Did you ever find yourself in a place in life where you had committed to something, and you couldn't make it work?"

"I was married when I was seventeen years old, and it was a huge mistake. For a few weeks, I was Mrs. Grant Withers. Did you ever hear of him?" Alda shook her head that she had not.

Loretta continued, "He was a big star, and I wanted to be. I had been working in pictures since I was four years old, and I felt like a grown-up. I eloped with an actor who I thought was in life as he was on the sound stage. Onscreen he was handsome and eloquent. Well, I learned the hard way that it's the writers that give us the lines—they don't come from the heart, if you know what I mean. Believe me, I'll never make that mistake again. Anyhow, I had to come home, beg for Mama's forgiveness, and get it annulled. So I understand making a commitment and feeling like a failure. But you shouldn't feel that way. You didn't make any dumb mistakes. The Mother Superior wrote a glowing recommendation for you."

"She did?"

"And Father McNally is very particular. He said you'd be perfect for me."

"I'll try."

"That's all I care about. We're going to learn how to do this together." Loretta patted Alda on the hand. She liked a challenge. Whether it was a complex character she had to crack, a problem to solve for one of her sisters, or a dilemma her mother might face, Loretta liked to fix things and lead whomever needed her out of the dark. Being useful gave her life meaning.

"How did you learn to be an actress?" Alda asked.

"I just watched when I was hired as background. I picked up a little something here and a little something there. I learned from watching Mae Murray and Colleen Moore—actresses like that. The best actors work the hardest but make it look easy. You have to master your nerves to do the job. You have to be willing to make a fool out of yourself. After a while, if you're smart and paying attention, bit by bit, line by line, you begin to understand how to interpret a character. Bela Lugosi was so kind. He told me to charge into the scene like a horse and keep my eyes on the action. You know, that's the tough part. When you're acting, you have to figure out where to look."

"It sounds difficult."

"No kidding. Tomorrow I begin again with a whole new crew and director. And a new leading man. He's from the theater. A stage actor. Did plays."

"Are you worried?"

"Nothing I can't handle. Theater actors waltz in high and mighty and ready to show everybody how smart they are and how dumb we are because we're in pictures. But I'm ready for him."

"What part is he playing?"

"Bill Ludlow. Sounds like a sap. I like his name in real life much better."

"What is it?"

"Spencer Tracy."

Loretta lit a cigarette without taking her eyes off the script. It didn't matter if she liked her costar, or if he liked her; she had a job to do. Tomorrow morning, Loretta would become a lost soul in Central Park named Trina. Whatever Mr. Tracy might have in store for her was beside the point. She would bring her skill and professionalism to the set, and her brand new secretary Alda Ducci to the lot. Their small army of two was about to invade the Columbia studio.

3

Frank Borzage, the director of *Man's Castle*, ran his hands through the wild curls on his head before he knocked on Spencer Tracy's dressing room door. When he entered, Spencer was sitting back on a couch covered in green plaid, his feet propped on a makeshift coffee table. His script lay flat and open across his chest. His hands were folded behind his head as he stared at the ceiling.

Borzage followed Spencer's gaze up to the ceiling. "What are you looking at, Spence?"

"I'm watching the picture."

"Is it any good?"

"Not bad." Spencer smiled.

"You're a comfort."

"All I can do is give you my version of this thing."

"You'll be great."

"We'll see. How's my leading lady?"

"She's in makeup."

"Does she need it?"

"No. Have you met her?"

"At the movies."

"Around town?"

"No, on the screen. Paid my ten cents like everybody else. Never met her in person. Is she that gorgeous in life?"

"Better."

"How is that possible? You should've cast Franchot Tone. He's pretty."

"I didn't want pretty. I wanted the best actor I could get."

"You're very kind."

"It's true."

"We need you on the set, Mr. Borzage," the stage manager called through the door.

"On my way." He extended his hand to Tracy. "Good to have you here, Spence."

"We'll see about that when you call action."

Borzage chuckled and closed the door behind him.

Spencer leaned forward and opened the script on the coffee table. He had memorized the entire script, dialogue and stage directions. Most movie actors learn their lines and cues for the scene work for that particular day, but not Tracy; he had to hold the entirety of the script in his head.

Spencer Tracy was thirty-four years old. He believed he was fifteen years behind his fellow actors in practical experience on camera. He could not afford to make mistakes; directors were generally impatient, and studio bosses were worse. He did not have the luxury of time to experiment and grow. Tracy knew he had to hustle.

Spencer scanned the page, saying his lines aloud without pausing, rapid-fire. He barely took a breath. Most of the sounds he made didn't sound like language, but the drone of a machine.

He got up and poured himself a cup of coffee, all the while muttering his dialogue. He stopped, closed his eyes, and pictured what he would do with his body when delivering the lines. He leaned one arm against the wall and shifted his feet. He dropped his shoulders, extended his hands, then buried them in his pockets. He nodded and muttered some more.

Spencer rocked up and down on the balls of his feet as he recited through a major speech in the script three times. He patted his shirt pocket and his pants pockets, finally finding a pencil behind his ear. His thick sandy hair, with natural marcel waves, was so unruly that it regularly swallowed pencils. He chewed the eraser and stared into the middle distance. He scratched a few words onto the page. Tracy circled a line of dialogue several times until it was encased in a thick gray oval. He looked down at the words inside the oval while chewing the pencil. He placed the pencil on the coffee table and closed the script.

Spencer paced back and forth in the small dressing room, only to stop and touch his toes. He stood up straight and shook out any tension in his body. He twirled his head slowly in a full circle to a series of pops and cracks, as his neck bones settled at the top of his spine. He washed his hair with his fingers with invisible shampoo. He pulled the hair at the root. He grumbled and sighed.

He walked out the door and onto the set.

Spencer Tracy was known in acting as an "everyman," which he took to mean as "nobody in particular." He blended in with the crew, moving in and out among them anonymously and effortlessly like a whipstitch, drawing neither attention nor curiosity. An actor should be a blank slate, Tracy believed, so he moved through the world without attaching to anyone, or any particular group, instead remaining free to be an ardent observer of others.

Unnoticed on the Columbia sound stage, Tracy circled back around the camera rig and eavesdropped as his director and cameraman talked shop. He looked up at the grid, then took in the expanse of the scenery, sizing up the joint as he walked the set, stopped, studied the entrances and exits, as if to kick the tires of the vehicle that would take him into the story of the movie.

A page of new dialogue was shoved under Loretta Young's dressing room door.

Loretta's hairdresser was asleep, snoring softly under the wardrobe rack. Loretta sat at her makeup table, lit brighter than an operating room in a city hospital, doing her own hair.

LaWanda Thompson, her makeup artist, a put-upon fortysomething matron with a brilliant smile and a suntan out of the old days of the gold rush, stood back and squinted at Loretta's face in the mirror.

"Can I get you anything?" Alda asked as she placed the new page of dialogue on the table.

"A new hairdresser," LaWanda groused.

"Let her sleep it off," Loretta said as she patted down the baby hairs that framed her face.

"What actress does her own hair?" LaWanda asked as she stirred black powder and water to make mascara for Loretta.

"An actress that doesn't want her hairdresser to lose her job. She has three kids."

"I got four."

"But you don't drink."

"I want to."

"But you won't, LaWanda, will you?"

"Nah."

"Because I can't do my makeup too."

"You could. It's simple. I layer a little powder, curl your lashes with mascara, a touch of pink on those cheeks, a tint of red on those lips, and you look like a rose."

"A rose doesn't have black pits. Get rid of those circles under my eyes." Loretta closed her eyes.

"Can do." LaWanda pressed a sponge gently on Loretta's under-eye circles.

"Do you know this Spencer Tracy fellow?"

"Word is good on him."

"Is he easy?"

"I didn't say that. He's good. Good actor."

Loretta swallowed hard. Whenever she started a new picture, she felt like she was back on the extras line at Players-Lasky, hoping to be chosen but afraid that if she was, she wouldn't measure up and they'd send her home.

Loretta was also nervous about the director. Borzage had won the first Academy Award ever given for directing. He was sharp, his style influenced by the great European filmmakers, which made Loretta feel inferior.

"You'll be fine. Borzage is a pro," LaWanda assured her. "And a good actress makes everyone on the set look better, including the makeup girl. So get out there and show them how it's done, sweetie." LaWanda removed Loretta's rubber cape and paper collar as she stood up.

The wardrobe assistant helped Loretta out of her robe and into her costume, a working-girl shirtwaist dress and coat. She centered a cloche hat on her head.

"You didn't need to do your hair," LaWanda marveled. "Love the hat."

Loretta's inner circle served up compliments and support freely, as they were both artisans and coaches. The more confident the actress, the faster the day's work for everyone.

When Loretta left her dressing room and walked out onto the set, she was met with stifling heat in contrast to the snowy winter set of Central Park in New York City. There were drifts of soap-flake snow on the ground, and trees flocked with white foam; glass icicles clung to a faux stone wall, and a coppery full moon hung in the distant sky like an old penny.

Borzage was known for his authentic sets, which were sprawling, ambitious, and built to actual scale. He thought painterly interiors looked fake on camera, so he had the scene designer use the entirety of the sound stage, in height, breadth, and depth, to re-create a portion of Central Park as close as possible to the real thing.

The set designer had built the small hills and footpaths of Central Park, the statues, park benches, and rock gardens. In the distance there were glints of light in the windows of the skyscrapers that surrounded the park, their walls made of faux sandstone and brick. Borzage's genius was in the details; a real squirrel ran up a tree, before he was retrieved and placed back in his cage by an animal trainer until the cameras rolled. Another cage full of pigeons, which would be used in the first scene, was positioned by the park bench. A bag of bread crumbs was placed on the park bench for Spencer Tracy to feed them.

Loretta smiled and nodded as the crew acknowledged her respectfully with greetings of "Good morning, Miss Young," "Nice to see you again, Miss Young," "Lovely as always, Miss Young."

Loretta's team surrounded her, yanking at the hem of her dress, dusting off the hat, powdering her face. Loretta greeted her stand-in, who was exactly her size.

"I guess I need a hat," the stand-in murmured.

"It's a sweat box in here," Loretta commented.

"Gonna get worse. It's going to break a hundred by eight this morning, and only going up from there," the stage manager said as he passed.

"You're gonna cook in those coats," the wardrobe assistant clucked.

"Snow scenes in July," a man's voice said behind her, dropping to a whisper. "Tells you something about the common sense of studio executives."

Loretta turned to find herself face to face with Spencer Tracy. In two-inch heels, she was almost as tall as he was. Tracy was stocky and broad-shouldered, a body more suited to a workingman than a leading man. She liked his face. He was blue-eyed Irish in the stevedore fashion, with a strong nose, wide cheekbones, and a smile that had a sly curve. He leaned in conspiratorially. She waited for him to say something more, but he didn't. Loretta pulled back and busied herself watching the crew add some snow around a park bench. Spencer Tracy shifted toward her again.

"I saw *Midnight Mary*," he said softly.

Following his cue, Loretta leaned in and whispered in his ear, "How did I do?"

"You killed every bum in the picture."

"It was in the script."

"What are you going to do to me?" he teased.

"Did you read the script?"

"Yeah."

"I save you in the end."

"Tough job. Are you up for it?"

"You'll soon find out. We're starting with scene one. Where's your tuxedo?"

"They're pressing it."

"We start at seven."

"I'll be ready."

He stood next to her, rocking back and forth on his feet and up on his toes. She didn't know what else to say, and he said nothing. She half smiled, looking straight ahead, thinking, Something is wrong with this poor man. He had to be the most socially awkward actor she had ever met.

Spencer must have sensed her feelings, because he turned and walked away, leaving her standing alone. She watched the oddball as he wove back through the crew, unrecognized.

"He looks like my uncle," the wardrobe assistant commented. "I'm all Irish on my mother's side."

"Mr. Tracy is as Irish as a boiled potato." LaWanda shrugged. "But there's something about him, don't you think?"

"Oh, yeah. Something," Loretta said. She was too polite to say what she was really thinking.

————

"Okay, Sis, this is where you work."

A production assistant, pencil-thin with a mustache to match, showed Alda the mail room, a dusty, ramshackle closet with a broken-down worktable and a few metal folding chairs placed around it.

"You sit there and you answer the mail." He put boxes on the worktable along with a stack of envelopes. "You can read 'em or not. If one of 'em makes you cry, you put it to the side for Miss Young. She enjoys a weepie. She likes to peruse a few here and there, but don't crush her with a bunch. Everybody, *everybody* that writes in gets a photograph. Columbia front office orders. The audience pays our salaries when they buy tickets, don't forget it."

"I won't," Alda promised. She looked at the windows, closed shut. The production assistant read her mind and opened them.

"It's hot in here."

"Thank you," Alda said.

He hoisted an oversize burlap bag full of mail onto the table. "Miss Young is popular."

"That is a lot of mail." Alda wondered how she could possibly answer all the letters.

"There's thirteen more bags where this one came from."

Alda opened the box on the table. A black-and-white photograph of her boss in a voile dress, with a matching umbrella shading her from the sun, was duplicated in a stack in the hundreds.

"Here's Miss Young's autograph stamp." The young man showed Alda how to stamp Loretta's signature on the photograph. "Easy peasy. Can you handle it? Stamp the photo, mail it to the return address. Write neatly. The boys in the front office don't like returns. Costs them money."

"Yes, sir."

The assistant left, leaving Alda alone with the bundles of letters. She opened the first one, with the return address Red Lodge, Montana. Alda began to read the story of a young woman whose husband had left her with three young children. She came upon the sentence "If you could please send me five dollars, it would go a long way to help."

Alda placed the paper off to the side, creating a stack for charity, and opened another. She took a deep breath, slipped off the shoes that Polly Ann Young had handed down to her, and settled in to read. This one made her laugh. It was from a man who had invented non-fade lipstick. She made another stack for inventors who wanted Loretta to represent their products.

Loretta peeked in the door. "Anything good?"

"I was told to send your photograph, but what they'd really like is a five-dollar bill."

"If we sent everybody money, I couldn't take care of my family."

"Should I send a picture anyway?"

"Just make a stack, and we'll figure it out. I've given letters to Father McNally, and he contacts the local parish if there's a real need."

"Is there anything I can get you?"

"I'm going to lie down during my break with an ice bag. I don't have any pain, mind you, I want to cool off." Loretta laughed. "La-Wanda will come and get you and take you to the commissary for lunch. It's fun. You'll see lots of stars over there."

Loretta peeled off costume pieces as she made her way back to her dressing room. The crew was rigging lights for the scene after lunch. She was about to turn to enter her dressing room when she saw her costar sitting alone on an extra park bench that hadn't made it into the scenery. Spencer Tracy was reading the newspaper, which he had folded into a square about the size of a page in a book.

"I could use a cold beer, how about you?"

Spencer looked up at her and smiled. "Only if I could take a bath in it."

"That's not a bad idea." Loretta sat down next to him on the bench. "Did you have lunch?"

"Jell-O."

"You must be starving."

"I had a cup of grapes with it."

"That must have been filling," Loretta said wryly.

"They tell me that the only other leading man with my waist size is W. C. Fields."

"That can't be right."

"According to wardrobe, it's right on the money. These are his pants."

Loretta laughed. "I was about to pay you a compliment."

"What for?"

"I think leading men should look like real men. And you do."

"You call that a compliment?"

"Yes, sir."

"And I was about to tell you that you're not half bad looking."

"I can't take any credit for it. I look like my mother. And she looked like her mother."

"That's usually how it goes." Tracy rolled his newspaper into a tube. "You're a fine actress."

"You're only as good as who you act with—"

"How do you think it went this morning?"

"All right."

"Borzage knows what he's doing."

"We'll see." Loretta stood and smiled. "I'm going to take a rest."

"What about that beer?" Spencer grinned.

"What are you doing for dinner?"

"Nothing."

"Would you like to come to my house?"

"I figured you liked me, but I didn't expect you to like me this much so soon."

"I don't mean to give you the wrong impression."

"Too late for that."

"Dinner at my house. It's a loony bin. I have three sisters, Mama, our priest, Father McNally, Alda, my new secretary, two cats, one dog, and a canary that can't sing."

"What time?"

"Seven."

"Right after work."

"Does that suit you?"

"I live at the Beverly Hills Hotel, and I'm sick and tired of room service."

"You theater people. Always in hotels. Movie people? We're homebodies. Home-cooked all the way. My family is on Sunset. A few blocks from the hotel. You can walk home after dinner."

"That close?"

"Five minutes."

"Thank you. It's a date."

"It's dinner," she corrected him.

Spencer Tracy watched Loretta Young walk back to her dressing room. She was slender, but there was nothing small about her. She was a talented actress, which was important to Tracy. A pretty girl was one thing, but pretty and talented, that was preferable. If he was going to sell out by acting in the movies, he hoped to at least bring serious skill to the proceedings.

The deep roots of respect are fed by admiration, and Tracy held Loretta in high regard already. He liked the way she worked. She was specific, kept her focus, and didn't fool around. She didn't seem to fear Borzage, and she didn't ask a lot of questions. She appreciated the work of the crew, treating them as she wished to be treated. She was without airs, and yet there was a distance between her and others; for sure there was one between her and him. Tracy was a man who couldn't abide artifice, on or off the set, but it was here, at work, that he sensed a conundrum regarding his costar.

For all of Loretta Young's warmth and professionalism, there was something aloof about her. In her company he got an odd sensation of simultaneous hot and cold. It reminded him of the magic hour in the desert, the brief interlude of twilight. The sun was going down, but there was still heat, and in an instant it was gone, as the world turned lavender and a chill set in. Loretta was mysterious, which intrigued him; she was sensual, which stirred him up. He was lonely, but he felt none of it in her presence. This was a girl who would matter to him, and he wasn't sure how he felt about that.

———

Father McNally, the fresh-scrubbed young priest and pastor of Our Lady of Good Shepherd Church in Beverly Hills, sat at the head of the dining room table at Sunset House. Ruby, the family cook since boardinghouse days, placed a pork roast at the center of the table. Like her boss, Ruby was from North Carolina. Ruby was a black woman who had the same goal in Hollywood as the Young family. She wanted to make it big. When she wasn't working for Gladys Belzer, she made cakes and pies for some of the popular restaurants on the strip. Ruby wanted to retire young and rich.

"May I help?" Father asked.

"Reverend, I don't need help in the kitchen. I need help everywhere else. Just keep me in your prayers," Ruby said wearily.

Gladys entered from the kitchen, carrying a basket of fresh biscuits.

"Mrs. Belzer, let me serve the table," Ruby groused. "That's why I'm here."

"Many hands make light work, Ruby."

"Many hands also make a mess, Mrs. Belzer. A mess that I have to clean up later."

Loretta and Polly came in, laughing, while Sally chased Georgie around the table. The girls greeted the priest before taking their seats. Alda sat at the far end of the table, the farthest seat from Father McNally.

"Who's the extra plate for?" Polly wanted to know.

"I invited a new friend."

"Is it a man?" Georgie complained.

"Yes. My fellow actor, Spencer Tracy." She checked her watch. "He should be here by now."

"Never heard of him." Sally poured herself a glass of ice tea.

"He's from the theater."

"Ugh. If you're going to invite actors to dinner, I wish you'd bring Clark Gable home." Sally unfolded her napkin on her lap. "Theater people have lousy clothes and bad teeth."

"There's some Christian charity for you, Father," Polly said drily.

"Sal, I hate to disappoint you," Loretta said. "I don't know Clark Gable. And I never will. He just signed a big contract at Metro."

"You could get loaned out."

"Won't happen," Loretta promised.

Alda's head was swimming. People didn't talk in the Belzer home, they prattled like the keys of a typewriter being hit by a crack secretary at a hundred words a minute. Words richocheted around the room like stray bullets, and when one of the girls made a point, she didn't stay in her seat—she stood up, as though called upon for her opinion.

"Alda, this is quite a household." Father McNally smiled.

Alda was surprised at how young Father McNally was—when she thought about Mother Superior dismissing her, Alda had imagined Father McNally as one of those older, imposing, autocrat priests, but here he was, the opposite. She couldn't believe that a man this young out of the seminary had changed the course of her life.

"Are you enjoying your work?" the priest asked.

"It's interesting. I like it, and I hope I'm doing well."

"What is she supposed to say, Father? We're all sitting here," Sally joked.

"You have all been very kind to me." Alda turned to the priest. "The girls shared their clothes with me."

"Lucky we're the same size." Polly grinned.

"I didn't want to leave Saint Elizabeth's because I felt useful there, but there's plenty of work for me here. Gretchen's fan letters are like reading the great novels."

"Really?" Loretta was surprised.

"People tell their stories when they write to you. They can be heartbreaking, but sometimes they're just ordinary bread and butter notes. People write to someone they don't know, but based on what they've seen on the movie screen, they feel they know you and assume you possess the qualities of your characters."

"Only the good ones, I hope," Loretta said.

Her sisters roared with laughter.

"If only they knew the real Gretch," Sally joked.

"Maybe they do. They consider you their confidante."

"What an honor for you, Gretchen," Father McNally said. "God gave you a talent that allows people to see your soul. You invite them in, so they want to share their stories with you."

"Sally and Polly get fan letters too," Gladys interjected.

"Oh, Mama, we don't care," Polly said. "We're happy for Gretchen."

"Besides, she wants it more," Sally teased.

"Mr. Tracy Spencer is here," Ruby announced from the doorway.

The girls laughed.

"It's Spencer Tracy," Loretta corrected her.

"That don't sound right. Tracy is a first name. Your momma got your name backward."

"That may very well be, Miss Ruby. Regardless, here I am." Spencer entered the dining room. He gave Mrs. Belzer a box of candy, greeted the priest, and took a seat.

As Father McNally said grace, Gladys watched with interest as Spencer made the sign of the cross. "Mr. Tracy, you're a Catholic?"

"All my life, Mrs. Belzer. Please don't ask me if I'm a good one."

"Alda was almost a nun," Georgie piped up.

"Your sister will tell you that I'm almost an actor."

"She only said you were intriguing."

Loretta blushed as Spencer laughed. Polly and Sally chided Georgie.

"Intrigue can mean a lot of things."

"No kidding." Loretta glared at Georgie.

"Alda, it must be a big change from the convent to a mansion in Beverly Hills," Spencer said.

"It's not that different from the convent. It's all girls, they just have better clothes and bigger rooms."

"And ice cream," Georgie said.

"And ice cream. Well, to be honest, we had ice cream at the convent on Christmas."

"We have it whenever we want it here," Georgie said.

"How do you stay so slim?" Spencer teased Georgie.

"I swim. You should try it."

"Georgiana!" Loretta shot her a look.

"She's right. I could stand to lose a few," Spencer said.

"You're just fine the way you are," Loretta assured him.

"Alda is Italian," Georgie interrupted. "What are you?"

"I'm from Milwaukee," Tracy said.

"Tracy is an Irish surname, Georgie," Gladys said.

"The statues at Good Shepherd came from Italy," Georgie announced.

"Who told you that?" Her mother smiled.

"We learned it in Catechism. Miss Spadoni said if we were going to spend every Sunday in church, we ought to know where the beauty came from."

"That's wonderful," Spencer said. "You know no one is sure where beauty began—am I right, Father?"

"Let me guess. You're a Jesuit."

Spencer Tracy laughed. "How could you tell?"

"Only a Jesuit would ask that question. Why don't we assume everything beautiful comes from God?"

"Fine with me, Father. Evidently, God was busy in this house."

"Thank you, Mr. Tracy." Gladys nodded.

"How's the roast?" Ruby asked Spencer.

"Did you prepare it?"

"Yes, sir."

"It's perfect."

"Good answer, Mr. Tracy. I might cut you a big slice of pie."

"I'd be grateful."

"Got a sweet tooth?"

"Legendary."

"Are you going to marry my sister?" Georgie asked.

"Georgiana!" Loretta glared at her.

"Which one?" Spencer teased.

"Polly is going to get married someday. She's almost bagged a big fish. At least, that's what she said on the phone."

"Listen here, you little snitch," Polly reprimanded, "it isn't necessary to repeat everything you hear."

"But it sure makes for interesting dinner conversation," Spencer said.

"Daddy!" Georgiana suddenly shrieked. She got up from the table and ran to her father. George Belzer stood in the doorway, extending his arms to his daughter. He was an attractive man around fifty, conservatively dressed with a receding hairline. He looked like an accountant, which he was by trade.

Polly, Sally, and Loretta looked down, and for the first time that evening, they were quiet. Spencer looked at Father McNally. George Belzer lifted his daughter off the ground and embraced her. He looked at the table and saw the priest sitting in his chair. Gladys smiled and stood up at the table.

"Won't you join us for dinner, George?" Gladys asked.

"No, thank you, I'm here to see Georgie's report card."

"All A's," Georgiana said proudly.

"Had to see it with my own eyes."

"I'll go get it." Georgie ran into the living room.

"This is my friend Spencer Tracy. Spencer, this is Mr. Belzer," Loretta said politely.

Georgie ran back with her report card. Her father looked at it. "Well, Georgie, you weren't kidding."

"I almost won the spelling bee too."

"Almost?"

"I couldn't spell *alabaster.*"

"You have to make flash cards," her father reminded her.

Alda placed her napkin on the table. "I can help you with that, Georgiana."

"That's not necessary," George told Alda.

"Will you help me with them, Dad?"

"Of course."

Georgie took her father's hand, and they went up the stairs together.

"Ruby, can you bring coffee up for Mr. Belzer and me? We'll be in Georgie's room." Gladys excused herself and followed them up the stairs.

———

Loretta and Spencer walked down the filigree steps in the Belzers' front yard to Sunset Boulevard.

"I never use these steps," Loretta admitted.

"Why not?"

"Who walks in Beverly Hills?"

"We are."

"I drive everywhere."

"Georgie tells me you're a bad driver."

"That kid!"

"She's the baby—she's the one with the goods on everybody."

"I guess. Did she also tell you that I never exercise? If I could drive from my bedroom to the dining room, I would."

"That's not what your figure says."

"I owe this figure to—"

"Your mother and her mother and the mothers that came before."

"How refreshing! A man that pays attention."

"A man pays attention when he's interested."

Loretta ignored his flirting and steered the conversation back to work. "Do you like the movie business?"

"I'm getting used to it."

"They say when you start your acting career on the stage, it never leaves you. You will always long for it."

"That's true for me."

"Are you going to get a house here?"

"I have one."

"Why do you stay at a hotel?"

Spencer walked along without answering the question.

Random thoughts swirled in Loretta's mind, as she imagined what Spencer's personal story might be.

After a few steps, he stopped, his hands in his pockets, turned, and faced her. He went up and down on the balls of his feet, which she had now come to recognize as a quirk, signaling that he was collecting his thoughts and was about to say something that mattered to him. Spencer Tracy had his own way of moving through the world, and Loretta was getting used to his cues.

"I'm separated from my wife."

Loretta was taken aback. There was no wedding ring on his hand, so she'd assumed he was single. Besides, Spencer seemed too lonely to be connected to anyone or anything on a permanent basis. "I'm sorry."

"It's not going well. But we have two children. Susie is a baby, and our son John is around Georgie's age."

"Is he as annoying?"

"No, he's a good kid. He has a problem with his hearing. We figured it out pretty early on. He's deaf, but he understands us and can speak. His mother spends all her time trying to find help for him—I kind of got into the pictures racket because of him."

"I don't follow."

"Salaries are better in pictures than they are in the theater."

"Oh, I see."

"It wasn't my intention to ever act in movies."

"Well, you're a natural at it."

"Thank you. Every day I don't get a pink slip is a win. Once they get a load of me on camera, they may change their minds and invest elsewhere."

"You're a great actor. That matters more than a pretty face. Unless you're a woman, of course. They want us pretty and young, although the biggest star in America right now is neither glamorous nor young. Marie Dressler is so good, her appearance is beside the point."

"So am I the male Marie Dressler?" Spencer joked.

"She started out in the theater, too."

"I feel worse now."

"Don't. I already told you that you're handsome."

"You didn't use that word."

"Well, I am using it now." Before another long Spencer silence could set in, Loretta filled the gap. "That was a long day. I was hoping that you'd be able to relax at our house. I'm afraid it was a circus."

"I liked it. It was a little strange when Mr. Belzer arrived."

"Wasn't it? My mother is divorcing him."

"That would explain Father McNally at the head of the table."

"We always bump the man of the house for the priest."

"Good to know. Was he a good stepfather?"

"Good enough."

"Where's your father, if you don't mind me asking?"

"I don't know."

"Your mother is an interesting woman."

"She's the center of everything."

"As my mother is in our family."

Loretta walked Spencer up the sidewalk to the hotel. "See you tomorrow, Spencer." She turned to go.

"This won't do," he said. "I have to walk you back home."

"That's unnecessary. Really. I know the neighborhood."

"What kind of a gentleman would I be if I let a lady walk home alone? Regardless of the swank factor of your neighborhood."

"But you can see my house from here!"

"Doesn't matter. What if you fall on those fancy steps? They wouldn't find you in that Garden of Babylon for months."

Loretta laughed. "I'll be fine."

"Come on," he said. "It's a couple of minutes more at the end of a long day. You're good enough company for a round trip."

Spencer took her hand on the walk back to Sunset House. It didn't make her nervous; it felt natural, almost too easy, as though they had an understanding and a history.

Spencer felt the same, but his longing for Loretta was far from simple and loaded with guilt. He knew that there was no hope at home with his wife, but his goal was never to leave her. Loretta surely wasn't the first woman he had walked home outside of his marriage. He'd had a few lovers of late that filled the separation from his wife, but the affairs never led to anything beyond sex. He wasn't proud of his dalliances, but in his mind, Loretta was different. Being with her and her family felt like a new start.

They walked without saying much, until Loretta let go of his hand and turned to him. "I'd like to meet your son sometime."

"Sure."

"We'll be fine friends, Spencer."

Spencer looked into her eyes and held her gaze. He smiled and took her hand. He wanted to kiss her, but didn't want to risk rejection. They were colleagues, coworkers, that was true, and even though they had just met, there was a connection that had nothing to do with work. He saw potential beyond platonic friendship for the two of them. He lifted her hand to his lips and kissed it. It reminded her that men could be courtly, but she pegged Spencer Tracy as way too down-to-earth for that sort of thing. Spencer Tracy, it turned out, was full of surprises.

He smiled at her, the funny crooked smile. "Good night, Gretchen."

Loretta stood and watched Spencer as he went down the stairs. "How'd you know to call me Gretchen?"

He turned and looked up at her. "I do my homework, you know." Spencer made his way down to the bottom of the stairs. When he reached Sunset, she could hear him whistling.

4

Loretta had never enjoyed making a picture more than *Man's Castle*. Perhaps it was her age: she was finally twenty-one, playing her first adult role. She played a character she could relate to, a young woman in love who worked hard to take care of those around her. Loretta quickly outgrew her trepidation about Frank Borzage and came to admire his vision of the movie and the way he ran the set.

Loretta would listen when Borzage and Tracy conversed about classic literature and the theater, committing the writers they discussed to memory so she might look them up later. She read the works of playwrights Eugene O'Neill and George S. Kaufman, and discovered *The Confessions of Saint Augustine* and essays by Erasmus, writers Tracy read time and again.

The Central Park setting in the heart of Manhattan inspired Loretta to make plans to spend time in the real place. Having spent a brief time there, she longed to visit the city's museums, libraries, and theaters, instead of just racing through to promote a movie for the studio.

Her esteem for Spencer Tracy grew with each day of work. What began as lunches on a bench outside the set or in the commissary became dinners after work to catch up on the day's events.

They became inseparable. They took long drives to find a dive diner on the outskirts of Los Angeles and, in relative anonymity, order scrambled eggs and coffee and talk into the night.

Alda observed Spencer and Loretta's simpatico relationship, and figured that this kind of connection happened between the actors on all movie sets. While Tracy didn't look like a typical matinee idol, Alda understood why he had such an appeal to women. He took an interest, paid attention to details, and listened. When Alda shared stories about her family home in Padua, a few days later Tracy brought her a mass card with a drawing of Saint Anthony on it. It was a small gesture, but a meaningful one.

Spencer became a part of life at Sunset House. He played cards with Loretta's sisters, ate seconds of Ruby's cuisine, and made himself at home by the pool. Gladys was worried about Loretta, but she also grew fond of Spencer, as all the members of her family had. Spencer's marital status was a concern. Loretta assured her mother that she and Spencer had not taken the relationship to a serious level, but it soon became obvious that Loretta, in her wildly romantic way, was deluding herself.

Spencer wanted Loretta to meet his son John. Susie was still a baby, but John, who Spencer could talk about for hours, was a delight. Tracy said little about his estranged wife, Louise, except that he had a deep respect and affection for her, and admired her as the mother of his children. He never complained about Louise to Loretta, though he held out no hope of returning to his wife and resuming life as it had been before he left.

Loretta had heard the rumors about other women in Spencer's life. She believed some of the stories, and ignored the rest. Leading men generally fell for their costars; Loretta figured that was a matter of proximity meeting opportunity. But it was different with Spencer. She knew for certain that when he was with her, he wasn't distracted.

———

Loretta parked her car behind a sea of automobiles in an open field next to the Brentwood Little League field. She wore sunglasses, a wide-brimmed hat, and a simple cotton madras sundress that she had made herself. She was finally going to meet Spencer's beloved son.

The game had already begun. The stands were full of parents who had their eyes focused on the field, which made it easy for the movie star to slip in unnoticed. Loretta climbed to the top of the bleachers and found a seat. She scanned the field, looking for Spencer and his son. Finally, she found them on the visiting team bench, watching the game with intensity. She didn't try to get Spencer's attention.

It was Johnny's turn at bat. Spencer took him by the shoulders and moved his face close to his son's. He coached his son, using sign language and gestures. The boy nodded intently, taking in his father's instructions. Loretta smiled; she knew when Tracy had a point, he could take his time making it. A few of the parents stood up and groused—"Move it along," "Get in the game, kid," that sort of thing. The carping from the stands didn't deter Spencer from taking his time.

Man's Castle was to wrap soon, and Loretta couldn't bear the thought. Movie after movie, job after job, she made friends, and then the company moved on to new projects. They promised to get together, which they seldom did, or simply said, "Hope we do another picture together." At the time, she always meant those words, but her friendship with Spencer Tracy was different.

As time went on, Spencer wanted a romance with her, and she longed for one with him. She tried to stay away, to balance her time away from work with other activities, but felt compelled to be near him. She felt sure that she was of use to him, that he had a need for her support, counsel, and advice. She couldn't help but notice that she made him happy. The brooding Irishman disappeared in her presence, leaving her to observe his earnest nature, his depth, and how ardently he rooted for her happiness.

There was also a spiritual connection. They went to mass together every Sunday. They didn't discuss their religion, but the act of meeting at church, sitting in the same pew, and taking their sacraments together week after week connected them in a way that was deeper than the physical attraction they shared.

They were buddies. Their interests were similar outside of work.

They liked hobbies they could get lost in; he painted, and she sewed. As much as they enjoyed their conversations, they could spend hours together in complete silence. He might refine an aspect of a painting; she might rip out a hem and reset it. This was the kind of relationship Loretta had hoped for, but whenever she thought about their future, she became confused.

Loretta watched as Johnny chose his bat. The boy had a laserlike focus on the game. He had his father's coloring, a smattering of Irish good luck freckles on his nose and cheeks just like Spencer, but a willowy build.

Johnny also had his father's intensity. Just like Spencer, he took everything in. He spied the boys on base, the pitcher, and the stands. He squinted and threw a few swings over home plate. He looked at his father, who gave him courage with a big smile and a two-fisted wave.

The pitcher threw the ball. Johnny hit the ball with force, a grounder to right field that sent everybody on the field scrambling. Johnny tossed the bat and ran to first base. Spencer was thrilled for his son, jumping up and down as though he had just hit a line drive that would secure the pennant. The crowd went wild.

Johnny was safe on first base. He stood tall, dusted himself off, and kept one toe firmly planted on the white rubber mat, the other safely inside the diamond's base line. He reached forward toward second base, catching the eye of the pitcher, who thought about throwing the ball to force him to run to second. Instead, the pitcher threw the ball toward the batter.

There was a bright sun, the dazzling baseball diamond, a determined boy, and eager fans hungry for a hit. And there was the father of the boy, full of admiration and belief in his son's ability. It was the picture of an authentic family life that Loretta longed for. She had never seen Spencer so happy. Free of his guilt and focused on his son, he was wide open, full of joy as a father and as a man. She would remember the purity of this moment.

Spencer shielded his eyes and looked up into the stands. Loretta raised her hand to wave to him just as she saw his wife, Louise, run behind the batting cage and join her husband on the green. Loretta sat back down, blending into the crowd in the stands as Spencer put his arm around his wife's waist. Louise buried her face in Spencer's shoulder, just as Loretta had dozens of times when she was weary at the end of the day and she needed to be close to him.

Louise was attractive, slim and simply dressed in a sunbonnet, skirt, and sandals. She looked like a fulfilled parent and a happy wife.

Loretta was neither envious of nor angry at Louise. Loretta was practical and knew that a marriage in its particularity was a deal; each had its own rules and interpretation. Spencer may have been separated from Louise when Loretta fell for him, but her conscience was beginning to bother her. What she saw between the Tracys was not so much romantic devotion as a deeper, more profound love between two people in a common cause to take care of their family and their son who was in need of their attention.

Loretta and Spencer were wildly attracted to one another on a physical level, and he was nurturing her young intellect, but neither of those truths would hold up against the sturdy marriage Loretta witnessed that day. Spencer may have insisted that he could divorce Louise to marry Loretta, but she didn't want him to; she couldn't break up their family.

As the next player took his turn at bat, Loretta seized the moment to slip out of the stands unnoticed. She ran for her car. She shoved the key in the ignition and backed the car out of the lot. On the road heading for home, she began to cry. What had made her happy was not to be. The months of confusion had given way to total clarity. Loretta couldn't be the other woman. She had to find the strength to say good-bye to the man she loved. She had to let go of Spencer Tracy once and for all.

———————

Clark Gable stood on the deck of the *König* and surveyed the waves rolling toward the bay of Monterey. The surf of the Pacific was blue as midnight, with low rolls of foam bubbles that bordered the shoreline like silver lace.

Gable checked the position of the sun overhead as he flicked his fishing rod and reel.

Close by, at his feet, a freshly caught three-foot marlin, quicksilver blue in the sunlight, thrashed in a metal bin.

The deckhand was nervous as he fumbled through the tackle box, searching for fishing wire.

"Look under the crate, kid," Gable instructed. At twenty-four, the deckhand was only ten years younger than the actor, but in Hollywood, that was the age difference between *pal* and *kid.*

The deckhand lifted the wooden sleeve out of the tackle box. Neatly arranged in small compartments below were circular bundles of wire, hooks arranged by size, and a compartment of colorful lures. It reminded him of his mother's jewelry box, filled with glittering crystal ear bobs, dainty bracelets, and a necklace of pearls.

"Hand it over, kid," Gable said. "What's your name?"

"David Niven, sir." The young man stood up straight. He was tall and slim, wore white trousers, a blue-and-white-striped shirt, and a cap embroidered with a *K*.

"You can cut the 'sir' stuff."

The deckhand swallowed hard. "But I'm British, Mr. Gable. We sir from the start."

Gable laughed. "With that accent, you shouldn't settle for swabbing."

"I assure you I won't."

"What are you doing in America?"

"Oh, this and that."

"You want to be an actor."

"Why not?"

Gable laughed harder still. "You got guts."

"No, this marlin has guts. I have something else entirely."

"Talent?"

"Not much, I'm afraid."

"What are you going to tell them in casting? Because they're going to ask you, you know."

"I will tell them that I have desire."

"Every background extra has that."

"I see. Well. I'm fairly well read."

"Nobody reads out here."

"How do you know?"

"Because I'm a reader," Gable admitted.

It was hard for Niven to believe that this massive man, with a head as large as a buffalo's and hands like the paws of a lion, could handle a leather-bound volume of anything. This was a man built for the outdoors and the hunting, shooting, skinning, hiking, and camping that went along with it. But Niven had learned to take people in Hollywood at their word, even if those words might not ring true. If Gable believed he was an intellectual, who was Niven to challenge him? Besides, the deckhand dreamed of becoming an actor, and that ambition was fueled by intense curiosity. Niven knew he could learn a lot from Gable.

"Do you find the men in charge of the studios intelligent?"

"They're good with budgets. You have your geniuses, like Irving Thalberg. He's a reader. The rest of them? Not so much. People read for them. Ida Koverman does most of the reading for Louis B. Mayer."

"If they don't read, what do the people in charge at the studios actually do?"

"They keep their noses in the wind and figure out which way it's blowing."

"Surely there's more to it than that."

"Here's a short history of motion pictures. About twenty years ago, the Schenk brothers were running an amusement park in Palisades, New Jersey. They noticed that people were spending a lot of money watching the nickelodeons, so they hatched a scheme to put words and music to the pictures."

"You make it sound pedestrian."

"Now the producers tell us that movies began in the theater, that plays were the inspiration. Classics. But that's a lot of hooey. We're a carnival amusement. They made movies in Australia, China, Germany, long before they came here. We didn't invent the movies, but just like anything American made, we take a good idea from anywhere and make it better. We've come a long way fast."

"Any advice, sir? How does one break in to the business?"

"The accent works for you. Work the Old Britannia for all it's worth."

"I will indeed."

"A ditch digger with a British accent could walk through the gates of MGM, and Louis B. Mayer would sign him up. An American ditch digger would walk through the same gate and be escorted off the lot. There's something about you people. You sound like you have culture."

"Lucky for me, they will never meet my family and disprove that theory."

"Commoners?"

"Mr. Gable, you have no idea."

"I might. I'm from Cadiz."

"Arabia?"

"Ohio."

"I passed through Ohio on the train. Lovely and languid."

"If you say so. I worked the oil rigs. Met a girl and got hooked on theater. Got out. Became an actor. That's how I ended up here."

"There's always a girl in the story."

"Every picture is a love story." Gable steadied his gaze on the water. "Even when they call it something else. They might call it an adventure, a mystery, a historical, or a Tom Mix western, but they're all love stories."

David Niven was aware that Gable had a reputation with the ladies. A lovely blonde had kissed him good-bye before he boarded the *König* that morning. Virginia Grey was a young starlet, her father a movie director, so she understood Hollywood and the life of a leading man. As Gable moved through the world, his way was made clear by women who could not get enough of him, or he of them. They had made him a star, and he owed them. Whatever he could do to repay the debt was fine with him, and in fact an obligation.

Niven studied the fan magazines to plot his course in Hollywood. *Photoplay* had reported Gable's recent passionate pursuit of the actress Elizabeth Allan, an English rose who had enchanted Hollywood with her regal bearing and delicate beauty. She had a British accent, which proved Gable's theory. It didn't matter that Gable was married; he was a contract player, at a salary of $3,000 a week, he could buy anything or anyone he wanted, including the press, who could be convinced not to write about his private life.

David Niven could only imagine how much fun it was to be Clark Gable.

"Things are changing in Hollywood. More eyes on us."

"I can be discreet," Niven promised.

"You don't have any choice in the matter. They can fire you over anything these days."

After a decade of gum-chewing flappers, the movie business left the Roaring Twenties behind and was ready for class and couth. By 1934, hemlines had dropped, bob haircuts grew out to chignons, and breeding replaced moxie as girls went back to being women. Good taste was in style, so were the traditional values of home and hearth.

The future of the movie business would be built on a moral high ground thanks to the Hays Code. The summer of 1934 changed everything. There was a binding clause in every actor's studio contract that said he or she accepted the responsibility of setting an ethical and decent example for the audiences that came to see them in the movies.

No longer could you play an angel; you had to *be* one.

The dramatic movies of the 1930s might have been filled with stories of gangsters and their molls—Gable himself had played his share of thugs and thieves—but there were consequences for bad behavior. If you sinned on the silver screen, you might die for it; if you repented, it made a splendid final scene audiences would never forget. You want them weeping on the way out. Hollywood was now in the business of hope, with plots centered on get-rich-quick schemes and love stories that brought riches along with wedding vows.

The art deco sets, layered confections of gleaming floors and vaulted ceilings, had audiences gazing up in aspirational wonder. Never mind that the Great Depression was in full force, with breadlines, unemployment, hunger, and need. The movies showed that dreams were as potent as reality. For a nickel, you could escape.

David Niven felt slightly guilty that he had access to the one place on earth that appeared to be unaffected by world events. It was as if the endless California sun beamed down on him, and only him, lighting a bright path to potential riches and romance.

"You're going to do all right. You have wet eyes, Niven."

"I'm a crybaby, sir?"

"No. The best cinematographer told me that wet eyes are the one requirement of all movie actors. The eyes make the close-up. And yours are big and blue, which doesn't hurt."

"I suppose every actor needs a gimmick."

"You know what I like best about acting?"

"The ladies, sir?"

"Nope." Gable threw the line into the water.

"Oh, I see. Fishing?" Niven said the word in such a way that it made Gable chuckle.

"And hunting and golf. I work for everything in between. The time off."

"You work to live."

"Exactly." Gabe smiled.

"My mother always says that's the key to being happy. Don't live to work, work to live. Of course, I hardly think my mother ever thought much about pursuing happiness. She rather thought it was a bird that landed on you. It was luck."

"I agree with your mother."

"A charwoman can be wise and better read than any queen."

"Your mother was a charwoman?"

"No. She just used to say that."

"England is far away. You can make up your backstory with any details you want. You wouldn't be the first actor to pretend that he came from royalty. The front office will cook your humble beginning and make fancy jam out of it."

"Oh, you make it sound so easy. Is acting as much fun as it looks?"

"If the director is enjoying his work, then I'm enjoying mine."

"How about the leading ladies?"

"They're all right." Gable grinned.

"I should say so, sir."

"I can't figure women out, and I guess that's what keeps me interested."

Gable surveyed the surface of the water. He tugged on the line gently. Niven stood at the ready to assist, marveling that Gable did not shrink against the vast horizon, but met its line. Other important actors and successful producers had rented the boat—Niven had swabbed for them too—but none stood out against the mighty ocean quite like this man. Gable was over six feet tall; he made the cruiser, with its wide deck and hefty sails, look like a dinghy.

Despite Gable's stature, there was an earthiness to the star that made him approachable, more field soldier than general. Niven decided Gable was impossibly likeable. This was a man he could envision becoming his friend, but only if he could one day be his equal.

Suddenly the boat creaked and leaned. Gable's reel bent, as he pulled back with steady force. Niven watched as Gable commandeered a ten-foot marlin out of the water, a swift arrow against a cloudless sky. With one graceful twist, Gable pulled the fish onto the deck, where it thrashed defiantly.

"Throw the baby back," Gable said. "We'll keep this one."

David scooped the bin up to the rig and dumped the baby marlin back into the water, where it disappeared into the foam of the surf. "Lucky bastard." Niven sighed. He hoped to be as lucky as the fish that got away.

Gable walked across the MGM lot on his way to his bungalow. Robert Leonard, his current director on his new film, *After Office Hours*, caught up with him.

"How do you like Connie Bennett?" Robert Leonard asked.

"She's a good kid."

"I have them rewriting the ending. I think we need to find out what happens to her."

"Fine with me."

Leonard looked relieved. He had been around since the silents, and felt lucky to still be working. The front office had assigned him to a Gable picture, which gave his career a desperately needed boost. Gable had been a Mae Murray fan, and seen all of Robert's movies, so he readily agreed to have him direct *After Office Hours.*

"Hey, Bob."

Robert Leonard turned to face him.

"What happened in New York?"

"You want the truth?"

"Yeah."

"Mae and I started Tiffany Pictures, and things were going along well."

"You put out some good movies."

"Yeah, we did. But we couldn't make a baby. Somehow Mae put the failure of that on the little studio we started, and she eventually divorced me because she couldn't face me."

"So you came back."

"I'm lucky they wanted me back," Robert admitted.

"Don't ever say that, bud. Working in the studio is like pursuing a woman. You never want her to know how bad you need her."

"I'll keep that advice in mind, Clark." Robert went to his office.

Gable stopped at a water fountain. He was wearing jodhpurs, a white shirt, and his riding boots. He removed his partial plate from his mouth and rinsed it in the fountain.

Anita Loos, a petite brunette and the most popular screenwriter on the lot, walked by with her secretary.

"Mr. Gable," she greeted him.

"What do you think of the King of Hollywood without his teeth?" He popped the plate back into his mouth.

Anita laughed.

"You writing anything new for me?"

"Always. I'm cooking up a little something for you and Miss Crawford."

"That's always a yes from me."

"I figured."

Anita and her secretary watched as Gable walked away.

"I've found religion," Anita said.

"The Church of Clark Gable?"

"Already a member. No, I'm taking up reincarnation. I want to come back in my next life and be whatever girl that man is sweet on. It'll never happen in this go-round, but I want to die knowing it's possible in the next. "

If the young people in the movie business weren't making pictures, they were going to them.

The Pantages Theater in downtown Los Angeles had a long line of eager customers that snaked around the block. A row of palm trees outside the theater was brightly lit with klieg lamps from the roots, which threw fingers of shadow across the boulevard.

Spencer Tracy pulled up on a side street next to the theater with a car load of girls. Loretta had convinced Spencer to take Alda, her sisters, and her to see a new blockbuster, *It Happened One Night.* They were piled into Spencer's car like chocolates in a box.

"You girls get the seats. Save me the aisle. I need an escape route."

"All the clamoring fans you want to dodge?" Polly joked.

"No, I think I can handle the two of them. I'm talking about the movie. If it's a turkey, I take off. I'm not a romance guy."

"We know," Loretta joked. "How do you feel about popcorn?"

"The bigger the tub the better. And don't forget the butter." Spencer reached into his pocket and handed money to Georgie. "I trust you with the funds."

"I go free because I'm only nine."

"I knew I liked you." Spencer reached across and opened the car door.

Alda smiled. She was beginning to feel like one of the Young sisters. They included her in everything from church to going out to restaurants to going to the movies.

"You having fun?" Loretta asked Alda.

"Can you tell?"

"I can't believe you're the same sad-sack kid who showed up at Sunset House a month ago. You're a different person. You're funny and gay and light—you were so somber when you arrived."

"I was scared. Mother Superior hadn't explained anything. She just said I was going to be a secretary. I didn't know what that meant."

"So you invented it. It's just like acting. You may not be the part you're playing, but you pretend until you get there."

"Mr. Tracy makes your job easy, doesn't he?"

"And how."

"I like him."

Loretta was wistful. "He's very dear. We're just friends, you know."

Alda nodded, but what she observed between Loretta and Spencer was more than friendship.

Loretta and Spencer were required to make publicity stills for the studio. A photographer came to the set, and Alda was to keep track of the number of photographs taken, and the context of the photographs. Spencer found a way, just by virtue of having to present particular scenes, to make the shoot last an entire afternoon. Loretta and Spencer had to hold one another, look deep into one another's eyes, and come up with romantic clinches that would sell the movie on a poster. For Alda, the emotions behind the poses seemed real. There wasn't a lot of romance to conjure up because it was obvious.

"I know the difference between acting and real life," Loretta assured her. Alda nodded, but she knew that Loretta was in dangerous territory. It may have been an innocent friendship at the start, but Alda could see that emotions that had evolved over time ran deep. She was worried about Loretta, and was convinced that she would end up with a broken heart.

The Young sisters took their place on the line. Soon they were recognized, word spread, whispers turned to chatter, and they were quickly surrounded by eager fans. The girls signed autographs, and after a while the manager of the theater came outside to control the throng.

Spencer had parked the car and come around the corner to find the girls in the midst of the frenzy. He stood back and watched them, getting a kick out of their popularity and the politic way they handled the crowd. Loretta felt Spencer's gaze. He winked at her and moved behind the shadow of the palm tree.

"Ladies, look! I think that's Spencer Tracy from *Man's Castle!*"

"Where?" the women shouted.

"Behind the tree!" She pointed.

The ladies made a stampede for Spencer Tracy, surrounding him. He shot Loretta a look. The Young sisters laughed as he was deluged with fans.

"He thinks he's invisible," Loretta said to Polly.

"He won't after tonight."

"Sir, will you please pry Mr. Tracy loose from the ladies?" Loretta asked the manager. "We'd love to see the movie."

The manager obliged, freeing Spencer Tracy and ushering him into the theater with the Young sisters in tow. He led them to a private viewing box over the mezzanine that overlooked the audience and stage, where the screen was obscured behind gold velvet curtains.

"I'm going to get you for that," Spencer whispered to Loretta.

"They love you, Spence."

"That's not love, that's fighting over a sweater in a bargain bin. I could've been George Arliss, and they would've gone batty."

"You're a star."

"Oh, big deal."

"It *is* a big deal. The bigger the star, the better the scripts, and the better the scripts, the bigger the career."

As the theater went dark and the newsreel jumped onto the screen, Georgie and Sally piled into the viewing box with bags of popcorn and bottles of cold soda. Georgie handed Loretta a sack of licorice and gave Spencer his change. Loretta shared the candy with Spencer. When Spencer took Loretta's hand in the dark, every muscle in her body relaxed.

The feature credits appeared on the screen. Claudette Colbert received applause, but when Clark Gable's name appeared, the audience went wild. Sally reached across and yanked Loretta's arm. "He's the king!"

Loretta leaned back in her chair. Spencer leaned forward and looked over the banister of the viewing box to observe the audience. He watched as hundreds of people sat up higher in their seats when Clark Gable walked into the scene. Whatever that guy had, Spencer figured, it was bigger than good acting. It was a mania, a kind of popularity that he could only imagine. But he had to admit, Gable had technique. He understood the camera and played to it well.

Loretta watched Gable work. He photographed with ease. His gray eyes had a depth in black and white; tall and lean, his posture was both confident and relaxed. Gable's acting had become less pre-sentational and more emotional, an improvement on his earlier roles playing crooks, gangsters, hucksters, and con men in pre-code melo-dramas. Over time, Gable had dropped the menacing leer, along with other bad stage habits, and begun to use his body to express feeling. He learned to play to the camera, to fill the shot, to use emo-tion and expression when he said a line instead of playing it in one dimension, as if on a stage. He had become a leading man. Usually it's the studio that decides who will become a star, but it doesn't stick unless the public concurs. As is the alchemy of all good fortune in show business, Gable had the backing of the studio and a fan base that was growing by the week.

Gable appeared polished onscreen yet masculine, his deep dim-ples giving away a wily humor, a knowingness that the joke was not on him. Loretta saw him with a new admiration and hoped to work with him someday, but she knew it was unlikely. Gable was in demand, and there was a line as long as Ventura Boulevard of leading ladies who wanted a shot at him.

"You're not falling in love with Gable, are you?" Spencer whispered.

"I'd be the only woman in the theater who didn't."

"Do me a favor, Gretch."

"What's that?"

"Be the only one who doesn't."

Loretta looked over at Spence. He didn't take his eyes off the silver screen.

Alda watched the exchange between her boss and Spencer and knew that Loretta was in deep. Alda had heard that Tracy's wife was due to visit the set of *Man's Castle*, and while Alda did not approve of infidelity, she didn't want Loretta to be embarrassed. Alda observed that all the men on the set fell in love with Loretta a little, but on Spencer Tracy's part, it wasn't admiration or a crush. It appeared to Alda to be the real thing, the most dangerous kind of love of all.

The Ides of March blew David Niven, part-time caddy, deckhand, and performer, into Bel Air, practically on horseback. The swabbie was making his move into Hollywood. One of David's equestrian pals from England introduced him to Loretta's sister, Sally Blane, who never met a foreign accent she didn't love. She immediately invited David to dinner at Sunset House, knowing he would charm Gladys and her sisters with his fine manners and scintillating conversation.

David excused himself from the table to take his plate to the kitchen.

Ruby was busy preparing the dessert. "Mr. Niven, get out of my kitchen."

"Miss Ruby, I grew up in a kitchen. I like to help."

"I don't need it. Take your English fanny back to the dining room."

"I've never heard it put that way."

"Welcome to Ruby's."

Gladys and the girls listened to the exchange through the door and tried not to laugh.

"Can we keep him, Mama?" Sally begged.

"He's not a stray kitten you found on the side of the road."

"He's so charming. And funny. I haven't stopped laughing since I met him."

"Sally, you've been laughing since the day you were born. That hardly qualifies as an endorsement."

"The pool house is ready for company. You said so yourself," Loretta reminded her mother. "Properties get gamy when no one lives in them."

"They start to smell like wet mattresses and old socks," Sally said. "Better to have a tenant."

Gladys had taught her daughters well. They were a business, on-screen and off. The girls pooled their money and invested it in houses. Gladys would buy them, fix them up, decorate them, and rent them. When the bank account got high, they'd purchase another property, renovate it, and rent it.

Loretta became the highest earner in the family, so she served as the bank. Real estate in the early days of Hollywood was a genius investment, but truthfully an innocent one for Gladys Belzer and her family. Gladys simply stuck to what she knew. A renter all her life, she understood what was required when it came to being a landlord. And as actors, directors, writers, and producers flocked to Hollywood from the Broadway stage, they needed good places to stay, ones that would increase their stature and send a message to the studios. "Does Mr. Niven have any referrals?"

"Mama, he doesn't need any. He has impeccable manners. He's British. He's in the horse business."

"What does that mean?"

"Racehorses. Something or other."

David returned to the dining room with Ruby.

"Mr. Niven, I understand you're looking for a place to stay."

"I could not possibly burden you with my troubles, Mrs. Belzer."

"What kind of horse business are you in?"

"I'm not actually in the horse business. I have friends who are, and I've been part of a rodeo show that traveled around the country a bit. The truth is, I'd like to get into acting." He sat down. "Why aren't you all laughing?"

"Why would we?" Loretta stood and poured the coffee.

"Have you tried?" Gladys asked.

"I've been background here and there. I earn my keep on the golf course as a caddy, and I swab for the upper crust on the marina rentals in Del Rey and Monterey. Wherever the wind blows through sailcloth, you shall find me. I fully intend to keep working my odd jobs until I'm cast in something. I would pay you rent, of course."

"As Loretta mentioned, we don't need it," Sally blurted. "I mean, right, Mama? The pool house is empty anyway."

"You're a hard worker?" Gladys asked.

"I'm afraid that's the one thing I'm good at. I'm a very determined young man, or so I like to think."

"We do have a furnished pool house here on the property. You're welcome to it. Ruby serves breakfast at seven if you want eggs. If you sleep in—"

"I leave out the bread, and you can toast it," Ruby told him.

"Sounds marvelous."

"If you're serious about acting . . . ," Loretta began.

"I am."

"Alda and I leave for the studio at four thirty tomorrow morning. You're welcome to come, but we'll have to sneak you."

"I've done some sneaking in my day." He turned to Gladys. "Nothing you wouldn't approve of, Mrs. Belzer."

———————

"I haven't done anything this low-rent since I seduced my sister's piano teacher on her sixty-second birthday. The piano teacher, that is."

"Get down," Loretta said, laughing, as Alda threw a tarp over Niven as he lay on the floor of the back seat of Loretta's car.

All the way to the studio, Niven kept Loretta and Alda in tearful hysterics as he made the sounds of a hostage under the tarp. At first he whimpered, and then he began thumping the floor of the coupe as though he were trying to wrestle his way out of captivity.

"Shush back there," Loretta commanded before she waved to the guard at Twentieth Century-Fox. The guard motioned Loretta and Alda through the gates, their big smiles protecting the stowaway.

Loretta was capable of following the rules, except when it came to people she cared about. She was game to break rules to benefit others, but never herself. If she liked you, as David Niven and Alda Ducci had found out, she welcomed you into her life, shared everything she had, made you family, and never let you go.

David followed Loretta and Alda into the dressing room bungalow. Loretta's team was ready to put her through "the car wash," as the actress called it. She was buffed, plucked, rolled, and pressed, ready for the cameras at 6:00 a.m. sharp.

David sat back and watched the proceedings with wonderment. He had not seen this aspect of the process up close. As an extra, he only saw the finished product, the actress fully made up and costumed, surrounded by her staff, shielded by an umbrella carried by a dresser lest the California sun age and scorch her on her way to the set, her bungalow, or the commissary.

David observed that once the studio believed in you, they protected their investment. Niven longed to be a contract player, vowing he would never complain, if he were so lucky as to go under contract, about any role assigned him. He said he would play a toilet plunger if Louis B. Mayer asked him to, and he meant it.

He observed as the makeup artist applied rouge to Loretta's cheeks. He could barely stand to watch as they made her creamy skin like glistening marble, her eyelashes as thick as the bristles on a push broom, and her lips a shade of pink that he could only recall on his favorite flower, the peony.

In the course of the previous evening, Niven's yearning and attention had spun through the Young sisters like a roulette wheel, his fancy landing first on Sally, then on Polly, and now on Loretta. He adored them all, with indiscriminate grace notes of lust. Like a man in a showroom full of new cars, unable to pick just one, he coveted all equally. Is there much difference between a roadster, a convertible, or a coupe? They all had their charms, and so did the glorious Young sisters.

Niven appreciated all women, but beautiful women were his weakness. He'd almost put up with the worst aspects of character in a girl if she had a pretty face and a fetching figure. He would endure a twit as long as her aesthetics held up in the hot light of the bright sun. There was plenty of that in California.

Niven was also vulnerable. He desperately wanted to sit on the merry-go-round, but it was spinning so fast that he couldn't get a running start to make the jump. He needed connections, and he needed them now. He had admitted to the Young sisters that he wanted an acting career. It was almost as brave to admit it as it was to find the determination to do it. Niven would have to dig deep for his acting ability, as it did not come naturally to him. Parlor storytelling was his gift, and he would do his best to apply those skills when it came to acting, but in the meantime, he'd have to charm his way into the movies.

Alda brought Niven a sandwich and a cold bottle of root beer while Loretta changed costumes for her work that afternoon.

"You're so kind, Alda. Will you join me?"

Alda looked around and took a seat next to him.

"We have a bond, you know," he said as he fished in his pocket for his Swiss Army knife with the bottle opener.

"You worked in a convent?"

"I wish. I don't have the stuff for saving humanity. My liver is made of lily, I hate to tell you." He snapped the lid off the soda bottle.

"I doubt that."

"I have no courage."

"You'll need it as an actor."

"I don't know how Loretta does it."

"She makes it look easy."

"She's made fifty pictures, you know."

"I imagine she was good in the very first one."

"You know, Mr. Niven, it's not a sin to want to succeed."

"It may be a sin to put an audience through one of my performances."

"You don't know that."

Niven sat up and smiled. "You know, you're right, I don't. I might be bloody good at acting."

"Loretta says you're only as good as who you act with in the scene."

"That's what Gable says."

"You know him? Don't tell Sally."

"Oh, she already dug those ten red talons into my arm when I told her I swabbed for him."

"Do you know Spencer Tracy?"

"We haven't met. He does not participate in the sporting life. No shooting ranges, no boats, no golf. At least, if he does, I haven't seen him."

"He's a good actor."

"Not much of a looker."

"It doesn't matter. You forget all that when he speaks. He makes you understand what he's feeling."

"Loretta is sweet on him, so he must be a good fellow."

"He is."

"But it's complicated, right? Isn't it always a tangle when a man loves a woman?"

"I wouldn't know, Mr. Niven."

Alda remembered the girls of Saint Elizabeth's. No matter their despair, they still believed in romantic love. They talked about movies, how a kiss could save a character, redeem her or elevate her to a higher social station. Kisses had not done much good for the girls at Saint Elizabeth's, though Alda encouraged them not to turn bitter. Even as their pregnancies advanced toward labor, the girls would hold on to their dime novels, to the possibilities of a storybook romance happening in their own lives.

"I'm very grateful to you, Alda," Niven said as he finished his sandwich. "You feed me. You quench my thirst." He toasted her with the root beer. "And you took me in on the spot."

"Everyone can see you're a good man."

"Now what do you suppose the value of that is in Hollywood? I don't think I'll rise very far with goodness as my calling card. If I am polite, agreeable, and good-natured, I will be a deckhand and a caddy for the rest of my life. Of course, I will have a marvelous suntan in the process. I'll have absolutely no film career, but I will look like Midas by way of Pismo Beach. I shall be a golden god with a sterling temperament who buses tables at the Pig N Whistle."

Alda laughed. She wondered if Mr. Niven knew how funny he was. He was so busy being suave and courtly, he might not have any idea how his real gift, the humor that came so naturally to him, was in fact the only talent he needed to become a star. It seemed to Alda that the people who were successful in Hollywood knew exactly who they were, and the parts they played were extensions of themselves and not a creation of someone new.

———

Father McNally knelt in the confessional booth, made the sign of the cross, and took a seat. He placed a purple stole around his neck, lit a small votive candle, and opened his prayer book.

The priest had noticed a long line of congregants in the front pew when he arrived for work, so he settled in for a long afternoon. His superior, Monsignor McNeill, was working the confessional on the other side of the church, but his line was shorter because he had a reputation for strict penance. Everybody, it seemed, even Catholics in search of absolution, rooted for the rookie.

He heard the door snap shut on the other side. A woman whispered in the dark.

"Bless me, Father, for I have sinned. The last time I went to confession, a few moments ago."

"You went to Monsignor McNeill?"

"Yes, Father."

"Across the way?"

"Yes, Father."

"Then you must follow his penance." McNally was in second command at the church. The last thing he needed was to return to the rectory that evening for his own penance and admit to the monsignor that he had overturned his absolution.

"There was no penance, Father."

"Monsignor must have thought your confession was not a sin."

"No, he said he could not absolve me." The woman began to cry.

"Did the monsignor say why?"

"Father, please. I need your guidance. I'm in love, and I can't think."

"You should talk to your mother."

"I already know her feelings on the matter. She told me not to fall in love with this gentleman, but it was too late."

"You should listen to your mother."

"But you haven't heard my side."

"I don't need to—I'm sure your mother is wise."

"I'm in love with a good man. He's Catholic. But he is separated from his wife."

"Are there children?"

"Yes."

"What has this man offered you?"

"We love each other."

"Is his intention to leave his wife?"

"I don't know for sure, but I believe so. He said he would seek an annulment to marry me."

"An annulment isn't like paying a parking ticket. It's an arduous process." The priest was exasperated. "There's a tribunal that doesn't guarantee a result in your favor."

"I know that, Father."

"If you know what you're doing is wrong, then you know what you must do."

"Even though I will give up any future happiness?"

"How can something you know is wrong make you happy?"

"It can't, Father."

"So you see, you didn't need to come to me. You know what is required of you. You have to end this love affair with this married man. He will not have the strength to do it."

"But I love him. He needs me."

"He is not free to love you, nor are you free to love him in the eyes of the church."

The woman began to weep.

"Whatever happiness this love affair gives you is fleeting. This man belongs to another, and he has a family. Years down the line he would look at you with contempt for forcing him to break his vows, leave his children, and abandon his faith. You must end it now."

"Please, Father."

Father McNally leaned into the screen. He recognized the voice, but before he could say her name, Loretta Young pushed the door open and exited the confessional. Mrs. Belzer had already come to him and asked him to speak to Loretta. Gladys believed Loretta needed a father figure, someone with a different point of view, one more practical and less romantic than her own.

Usually, after confession, Loretta knelt before the shrine of the Blessed Lady and recited her rosary, but she was too upset to stay inside the church.

Loretta was turning to go when she saw Spencer, his back to her, kneeling in the first pew before the altar. Loretta couldn't face Spencer, so she slipped out the back of the church.

———

Spencer Tracy turned and saw Loretta leave. He thought about going after her, but he didn't want to make a scene. He helplessly buried his face in his hands. Tracy resented the constraints of his marriage, career, and religion. It seemed that there was no solution to his dilemma, which over time had become a conundrum that he could not solve to his own or anyone else's satisfaction. He never seemed to get what he wanted on this side of heaven, and he knew that would probably be the case for the rest of his life unless he made the changes necessary to pursue personal happiness. He was a fatalistic Catholic, but he was also becoming a movie star, and that meant he would soon have all the things of this world that he desired.

He loved Loretta. He would press Louise for the divorce and pursue the annulment from the church that Loretta would require. Surely that would clear the path for the sacrament of marriage, and satisfy the priest and Mrs. Belzer. Tracy could not predict whether his plan would suit Loretta or be too great a sacrifice for her, but he was willing to do whatever it took to find out.

———

The Cocoanut Grove was a homestyle pot roast and banana cream pie restaurant in a fantasy Hollywood setting. The decor was inspired by the colors and landscape of the South Seas, while the kitchen was an homage to Grandma's home cooking. The fronds of papier-mâché palm trees tickled the ceiling, their trunks obscuring dark booths convenient for trysts. Murals of marine life draped with glittery nets decorated the walls.

"The Grove is the perfect place to get caught in the nets," David Niven had said. "If you want your wife to catch you with your girl-friend, book a table at The Grove."

Loretta drove to dinner that night, straight from the studio. She'd had a stomachache all day. She hadn't seen Spencer since the priests denied her absolution, and she couldn't bring herself to discuss it with him over the phone.

Spencer had suggested several nights out, but she'd begged out of all of them, using her heavy work schedule as an excuse. Spencer was intuitive, and he knew he was getting the bum's rush.

Loretta knew something had changed when she slipped into the seat next to him in a booth.

"How was work?" He looked at Loretta, but she could not look him in the eye.

"Long day. How about you?" She studied the menu.

Spencer could have spent the entire evening looking at her, saying nothing. He was enamored of her beauty, but his feelings were deeper. Her presence sustained him. Even sitting in silence near her replenished the deepest wells of emotional need within him. She had him, and he knew it.

"I did my share of bad acting today," he offered.

"I doubt that."

"I was distracted. And I think you know why, Gretch."

The waiter came by for their order.

"What are you having?" Spencer asked.

"I'm not hungry."

"I'm starving." Spencer ordered a rare steak and a baked potato. "Bring the lady a bowl of soup. Whatever you got that's plain. Consommé."

The waiter left them alone. Spencer took her hand.

"Come on, Gretch. Look at me. You look pale."

This had been her first real romantic relationship, despite her short-lived marriage. Loretta was prone to crushes on her costars, feelings that built to a fever pitch and went nowhere.

"Spence, my mother is worried."

"About what?"

"She heard around town that you drink."

Spencer chuckled to himself. "Have you ever seen me drunk?"

"Never. I told her. I thought maybe they were mixing you up with Lee Tracy."

"Let's hope he's not getting offered the same roles," Spencer said wryly.

"You know Grant Withers had a drinking problem, and I couldn't take it."

"Which is why I've never had a cocktail around you."

"Is that any way to live? You behave a certain way around me?"

"I believed I was being respectful and thoughtful."

"You would." Loretta shook her head.

"Let's talk it out, kid," Tracy said softly.

Loretta looked into his eyes, but she loved him so much that she had to look away.

"What's the problem?"

"You know what the problem is," she said quietly.

"And I'm working it out."

"We can't work it out."

"Why not?"

"I went to see the priest, and he refused me absolution."

"You're not the one who's married."

"It doesn't matter. I'm keeping you from Louise and your family."

"We've been through this."

"It isn't right."

"I was separated when I met you."

"It doesn't matter. You know this isn't right."

"I could never say that about you."

"You know what I mean. You're a man of faith. You're a believer, and that comes with a responsibility. It's one of the things I love about you."

"You can't have redemption without sin."

"I'm your sin?"

"I didn't say that."

"But I am. Do you want to be with me and lose your faith?"

"You've shored up my faith, Gretchen."

"Do you want me to give up mine?"

"I'm not asking you to give up anything. Together we're strong, we're better. You know that."

"There's no absolution for us. Even if you got an annulment, even if we could start over, we still know the truth. We'd have a brand-new life based on a lie. I can't do that to you."

"I don't want to say good-bye."

"You love your wife and family. They need you more than I do."

Spencer put his arm around her. "Gretch, it's a little more complicated than that. I'm in love with you. You're the most magnificent girl in the world, but it's more than your pretty face, which, if I'm honest, has sustained me through a lot of dark hours. But all that aside, I can talk to you. It isn't that way with anyone else. Maybe it's our situation—maybe because I can't have you, I feel the loss more deeply when we're apart. But the truth is, you get me. I can share my feelings. It's very simple. I can't face life ahead without you. I don't want to, and I don't think you do either."

"I don't want you to leave your wife."

"I've already left her."

"Go back."

Spencer sat back in his chair. "You've fallen out of love with me."

"No, I haven't," she said quietly.

He pulled her close and kissed her. "That would be the only reason I'd let you end this. Gretch, let me handle this. I'll go see the priest. I'll explain. I'll tell them I met you months after leaving Louise."

"It doesn't matter. It's still wrong."

"Will you let me work this thing out?"

Loretta didn't want to argue with him, not ever. She had seen his temper before; his anger didn't frighten her, it pained her. She especially didn't want to break his heart. She knew it had happened to him before, in so many ways, as a man, a husband, and a father. Loretta had seen the dark corners where Tracy hid. She understood his torment, empathized with his suffering, and observed how he prayed for serenity, something that had eluded him all of his life. She didn't have to be told he was an alcoholic. She knew something was wrong. Tracy handled conflict by burying it, and temptation by yielding to it and then punishing himself for having indulged. Spencer Tracy was at war with his needs. Loretta could see it was a hopeless struggle.

Still, they had such glorious connections. Tracy loved her family, understood her work, and shared her faith. And now she had the memories they had made during *Man's Castle*. She reached out to him when she had problems with her role, and with simple, clear directives, he worked her through the script. If she had a tussle with her sisters, he said just the right thing. There was more than romance at stake; underneath the mutual attraction was an abiding friendship based on common interests. She didn't spend hours on the phone with any other friend, male or female, but Spence was different. Just as he was an actor who listened, he listened in life. Loretta strengthened her resolve.

"I want you to pretend that I'm not me, and that I'm coming to you with a problem. Our problem. What would you say to a twenty-one-year-old woman in this circumstance?"

"I'd tell her to say good-bye and don't look back." Spencer leaned back in his chair, resigned. "Even if it hurts."

"And it does, Spence. It hurts."

"You know, I'd only let you go if I knew you could find happiness without me."

"It doesn't feel like it tonight." Loretta's eyes filled with tears.

"I'm older, and I know your sadness will pass. I'm the one who will drag this ending around with me for the rest of my life. You'll be all right."

"I wish I didn't care about doing the right thing."

"Naw, that's what I admire about you. You have standards. Principles. They say good roles are rare in Hollywood, but a moral compass is almost impossible to find."

"I will miss you. I'll miss how innocent we were when we were palling around. Why did I have to fall in love with you?"

"You know what the worst part of this thing is? You go your whole life looking for this exact thing, and you swear you'll never find it, and then you do, and then you can't have it. It is parceled out to everybody else, so you see it and recognize it, and patiently you wait for your portion, and by the time your turn comes, there isn't enough to go around. Hell of a thing."

"If it helps, you're not alone, Spence."

"It makes it worse, actually."

Loretta leaned against Spencer's shoulder, a place that had given her comfort in ways that delighted her and strengthened her since they met. She wanted to remember this moment, his scent of bergamot and cedar, his hands that enveloped her own and made her feel safe. She closed her eyes and was still. She waited for the answer to come, the one she hoped for, the one that would tell her to fight for him. But instead of an answer, she saw Louise in her mind's eye. She pictured that day at the baseball diamond, when Louise placed her head on Spencer's shoulder. Loretta had seen with her own eyes what Spencer meant to Louise, and together, what their son Johnny meant to both of them. She could not in good conscience take him away from them. She couldn't live with him, knowing she had hurt Louise and his family. She lifted her head off his shoulder.

"Are you all right, Gretch?"

"Eat your dinner," she said. "It's getting cold."

————————

Alda sat at Loretta's messy desk in her bedroom, which was piled with pages torn from her scripts, gum wrappers, receipts, fabric swatches, and reminder notes. She sorted the papers into neat piles. She found Loretta's retainer under a stack of party invitations. She took the retainer into the bathroom, rinsed it, and placed it in its container on the sink.

Alda returned to the desk to finish straightening. When she got to the bottom of a stack, she found a letter that Loretta had written in draft form several times. It was her final farewell to Spencer. She was breaking off their relationship for good.

The practice letters, with misspelled words and jumbled letters, were marked with the same symbols she used on her scripts. Loretta had taken to using dictation for all her correspondence, and Alda was getting pretty good at it. But this time Loretta had done the composition herself. As Alda continued to organize the desk, she found the finished letter, in Loretta's simple cursive penmanship, tucked into an unsealed envelope. Alda held the letter, remembering one that she had written. Letters that end a love affair are always short, each word selected carefully, for exact meaning.

Alda placed the envelope on top of the desk. She collected the practice letters, the scraps of notes, and went to the fireplace. She threw the papers on to the grate, lit a match, and burned them. As they burned, they turned the deepest red, the color of roses.

5

Loretta sat cross-legged by the swimming pool at Sunset House. The late-afternoon sky over Bel Air was faded coral as the sun slipped behind the Hollywood Hills. She dipped her fingers in the satin waters, spelling out the name Spencer Tracy with her index finger, then erasing the letters with a splash.

"Stay away from the edge. You're a horrid swimmer, Gretchen." David Niven stood near the shallow end, in a proper suit and hat. "I cannot possibly save another woman from herself today."

"Mama said to tell you that they fixed the heat in the pool house."

"It's about bloody time. October can be cruel in California. It's so cold in there, I'm storing oranges in my sock drawer."

Niven sat down beside Loretta. "Bad day?"

"The worst."

"You can cry on my shoulder."

"The suit is Savile Row. The wool is Italian. No, thank you. You can't afford the shrinkage. You're a working actor, remember?"

"Sort of."

"You need your suit."

"I saw the paper."

"Nicely worded, don't you think?"

"They're going to call you Saint Loretta in print from now on. You were generous, contrite, and absolute. Maybe for once Mother Publicity got it right. The Iron Butterfly—that's you, darling—can actually fly. Maybe you are a saint after all."

"Hardly."

"You know I don't believe in a chaste romance."

"How do you know it was chaste?"

"I live in the pool house. I never once saw you scale the tree at midnight and sneak back in at dawn. Never saw Spencer climb the same tree up to your window. Never saw you roll that pathetic roadster of yours down the drive in neutral so Mrs. Belzer wouldn't wake at the sound of that dreadful engine. Never caught Mr. Tracy in the hedges."

"And you never will."

"Poor dear. You got all of the aggravation of a love affair with none of the fun."

"We had fun."

"All right, then. Let's be sensible. If you want him this badly, convert. Join the jovial Protestants who clutter up the Church of England. It's all the familiar bells and whistles and incense of the Holy Roman Church with the option of divorce. You can have your Spencer Tracy and wedding cake too."

"There's a thought. Hop around until some church gives me permission."

"Many died in the Crusades for less. Besides, it's better than being miserable."

"I guess."

"Do you really love the man?"

"David."

"No, seriously. I think if you truly loved him, no church could stand in your way."

"I don't know what love is anymore. I thought I knew, but clearly I have no idea."

"I rather think you wanted to save him."

"Isn't that what we do when we fall in love?"

"Not generally. The saving comes later, if at all. When in love, we frolic and play and go at it like rabbits."

"Where do I sign up for that?"

"For starters, pick someone who doesn't drink."

"I never saw Spencer drunk."

"That's because he was on his best behavior around you. Take it from an occasional tosser. He's a tosser."

Loretta grew wistful. "We could talk for hours."

"*We* talk for hours."

Loretta managed a smile. "It's not the same."

"You're telling me. I've never so much as gotten a passing snog off of you."

"You're my pal."

"The price of friendship! No one tells you."

Loretta laughed. "Thank you, David."

"Now you go upstairs and get out of those unsightly jodhpurs and put on one of those dresses with the cancan ruffles and tell the gaggle of geese—yes, I mean those obnoxious sisters of yours on the second floor—to do the same. Lipstick, powder, and hairpins, man your stations, girls! Make sure Alda sparkles—that girl has a grim side. I'm taking you all out to dinner. I have a yearning for the brisket at the Clover Club. I'm in the money. I took Mr. Chaplin out on the boat, and who knew, he's a lousy fisherman but he's a big tipper."

David stood up, extended his hand, and helped Loretta to her feet. "Now, no weeping. It's bad for the skin. We don't need you turning into a grizzled hag over an unrealized love affair."

"No, we don't."

"You need to work, Gretchen. That's what you tell me, and now I am happy to throw your own advice back in your lovely face."

"I just took a job."

"Splendid!"

"*The Call of the Wild* with Clark Gable."

"I adore the man!"

"You know him?"

"I'm his swabbie on cruisers in Del Rey. Motorboats on Monterey. And his caddy in Pebble Beach. Whenever he needs me."

"I'm doing this picture for Bill Wellman. He gave me a couple of breaks, and I owe him. He said we're going up to Washington State, going to film on location in the actual Yukon."

"How delicious!"

"We'll be on location in the worst of the winter. If I could leave today and walk there, I would."

"Darling, you're going to make a movie, not hike Calvary."

"Why does it feel like it?"

"There's nothing worse than a love affair that never bloomed. You have to think like the gardener who snips the heads off the buds that never blossom. It brings down the beauty of the garden. We are meant to bloom," Niven assured her.

————

Loretta went into the house to find her sisters and her secretary as David made his way back to the pool house. His silly crush on Loretta had ended as the sun went down that chilly afternoon. He felt like an older brother, a half-wise one who'd helped his baby sister navigate her sadness from a broken heart. He wasn't sure that he was of any use, but figured perhaps there was some meaning in his stay on the grounds of Sunset House—a purpose greater than the pursuit of a breakout part and the fame and fortune that come with acting in a surefire hit. He felt needed, and for a man who tried to dodge the responsibilities that came with commitment, he liked having a higher purpose. It made him feel useful, in the British fashion.

————

Clark Gable crouched low to the ground and wiggled a fat stick in front of Buck. The dog teased a low growl, lunged for Gable, and grabbed the stick in his mouth. The actor kept a firm grip as the dog thrashed around to steal the stick out of his new master's hand.

Buck weighed in at two twenty, a good forty-five pounds heavier than his master. A Saint Bernard with a massive head, the dog could put his paws on Gable's shoulders if he stood on his back haunches and dance a waltz, like Fred Astaire leading Ginger Rogers.

Bill Wellman, the director of *The Call of the Wild*, perched on the fence of the holding pen on the lot at Twentieth Century-Fox. In full sun, Wellman had the face of a war hero on a bronze monument, all angles, deep lines, and determined chin. He moved through the world with authority, long-legged and tall; it appeared he could take any man in a fight. The director used his imposing stature and deep baritone voice to control his movie set and the actors.

Gable, who was raised on an Ohio farm and had worked their oil rigs, was a physical match for Wellman. The actor was at home training the dog and navigating the pen typically used to hold horses for scenes in westerns. Wellman had reserved the pen for two weeks, or as long as it took for Gable and Buck to bond.

"How'm I doing, Bill?" Gable asked his director, brushing his thick black hair out of his eyes.

Wellman was an experienced hunter and fisherman, but that day all six foot four of him looked more professorial than outdoorsy, resting on the fence as he smoked a pipe, wearing a fedora. "Don't ask me."

"You have to direct this animal."

"Yeah, but you have to act with him."

"Thanks."

Gable led Buck to a trough, where the dog lapped up the fresh water.

"Does anybody know how this dog will do in snow?"

"We know he likes it," Wellman said.

"It's going to take me another week to get him under control."

"Then it's Christmas. You have a couple of days off by the tree, with Ria and your stepchildren."

"You're making plans for me?"

"I took you for the kind of guy who likes to sit by the fire and read *The Night Before Christmas* to the kiddies."

"You really want me to come over there and knock you off that fence?"

"I'd like to see you try. I'm the one who got you the Zanuck bonus."

"I had no idea Zanuck gave out bonuses." Gable put his hands in his pockets and grinned.

"He doesn't. You got the first and the last."

"I must be worth it."

"Must be."

"Tell me about Loretta Young." Gable threw a rawhide ring to the far side of the pen. Buck went to fetch it.

"You're gonna keep your paws off of her."

"Mr. Wellman."

"I mean it, Clark. She's a good kid."

"Are you her father?"

Buck made a wheezing noise, trotted over to Gable, dropped the rawhide ring, and sat obediently by his feet.

"After a nap," Gable said to the dog, "the trainer is coming to work you with the sled. Can you handle it, boy?" He ruffled the dog's ears.

"You're better than the trainer."

"Only two things you need to know when training a dog: reward good behavior and don't reward bad behavior."

"So simple." Wellman shrugged. "If only it worked with women."

"Who said it doesn't?"

"You're a better man than me," Wellman admitted.

"Was there even a question?"

Wellman puffed his pipe as Gable wrangled Buck. It would take an ego the size of Clark Gable's to conquer the wild on Mount Baker, and Wellman was betting he had cast the perfect actor to do it.

———

Southern Pacific Railroad provided the Daylight Limited, a train with twelve cars chartered by Darryl Zanuck and the team at Twentieth Century-Fox to transport the actors, crew, film equipment, and Buck the dog from Los Angeles to San Francisco, and on to Bellingham, Washington, to the location for *The Call of the Wild*. The charter express was scheduled to leave at 5:00 a.m. sharp on Tuesday morning, January 1, from Central Station in Los Angeles.

A phony press release had announced that the train was leaving on the morning of January 3. From the looks of the platform, the ruse had worked. The company of *The Call of the Wild* had Track 4 to themselves. There wasn't a reporter or photographer for miles, and if there was, he was probably sleeping off the New Year's Eve party from the night before and wouldn't have the pep to make it downtown to the train station.

Alda, in her best tweed suit, stood by the luggage on the train platform. Loretta Young was busy saying good-bye to her sisters, who gathered to see her off to the wilds of the great Northwest, on the first film their sister had ever shot so far from home. When any of the Young girls traveled by train, the remaining sisters formed a farewell entourage, complete with handkerchiefs to wave as the train rolled out of the station.

A bellman lifted Loretta's and Alda's luggage onto the train.

"Go ahead, Alda. Check out the digs," Loretta said to her secretary.

The bellman helped Alda onto the platform. She pressed the button that opened the glass doors to the third car, the sleeper. There was an elegant seating area with an L-shaped sofa. Small lead-glass tables holding Tiffany lamps were set to either side of them. The walls were polished cherry wood, as fine as Alda had seen in any Hollywood mansion.

Alda followed the bellman back to the berths. Loretta's room was decorated with a white satin comforter and matching plush pillows. Frilly organza curtains flounced over the pull shade, which Alda raised to let in the light.

"Is this berth to your satisfaction?" the bellman asked.

"Yes, sir." Alda smiled. She had never seen a train like this. The train from Padua to Naples consisted of one car of people, one car of cattle, one car of people, one car of cattle, and so on until the caboose. There were no beds, no mirrors, no draperies, just people herded into the cars on simple benches with a shared window. Whenever a Hollywood studio greenlit a movie to go on location, they simply packed up the glamour and brought it with them. Every once in a while, Alda thought she was in one of Loretta's movies that brought the sparkle of the 1930s art deco era to life. She certainly did that morning.

Alda's room was smaller, but just as lovely. She tipped the bellman, took off her hat and gloves, and went back to Loretta's room to unpack her clothes.

Alda looked out of Loretta's window when she heard a racket outside on the platform. She could see Loretta and her sisters huddled there, laughing and talking. The noise came from down the way, where a polished forest-green Packard had pulled up to the platform. As Loretta hugged Georgie good-bye, they looked down the track to see what all the fuss was about.

The crew, including cameramen, electricians, gaffers, set builders, and scene painters, had gathered to welcome Clark Gable. The boys whooped and whistled as Gable jumped out of his car, removed his hat, and greeted the men with back slaps and handshakes.

Gable's jet-black hair was shaggy, and he brushed it off his face as the bangs fell back into his eyes. Tall, trim, and camera-ready, he stood above the crowd, his dazzling grin flashing like the white of the moon in the daytime sky.

"It's Clark Gable!" Sally fake-fainted into the arms of her sister Polly, who nearly dropped her to the ground to make a point. Loretta shushed her sisters. The last thing she wanted was to have her costar believe that she was as silly as Sally.

Clark Gable helped his wife out of the car. The petite Ria Langham Gable stood up straight, lifted her chin, and smiled. She was dressed in regal purple from head to toe, topped with an architectural hat anchored with a tasteful cluster of amethyst jewels. Gable kissed her on the cheek, careful not to disturb her hat, before going behind the car to the trunk for his bag.

"She's older than Mama," Polly commented. "And she looks like a bunch of grapes."

"Nobody's sure how old she is. It's a mystery. That's what it said in *Photoplay*."

"It's nobody's business," Loretta said politely.

"She's seventeen years older," Sally told them. "I'm the Gable fan in this family, and I know the truth."

"You should dig for truth in places besides fan magazines."

"Here's what's true. Her suit is too formal for daytime," Polly said.

"She thought there would be cameras." Sally shrugged.

Clark Gable bolted up the steps on the last car on the train. He carried his own suitcase, and was followed by the raucous crew.

Loretta's stomach turned from nerves. It seemed the crew and her costar were old pals. She tried not to feel left out. She was happy her mother had insisted she bring Alda; at least Loretta wouldn't be alone on Mount Baker.

Ria Gable stood by the car and waved to the train. Gable did not appear in the window to return the courtesy. Dutifully, Ria continued to wave.

"I can't believe that out of all the women in the world, he married her," Sally groused.

"She's a socialite," Polly reminded her.

"Big deal. They don't look good together."

"People get married for many different reasons," Loretta told her.

"I can only think of one when I look at her."

"Sally, you're being rude," Polly chided.

"Here's the story. Gable's first wife was his acting coach. She was twenty years older than he was. They divorced. He met Ria when he was touring through Houston in a play. He was twenty-seven, and she was forty-four. She had been married three times herself."

"Sally, knock it off. I don't want to spend my final moments in Los Angeles gossiping."

"I think it's fascinating," Polly admitted. "Don't you want to know about your costar?"

"Not really. I think I've heard enough. Lord knows I've already seen enough."

Alda appeared on the train steps between the cars. "Come aboard, Loretta!" she called.

"Save Mr. Gable for me!" Sally called to Loretta.

Loretta turned around and shot her sister a look as Polly grabbed Sally and covered her mouth.

"Thank you, Pol," Loretta said before climbing the steps. She turned and gave her sisters a final wave. Sadness rushed over her as the train began to chug out of the station. She was sorry to leave her family, but figured putting some distance between Spencer Tracy and her was the wise thing to do, though she couldn't help thinking she was running from her problems. One thing she knew for sure: she wasn't going to look to Clark Gable for consolation. In her opinion, he was a cad with a mother fixation, and she need not get to know him further to prove her theory.

———————

Loretta organized her makeup on the vanity in her berth, making herself at home on the move as actresses do. The bellman appeared at the door as the train rattled through the flats outside Los Angeles.

"Breakfast in the dining car, Miss Young."

Loretta hadn't thought about food that morning. No matter how many days she'd had to plan, she didn't feel ready for this trip.

Loretta felt emotionally frozen. Perhaps playing Claire Blake would bring her back to life. She was looking forward to the physical demands of the part—hiking mountain trails, navigating a canoe on the river, and sledding through the deep snow of Mount Baker. She was also looking forward to being anywhere but Hollywood, safe from running into her former flame on the lot or in restaurants. This was a chance to put Spencer Tracy in the past once and for all.

Loretta checked her hair in the mirror. She applied some lipstick, smoothed her eyebrows, and tucked a handkerchief into the pocket of her traveling suit, which accentuated her gray eyes with its gunmetal and pale-blue plaid.

Loretta gripped the railing as she made her way to Alda's door.

"Come on, Alda. I'm hungry."

Alda opened the door. "I'm ready."

Loretta sized her up. "Alda, you're seven months out of the convent. It's time you wore lipstick."

"I don't know how."

Alda followed Loretta into her berth. She flipped open the lipstick satchel, which had twenty gold tubes nestled in velvet pockets. Loretta chose one and demonstrated the proper technique for applying lipstick. She handed Alda a fresh tube of lipstick.

"You've got black hair, so you go with any red in the cherry family. No coral. Never orange. Always blue reds. If something ever happens to me, I want you to remember that."

Alda smiled. Loretta often joked about her mortality. Usually the comments were about something in her closet. "If something happens to me," she'd say, "see to it that Sally gets the alligator bag. Don't fight over my Jean Louis opera cape, it goes to Polly"— that sort of thing. The people that joke about dying young never do.

Alda applied the lipstick to her well-shaped but small lips and blotted as Loretta coached her. The lipstick gave Alda instant sophistication, with her straight nose, large brown eyes, and thick lashes.

"Here, put this in your pocket." Loretta looked at Alda's reflection in the mirror. "The problem with lipstick is that it's not cheese. It should never stand alone. Now we need to powder your face."

Loretta shared a fresh chamois puff and a container of pressed powder with Alda, and gently powdered Alda's cheeks and nose. Alda looked in the mirror. She looked fresh and pretty. The powder took away shine and added a veil of translucent allure, like the luster on a flawless Hurrell photograph.

"I've never looked this nice."

"Powder and lipstick are the tank and the rifle in a woman's beauty arsenal."

The ladies made their way to the dining car, gripping the railing as the train swerved around corners, laughing and holding tight as the train dipped in the pits of the tracks along the coastline of California.

Loretta pushed through the glass doors into the dining car, followed by Alda.

The dining car was filled with smoke from pipes, cigarettes, and cigars. It would seem that there was less smoke at the gates of hell. The men were laughing and carrying on as though this were an all-male whistle-stop tour to a gold rush town, and the train car was their private saloon.

Whenever a lady enters an all-male enclave, men remember that they have mothers. Instantly, they behave. There was a mad scramble to clear a booth for the women to sit. Loretta nodded graciously as she and Alda angled through the admiring crowd and took their seats.

The porter presented their menus. He too was smitten at the sight of Loretta Young. When she smiled warmly at him, he stood taller.

The men looked to Gable to check his reaction. He appeared aloof and disinterested. Jack Oakie, their costar, slipped into the booth next to Loretta. His brown hair was shaggy, and he had a three-day growth of beard. "Are you ready for the snow, Loretta?"

"Are you?"

"Got on three sets of long underwear. I'm actually slim under here."

"Really."

"My wife said if I came back with frostbite, it was my own damn fault."

"She's right about that."

"Who is this lovely young lady?" Oakie leered just enough to let Loretta know she might have gone too far with Alda's lipstick and powder.

"This is Miss Ducci, my secretary."

"Oh, an Eye-talian girl."

"Nice to meet you, Mr. Oakie."

The men gathered around the booth as though the ladies were behind glass in an exotic fish tank at the Mocambo.

Jack Oakie waved across the train car. "Chet, come here and say hello. She's one of your own."

Luca Chetta pushed through the crowd. He was five foot nine and black-haired, with wild curls. He wore a charcoal gray suit with a gold pocket watch tucked into the vest. He was handsome, of the sprite variety. His eyes were brown like Alda's, and he had a sweet smile.

"May I sit down?"

Alda looked at Loretta, who nodded her approval.

"He seems all right," Loretta whispered to Alda.

Alda shifted over in the booth to make room for Luca.

Luca Chetta was shiny and new in that first-day-of-school way, clean, pressed, and bearing the scent of sandalwood. Alda leaned against the window to give this blast of pure energy some space. He placed his arm on the back of the booth, his hand near her shoulder. This move was not slick or untoward but his attempt to include her, to make her feel welcome and part of the crew. It was obvious that this wasn't his first location shoot.

Luca's wide, white grin took her in. Whoever this man was, and whatever his trade, Alda felt the instant and soothing familiarity of being among one of her own. Luca was also respectful, which impressed her.

As secretary to the costar of the movie, Alda held a prestigious position. Finally she was no longer a nun pretending to be a secretary but a full person in her own right, earning her keep by hours on the job. She sat up a little higher in the booth, knowing her value.

"Where are you from, Luca?" Alda asked him.

"Brooklyn."

"Before Brooklyn." She smiled.

"His people were on a boat," Oakie joked.

The crew roared with laughter.

"So was I." Alda gave Oakie a look.

"I am Neapolitan," Luca began. "My parents came from Naples and settled in New York. I was born here. I'm as all-American as a hamburger and a glass of cold beer."

"I'm from Padua," Alda offered.

"The home of Saint Anthony," Luca said.

"It means I never get lost. And when I lose something, I find it."

Noticing the spark between Alda and Luca, Loretta kept her eyes on her menu.

"Get the ladies some breakfast," Jack Oakie called to the porter. "Hot coffee to start. Cream?"

"Yes, please," Loretta said.

"That's where that peaches complexion comes from."

"Stop flirting with Loretta, Jack." Bill Wellman looked up from his newspaper.

"You call that flirting? I will have you know that line isn't even circling. It's not even for starters," Oakie protested.

"That's a good thing, Jack. Because it will get you nowhere," Loretta promised.

The train car erupted in laughter, including a chuckle from Clark Gable.

"I better get tight with Buck the dog," Oakie joked.

The porters had turned down Loretta's berth. The satin comforter was folded back and the pillows fluffed. There was a pot of hot tea on the table, two sugar cookies beside it. Loretta studied her script on the coffee table, puffing on a cigarette without taking her eyes off the words. Wellman had given her two new scenes. She had marked them with her symbols, and was learning her lines.

As the train snaked up the coastline, the wheels settled into a soothing rhythm. Loretta raised her shade, turned off her lamp, and looked out. The ocean rolled out before her like a bolt of black velvet, while the stars overhead were fixed like silver sequins. The night sky was so clear it seemed that Loretta could see all the stars in the heavens.

She closed the window and was turning back to the script when she saw a shadow pass by her door. Loretta waited a bit, and then slowly rolled open the door to peek out. Looking down the hallway, she saw Alda entering the club car. On this train, with this clientele, Loretta figured she would be safe.

Loretta closed the door and went back to her script.

As the distance from Los Angeles grew, so did the distance between Loretta and Spencer Tracy. She began to feel free of her problems and more like herself again. Father McNally had promised that the pain from her broken heart would lessen with each passing day. Maybe he was right. It helped that she had seen Spencer and his wife at midnight mass at Good Shepherd. While her heart was full of love for him, she felt relief from the guilt that had weighed on her for so long. She hoped Spencer was free of it, too.

Loretta had gone for counseling every Friday evening since she was denied absolution, and it had helped. She had gone to see Father McNally before the trip so he could give her a special blessing. He had given her a book of prayers to read on Sundays, since in the remote area there was no way she could make it to mass. Father had helped in other ways as well.

Loretta learned that she had to be specific when she asked God for something; she had to trust that He would come through for her in His fashion, in His time. Loretta prayed for wisdom, and that night she also prayed for stamina. Once they reached Bellingham, she had to match these men, task by task and scene by scene, in treacherous conditions. That night she prayed for strength. She figured God would take care of the rest.

————

When Alda pushed the door open on the club car, the first thing she saw was the back of Luca's head, a storm cloud of black curls. She pressed her lips together, having just reapplied her lipstick. She tucked her hair behind her ear and joined him. Luca sat up in his chair and smiled, happy to see her.

"*Parla Italiano*?" she asked.

"*Poco*," he replied. "You'll have to teach me." He grinned.

"Didn't your parents speak Italian?"

"They spoke it to each other, but didn't teach us."

"Why not?"

"We're Americans."

"But they named you Luca."

"My father's name. There are eight kids in my family. We all have Italian names, except the baby. She's eleven."

"What's her name?"

"Nancy."

"Now that's American."

"No kidding."

"Mr. Gable calls you Chet."

"He gave me my nickname. I've known him since *Manhattan Melodrama*."

"What do you do?"

"I'm a scene painter. What did you think I did for a living?"

"I wasn't sure. I haven't learned all the jobs on a film set. I've only been with Miss Young for a few months, and most of the time I'm in a storage room answering fan mail."

"Do you like it?"

"She's been very kind to me."

"People say she's nice. Had a big bust-up with Spencer Tracy."

Alda blushed. "I wouldn't know about that."

"That's very politic of you."

"Tell me more about your work."

"I paint whatever they need. I spent the last month painting the interior of the mansion in *It Happened One Night.* I made plywood look like Italian marble. I go from one picture to the next."

"Like the actors."

"Just like the actors. We finish one job and start a new one."

"How did you get into pictures?"

"I went to art school in New York, and one of my professors thought I could handle this kind of work. So I came out to California with a letter of recommendation from him, and they put me on a crew at MGM that same day. I learned about white paint. When you work for Cedric Gibbons, you realize how many shades of white there can be. How did you get your job?"

"I was in the convent."

Luca Chetta turned pale. "You're a nun?" Every impure thought that Luca had about Alda rose to the surface of his skin like a case of measles. "I'm sorry, Sister."

"No, no, I'm not a nun. I didn't make it."

"Whew." Luca exhaled. "Why were you in the convent?"

"Most people would wonder why they let me go."

"I can see why they let you go. You don't look like a nun."

"I can thank the Young sisters for that."

"Maybe I should thank them." Luca leaned in close to her.

"If you want to thank anyone, you might want to thank my Mother Superior. She's the one who dismissed me and sent me to Los Angeles."

"I'll send her a box of chocolates parcel post the minute we hit Seattle." Luca took her hand.

"Mr. Chetta."

"Yes, *bella*?"

"There are two women on this train. One is the star of the movie, and the other is me."

"And there's a cook, Elvira."

"I haven't met her yet. My point is, I might be pretty to you because I have no competition."

"Not true."

"You don't have a lot of choice here."

"But you do."

"But you don't."

"Are you saying that I'm not picky?"

"That's exactly what I'm saying."

"Alda, I'm thirty-four years old, and I'm not married. I'm past picky. I'm on my way to old bachelorhood." He took Alda's hands in his.

"You move too fast, Luca." Alda pulled her hands away.

"No such thing."

"Yes, there is such a thing! I met you at breakfast."

"Nope. Time is a tool to use however you wish. You never know anything about anything. That's why you have to grip the rope and climb it. Right now. Right here. In this moment. This could be it for us. There could be an avalanche in Bellingham. This train could take the wrong turn, and we're at the bottom of the ocean. We could get to Mount Baker and be eaten by wolves."

"Or not."

"Oh, Alda. Take it easy. I'm already crazy about you."

"But you don't know me."

"I don't? How about this? You got a big, sad heart. And big opera eyes. I want to understand why you're sad. And I want to look into those eyes of yours forever."

"You sound like a movie script."

"A good one, I hope!"

"I'm not sure."

"I am. I can see everything. You've been alone so long, you don't even know what to look for in a man, but I'm telling you, I promise you—you don't have to look. I'm right here. I'm all you need."

"I should go." Alda stood.

The train took a turn, and she tumbled back into the seat. Luca jumped out of his and helped her up.

"We aren't going into the ocean, are we?"

"No, that was a glitch. Probably some kids put a penny on the track. That's all it takes for a bump."

"I think I should go back to my berth now."

"I'll take you."

"I know my way." Alda stood, but her knees were buckling. She wondered if it was the train, or the things that Luca Chetta had said to her.

"Outside the convent, a man walks a woman home."

Luca pushed the button on the door. He took Alda's hand and helped her jump from one car to the other. He pushed open the door to the sleeper car and walked her back to her berth.

"Good night, Mr. Chetta."

He placed his hand over hers as she attempted to unlatch the door quickly.

"Alda?"

She turned to him. "Yes, Luca?"

Luca took her in his arms and kissed her.

"Good night, Miss Ducci." He bowed ever so slightly to her.

She went inside her berth and shut the door behind her. She went to the window, rolled up the shade, and opened it. It seemed she had forgotten how to breathe. She leaned out of the window and gulped in the fresh air, taking in the black night, the silver stars, and the scent of night-blooming jasmine.

Alda tried to imagine where she would be had Gladys Belzer never sent the letter to Father McNally, who had contacted the Mother Superior. Alda might have taken her final vows, worked in the convent orphanage, or discovered meaning anew in a prayer recited at vespers: just another day in the life of a nun. Instead she was on this train, off for an adventure.

Alda's world had opened up like a night sky in full moonlight. Without ever having dreamed of it, she was working in Hollywood in the movies. She bore witness to the creativity and ideas, arguments, and struggles that went into making pictures. She saw a costume designer agonize over fabric swatches, a makeup artist take a few minutes to attach a single eyelash to a leading lady's eyelid, and a cameraman invent a new angle on the fly just moments before a producer exercised his ultimate power by actually turning off the electricity when a director went into overtime after promising he would not.

Alda owed all these experiences to Loretta, who included her in her life at home and at the studio. Loretta never made Alda feel backward, even though she could be. Loretta was incapable of being dismissive, and she was strong, which some took as a star turn or less than feminine. Alda appreciated Loretta's honesty, though, and looked to her as an example of how to be a modern woman and conduct herself professionally.

All around the movie studio, Alda observed working women—actresses, artisans, writers, costumers, musicians, and secretaries. Some had families, others longed for them, but they were all hardworking and, no matter their level of education, eager to learn and advance in their departments.

Alda had come to appreciate the chorines, who by reputation were considered flip and silly. Rumors of their brief yet numerous love affairs scandalized the lot, but when it came to their work, they were complete professionals. They danced in multiple movies, shooting several at a time on the lot. They went from set to set in their rehearsal clothes, took a quick look at a dance notator's grid and would, in one run-through, master a difficult routine. They were the athletes of the studio system.

Whether the young women employed at the studio were living in the frivolous years of youth or had mouths to feed at home, they threw themselves into the industry of making movies, grateful for jobs that paid decently. They didn't think much about artistry because they were there to please the director.

Everyone lived in fear of the director and the clock.

Alda was already plenty scared of Bill Wellman. She had no idea what lay ahead on the mountain. For the rest of her life Alda would remember her feelings on this black night—the sweet scent of the jasmine, the kiss she hadn't agreed to but liked—and it would pull her back to this moment, when she was free. Alda had finally let go of the past in Italy and her years in the convent, determined to live in the world on her own terms. Alda felt the train move beneath her as it picked up speed, charging through the dark, taking her out of her old life and into a new one.

Loretta rolled up the shade on her window as the sun came up, and looked out over the mountains of northern California. The sky was gray except for a stripe of orange on the horizon.

An early riser by habit, Loretta was dressed for the day and hungry. She grabbed her script and went to the dining car, pushing the button that opened the glass doors. Stale smoke and the scent of good bourbon hung in the air from the all-night party that had ended a couple hours earlier. The dining car was empty except for Clark Gable, who was sitting in the same booth in the same clothes he had worn the day before.

"Good morning, Mr. Gable," Loretta said, taking a seat at the booth farthest from him.

"Miss Young." He nodded.

Loretta wore a red corduroy skirt and matching sweater. Her lips were as ruby red as the cashmere. She placed her script on the table and studied the menu.

"Would you like to sit with me?" Gable said softly.

Gable's sweet humility moved her. She smiled. "Would you like me to?"

"Please."

Loretta got up and joined him in his booth.

"Did you get much sleep?" Taking a good look at him up close, Loretta could see that he hadn't.

"A little."

"Do you always celebrate before you work?"

"Not always. Do you always go to bed at nine?"

"Not always." She smiled. "I need my beauty sleep."

"I don't think so. I don't think you need anything."

"You'd be surprised."

"Would I?"

"I'm not even the looker in my family. My sister Sally is a blonde, and she has a wicked crush on you."

"She does?"

"Has since *Night Nurse*."

"I was lousy in it."

"I thought so too."

Gable threw his head back and laughed. "You mean it?"

"Of course I mean it. I only signed on to this ship of fools because I saw *It Happened One Night*. You're really good in that."

"Thank you."

"Now you're supposed to return the compliment. Have you seen any of my pictures?"

"Here and there."

"And what did you think of my work?" she asked.

"Would we be on this train together if I wasn't keen on you?"

"I guess not. You just worked with Robert Leonard. He was my first director. In 1917."

"Were you even born then?"

"I was four years old. Played a fairy."

"How did you do?"

"I flew. And I liked it. Did you ever fly?"

"In *Hell Divers*."

"Not at work, not in an airplane. In your dreams. I get those flying dreams before I start a picture. How about you?"

"No dreams. Just garden-variety anxiety. I mostly worry if I'm going to look an idiot."

"That's why you stayed up all night. If you stay awake, the fear won't get you."

"Oh, it'll get me regardless."

"I wouldn't worry. As long as you're acting with me, we'll get it right."

"How big of you to give me a chance after *Night Nurse*."

"Why wouldn't I? Every actor I know has one or two pictures they'd like to bury in the desert."

"What would you bury?"

"Oh, I don't know." Loretta thought it over. "I've made around fifty, so I'd say forty-nine of them."

The porter brought the newspaper to Gable. "We stopped in Big Bear last night. Got the latest for you, sir."

"Thank you."

Gable opened the newspaper and scanned it.

"Anything interesting?"

"Just checking if my buddy Niven is in prison yet."

Loretta grabbed the newspaper. "Oh, no!" She scanned the paper quickly for his name, but couldn't find it.

"I was teasing." Gable laughed.

"Thank goodness."

"Had to get you back for your bad review of my work."

"That wasn't David Niven's fault."

Gable tried not to smile. "You like Niven?"

"He's a good and loyal friend."

"If you have one of those in Hollywood, you're lucky."

"It sounds like we both do."

Loretta opened her script and started to read the new scenes.

Gable took note of her focus and concentration. He ordered a pot of black coffee. Loretta wasn't just any starlet, she wasn't just any girl—she was something entirely new, and Gable knew he'd have to be stone cold sober to keep up with her.

6

As a general leads his soldiers into battle to win, the director leads his actors into a movie with high hopes to create a surefire hit. Bill Wellman led his cast and crew out of Los Angeles on a train, through two states, into Seattle and on to Bellingham, Washington, for a final trek across a snow-covered field to the Mount Baker Inn. Wellman had convinced the studio that the adventure story was best served on location, where dramatic vistas, painterly skylines, and snow were in abundance.

The Mount Baker Inn served as their base of operations as they filmed *The Call of the Wild*.

There were a hundred of them, cast and crew, laughing and joking as they traipsed through the frozen tundra. This was all new to them, and for the first few hours, the novelty of winter was exciting, as they imagined the fun to be had marooned on a mountaintop with the studio bosses hundreds of miles away and enough crates of Glenfiddich whisky to keep them smiling through the cold.

This movie was written as a great American adventure story of ambition and greed during the Gold Rush, one that Wellman insisted should not be told on a sound stage with sets built of plywood and soap flakes, no matter how artful the results. Wellman wanted the real thing, and he got it. Mount Baker was drenched in new-fallen snow over a hardened shell of layers of ice. The mountain peaks pierced the pale blue sky like knitting needles in skeins of soft wool. If it was treacherous, that reality was hidden on the morning of their arrival, as a gold marble sun hung low and bright in the sky over fields of white-hot diamond dust.

Bill Wellman pushed the door of the Mount Baker Inn open and invited his cast and crew inside.

Jack Oakie, the headliner on the I Want to Impress Loretta Young Tour, had volunteered to carry Loretta's luggage, while Luca had picked up Alda's. They ushered the ladies through the door and into the hotel.

The lobby was a massive great room with a double-sided hearth that crackled with a roaring fire. It was the only touch of warmth in the inn. It was so cold inside, the floorboards creaked like evergreen branches loaded with snow. The decor was simple, as the hotel was typically open only in the summers for swimming in the lake and fishing on the river.

The management made attempts to accommodate the cast and crew by providing them with an old overstuffed sofa, a matching love seat, and a set of club chairs covered in cinnamon chenille pushed close to the hearth. This was as close as the decor came to cozy living.

"Where's the dining room?" Luca asked.

"The Italian is always worried about the grub," the camera operator said as he dropped his bags on the floor.

"By suppertime, you'll be glad I do," Luca said.

"Dining room is out the building, to your right. " The clerk pointed.

Alda looked out the window and saw a barn with a tin roof behind the hotel.

"Now we know who put the rust in *rustic*," Loretta whispered to Alda.

The production manager handed out envelopes with keys and room assignments.

Gable, disheveled after the long trip, was looking forward to a shower and a shave. He slung his leather duffel over his back and climbed the stairs.

Wellman called after him, "I'd like the actors to gather in the meeting room in an hour. We're going to go through the script."

"You got it, Captain." Gable disappeared at the top of the stairs.

Jack Oakie was eager to take Loretta's bags to her room. She thanked him but demurred. "I can take it from here, Jack."

Alda took her bag from Luca. "Thank you."

"What are you doing this afternoon?"

"Whatever Miss Young needs."

"She's going to be busy rehearsing. I could use your help."

"Let me ask her."

"I already did."

"What did she say?"

"She said you're free."

Alda felt cornered, and yet she liked Luca. He was energetic and full of fun. And he was the first man she had kissed since she left Italy seven years ago. "What do you need?"

"We're going to be creative."

———

Gable was particular about his wardrobe. He unpacked his suitcase, hanging his pants and shirts neatly in the closet. In the dresser, he lay his undershorts, socks, and thermals next to his belts, coiled tightly. He unpacked his toiletries and lined them up on the sink in his private bathroom. Ria had bought new bottles and tubes of his favorite toiletries to last through the shoot. He smiled. Ria's best attribute as a wife was that she anticipated his needs and took care of them without his having to ask.

As the tub filled with water, he built a fire. He turned the lamps on and put up the shades. He needed light; he thrived on it. He sank into the tub and scrubbed himself head to toe, paying special attention to his nails.

Gable shaved carefully; a nick could set a picture back while a cut healed. He brushed his hair until it had the sheen of black patent leather. He rubbed cologne in his hands, a mix of pine and bitter orange, his own custom blend. He rubbed it on his face and neck and pushed back his hair, which was long because Wellman had asked him to keep it shaggy.

The actor wore a pair of Levi's, lined with blue-and-green flannel, which he belted with a blue suede belt with a gold buckle. He pulled on a hand-knit turtleneck sweater his wife had commissioned from a weaver in Ireland, his Christmas gift from his stepchildren. The weave of blue and green complemented his gray eyes, but he wasn't concerned about the aesthetic appeal; he was trying to keep warm.

The actor looked at his watch. He had a half hour before the cast was to gather and read through the script, and he wanted to run through it one last time. He had his own specific ritual with the script.

Gable read his lines aloud, on his feet, every exchange of dialogue. When he finished, he took one last look in the mirror, grabbed the script, and went to meet his director and fellow actors for the table read.

———

Loretta was sitting by the fire in the lobby, reading through her script, when Gable appeared on the landing of the stairs. When she looked up at him, it was as though she were watching him on a silver screen. He had a casual elegance. No other man in the world could have pulled off that sweater, but on him it was fashionable. No wonder Gable had enchanted every woman in Hollywood, from Joan Crawford to Jean Harlow. He was scrumptious, and there were plenty of women hungry for him.

As Gable turned on the landing, a hotel maid, a girl of around twenty with her hair pulled back in a single gold braid, came out of the office behind the desk and turned to go up the stairs. She stopped and greeted him and then tried to move past him, but he blocked her. He made her laugh. He leaned in and said something in her ear that made her blush. She was not shy; she whispered in his ear, and he got the look of a hungry wolf. Gable's face turned into a pen-and-ink line drawing of a scavenger, all bulging eyes and wild mane and black pits and dark shadows and teeth looking to bite.

Loretta's stomach turned. She was dismayed by what she'd witnessed—or was she? Was she jealous? Or was it simply the cheaper version, pea-green envy? Did Loretta long to be an ordinary girl with some pleasant aspects—in the case of the hotel maid, say, lovely hair and eyes—who was free to flirt with a man, in this case, Clark Gable, and want nothing in return? Well, Loretta was certain that Gable wanted something, but she could not be sure about the hotel maid. It certainly appeared like they had a lot to say to each other. It seemed to Loretta that they had made plans to see each other, to continue the conversation.

The maid took her bucket and mop and ascended the stairs. Gable watched her climb as Loretta watched him. He didn't take his eyes off the maid's ample fanny, watching it wiggle from side to side, step by step, as she went up the stairs. Usually Loretta would mind her manners, look away, and pretend not to have caught the wolf in the act, but this time she thought differently. She sat up in the chair and closed her script. Her gaze bored through Clark Gable like the sharp blade of a knife through a fresh pie.

Gable felt Loretta's gaze and met it. He extended to her, across the room, the same knowing leer he had offered the hotel maid. She, actress that she was, without words, sent Gable a return message that withered him. *You don't have a chance with me, bud. Stick to the hotel maid.*

Gable took in her meaning, rebounded with arrogant bravado, and walked past her without saying a word.

"We're here to work," Bill Wellman said from behind her.

Loretta turned to him. "I love the script."

"Do you think your leading man has read it?"

"We read it together on the train."

"That's good to know."

"We're going to make a swell picture, Bill."

"As long as that big goof keeps his mind on his business."

Loretta figured that Wellman had observed the flirtation between Gable and the hotel maid, too. "Now, Bill, you know you'd have more luck stopping an avalanche with your bare hands than you do keeping Mr. Gable from that hotel maid."

"I'm not worried about her. I'm worried about you."

"I have to learn how to navigate a raft on a real river, shoot a bear between the eyes, and hike a mountain peak. Don't worry about me. I've got plenty to keep me busy."

Wellman followed Gable to the meeting room.

It bothered Loretta that she had a reputation for falling easily and hard for her leading men. She tried very hard not to, but between the long hours she kept at the studio and the few she had off to prepare for her roles at home, it was likely that the only place she would meet potential beaus was on a sound stage. Wellman loathed publicity, puff or negative, and probably had judged her because of the press release she had authorized about her breakup with Spencer Tracy. She couldn't worry about that now, and besides, the personal life of a director was not scrutinized like the life of an actress. Wellman could not possibly understand her position.

Loretta gathered up her script and followed the director, looking forward to the first read-through of the script. After all, the classic Jack London story was why she agreed to act in the movie and climb this particular mountain in the first place.

———

Alda followed Luca as he trudged through the snow to the dining hall. He pushed a metal sliding entrance door open, revealing long community-style tables set up for meals.

A set of a dozen windows overlooked the snow-capped mountains behind them. The view—rolling fields of white that sloped away like dollops of whipped cream—was luscious, a contrast to the barn, which was strictly utilitarian: the mottled trusses on the ceiling were held together with rusty bolts; the walls were weathered beams of knotty pine, with light pouring through tiny slits where the wood had worn away.

Beyond a serving island was an old service kitchen. Alda could see every pot and pan, an open coal stove with burners, and stacks of industrial white ceramic dishes. The roaring fire in the flagstone fireplace was the only heat source in the barn. Luca moved around the room, surveying it.

Alda wondered how the cook could possibly prepare meals for their group. The work space was about the size of Ruby's in Sunset House but without the beauty, convenience, or modern appliances.

Luca unfolded his paint kit on the floor of the dining room. He selected brushes, chose the tubes of paint, and set up his palette.

"Over here, Alda," Luca called.

"What's this big project?"

"This place is giving me the heebie-jeebies. Look at it. It's an old barn—all that's missing are the cows and pigs. There's no pizzazz. No color."

"What are you going to do about it?"

"You're going to help me give this place a little personality. We're going to be eating three squares a day here, so we need to make it pretty. Help me pull down the shades."

The long windows that overlooked the mountains had no draperies, just simple paper pull shades with a ring hook on a string. Alda pulled the shades to the sill.

"Wellman wanted me to paint a welcome sign for the cast and crew. Look at these."

Luca gave Alda a set of small fabric samples.

"The costume designer and I collaborated on the fabrics. We had this idea that if we put Eskimo symbols into the costumes, wove them into the fabric, or painted them on leather or suede, it would feel like the turn of the century, and give a sense of authenticity to the picture. I thought it would be fun to paint these symbols on the shades."

Luca went to the first shade and, swirling the brush into the vivid red on the palette, created a symbol that looked like a cross made of knife blades. He filled in the blades with a deep coral, splashed yellow outside the red, then blended into the background with a smaller brush. "Want to try?" He handed her the brush.

She shook her head.

"You can't make a mistake, Alda."

"Oh, yes I can."

"There are no mistakes."

"I've seen great art, and I disagree."

"That depends upon what you think great art might be. I think great art is as simple as where you're standing and what you're looking at. Does this color make you feel something?"

"Happy." She shivered. "And warm."

"So tell me, Alda, what greater purpose is there for a painter?"

"I don't know."

"You do know. There is no greater purpose for art than to move you, to elevate your mood, to make you think, to remind you of places you have been or places you want to build. It does everything—nourishes the soul and lifts the spirits of the people."

Luca put a brush in Alda's hand. He guided her on the next shade. They made giant circles together.

Alda took over and painted colors within the swirls. It felt good to stretch and reach high with the brush to the top of the shade, then drag the ruby-red paint down the length of it. She could only describe the feeling as total freedom.

Luca was, as an artist by profession, more particular. He had a notion about the designs on the fabric, so he followed them. Alda and Luca spent the afternoon painting, and they did not rest until every shade was filled with color.

The late-afternoon sun poured through the paper shades, revealing the brushstrokes through the light. It was all there—color, form, line, and perspective—in the swirls, broad strokes, and sweeping details. Alda's rudimentary skill was on display, contrasted by Luca's craftsmanship.

Alda stood back as Luca gathered the supplies and took the brushes to the shed behind the kitchen to clean them. She stayed and watched the sun as it played through their creations. Luca was right. Art changed everything: mood, climate, perception.

Alda was beginning to see the world through Luca's eyes, something she believed wasn't possible. He loved life and art with such enthusiasm, he made everyone around him seem bloodless by comparison, including her. She longed to be free like him, to choose colors without judgment, to say exactly what needed to be said, to embrace life and squeeze every moment out of it with intention. Luca had the ability to meet any challenge. She wondered if he would accept her once he knew the truth about her. She doubted it, but she knew the time had come to tell him about what had happened to her.

———

Alda knocked on Loretta's door.

Loretta had the day to herself, as Wellman decided to shoot the scenes with Buck before getting her material. She had done some reading and written some letters, but it wasn't enough to fill the long day.

"Am I disturbing you?"

"No, no, come in. I'm bored to death."

"You don't like a day off."

"I hate them. I never know what to do with myself. When I'm home, I can drive into town and putter around, but here, there's nothing but snow."

"I need your advice." Alda sat in the chair by the fire.

"You don't want to quit, do you?"

"No, no, nothing like that."

"Whew. Because I can't get along without you."

"Thank you."

"So what's the problem? Let me guess. It started in Brooklyn."

Alda blushed. "Yes."

"What's the problem?" Loretta leaned in, loving a moment where she could talk about men, and it wasn't her issue. "Tell me everything."

"Luca is very determined."

"That's because he's crazy about you."

"How can you tell?"

"He waits for you by the door at the barn when it's mealtime. He makes up excuses to sit with us when we're reading by the fire. He's the first to jump up when you need something. Mr. Chetta has it bad. He gets goof eyes when he looks at you."

"I was afraid of that."

"Afraid? You don't like him."

"No, I do."

"Oh, you're out of the convent, and you have no experience with men."

"Not exactly."

"What does that mean?"

"I had a beau in Italy."

"Oh."

"It wasn't meant to be, though. I feel like I should tell Luca about him."

"Holy Hannah, don't tell him!"

"Why?"

"He'll be jealous of a man he'll never meet. It'll make him feel small. He'll wonder if you like the man overseas more than him. No, don't tell him."

"What if it was a serious relationship?"

"Hmm." Loretta had to think about this. Her serious relationships always wound up in the newspapers. She knew that if she ever had a secret, it would be impossible to keep. But Alda was different. She had a private life; she actually owned her privacy, and could dictate the terms of her life and relationships. "I need to think about this."

"I think it's best to be honest."

"Maybe. I'm not saying be dishonest, but you need not volunteer details that will make him unhappy and therefore make you miserable."

"I wouldn't want to hurt him."

"No, you can't. He's a good one."

"Do you think so?"

"Oh, yes. He's kind. He's fun. He's talented. Let me see, what else can I say? He gets you because he's Italian too. That's important, you know. Any common ground is good. I really want to marry a Catholic when the time comes. I would just feel understood."

"My mother said to fall in love with a man from your own village."

"She's right. But I've had a little too much of my own village lately, if you know what I mean."

Alda laughed. "Hollywood." She stood to go. "Thank you."

"Don't thank me. I have never had a single romance work out. I should be coming to you for advice."

"I think Mr. Gable is interested in you."

"Please God no! He's a wolf."

"Even with you?"

"The only reason he has decent manners around me is because I'm the only woman in his sightline. And you know what? That's all right with me. I've had enough of the dramatics. I like being alone."

Loretta meant it. She wanted no part of an on-set love affair with a man who was famous for them. To that end, Loretta kept the image of Mrs. Gable at the train station at the front of her mind like a purple billboard. She'd had enough of married men, their problems, their indecision about whether to stay or go, and especially their desire for amusement outside of their responsibilities. She hoped that someday she would meet a nice fellow who was kind and devoted to her. If he didn't come along, that was fine too. She made her own money, owned her own home, invested in real estate, and took the best scripts she could get from the offers that came her way. The rest was up to fate, and for now, she could live with that.

———————

"How does this look?" Loretta asked Alda, placing a freshly baked apple pie on the rack next to the dozen she had baked that afternoon. The crust was golden brown. Loretta brushed it with butter, glazing it, and sprinkled sugar on it.

"Looks like snow," Alda said. "Ruby would be proud of you."

"I didn't think I could bake a pie. Much less a baker's dozen of them."

"All it takes is a recipe," Elvira the cook said as she stirred the stew on the stove. The cook was only in her thirties, but she had the countenance of an old gray barn, weathered with loose hinges on all the joints.

"And time. Nobody saw how bad that first batch of dough turned out."

"And they'll never find out neither," Elvira said. "I don't believe in showing weakness in the kitchen."

Clark Gable burst into the kitchen, with Bill Wellman and Jack Oakie in tow.

"What's for dinner, girls?"

"Stew," said the cook.

"Again?" Gable complained.

"I don't know how to feed a hundred people if I don't make stew."

Gable took the ladle from her and stirred the stew. "Now, Elvira, surely you have some recipes in your file that you can make for us that don't involve carrots, potatoes, and chunks of meat so tough it's like chewing rubber stoppers."

"I am following the menus approved by Mr. Wellman."

"Don't blame me, Elvira. I checked chicken cordon bleu for dinner tonight."

"Yeah, well, the truck with the chicken got stuck in the ice in Bellingham."

Gable assumed a full-tilt flirt. "There's got to be something else in that icebox. Elvira dear, couldn't you change it up it for me?"

"Why should I do it for you?"

"Because he's Clark Gable," Loretta interjected.

The men laughed. "You could do it for me—I'm Jack Oakie."

"Elvira is not impressed by Hollywood," Loretta reminded them.

"The last picture I saw was *Birth of a Nation*. I have no idea who you people are."

"Don't you find us charming anyway?" Gable teased.

"Not really. Your girlfriend made pies."

"My girlfriend?"

"She means me," Loretta said. "I guess I left the script lying around and Elvira read between the lines."

"You made these?"

"I have many skills. Many I didn't know I possessed," Loretta admitted.

"Tell the folks dinner will be ready at six," Elvira announced.

"I'm going to put my feet up till then," Wellman told Oakie.

"I'm going to have a cocktail myself," Oakie said, following him out. "Don't even need a glass."

"I'll let the front desk know about dinner," Alda said, following the men back to the inn.

"The pies look delicious." Gable was impressed.

"Thank you."

"I haven't had a woman cook for me in years," Gable admitted.

"How's that possible?"

"Well, I've had women feed me, but they didn't do the baking. They hired a cook for that."

Elvira rolled her eyes.

"I like a woman who knows her way around a kitchen." Gable smiled.

"You must be madly in love with me," Elvira said. "I live at this godforsaken stove."

"I will fall madly in love with you if you come up with something for supper besides that godforsaken stew." Gable laughed and left for the inn as Loretta sprinkled the pies with sugar.

"That one there is trouble," Elvira said. "Long, tall licorice whip. Those eyes are like cue balls rolling around looking for the corner pocket. That one could hurt you."

"You think so?"

"Who does he think he is? Rudolph Valentino?"

"I hate to tell you, he might be bigger than Valentino."

"Not to me."

Loretta smiled to herself as she finished her chore. Women hold on to their first crush at the movies until the day they die. Of course no one could top Valentino—he was Elvira's youthful ideal. Loretta hoped Gable held the same allure for the audiences of 1935—she could use a hit. Nothing wrong with a screen idol who could pack them in all the way up to the last row in the balcony. Gable was good for business, which made him good for her business. Loretta had her eye on a hotel she wanted to buy, one that was close to home, one she could see from her driveway. If *The Call of the Wild* did well, she was going in for a piece of the Beverly Hills Hotel, figuring it was a smart investment. Mr. Gable didn't need to know that he was part of her business plan, a means to an end, but the thought of it made her chuckle.

———

The sun had set on Mount Baker. The hotel had placed oil lamps along the path from the hotel to the dining hall. The snow crunched under Loretta's feet as she walked between the pools of light. She had gone back to the inn to catch up on her mail and bathe before supper. She wore dungarees, a plaid workshirt, and chamois-lined leather boots that laced from her ankle to her knee. Over her ensemble she wore a fluffy ankle-length fox coat that, while it was stylish, was the warmest coat she owned.

Loretta smiled to herself. She had packed stylish clothes and shoes for the location shoot, including silk slippers, velvet slides with a kitten heel, and high heels. Every single pair was inappropriate, and every pair remained in satin shoe bags in her suitcase in the closet. She had lived in these utilitarian boots since they dropped their luggage.

As she approached the barn, lit up from within against the black sky on the white mountain, she could hear the laughter and conversation of the crew. Their joy spilled out into the dark night, the only sign of life in the wilderness. She pushed the barn door open and stepped into the dining hall, which was hot and noisy. Loretta scanned the community tables, but it seemed all the seats were taken. At the far side of the room, Alda sat with Luca and his crew. She stood up and offered her seat, but Loretta waved her off.

The mood was raucous, rolling big laughs filling the big barn, underscored by the chatter of conversation and the clatter of pots. Elvira directed the kitchen staff to place baskets of fresh cornbread on the tables. She shook her head as the men seized the squares like panhandlers grabbing gold nuggets.

As Loretta looked around the room, she noticed the hotel maid sitting with the assistant cameraman, which didn't surprise her—if there was a woman within a hundred miles, and she could make it up the mountain, she'd probably end up with one of the crew from *The Call of the Wild*. Loretta chuckled to herself. *I guess Gable wasn't the maid's type, after all.*

Gable was sitting at the back table with Jack Oakie and some of the crew. He motioned to Loretta to join them and kept his eyes fixed on her as she made her way through the crowd.

Loretta slipped into the seat next to her costar, who was in midconversation when she joined them. Gable served Loretta a slice of cornbread and handed her the butter. She listened as they recounted how difficult the filming had been that day—the camera had frozen, Buck was contrary, and Oakie went down in a snowdrift so deep he sank like an anchor.

Gable reached under the table and squeezed Loretta's hand.

"Rough day."

"It's a monster out there."

"How are we going to navigate that river?" Loretta wondered.

"We're not. It's got whitecaps."

Loretta exhaled nervously.

"Don't be afraid," Gable said. "I'll be with you."

"You're going to save me?"

"Only if you need it."

Loretta poured herself a cup of hot coffee. "And who will decide if I need saving?" She poured Gable a cup too.

"Me, of course. I'll have to keep my eyes on you at all times."

"Too late for that."

Gable threw his head back and laughed.

"I'm from a family of girls—one brother, but really, it's a sorority. And I don't mind being second place, or even third."

"What do you mean?"

"How did you lose the hotel maid?"

Gable blushed. This time it was her turn to laugh.

"Turns out she doesn't like actors," Gable grumbled.

"Smart girl."

When it came time for dessert, Gable stood up and hit a fork against his bottle of whisky. "Folks, I have an announcement."

The chatter in the room died down. "Now, we've been on that mountain all day, risking life and limb. And we did our best, and evidently, according to Mr. Wellman, we got some great stuff."

The crew cheered.

"But that wasn't the only hard work today. Our own Loretta Young was in the kitchen, baking pies like our grannies of old. She sliced the apples and rolled the dough and practically spun the sugar. So, my friends, please, a round of applause for Miss Young, who is not only a fine actress but a great baker."

The men stomped their feet, whistled, and applauded. Loretta took a bow. She grabbed Gable by the neck and mimed strangling him. He pulled her onto his lap. There was a medley of wolf whistles.

———

Alda looked across the room at Loretta and Gable. The last thing Gladys Belzer had whispered to her as they were getting in the car to go to the train station was, "Keep Gretchen clear of Clark Gable." It was obvious to Alda that she had already failed.

———

Loretta sat by the fire in the great room. Most of the crew had retired for the night. A few stragglers sat on the opposite side of the
fireplace, their feet propped on the stone bench in front of the grate.

"I don't think I've ever been this cold," Gable said.

"If I could crawl into that fireplace, I would. We're spoiled. Just a
couple of southern California crybabies," Loretta said. "I thought you
turned in."

"Can't sleep."

"Me neither," Loretta admitted.

"I get the feeling you're missing someone."

"A little. How about you?"

"A little."

Loretta laughed. The thought of Gable missing anyone *a little* was
funny to her. He was so big in every way. Loretta wondered who he
was missing, and in what numbers. Was he was missing the divine
Joan Crawford, who gave up Douglas Fairbanks for him? Loretta had
read all about it in *Modern Screen.* Turned out the actors checked the
magazines for updates on their peers, just as the fans did. Fairbanks
was a good man, so Gable must really be something, for Crawford to
have ended her marriage over the affair.

Gable sat down next to Loretta. "You have a boyfriend?"

"Maybe."

"It's a secret."

"Or maybe mystery is all I have left on this mountaintop. Look at
me. I look like a lumberjack. I'm hardly alluring."

"I disagree."

"You would. It's either me or Elvira. You don't have much of a
selection up here."

"That's true."

Loretta pretended she was insulted. "Anyway. Doesn't matter. I'm
here to do a job."

"Wellman told you to steer clear, didn't he?"

"Yep."

"You only have to listen to the director on the set."

"He's pretty persuasive."

"So am I."

"I've heard."

"What do I have to do to get you to like me?"

"I haven't thought about it."

"So you don't like me."

"I don't know you well enough yet."

"That's fair."

"You're married."

"Mrs. Gable is not happy with me."

"She seemed fine at the train station."

"She was being polite. We're separated."

"Agh." Loretta turned away from Gable.

"What's the matter?"

"Why does every married man say that?"

"In my case it happens to be true."

"Does your wife know? It didn't look like it on track four. She was waving that white hanky like she was docking the *Queen Mary*."

"That's because she cares about bad publicity."

"And you don't?"

"In my fashion."

"Mr. Gable, why don't we try something novel?"

"I'm game."

"Let's be friends."

"Friends. Okay."

"Great." She smiled.

"But if your feelings change?"

"They won't."

"How do you know for sure?"

"Let's just try and stay alive and get this picture made. I'd like to see a palm tree again."

"Me too, Gretchen."

"You know my name?"

"Made it my business. I have a little file on you. I know a lot of things. You know, things I've read in magazines."

"You should never read those magazines. They're trash."

"I find the information in them very helpful. I got to know you before I met you. Found out some fundamentals."

"Like what?"

"You sew."

"That's true."

"They got your eyes wrong. They call you blue-eyed in the magazines. You have gray eyes."

Gable liked to think that he was an arbiter of feminine beauty. He found something to like in almost every woman he met. Sometimes it was something small, like a delicate wrist or brown eyes the color of chocolate or a laugh that sounded like music, or it could be the entirety of the woman. If she was a dancer, the graceful line of her back and legs could send him into a tizzy.

Loretta Young was more than the sum total of her beauty. When he closed his eyes to envision her, he didn't revel in one aspect of her physical attributes because he couldn't choose. He liked to fall in love with his leading ladies; it was good for the work. Loretta made him feel things. He wanted to impress her and please her, but more importantly, he wanted to get to know her. That was not typical for Gable, as he liked to keep conversation light, and promises of any kind to a minimum. When he was around Loretta, his emotions were on high alert. It was more than sexual attraction, though that was present, and he appreciated it always. Loretta was something more altogether, and he looked forward to solving the mystery.

Gable remembered how she'd moved so elegantly through the train car infested with men, her tapered fingers touching the shoulders of the crew as she made her way to the booth. Gable liked beautiful hands on a woman. He didn't know why, but it was the first thing he looked for. He also liked the way Loretta's front teeth had a slight overbite, which pushed her upper lip out in a way he found sensual. Her face was luscious. He had studied countless women along the way, but her full lips and cheeks and her gray eyes framed in dark lashes were irresistible. "Gray eyes are very rare, you know."

"Mama calls them rainclouds. You have them too. What are your rainclouds?"

"You first." He sat down across from her before the fire. "If we're going to be friends, I want to be useful to you. You have to know what makes a person sad to figure out how to make them happy."

"What makes you think I'm sad?" The last thing Loretta wanted to share with her new costar was the story of her romantic travails. Hadn't she spent an afternoon telling Alda to keep her past to herself?

"Is there anything you'd change, if you could?"

Gable was so sincere in his question, she didn't hesitate to share, just as she would in a confessional. "I did a stupid thing. I got married when I was seventeen. My mother almost killed me. You know how when you're in a scene and the director is watching you, you can be inside the scene but watching yourself at the same time?"

"Yeah."

"I stood outside myself as I said 'I do,' knowing it was wrong."

"You were a kid. What does a seventeen-year-old girl know about anything?"

"I've been working since I was four years old. I knew the score." Loretta sighed. There was a deeper meaning in admitting her mistake, and Gable picked up on it.

"You have a right to make mistakes."

"Not when you know better." Loretta pulled her knees to her chest, locked her arms around them. "And I know better."

Loretta hoped that Gable got the point. She'd had enough pain with a man who was unavailable, and she certainly wasn't going to repeat the drama with Gable.

"Why were you waiting for the mailman?"

She smiled. "I like getting mail."

"Fan mail?"

"Alda handles that. I look for 'Confidential' on the envelope. I like letters from friends who really know me."

"Or want to get to know you better."

Loretta's work in pictures had taught her that there was no closer relationship than the creative one, actor to actor, nothing but the task at hand, a scene to perform, with words written by others, to convey emotion and sentiment between you.

The actor is required to dramatize his emotions. He mines

everything: the moment, the past—anything he can conjure to deliver the meaning of the words in the script. The job of acting is to
feel. An actor displays his emotional template in full view for all to
see, and a director to judge. It's in the bubble of vulnerability that
chemistry is born. Chemistry is what makes a movie work, or at least
makes the story believable to the patron who took her seat in hopes
of sparking her own passion or escaping her lack of it.

Gable knew it, and so did Loretta. This rhythm between them,
their ability to communicate with one another in a way that was interesting and illuminating, was the very thing that made them valu-
able commodities to the studio. It was obvious to both of them that
there was something between them. Loretta, however, did not want
to make it personal.

Gable sat down on the floor next to her. The logs crackled; a blue
glow under the grate fed blazing orange flames that jumped high
into the flue like ribbons.

"Do you like it up here?"

"It's growing on me."

"You like camping?"

"I'm not the outdoorsy type. I could never figure out how to get
warm in front of a fire. If you face it, you burn up in the front and
your backside is freezing. You turn and warm your backside, and
your front freezes."

Gable laughed. "You have to keep moving."

Loretta could see Gable clearly. Even in bright light, he had a darkness, a depth of tone and hue that was perfect for the cinema, for the
shading of black-and-white film. His forehead was etched with deep
lines—thought lines, she imagined. She wondered if he was as intelligent as he seemed, or if that was simply the years between them.
His experience trumped hers in every conceivable way.

"How about you? Are you as perfect as everyone tells me you are?"
Loretta asked.

"Who are you talking to?" Gable smiled. "I make the same mistakes over and over again."

"If you know better, why do you make them?"

"Because I'm thick. Or maybe I'm just human. Life isn't a class where you can get a perfect score. It seems to me you have to keep trying."

"Maybe you should pray about it."

"I'm not a believer."

"Were you baptized?"

"Catholic."

"And it didn't take?"

"Couldn't. My mother died when I was a baby. If you're going to get religion, you get it from your mother."

Loretta nodded. Her mother, with her conversion to Catholicism, was faithful, but she also felt she owed the church. A priest had suggested she get into the boardinghouse business, and had helped her with a loan to start one. If she ever had a lapse of faith, it wasn't apparent to her children. She walked in gratitude and expected her children to do the same.

Gladys Young Belzer had never gotten a break, which made Loretta value her own. Gladys had worked hard at the boardinghouse, and no job was beneath her—she cooked and scrubbed and ironed and cleaned as though every gleaming surface was a reflection of her own sterling character. When she remarried, she did so to benefit her daughters and son, knowing that a proper marriage in a pillared church gave her family stability and placed them on a moral high ground, which in Gladys's eyes would keep them above the tawdry aspects of show business. As determined as she was to take care of her children, she knew that giving them a traditional structure would send the message that she had a fine family, deserving of respect. When a single mother is raising daughters, nothing is more important than that.

When her first husband walked out, Gladys did not delude herself. She didn't delude herself or the children that John Earle Young would come to his senses, return home, and resume his responsibilities by earning an honest paycheck to care for his family. Instead, she leveled with her children, telling them that she would need their help in order to stay together as a family.

Fear drove the Young children to be loyal to one another, but love was the glue. They had to study, behave, and work hard; their father wasn't going to return to keep them safe or provide security. Gladys was all they had. Their mother promised them that she would put them first and ensure their happiness. She told her daughters they were blessed with beauty and talent—and that it wasn't just luck, but a gift.

Gladys encouraged her children to honor answered prayers, and pay attention to the signs that would lead them to prosperity. The hand of God had placed them in a house across the street from Lasky Studios, and that too was a sign. A dollar-a-day paycheck as extras from the studio from each of the girls placed in a common kitty would provide handsomely for their survival, and the weekly rent collected from the boarders would do the rest.

For Gladys, there were no accidents; only the twists, turns, and sudden sharp corners of destiny determined by prayer and hard work would write the family story. She believed those who were good were blessed, and if blessed, could handle any challenge. Poverty was a temporary condition that could change from a Monday to a Friday if every room in the boardinghouse were full, and if the guests paid on time.

Loretta wasn't going to be a working actress, a model, or a day player who waited patiently to be chosen for background, then stood on the same line that night to receive her pay. She was going to be great—mentally sharp, physically perfect, and spiritually bound, believing that this holy trinity of show business attributes would in time turn her into a movie star. Loretta would learn how to choose the best roles for her skill set and, beyond that, make certain whatever movie she was in reflected the values her mother had inculcated within her. Loretta also learned not to count on a man to take care of her, her mother, or her family. The starlet's first marriage had made this painfully clear. Gladys had been devastated when Loretta eloped, and since then the mother and daughter talked things through when it came to romance, instead of keeping secrets.

Loretta was curious about Clark's mother. She believed a man's relationship with his mother determined his point of view about women. She had learned from Grant Withers that a mother who abandons her son sets in motion the worst qualities in him as a husband. If she had known about Grant's mother before she married him, she would never have eloped in the first place.

"What was she like? Your mother?"

"I don't know."

"Your father never talked about her?"

Gable smiled. "He wasn't the type."

Gable reached into his back pocket and pulled out his wallet. He carried the flat style, like an envelope, made of fine, oxblood leather. It was neither new nor old, but Loretta noticed he took care of it: the wallet was neat, the bills organized. The money was arranged in numerical order, with crisp one-dollar bills resting on the fives, and so on.

Loretta couldn't help but compare Gable to Grant Withers. Withers had kept his money loose, tucked in his shirtsleeve, crumpled in coat pockets, as if it mattered little and meant even less. Withers disregarded money, and therefore he was always searching for it, patting his pants pockets, jingling random coins, hoping to find some treasure.

Gable thumbed through his wallet in search of something. Bits of paper were neatly folded in the sleeve. Gable had large hands, but his fingers were tapered, the nail beds deep, the nails themselves clipped straight across and square. In her opinion, they were exquisite hands. She figured he was handy, being an outdoorsman and all, but there was also art in them, a craftsman's elegance.

Gable pulled a small black-and-white photograph out of the wallet and handed it to Loretta. A pretty woman of around twenty, in a cotton voile dress trimmed in white piping, smiled at the camera. Her black hair, parted neatly on the side, extended down to her waist in a single shiny braid. At the tip end of the braid, she had tied a white ribbon. "This is my mother," he said, his voice breaking.

"She's lovely," Loretta said. "You look like her."

"It's the only picture I have of her."

"What was her name?"

"Adeline."

Loretta gave the photograph back to Gable, who returned it to its place in the wallet.

"Did your father ever remarry?"

"A nice woman named Jenny."

"She was good to you?"

"She read to me. Was forever giving me books."

"You're a reader?"

"I like the classics. Shakespeare."

"Well."

"Dickens. Melville. O. Henry." Gable shook his head. "You thought I was an ape."

"No, not at all. I just didn't think you'd be a reader—you hunt, you fish, you take apart engines."

"How do you think I learned how to take apart an engine? I read a manual."

"That's different from literature."

"Not really. A poem is just a set of instructions. Tells you how to live."

"That's lovely."

"How to love." Gable moved closer to Loretta.

"You're a married man, Mr. Gable."

"I'm pretty lousy at it."

"You should try to do better."

"I am."

"Not with me, you sap, with your wife."

"Do you always tell everybody what to do?"

"I'm a little bossy."

"A little?"

Loretta laughed. "Sometimes things are simple."

"They're never simple."

"But they are. There's right and wrong."

"And in between them is a mighty river. Ever been fly fishing?"

"No."

"The river is never what it seems. Now you can look at that river, and see the stones on the surface, and think, The water's shallow. I can handle it. I can make it across. I'll just stay right on those rocks and get to the other side. And then you get out there, and pretty soon you're up to your waist. The stone, it turns out, is an old volcanic plate that goes so deep, there's a mountain under that river that you couldn't know was there. There's an undertow. The surface seems calm, but it's only there to trick you. There are deep pits in the rock, so deep the force of the water pulls you in and under. The water is now raging, and you didn't plan on it. You're doing the right thing, you're trying to get to the other side, but you couldn't know what you'd find when you got out into the middle of the river. That's the mystery. You can do everything just right, and the river moves through anyway, and it takes you with it. When you go deep, that's where the trouble lies."

"I'd turn back," she blurted.

"What if you can't? What if the river is what it's supposed to be, and you have to go forward?"

"I'd try to do the right thing."

"You can't know what you're going to feel, and you can't control what you feel. You only know what you know."

"The way I was raised, that's the devil talking."

"Or maybe an angel who's been sent to save you."

"That sounds like a real line to me, Mr. Gable." Loretta gathered up her script.

Gable watched her sort the pages in order and stack them neatly with a rap on the table. "May I see you home?" he asked.

"I think I can find the second floor."

"It's good manners to walk a lady home."

"Okay, okay, good point. I would not want to deprive you of your courtly gesture."

Gable followed Loretta up the stairs. This time he took in the sway of her hips and her movement on the stairs, the same way he had observed the hotel maid.

Loretta spun on her heels. "I know what you're up to."

Gable held his hands up innocently. "You have eyes in the back of your head?"

"Don't need 'em."

"I'm appreciative of beauty."

"Oh, that's it."

"I'm a simple man."

"I'll say."

"I can't help it, Gretchen."

"That's too bad. Mrs. Gable will be very sorry to hear that."

"Why do you bring up my wife?"

"Because she's your wife."

"And I need reminding."

"Exactly."

"Since you're so obsessed with Mrs. Gable—"

Loretta gave Gable a playful shove. "I am not."

"You're such an expert about my situation, so indulge me. What happened with Mr. Withers? On the level, tell me what happened."

"He drank, and I wasn't ready for that."

"What did you think marriage was going to be?"

"Happy. He was handsome and sharp. He dressed like a duke. He courted me. He was an actor, and I liked his work. He was good at it. It came naturally, so I assumed that all those elegant gents he played in pictures were real."

"You're just like the girl who sits in the balcony. She thinks it's real."

"I've lived it, so I know it isn't. To tell you the truth, I don't like to think about it. I am like the girl in the balcony. I was devastated when I found out the truth." Loretta fished her key out of her pocket. "Good night, Mr. Gable."

Gable stood next to her as she unlocked the door. He leaned against the frame. "I'm sorry I brought it up."

Clark leaned down and kissed Loretta on her forehead. This was something Loretta's father might have done had he stayed. Gable was twelve years older than she was; maybe he was feeling protective, or this was his way of making her comfortable before the cameras rolled in the morning.

"Good night, Gretchen."

It was cold in Loretta's room. The ruffles on the satin bedskirts were like ribbon candy, stiff to the touch. The maid had left a pot of fresh snow water boiling in the kettle on the hearth. Loretta changed into her nightgown. She covered the warming kettle in a flannel sleeve and placed it under the covers. She brushed her teeth, snapped her retainer in place, and brushed her hair.

Loretta threw another log on the fire, and soon the flames were roaring, the bits of dry wood crackling and spitting small blue sparks. Loretta placed three lumps of black coal on to the burning logs, where they glistened like black diamonds as the flames engulfed them.

Loretta stood there for a long time, trying to warm herself. She rubbed her hands together.

"Come on, Gretch." She jumped in place—anything to make heat, anything to shake off what she was feeling for Clark Gable. She had flirted with him, joked around, but it was all for fun, all for the movie.

She admonished herself, shook her head and rejected the thought of him. This was a set crush, that's all. It was simple. It was sex. She found him wildly attractive, and they were stuck on a mountaintop. She could control this situation. She was not going to let anything happen; she refused to fall for a man who belonged to another. Again. She would keep this situation platonic. He was fun, she liked flirting with him, liked being around him, and nowhere—not in any sermon, church, or penance given by a priest—had *that* ever been a sin. That's what she would hang on to—it was just a friendship. And who doesn't need a friend?

There was a knock at the door.

Gable stood in the dim hallway holding a blanket folded neatly. "Thought you could use another blanket."

"Thank you." She smiled and then realized she was wearing her retainer. "See you in the morning." Loretta closed the door.

Gable pushed it open before she could lock it and looked at her with a smile that made her heart beat faster.

He made her so nervous, she blurted, "I wear a retainer. If I don't wear it, I have buck teeth. The studio wanted to pull them, and Mama said no, so I have to wear this thing for the rest of my life."

Gable laughed. "Last summer I got sick and they pulled mine. I have a few left."

"Doesn't look like it hurt your career. Or that smile."

"You can buy teeth." Gable stood in the doorway. Just as he filled the screen in the movie theaters, he filled the doorway to her room. He leaned against the doorjamb and folded his arms across his chest. She swore he was holding the entire building up, maybe even all of

Mount Baker. The fire threw a golden glow on him. The greatest cinematographers in Hollywood could not have possibly lit him better in this moment. Whatever this man was, Loretta thought he looked part god in the firelight, and she hated him for it.

"Thank you for the blanket. See you tomorrow." She smiled, lips together, no teeth, no gleam from the silver bands of her retainer to blind him. She pushed the door closed.

He pushed it back open. "Is this good night, Gretchen?"

"Yes, Mr. Gable."

Loretta pushed the door closed, and locked it.

Gable heard the click and chuckled.

7

Buck had been living in a dog shed off the back of the kitchen of the dining hall at the Mount Baker Inn until director Wellman decided that it was inhumane. At night the temperature on the mountain would drop to ten degrees below zero, which evidently was too cold even for a Saint Bernard.

Buck was granted permission to stay in the hotel with his trainer. The crew found the dog much easier to handle once he had moved inside. Gable figured that Buck had somehow seen the rushes, decided he was a star rivaling Rin Tin Tin, and renegotiated his contract to include posh digs for the duration.

The hotel was remote, cold, and—now that Zanuck had ordered the plows—noisy. A group of local workingmen had been hired to keep the road clear between the exteriors and the hotel. The workers plowed incessantly in shifts, covering miles of road in trucks that ground surface ice and cleared snow from morning until night.

Mount Baker was 5,000 feet above sea level, and while Darryl Zanuck loved to brag that it was the highest location ever used on a Hollywood picture, he left out that it was also deadly, and nearly impossible to navigate. Wellman certainly was the best director for the job. Nothing scared him; no climate, no actor, and no stunt was too great a challenge. He made a personal mission out of professional challenges. He wanted to win.

The stretch of the Bellingham River that Wellman had scouted the previous spring appeared safe, meandering through the foothills of Mount Baker in ruffles of clear blue. At some points the water was shallow enough to cross, yet in a turn it widened, veins of small streams feeding the river. The water was deceptive; it looked deep but was actually shallow. The swift movement of the waves gave the illusion of a raging river, with plumes of white water rushing over rock formations before pouring into the rapids before a waterfall.

Gable, Jack Oakie, and Loretta had rehearsed the raft scene on dry land. There was a good stretch of witty dialogue, and the words were important to the story. Wellman needed the trio to master the raft, navigating it down a cleft of the river. He blocked the scene so the actors' backs were to the camera; this way, he could artfully cut in any dialogue he chose later. Wellman often made story points in voice-over, over the shoulders of actors. It was a trick he employed because he was more interested in getting the visual right. He wanted as much wild as he could get in *The Call of the Wild.*

Loretta was wearing a layer of long thermal underwear and a flannel shirt tucked into work jeans trimmed in sturdy oilcloth. The high-waisted pant had a thick belt upon which she had hung hooks, a circle of rope, and a small hammer. Her workboots were laced to the knee. For authenticity's sake, she tucked a small prop pistol loaded with blanks under the belt on her hip. Her character Claire was savvy, brave, and an equal partner to her missing husband, an explorer in the wild. She was wigged in a low chignon with curly bangs. Alda had artfully sewn lace on the collar of the flannel shirt; Loretta was certain that without a feminine touch, the camera would mistake her for a man in the wide shots.

"Come on, Gretchen," Gable teased Loretta, who surveyed the bank of the river carefully.

Gable had boarded the raft, and dug a guide stick into the river.

Loretta gripped the safety line and stepped into the shallow water before pulling herself up onto the raft. Gable was there to lift her. Oakie trudged through the shallow water and sat on the edge of the raft, nearly tipping it over. Loretta and Gable hollered and hung on as he threw his legs out of the water and onto the raft, then crawled to standing position. From the shore Wellman cursed Oakie, who pretended he couldn't hear the director.

"You've really done it this time, Oakie," Gable chided him.

"The minute this stops being a goof, I quit."

"Have all the fun you want on dry land, but not on the water. I don't want to freeze to death out here," Loretta told him.

"That water's as cold as a sloe gin fizz." Oakie chuckled.

Wellman picked up a bullhorn. "Stay on the raft. We have a problem with the camera."

"How long, Captain?" Gable shouted.

"Don't know. Just stay put!" Wellman hollered back.

"Listen kids, I got a plan." Oakie rubbed his hands together.

"Don't ad lib. You're killing us," Loretta told him.

"I'm not talking about the movie. I think I can get us a car."

"For what?"

"We can get out of here on the weekend."

"Where are we going?"

"Seattle."

"Count me in," Gable said. Gable was not a man who liked being cooped up, and this movie was beginning to feel like a stint in beggar's prison.

"Count me out," Loretta said.

"If you go, he"—Oakie pointed to Wellman—"won't get mad."

"Come on, Gretch," Gable implored.

"You too?"

"Yes, I'm begging," Gable flirted.

The flirting didn't sway Loretta; she'd seen him use his wiles on everyone, including Buck the dog.

"It won't be any fun without you," Gable insisted.

"You'll do all right. You two on the town, with your fat wallets, liquored up like a couple of bums, and looking for love when you're not looking for a couple of suckers to take in a card game. No, thank you."

Oakie and Gable laughed.

"This isn't my first river raft," she assured them.

"Gretch, wouldn't you love a juicy steak and a baked potato? How about a cream puff? A hotel room with fluffy goose-down blankets and soft pillows and heat from a coal furnace, not a fireplace? Think about it. You could put on a pretty dress for a change. And shoes that don't have laces," Gable promised.

"We'd treat you good," Oakie added.

"I'll think about it."

Loretta hadn't told anyone that this was her twenty-second birthday. Her sisters had written to her and asked her what she wanted, and she wrote back with a single request: wool socks.

"Okay, we're gonna go, kids," Wellman shouted from his bullhorn. "Set dec is gonna let the raft loose. Clark, take it as far as the turn."

Gable waved that he understood.

Wellman continued, "The guys are below, ready to pull you in—just anchor the raft with your guide stick when you get there."

Gable waved again. He said to Oakie, "You must be worth more at the box office than I thought."

"I'm gold. Comic relief. You can't put a price on funny."

"Mr. Zanuck puts a price on everything," Loretta commented. "I'm sure he told you what you were worth with your last paycheck."

"You know, Loretta, you piss on the fire with the best of them."

Gable navigated the raft to the center of the river, the undertow tugging the raft down the river toward the cleft. It picked up speed and hit a rock. Loretta lurched toward the side; Gable grabbed her by the waist, keeping hold of the stick.

"I got it!" Oakie grabbed the guide stick. He moved it to stop the raft in the rush of the water, but instead of hitting river bottom, the stick went deep into a pocket of sand in the riverbed, pulling the stick into the water. Oakie got down on his stomach and reached for it. The raft rocked to and fro. The assistant director hollered from the banks as the raft slipped past the point of anchor.

Wellman and his team ran along the riverbank to meet the team at the cleft.

"Keep rolling," he shouted as he ran.

Gable kneeled in the center of the raft, telling Loretta to lie down in the center to stabilize the raft. Oakie was hanging on, but he'd taken in the waves, and they rushed over the side of the raft. Gable scooped up the lifeline rope, stood, and with the raft moving down river, threw it back to Wellman, who waded into the river and grabbed it. Soon the entire crew was in the water, pulling the raft back toward shore.

Loretta could feel the undertow of the river pulling them forward. She thought about jumping off and swimming, but worried about the black pockets in the river bottom. They could pull her in, and she'd drown. Gable was cursing, using words she had never heard before. He was angry at the raft, the river, and Wellman.

Oakie stayed on his stomach, trying to ride the torrents and stay on the raft. Loretta reached for him.

The raft tipped, and Oakie fell into the rushing water like a stone. Loretta slid to the edge, reaching for him. Oakie surfaced and bobbed in the water like a hunk of driftwood. He went under, and the crew shouted from the shore.

Gable pulled Loretta back to the center by her feet. "Don't move!" he shouted.

Gable lay down, balancing his body on the edge of the raft as he reached for Oakie. He grabbed Oakie's forearm before he went under again. Oakie sputtered and cursed as Gable pulled him to the raft, now stationary in the middle of the river, thanks to the lifeline rope. He pulled Oakie onto the raft.

Oakie began to shiver from head to toe. "It felt so warm in the water," he whispered.

Gable looked at Loretta as she prayed silently to herself. Oakie could've died in the accident, and he almost had—but Gable had saved him. Loretta had never witnessed that kind of courage. She was more than impressed, she was in awe.

Wellman shouted from the shore, "We're pulling you in!"

Loretta sat up to help Oakie.

"Stay down, Gretchen," Gable hollered.

"Don't yell at her, it's my fault," Oakie said.

The raft inched toward the shore. A dozen men, with all their strength, water to their waists, pulled the raft against the mighty flow of the river. The raft creaked and rocked. Loretta closed her eyes.

She could hear the water rushing under the raft with such force, she wondered if twelve men were enough to pull them safely to shore.

Gable reached across the raft and put his hand on Loretta's. It was the only warmth she felt as the crew towed the actors in. As the raft bumped up onto snowy banks, the crew reached for the actors.

"You're buying dinner in Seattle, bud," Gable said to Oakie.

"I'll buy the entire town dinner, and French whores for everybody! Sorry, Loretta. I'll get you a Russian prince."

"No, thanks. You can keep him, Jack."

Loretta looked at Gable, who kept his eyes on Oakie. She lay still as the crew pulled them to the shore.

"Secure the raft!" Wellman shouted.

Loretta looked over at Wellman, who seemed as concerned about the raft as he was about his actors.

Wellman believed Gable didn't take his acting work seriously enough, but Loretta did not share that opinion. She had come to appreciate the way her costar approached his work. Gable was all in, for anything that might happen. He was present in the moment, alert and intent when the cameras were rolling. It might not be Wellman's idea of great acting or technique, but as far as Loretta was concerned, it was as fine a method as any she had seen.

The crew helped Loretta off the raft. Sitting down on a snowbank, she took deep breaths to steady her heart. The costume crew draped Oakie in blankets to take him back to the hotel. Gable came off the raft, and in a few feet of water, helped secure it to the shore. He trudged out of the frigid water.

"Reset, Mr. Rosher?" Gable said to the director of photography.

"Hell, no. Got the whole debacle."

"Print?" Gable asked.

"Oh, yeah, we got it," Wellman said.

Loretta wearily climbed the steps to her hotel room. She pushed the door open, closed it behind her, and immediately began to undress, laying her wet costume pieces on the bathroom floor. She pulled on a warm chenille robe.

When she returned from the bathroom, she saw a large box at the foot of her bed. She was elated to see the return address: Sunset House in Bel Air.

Loretta removed a hairpin from her chignon and ripped into the package. There was a frilly birthday card signed by her mother, her sisters, and Ruby. Polly wrote a newsy note about her new beau Carter Hermann (Gladys-approved). Sally was out on the town with director Norman Foster (Gladys-approved). Life was going on without Loretta in Los Angeles. She was happy for her sisters but painfully aware that she was alone. Her sisters tried to make Loretta's birthday a happy one. The wool socks she had requested were tied with string, a lollipop anchored in each sock.

A stack of fan magazines was tied with a ribbon. Loretta quickly shuffled through them, finding Joan Crawford, Janet Gaynor, and Myrna Loy on the covers. The sight of them in their furs and finery made her long for home. She set them aside and dug into the contents.

The box was filled with glorious food: cellophane packages of noodles, German cured sausages, wedges of hard cheese, a bottle of olive oil, and a jar of Greek olives. Ruby had mixed dry biscuit ingredients in a mason jar, with instructions to add eggs and bake. Another jar held the dry ingredients for chocolate cake. There was a box of See's Candy, Loretta's secret vice. A large square baker's box was nestled in the center; she lifted it out carefully and opened it. As soon as she did, the room filled with the scent of lemon, rum, and butter. Her mother had made her favorite cake for her birthday, wrapped in layers of tinfoil: a southern rum cake, an old recipe handed down from her great-grandmother in North Carolina.

The first person Loretta thought to share this bounty with was Clark Gable.

She knelt next to the box in her robe and began to cry. She tried to understand her tears, to put her feelings in some rational context, but she couldn't. Maybe it was being so far from home on her birthday, or perhaps it was where she was, frozen on a mountaintop in the bitter cold, adjusting to the short days and long nights, that made her miserable.

Or was this wave of sadness about the abrupt end of her friendship with Spencer? She missed their conversations, his view of the world, his take on things. He could talk for hours about anything—acting, baseball, or spiritual matters. He had common sense. He taught her about polo, which on the surface of things bored her, but when he was describing the sport, she was riveted.

Loretta missed those talks, and she missed *him*. She wondered who she was alone, without someone to love, and the mirror reflection of someone loving her. She pondered her worth. Good actresses were like the oranges in the groves in California, plentiful, shiny, and sweet, an endless bounty that seemed to multiply in the heat of the California sun.

Now that movies were available in every small town across the country, the dream of acting in them was available to every girl who had the beauty, youth, and moxie to give Hollywood a try. Loretta had seen every variation of the story, but believed if she worked harder than the rest, she would continue her ascent, to earn roles in scripts worthy of talents like Jean Arthur and Bette Davis. But here, far away from her studio routine and all she knew, she questioned the talent she had worked so hard to nurture. Was she really strong? Had she been afraid on the raft that afternoon? Had she been brave, or was she simply acting? Was she good enough? Did she have the stamina to endure a career that would take her away from family and friends? What kind of life was this for a young woman who hoped to marry and have children of her own someday?

There was a knock at the door. She dried her tears and went to answer it.

————

Alda looked at Loretta and knew something was terribly wrong. "I heard all about what happened on the river. How can I help?"

"I'm all right," Loretta assured her.

"Have you been crying?"

"A little."

"Why?"

"I'm tired," Loretta said. "I'll tell you what. I want you to help me make dinner tonight. I can't bear that bad food any longer. Mama sent a box of great stuff."

"I know. I didn't want to open it." Alda looked through the box. "Spaghetti!"

"When the crew has eaten and Elvira is done with work for the night, ask her if I can borrow the kitchen. Invite Luca. I'm going to invite Mr. Gable. We'll have a good time, just the four of us."

"Should I extend the invitation to Mr. Gable?"

"I'll take care of it."

Alda left to make the arrangements in the kitchen.

Loretta sat down at her desk. She drafted a short letter. She corrected her grammar and spelling, then wrote it out slowly and perfectly for delivery.

> Dear Mr. Gable,
>
> An astonishing stroke of luck has occurred that does not involve wild river rapids. I have received reinforcements from Hollywood (the food kind, not the chorus girl variety) and would like to invite you to dinner this evening at eight o'clock in the dining hall kitchen. Dress casual.
> Your friend,
> Gretchen Young

Loretta threw her fur coat over the robe and snuck down the hallway to deliver the invitation. As she approached Gable's room, the last room at the end of the hallway, she followed the scent of sweet tobacco and heard him talking on the phone. "Minna, I'm telling you, it was unbelievable! Bill said he never saw anything like it."

Loretta slipped the invitation under the door and heard Gable's heavy footsteps coming toward her. She ran down the hallway and into her room, closing the door behind her.

Minna Wallis was Gable's agent. Loretta would never think to call her agent from a location, but that was the difference between them. He was busy acting in one picture while he was planning the next. Only a star connects one role to the next like glistening pop beads. Box office popularity could only be sustained by a star's constant presence in the local movie house, and that meant cultivating the next role while acting in the current one.

Loretta ran a bath. She placed the kettle on the hearth to make a cup of tea. She bathed quickly; the last thing she wanted to do after the raft scene was soak in water. She pulled on the robe and slippers and curled up on the bed with the fan magazines, the box of See's Candy, and a cup of fragrant Earl Grey. She opened *Photoplay.* In it was a full-page article about Gable and his wife, Ria. She sat up and read it carefully.

Under a photo of Gable wearing black tie and tails and his wife in a slim white gown, was the subhead RAISE FOR GABLE. Loretta read that Gable was earning $3,000 a week. She whistled softly at the sum. He was quoted: "I do all right in pictures. My wife, no matter my salary, feast or famine or suspension by choice, always finds ways to spend what I earn on draperies and furniture."

Loretta shook her head. That quote didn't sound like a man who was separated; it sounded like one who was very married. But the article went on.

> *Clark Gable is at the precipice of greatness. Box office gold, they call him. And while Mrs. Gable is busy decorating their mansion, Gable has an open lease on a bungalow at the Beverly Wilshire, where he lives most days and nights, fueling rumors of divorce. His complaints about his wife's spending habits cannot help the situation. Time will tell.*

Loretta stretched out on the bed, recalling the scene at the train station. Mrs. Gable had kissed her husband good-bye as if she were his aunt, not his wife. Loretta could not reconcile the Gable she was beginning to know with the wife he had chosen. There must be something more to it, but she couldn't imagine what that could be.

Loretta heard the soft brush of paper under her door. She lay still, lest the squeak of a bedspring or the creak of a wood slat reveal her. Only when she heard footsteps walk away from her door and down the hallway did she dare to slide off the bed and creep over to read the note. It read:

I'd be delighted. See you at 8.
—Jack Oakie

Loretta didn't find it one bit funny, but she laughed anyway.

————————

"My mother used to say, if you have a lemon, a clove of garlic, some salt, olive oil, and spaghetti, that's all you need to live." Luca stirred the sauce.

"What about cheese?" Loretta placed the wedge of Parmesan on the counter.

"Love it. But cheese is a luxury. Somebody has to make it. It takes time. Pasta, you can make from scratch if you have flour and eggs. Lemons—if you live in California, they're everywhere. Garlic, that keeps well, and olive oil—well, a home without olive oil is not a home. It's just a place where people sleep."

"You have strong opinions on the subject," Loretta said as she set the table in the kitchen.

"When Italian food catches on in America, look out," Luca promised.

Loretta went to the stove and turned the sausage over in the cast iron skillet until it sizzled crispy brown.

Alda checked the pot of boiling water on the stove. "Should I throw the spaghetti in?"

Loretta checked her watch. It was almost 8:30. "I guess he's not showing up."

"Oakie or Gable?" Clark Gable said from the doorway.

"Throw in the spaghetti, Alda," Loretta said. "Mr. Gable, try as you might, you will never have the stature and sex appeal of Jack Oakie. So stop trying."

Gable smiled. He got a kick out of Loretta. Usually women didn't make him laugh, and not usually at his own expense, but he liked her. A sucker for a pretty girl he had always been, but now, in his mid-thirties, he was beginning to appreciate the clowns.

For Loretta, the slow emotional tumble had begun. She felt the flutter of desire, and her heart raced as though it was trying to outrun her feelings. It didn't hurt that Gable looked divine, fresh scrubbed and eager.

"This is a celebration," Loretta said as she placed a platter on the table.

"What are we celebrating?"

"We didn't drown in the river."

"That? That was nothing. No harm was going to come to you," Gable assured her.

"Because it came to Jack Oakie."

"He's all right. He's in an all-night card game with Wellman. The only thing he's going to lose tonight is his shirt."

"Your response to my invitation was funny."

"I always sign my contracts and important correspondence with the name Jack Oakie."

"Keeps the riffraff off your tail, Luca said."

"That's right, Chet. It's the old dodge-and-weave."

Gable went to the stove and peered into the pots. "What are you making, kid?"

"Spaghetti with olive oil," Alda said.

"Never had it."

"Please, sit down. We're almost ready."

Alda and Luca worked together in the kitchen as though they had been raised in the same one. He lifted the boiling pasta off the stove and drained it into the sink, while she stirred the lemon and butter sauce. He brought the noodles to the pot and threw them in; she tossed them while he grated fresh Parmesan on top of the mixture.

"You two are like an old married couple," Gable remarked.

"Do you think she'll have me?" Luca asked.

"I don't know. If she's as picky as you are, you may never get together. How many pictures have we worked on, Chet?"

"This is number eight."

"Everybody wants Chet. Nobody paints like him. Nobody sees the world like he does. Wellman paid you double to come on this picture, didn't he?"

"I don't like the cold."

Loretta and Alda and Gable laughed.

"I left Brooklyn because they have four seasons. I like one season. Sunshine. In this respect, I am a true Italian."

"After this, I almost agree with you," Gable said.

"I can't mix my paint, it's so cold up here."

"You'll figure something out," Gable assured him.

"I always do."

Alda and Luca sat down at the table. Luca reached under the table, produced a jug of homemade wine, and poured it into lead-glass tumblers from the kitchen.

"Where'd you get the wine?" Loretta asked.

"I made it myself. Best part of living in California. I drive up the coast, buy my grapes, then make the wine in my basement in the valley. Go on, taste it."

Loretta and Clark took a sip.

"It's delicious," Loretta said.

Gable said, "I'm not much for wine, but I like it."

"You can't eat macaroni without wine. It won't digest properly," Alda said.

"She learned that in the convent," Luca joked.

"I learned that in Italy," Alda corrected him.

"Were you really in the convent?" Gable asked.

"Yes, I was. And they didn't think I had what it took to be a nun. So here I am."

"In show business." Gable laughed.

"I try to help Loretta."

"And you do."

Gable tasted the spaghetti. "This is good."

"Do you think two Italians would make you dinner, and it wouldn't be?"

"Buddy, the food has been so bad up here, it's ruined my taste buds."

"We wanted to make something special. It's Loretta's birthday."

Gable turned to her. "Really?"

"Yes."

"Happy birthday."

"Thank you."

"I didn't get you a present."

"You sure did. You didn't let me drown today. This is my present. Good friends, good food, and homemade wine."

"You're a simple girl," Gable said.

"You have no idea."

"When I was a kid in Brooklyn, we did this all the time. The whole neighborhood came over on a Sunday, and my mother would make manicotti, and another family brought bread, somebody else made meatballs, another family brought a cake, and we all had a meal together."

"We had that in Italy," Alda said.

"And we have it every Sunday after mass." Loretta smiled.

"And I never had it," Gable said. "Never had that kind of family life growing up. It must be great."

"It is," Luca said. "But that doesn't mean you can't have it now."

"You have to have a wife who wants that sort of thing, I guess."

There was an awkward silence. Alda looked down at her plate, and Loretta slowly twirled her spaghetti.

"I want a ranch. A big ranch with a little farmhouse," Gable said.

"Why the small farmhouse?"

"So I can find the one I love. Big houses, those Beverly Hills mansions, might as well be airport hangars. They're so big, you can't find anybody in them."

"Maybe people live in them so they can't be found," Alda offered.

"You need to have Gladys Belzer decorate your mansion—she makes them cozy," Loretta said.

"I'm not talking about wallpaper. I'm talking about sharing your life with someone who wants to be with you—just because they love you. A couple of rooms, a kitchen, that's all you need."

"I have a big dream too. I want to buy a house and have enough land to grow my own grapes to make my own wine."

"And will your wife stomp the grapes?"

"She'll have to." Luca looked at Alda. "A man can think clearly on a mountaintop."

"And what is the man thinking?" Loretta wanted to know.

"Alda?"

"He's thinking he has all the answers, and I think he's rushing things."

"There's no such thing," Luca said. "Why don't you believe me?"

"Now, Chet, if you want to win Alda's heart, you need to listen to her. You don't want to rush a lady. Her feelings are more important than yours in this situation—if your goal is winning her heart, of course," said Gable.

"That's my goal."

"Then slow down."

"Thank you, Mr. Gable."

"What's your dream, Alda? We know Chet's, and we know mine—what's yours?"

"Since I left Saint Elizabeth's, I haven't had time to think about it. I know I want to go home and see my family in Italy."

"No vineyard, no farm?"

She shook her head. "I don't know."

"And how about you, Gretchen? What's your dream?" Gable asked.

"A simple life."

"I never met a leading lady who didn't want a simple life. And then they break through in pictures and live everything *but*."

"And since you know every leading lady, we'll take that as gospel," Loretta said.

"Just my opinion, kid."

"I dream of a house with a fence covered in roses. A husband who loves me. A baby or two or three . . . maybe more."

Loretta cut her birthday cake, placing ample slices on the dessert plates.

"This is bad luck. You didn't blow out candles," Gable said.

"Because we don't *have* candles," Loretta reminded him.

"Make a wish anyway."

Loretta closed her eyes and made a wish.

Alda, Luca, and Clark applauded when she opened her eyes.

"You want to know what I wish for?"

"Let me guess. That you get William Powell in your next picture," Gable joked.

"I wouldn't mind that. I wished that we would all stay as friendly as we are tonight."

Luca held up his glass, and they toasted one another in honor of Loretta. As she sipped her wine, she decided that this had been her best birthday yet.

———

The wind howled as the couples trudged back to the hotel.

A half moon glowed overhead through the black sky and onto the white snow. They gripped the rope the management stretched from the dining hall to the hotel entrance. The wind was so fierce, it kicked up an icy dust that stung their faces. Gable pulled Loretta close and Luca held Alda tightly until they made it inside the hotel.

"Thank you for a delicious meal." Loretta gave Alda and Luca a hug. "And thank you Mr. Gable for coming to the party."

"May I see you home, Miss Young?"

"Yes, you may, Mr. Gable."

"We're going to warm up by the fire," Luca said. "See you in ten years. That's how long it will take me to defrost."

"Good idea." Gable winked at him.

When Loretta reached her room, she fumbled for her key. Gable took it and unlocked the door.

"Thank you for inviting me."

"It was fun."

"Why did you invite me?"

Loretta blushed. "I like you."

"You do. At long last. The Miracle of Mount Baker." He leaned against the doorframe. "What do you like exactly?"

"You've got guts. I like that. And you're kind to everyone. And you look out for me."

"You make me sound like a crossing guard."

She laughed. "I don't mean to."

"I feel like a sap."

"Don't." Loretta placed her hands on his face and looked into his eyes. She ran her fingers through his hair. "Good night."

"You'd rather not kiss me?" he whispered.

"Where'd you get that idea?" Loretta put her arms around him. He lifted her off the ground, and with tenderness, their lips met. She relaxed into his arms. After all, it was her birthday, and she had been so lonesome that the thought of letting it go by without a kiss made her feel worse. Besides, she could file this tender moment under "rehearsal."

Clark Gable was strong, and whatever he held dear, he protected. She let him protect her. His lips traced her nose, and he kissed her again. This time he didn't stop and she didn't let him. She buried her face in his neck. His skin, his scent, were familiar to her. He made her think of home.

"May I come in?" he said softly.

"No."

He smiled. "Why not?"

"I need eight hours of sleep with my retainer."

"Let's make it a late morning." Gable kissed her neck.

"You can be late. I can't. I promised Wellman."

"It's unprofessional," Gable agreed.

"Terribly."

"You should never fall for a costar." He kissed her hands.

"That advice is the best birthday gift I ever received."

"I thought you said it was the spaghetti," he teased her.

"If I'm being honest, the See's chocolates were the best."

Gable put his arms around her. Loretta looked up and down the hallway, making sure that they had not been discovered.

"We can be friends, but that's all," she said firmly.

"Right."

"I don't kiss friends."

"Absolutely not." He softly kissed her cheek, her eyes, and found her lips again.

"That was just rehearsal."

"Right." He tried to kiss her again.

She pulled away. "I think we've mastered the kiss for now. Good night, Mr. Gable."

"Happy birthday, Gretchen."

Gable made his way down the hallway to his room. He opened

the door to be met with a dusting of snow blowing into his face. He rushed across the room and closed the window, catching his hand under the sash. He cursed and pulled the window shut.

He stoked the fire, which was down to orange and blue embers, crackling softly in the grid. He added a log, and soon the dry wood was engulfed in flames, throwing heat. He leaned against the mantel and looked into the fire as a terrible sense of dread came over him.

At first he thought it might have something to do with work, but soon he was thinking about Ria. The life she had made for him was precisely as she had promised. She made a lovely home: cushions covered in brocade, draperies of fine silk that rustled in the breeze, a dining room that was a stage setting for important guests, set with so much silverware and cutlery, it might as well be Buckingham Palace. Queen Ria served dishes made by a staff, based on menus she had crafted from books she read about the living habits of the crowned heads of Europe. Her typical fare was duck in aspic, pheasant, and trifle—the food of royalty, or Ria's view of what that might be.

There was never hearty food or plain food, the kind he grew up on. Gable longed for simplicity—for flapjacks, chicken pot pie, and mashed potatoes. He imagined chairs wide and deep enough to accommodate his height, covered in fabrics that could take a whiskey spill or the ash of his pipe. He preferred baseball on the radio or the occasional mystery theater, not the Philharmonic playing the classics. Gable's life was filled with music that put him to sleep, food that didn't satisfy him, people that bored him, and a wife that sparked neither his libido nor his intellect. He was stuck in a private life that offered none of the comforts he required.

Gable wanted out.

Gable had relished the spaghetti that night, and not just because it was delicious. He'd enjoyed the conversation, the jokes, the ease and camaraderie of friends. He couldn't remember the last time he'd had a home-cooked meal with people whose company he enjoyed. Ria would have taken one look at the Italians and hightailed it out of the room. Working people were of little interest to her, the things they made, even less. Ria would think a rum cake was common, and homemade wine a poor substitute for any with a label in French.

Gretchen took delight in the very things Gable treasured. Gretchen thought of others and their needs. She was a girl who took an entire day to bake pies for the crew, the kind of pies he grew up on, the kind of dessert the men appreciated because it reminded them of their mothers, of home.

Ria loved the idea of Gable and his potential stature in Hollywood. She was a career-building architect, trained in the grand Texas style, which she'd invented from the scraps of her meager childhood. Ria went big and wide with her ideas. Ria may have cared about Gable as a part of her aspirational vision, he was certain of that, but there was no romance. At first there had been. When she was in a bad marriage, she'd been hungry for him. He'd obliged, and he'd shared his dreams, which she promised to make come true. She swore she knew how, and Gable had been grateful as she took him from a player in a stock acting company and moved him to Hollywood to become a star. Never mind that his first wife, his acting coach Josephine Dillon, twenty years his senior, was punted in the process. Gable took care of Josephine financially, buying the home they had lived in and willing it to her. Upon his death, she'd own it outright. It was the least he could do.

Of late the second Mrs. Gable and Clark had put on an act in public as phony as a publicity still—"a Hollywood two-step," Gable called it—but he could as easily have acted the part of chauffeur or gardener as he did the part of husband in the moving picture of their marriage. He wondered if he had bollixed up the works, the entirety of his life, with a home that was strictly symbolic, a wife who was one in name only, meeting his needs outside his home by working the kick line of chorus girls who graced the MGM musicals. Sex was as easy to get as ice cream, and about as filling.

———

Loretta sat in the window of her room at the inn.

The moonlight made the rolling fields of snow look like layers of chiffon. She couldn't sleep, which was unlike her.

She couldn't shake Gable's kiss.

Loretta had been kissed onscreen by every type of actor. Granted, they were acting, but none could compare to Gable. Her chaste kisses with Spencer had been so guilt-ridden that not only were they not much fun, they were loaded with all the drama that comes from being with a man who belongs to another woman. It's impossible to stake a claim on a man who is already taken.

Loretta hadn't known that Spencer Tracy was married when she met him. Gable was different. Perhaps she had too much information; his romantic dalliances had been chronicled in every fan magazine since 1930, and what she didn't know from reading about him, Sally was happy to fill in. Loretta knew of him—but what she'd discovered in person did not square with the fan magazine narrative or the public's perception. He was much more handsome and goofy than he appeared in print. "Fun-loving" wasn't a phrase often used to describe him, but in her mind, he was. Gable was a he-man; he could hunt and shoot with the best and make love with anyone he chose whenever he wanted to, which also appealed to her young heart. He liked her, and it seemed he was choosing her; how could she not be flattered by the attention?

Still, Loretta was wary of getting involved with an actor. Temptation came with every rehearsal of every love scene. The hours between scenes when the crew was setting up were an opportunity to converse and connect, to learn about one another, and as an extension of that, an excuse to make plans outside of work. In her mind, the birthday kisses with Gable at the door were just that. She had no intention of pursuing a relationship with Gable beyond Mount Baker, and while she was here, all her efforts would go into reining in her feelings. She just wished it wasn't so cold, and that she weren't so lonely.

She could only justify her feelings and their kiss with what she'd observed of Ria and Gable on the train platform. Gable wasn't lying to Ria, and she wasn't lying to him. She wasn't the dutiful wife in an authentic marriage; she was the presentational wife, strictly scenery, like the painted backdrops in the silents that flew down from the flyspace on to the sound stage. On camera the bricks looked real, but upon close inspection the wall was just a veneer. Ria was playing a part for all to see. Loretta knew an actress when she saw one.

The Gables' marriage was an arrangement, and while Loretta didn't know what it meant, she was certain it was not love. She'd promised herself she would never be involved with a married man after Spencer Tracy, but the situation with Gable was different. She felt in control of her feelings for Gable because she understood him. When a woman falls for a man with a roving eye, she had better plan on being on the move.

All movie sets are an alternative to real life. Like life, it's a living story, with words and settings, expectations met and unmet, relationships, and within them, feelings. The difference between life and a movie is that in a movie, everybody shows up the first day knowing the ending.

The cast and crew of *The Call of the Wild* were living on a mountaintop, in a snow globe, removed from the ordinary world to one that they had created on their own. The air was thin on Mount Baker. It made breathing shallow, hearts beat faster, heads light. If an actor was prone to poor judgment at sea level, he didn't stand a chance at this altitude.

The actors had been removed body and soul from the place that anchored them in reality, away from home, far from the bonds of marriage and the pull of family responsibility. It was possible to forget loved ones temporarily; the work at hand was so intense and required such concentration, there was no room to think of anyone else. When the work was dangerous, and the days long and rigorous, there was no time for anything but work, and the work itself bound everyone together.

Even if you wanted to connect to loved ones at home, it was impossible to call. Telephone lines were unreliable in bad weather, and it was difficult to write letters, as an actor's time was not his own. Every wife left behind was afraid that she and the children would fade like an old memory in the face of the excitement, romance, and danger of making a movie.

And danger was everywhere. It wasn't likely that the worst would happen—but if it did, how would they make it off this mountain? How many search parties had disappeared above Bellingham in blizzards, in the cliffs of Mount Baker in the event of an avalanche?

Why else would Zanuck have insisted on round-the-clock plowing, to keep the road open for his crew and stars? He must have thought the danger through—but in Loretta's mind, the danger was a reminder that there is only the moment. It was essential that she be honest about her feelings. She'd invited Gable to dinner because she wanted to get to know him better. She wanted his attention, but she also wanted to understand him.

Loretta piled the blankets on to her bed. She was slipping out of her clothes and into her pajamas as the phone rang.

"I'm sorry I got out of hand there," Gable said.

"It's my birthday."

"That's not an excuse. The circumstances of my life are complex."

"I know."

"And I don't have anything to offer you."

"I'm not looking for anything."

"You want that fence with the roses."

"That's a dream."

"You should have your dream. I hope it comes true. Some man should love you enough to give it to you." Gable paused. In that moment, Loretta could read his thoughts. He wanted to tell her that he wished he could be the man to give everything to her—the house, the fence, and the roses—but he learned long ago to never make promises he couldn't keep. Gable was used to getting everything he wanted without making commitments. She could see that he wanted to, so that would have to be enough.

"Thank you, Clark. For looking out for me."

Loretta pulled the covers over her. She was drifting off to sleep on the wings of the kisses of Clark Gable when she felt something in the bed.

She reached under the covers and found the stack of fan magazines. She picked them up and dropped them onto the floor beside the bed. Tomorrow morning, she'd use them to build her morning fire.

———

Alda and Luca were curled up in front of the fire in her room. Since they returned from dinner, they'd spent most of the night kissing. Perhaps it was the wine, or the fire, or the fact that two sticks rubbed together make sparks and therefore heat, but whatever the reason, they were in love, and basking in the warmth of it.

"What do you really know about Mr. Gable?" Alda asked suddenly.

"Are you kidding me? I'm kissing you like my life depended on it, and you're asking me about Gable? God, I hate the movies sometimes."

"I'm curious."

"I knew him when he wasn't a star. He's the same guy, really. He just wears better shoes."

"I like him."

"He's a good one. He's a bit of a hound with the ladies, but they all are. Women see them up there on the silver screen, and they feel like they know him, so they skip the chitchat and head straight for the bedroom. It's not his fault. He walks into a room, and there's no mystery. Not if they saw *Red Dust*."

"But he's acting."

"He's so natural it doesn't look like it. I'm telling you—I've been with him when he's minding his own business, fixing something under the hood of his car, and women flock, like they're birds and he's the sun. Who wouldn't take advantage of a situation like that? A guy would have to be crazy."

"Would you?"

"I'm not Clark Gable."

"As Luca Chetta, do you take advantage of those situations?"

"What are you asking?"

"Have there been a lot of women in your life?"

"Alda—"

"I don't want a number."

"I'm thirty-four years old. There have been many women. I am a normal, flesh and blood male." Luca leaned in to kiss her.

"Any special woman?"

"Not until you."

"I like that answer."

"When I saw you on the train, I knew you were for me."

"How did you know?"

"Something about you. Something familiar."

"Because we're Italian?"

"Maybe. It's a bond that seems natural and easy too. I don't have to explain myself. It's just one of those things that you know. Hits you on the head like a steel beam."

"Luca, there's something I want you to know about me."

"Sure." Luca made himself comfortable in front of the fire. Lying before the hearth, he looked at her.

Alda looked down at her hands, searching her empty palms for the right words as though there was an open book with the answers. "I didn't go from my parents' house to the convent."

"Where did you go?"

"I fell in love."

Luca sat up and looked at her. "Go on."

"I got in trouble."

"What kind of trouble?"

"I was eighteen and foolish. I fell in love with a boy who came to Padua during the summers."

"Okay," Luca said.

His frosty reaction was not what she had anticipated. "It's not important."

"Sure it is. If you felt the need to tell me about it, it must matter to you."

"At the time it did."

"Do you still love the guy?"

"No, no."

"What kind of trouble did you get into?"

Alda didn't appreciate the accusatory tone in his voice, and she was surprised by it. "I am not going to talk about this anymore." She stood and went to the window.

"You might as well tell me the truth."

"I always tell the truth."

"You're keeping something from me."

"If that were true, I would have not brought this up."

"What were you waiting for?"

"I waited for my own reasons."

Luca stood and faced her. "So I'd fall in love with you, and there would be no turning back?"

He was spoiling for a fight. Alda recognized the signs; she'd been raised by a traditional Italian man in a country full of them. But that was the past; now things were different. Alda was an American, and with that came the gift of reinvention and the notion that a woman could work and take care of herself all of her life, whether she chose marriage and motherhood or not. Gladys Belzer and Loretta Young had taught her this by example, but instead of enjoying the great gulps of independence that were pure oxygen to her growing intellect and character, Alda found herself in love with a man whose progressive ideas were fine for everyone else but not for her.

"You should go," she said quietly. She wanted to be alone to sort this out in her own way.

"I'm not leaving until you tell me what happened with this clown in Italy."

"He's not a clown."

"Now you defend him."

"You don't know him."

Luca threw his hands in the air. "You're not a virgin."

"No, I'm not."

"You said you were in the convent. Is that a lie?"

"No."

"But you're not a virgin."

"It's not a requirement of the convent."

"It should be."

"It's a good thing you don't make the rules. If you did, there would be few nuns and practically no priests in the Holy Roman Church."

"I don't care about the church. I only make the rules for me, for my own life, for the morals I believe in, and I demand the same of my woman."

"Your woman. Who is she? Who is this virtuous virgin without sin who is so perfect in every way that she has lived alone on a mountaintop waiting for you to claim her? Please, introduce me to her. Shall we pick one from the long list of women you have bedded? Where are they? I'm required to accept your past, as though your experiences are a gift that will only enhance mine. I'm to believe that everything you've done to this point made you a better man, but I confide that I was in love once, with one good man, and that makes you angry. This is not love."

Luca had not heard a word Alda had said. He spun on his heels. "I can't believe this. You're spoiled."

Alda drew a deep breath. "I'm not a bin of potatoes. There is nothing spoiled about me."

"I was raised a certain way."

"I'm sure your fine upbringing came in handy when you made love to numerous women whose names you can't remember. You're allowed to do whatever you want, while your wife gives up everything to you, including her innocence. You belong on the pages of a dime novel."

"You should have told me."

"I told you the story not because I'm ashamed of it but because it's a part of who I am. You have not only disappointed me, I pity you for your ignorance." Alda quickly gathered Luca's coat and hat and gloves. She flung the door open and threw the clothes at him. "I am not going to atone for my sins twice, once to my God and the second time to you."

He turned to say something more to her, but she was finished.

"Get out."

Alda slammed the door in his face, bolted the lock, and slammed the chain into the slide. Twenty-six years of rage rose within her. She had spent her life in service to others—first to her parents, then to the sisters of Saint Vincent. She was angry on behalf of every woman who had to live in a man's world by a man's rules.

Alda had missed the roar of the American 1920s, as young women broke away from the Victorian constraints their mothers had known and got jobs, bobbed their hair, and dared to travel without chaperones. Alda had come into her own with the first paycheck she received from Loretta Young Enterprises. She remembered the moment she opened her first bank account, deposited her first paycheck, and began to save money. It was a transcendent moment when Loretta showed Alda how to wire money to her family in Italy. Alda felt empowered by her ability to earn money and decide how and when to spend it. With financial independence came self-confidence, and with that came the peace of putting the past behind her, including her mistakes. She didn't need Luca Chetta to take care of her, she only needed him to love her, but that he could not do unless she met his criterion of moral perfection. He could keep his requirements!

This would be Luca and Alda's first and last argument. Loretta had been right. *If you want to keep a man, tell him little of your past and keep your feelings to yourself.*

If Luca Chetta thought he was better than Alda Ducci, it would be her pleasure to spend the duration of the filming of *The Call of the Wild* proving him wrong.

Gladys Belzer had placed antique Tuscan urns spilling over with bright red beach roses on either side of the entrance of Sunset House. The January sun flickered overhead as warm breezes floated through Bel Air.

Gladys had opened the windows, letting in the fresh air, as she repainted Loretta's room and wallpapered her bathroom while she was off on location. The scents of fresh paint and glue were all but gone from Loretta's suite; gone too was the color scheme of pale pink and cream, replaced with soft green and a wallpaper of periwinkle-and-gray toile.

Ria Gable drove up to the entrance of Sunset House unannounced. She got out of her ice-blue Ford coupe and surveyed the exterior of the house and the view, deciding it was a better setting than her own on the other side of Doheny. Mrs. Gable's hair was done in black marcel waves, cropped to a lacquered bob. She wore a trim navy blue suit with a foxtail fur slung over her shoulder. Her kelly-green leather pocketbook matched her pumps, all custom-made.

"Mrs. Gable." Gladys smiled warmly and came from behind her desk. "What a lovely surprise." Gladys occasionally ran into Mrs. Gable at the fine design houses in Los Angeles, where they could both be found poring over large sample books of wallpaper, fabric swatches, and paint colors.

"Mrs. Belzer." Ria forced a smile as she removed her gloves and took a seat. While Mrs. Gable was not a beauty, she made up for it in sartorial splendor. She dressed in couture clothing, topped with unique hats, courant accessories, and expensive jewelry. Ria looked as good as she possibly could for a woman seventeen years her husband's senior.

"Would you care for tea?" Gladys offered.

"No, thank you," Ria said. "I hear an accent. I hadn't noticed it before. I didn't know you were from the South."

"My mother was a native of North Carolina."

"To a Texas lady, the Carolinas might as well be Canada."

"Oh no, it's still the South. If you need proof, I can make you a pot of soup beans and a pan of cornbread."

"That won't be necessary." Ria smiled, but it was more of a polite clench. "I don't usually intrude without an invitation, but I was driving by, and I thought we should have a talk."

Gladys had figured out as soon as Ria walked in why she might have dropped by, but she was going to make Mrs. Gable work for the pleasure of confronting her. "I understand that you do your own decorating, and admirably, so I don't believe you're here to talk draperies and rugs."

"I'm here about your daughter."

"Which one?" Gladys asked innocently. "I have four."

"I'm here about Loretta."

"She's on Mount Baker, shooting a picture for Bill Wellman."

"With my husband. I wish you had accompanied your daughter to Bellingham."

"I didn't have to—she's with her secretary, Alda Ducci, who is a former novice from the convent at Saint Elizabeth's."

"She's with a nun?"

"A splendid chaperone, don't you agree?"

"Perhaps the nun has her head in a prayer book. From all reports, she's not keeping an eye on your daughter."

"I'm not aware of any reports."

"Your daughter is making a play for my husband."

"That couldn't possibly be true."

"And why not?"

"She's not interested in him."

"Every woman in the world wants Clark Gable." Ria removed a tiny shred of lint from her skirt.

"That puts you in a terrible position." Gladys could see that Ria was desperate. She could empathize with her pain, having survived two unfaithful husbands.

"I want you to talk to your daughter and tell her hands off Mr. Gable."

"I won't do that," Gladys said politely.

"I should have known you have no control over her. I suppose it's fine with you that she seduced Spencer Tracy, also a married man, and has now moved on to my husband?"

"It's none of your business who Loretta spends time with, and you don't have your facts straight about Mr. Tracy, who happens to be a good friend of our family."

"I think I do. I have eyes. I read. Your daughter falls in love with all her leading men. She's known for it. She admits it herself! Her reputation precedes her."

"As does yours. And mine. And whomever else you want to gossip about."

"I don't believe this is gossip."

"Ah. So it's gospel truth. Look, Mrs. Gable. It must be difficult for you. You are relatively new to Hollywood, and you don't have the benefit of my years of experience in and around show business."

"Why should that matter? Whether Beverly Hills or Dadgum Holler, marriage vows should be respected. This isn't a matter of experience."

"But it *is*. The story of the starlet and the leading man is as old as the urns on my front porch. It's an easy story to repeat because it's tantalizing, mostly because it brings about the ruination of the young lady, who hasn't the fortitude or sophistication to fight the lies and correct the facts. The leading man, on the other hand, comes off looking virile and desirable, both bankable commodities at the studio. Surely you know that a man's sex appeal has a direct effect on his salary negotiations."

"I'm aware of my husband's allure."

"Then let me make you aware of my daughter's. She has to get by on talent. While your husband might benefit from an affair with a starlet, the same affair would lead to her professional demise. Do you think that my daughter, a hardworking veteran of fifty films, would squander her good name on a fling? If you do, you don't know Loretta Young."

"I have a daughter too, Mrs. Belzer. And I would defend her to the death."

"Then you must understand how I feel when lies are spread about my daughter."

"I was hoping you would take control of the situation."

"I understand your exasperation. You and I are of the same generation. We're also mothers. So, I'd ask you to give Loretta the benefit of the doubt. She's intelligent."

"Which can also mean that she is cunning."

"Loretta is also a devout young woman."

"That hardly has anything to do with her sex drive."

"Oh no, it has everything to do with every drive. She considers the feelings of others. She is compassionate. She would go as far to forgive you for your rude assumptions and advise your husband to go home to discuss your concerns with you."

"My husband and I discuss everything."

"That's why you chase down rumors in fan magazines—because you trust him. Ria, I know all about you. I know you grew up poor and hungry. I know about the three husbands before Mr. Gable, each one a little higher up the financial ladder than the last one. I know you're a hard worker who took a position in a jewelry shop because the high-end clientele would be better catches than the men on the oil rigs. You are ambitious, and there is nothing wrong with that. But don't accuse my daughter of the things you have been guilty of—I won't have it."

"You're out of line, Mrs. Belzer." Ria stood. "You don't have your facts straight."

"It's not easy to track down the truth when one has had so many surnames. Mrs. Gable, let me make something very clear. No one comes between me and my daughter, or me and any of my children. We are a team. Our family has built a life with hard work, fair play, and good morals. For you to assume that my daughter is anything less than the gracious, talented, and kind-hearted young woman she is, is an insult to my entire family."

"I'm not wrong about Loretta Young."

"Then prove it. Trade in the Schiaparelli suit for a pair of dungarees and waders and hire a dogsled. Climb Mount Baker to see with your own eyes what is going on up there. Knowing my daughter, you'll find her turning in a great performance, minus any monkey business. However, I can't vouch for your husband."

Gladys waited to hear the engine turn in Ria's car before she jumped on the phone.

"Room fourteen, please. Alda? What the hell is going on up there?"

"We were hit with another snowstorm. Production is delayed again. This one could take a few days to clear."

"I'm not interested in the weather. Is Gretchen carrying on with Mr. Gable?"

"They're good friends."

"Is it a romance?"

"Loretta is steering clear because he's married."

Gladys heaved a sigh of relief. "Why the rumors?"

"There are only three women on this mountain—four, if you count the cook."

"So the gossip is just that."

"Yes, Mrs. Belzer."

"Mrs. Gable just left, and she's hearing things. I'm not so worried about Gretchen, but Gable is another story. Don't let my daughter out of your sight."

Alda wanted to share that it was not Loretta but *she* that had fallen in love on Mount Baker, and had a nasty breakup, and perhaps therein lay the confusion. Evidently the facts had been twisted as they snowballed down the mountain in a typical *Modern Screen* fashion. Alda hoped she had reassured the woman who brought her to Hollywood that her mind was solely on the business of Loretta Young.

The cabin fever was so intense at the Mount Baker Inn that the company of *The Call of the Wild* would do anything to break it. Bill Wellman had called off filming exteriors when a powerful blizzard made it impossible to navigate the roads the studio had carved out in the snow. It was so cold the cameras froze.

After the storm had passed, the mountain was theirs once more. The company huddled together and thought of new ways to entertain themselves. The crew, headed by Luca, took a day to build a fire pit in the field between the inn and the barn, with a circular bench made of packed snow and ice, igloo style, around it. Gable helped chop wood to make the outdoor fire, relieved to do something, anything physical after being cooped up.

In the kitchen, Elvira was forced to be creative; staples were running low for the hungry company. Elvira operated the waffle iron as Alda and Loretta made a third batch of batter. Fresh, delicate, buttery waffles were stacked on trays all around them.

"Almost ready for the snow," Elvira said.

"I'll get Mr. Gable," Loretta volunteered.

"I need about six gallons—so tell him to fill the silver tub on the porch. I need icy snow—not top layer, but white ice below the surface."

"Got it."

Alda hadn't spoken to Loretta about her mother's call, but she had been diligent about being present whenever the costars were together. There seemed to be nothing between them deeper than on-set flirting. They had long conversations and took their meals together, but Alda had seen the same behavior with Loretta's costars on other movies. But to be safe, and mind Gladys Belzer's request, Alda asked, "Do you want me to go with you?"

"Nope, finish the waffles."

Loretta pulled on her coat, hat, and gloves. The kitchen was hot, and the cold night air felt good against her face as she pushed the door open. The crew was gathered around the fire, laughing, talking, and smoking. As Loretta passed, a grip offered her a cigarette, which she happily accepted.

"Where's Gable?" she asked, puffing the cigarette.

"Gathering wood," the grip said.

Loretta trudged to the woodpile behind the inn. She found Gable, in his full-length lynx fur coat, picking up logs to bring to the fire.

"Need your help, Clark. Elvira's ready to make the snow cream."

"Here." Gable handed her logs, then picked up more on his own. Loretta dropped the cigarette in the snow and followed him to the pit. The crew cheered as they dumped the wood into the fire, which roared to a mighty blaze.

"Come on, sis," Gable said to Loretta.

He took her arm as they hiked across the field to the barn. On the porch, he grabbed a saw from a hook, a flashlight, and the silver tub Elvira had washed and prepared for the blocks of snow.

Gable flipped on the flashlight to guide their way. The beam danced on the snow, making the surface sparkle like diamonds in a store window at high noon.

Loretta followed Gable over the hill to the middle of a pristine field that rolled out before them like an expanse of white velvet. The sky overhead was a clear midnight blue, speckled with tiny pink stars.

"Heavenly," she said, taking in the view.

"You can think in a place like this," Gable said as he set up the tub and saw. "Away from the world and all its problems. I'm going to have this someday, kid."

The laughter of the crew traveled across the snowy fields like music as Gable knelt down and sawed a block of snow from the drifts. Loretta helped him lift the solid block into the tub.

"May I try?" she asked. "Looks like fun."

Gable handed her the saw.

Loretta plunged the saw into the snow. She couldn't get the blade to budge. "What am I doing wrong?"

Gable laughed. "Everything." He took the saw from her and cut another block from the field.

"You make it look easy," she said as he sawed another square.

"You know I haven't tried to kiss you since your birthday."

"I noticed."

"Do you want me to?"

"Not really."

"Is that a yes or a no?"

"It's a 'not really.' A soft no."

Gable shook his head. "I don't know any girls like you."

"What a compliment."

"Now you know how I feel." He lifted one handle on the tub and indicated that she should lift the other. Together they hoisted the tub, and the load was instantly easy to carry.

"If I get a choice with a man, I would always rather be friends."

"Why is that?"

"It lasts."

"Romance can last," he said. "You have to give it a chance."

"With who?"

"Maybe with me."

"Where's the flashlight?" Loretta asked.

"Why?"

"Shine the light on my face."

Gable and Loretta placed the tub down in the field. He shone the light on her face. She rolled her eyes.

Gable laughed. "In silent movies that was called the kiss-off."

"And there's your answer." Loretta laughed and ran ahead, leaving him to carry the tub of snow. He called after her, but she kept going, leaping through the drifts like a doe.

Suddenly, Loretta was smothered in fur. Gripped by two giant paws, she fell into the snow. At first she was afraid; the attack had come out of nowhere. But the familiar scent of bitter orange and pine revealed that it wasn't a brown bear or a big bad wolf, it was Gable. They began to roll in the snow.

"You're scaring me!" She laughed as they spun through the drift until he was on top of her.

"So you do feel something for me." He grinned. He rolled off her and onto his back in the snow. They lay there, laughing. The scent of the fire pit, of cedar and smoke, carried by night winds, filled the air overhead. Clark and Loretta lay in the open field and looked up at the night sky.

"What does the sky look like to you?" she asked him.

"Heaven."

"You don't think heaven is bright, like a morning?"

"I don't know. I think this could be it. What do you think it looks like?"

"When I was a girl, my cousin Carlene and I used to play dress-up in Mae Murray's closet."

"No kidding." Gable rolled over, propped himself on his elbow, and looked at her.

"Long story. Anyhow, Mae had a closet filled with gowns and shoes, and capes made of velvet and feathers. And she had these long black satin evening gloves with tiny pink pearl buttons all the way up the back. That's what the sky looks like to me."

Gable leaned toward her and kissed her on the neck.

"Elvira needs the snow," Loretta said.

Gable stood up and helped her to her feet.

———

"Where are they with the snow?" Elvira wanted to know.

"On their way," Alda said nervously. Alda watched Gable and Loretta through the window of the barn. She was now officially worried that she had misread the situation between Loretta and Gable. It looked like something was bubbling up; something deep was heading for the surface, and given enough time and the right elements, it could blow.

Loretta was covered in snow as she entered the barn. Gable swatted the snow off her coat as she stamped her feet to remove the snow from her boots.

"Did you fall off the mountain?" Elvira clucked.

"I was attacked by a wild animal."

"Nothing you can't handle," Elvira said.

Loretta and Gable looked at one another and laughed.

"Come over here and help me make the cream. Those boys are howling for dessert out there."

Alda scooped four cups of white sugar into a large ceramic bowl as Loretta cracked four eggs over the sugar. Elvira whisked the mixture. Alda drizzled vanilla extract into the mixture. Slowly Loretta poured six cups of fresh cream into the sugar, followed by two cups of condensed milk, as Elvira all the while whisked.

"That's it," Elvira said. "It's ready to hit the snow."

Gable lifted the bowl and brought it outside, pouring it over the tub of snow.

Elvira mixed the sweet, creamy mixture through the snow with a large spoon. "Mr. Gable, you're such a know-it-all, take a taste." Elvira fed Gable a taste of the snow cream.

"It's good, Elvira."

"All right! Grab the tub. Girls, fetch the waffles. Follow me to the fire pit."

The crew gathered around as Elvira, Alda, and Loretta formed an assembly line to make snow cream cones. Loretta and Alda took the delicate waffles and folded them into triangles as Elvira filled them with snow cream.

Luca pulled the cork from a bottle of Fra Angelico and went around the bench of the fire pit, drizzling the liqueur on the cones.

"Does everything around here have to have booze in it?" Elvira complained.

"Yes, Miss Elvira. And when they figure out how to make soap out of it, we'll bathe in it too," Gable said.

The company cheered.

Loretta handed a cone to Luca. Alda looked away. Loretta looked up at Gable, who caught the exchange.

Gable sat next to Luca on the ice bench.

"You're still in the doghouse?"

"Yep," Luca admitted.

"Did you write her a letter?"

"Yep. She hasn't budged. Assuming she even read it. I bet it went straight into the fireplace. All that's left of my heart's desire are little black feathers in a big black flume."

"You have to be persistent."

"She hasn't given me any hope at all."

"She's hurt."

"I know that. And it pains me." Luca watched Alda as she walked back to the barn with Elvira. Loretta sat down next to Gable and Luca.

"Mr. Gable, you know how to find good snow," Loretta said before taking a bite of the snow cream cone.

"Thank you, Miss Young."

"Luca, what's the status?"

"Not great," Gable answered for him.

"You have to keep trying," Loretta advised Luca.

"That's what he says." Luca pointed to Clark. "I tried all his methods. Letters. Calls. I hang around to talk to her. She walks by me as though I'm not there. She's a real ice princess, that one."

"But she isn't," Loretta assured him. "She's heartbroken."

"You're making the mug feel worse," Gable said.

Loretta handed Gable her ice cream cone to finish. "How long did it take you to realize that you hurt her?"

"I knew the minute the words were out of my mouth."

"You should tell her that you were impulsive, and realized that you hurt her immediately—that you don't really believe the things you said to her."

"She's not buying it."

"Maybe Mr. Gable has some advice for you. He's been married eleven, twelve times or so. Clark, impart some wisdom here."

"I ought to smash this cone in your face," Gable said sweetly.

"I blew it. It's over," Luca said.

Loretta patted Luca's knee. "Well, you still have a shot at Elvira."

"You're not helping." Gable nudged her.

Loretta turned to Luca. "Alda was almost a nun—she spent most of her youth in the convent. There's still a lot of that in her. She likes order and rules. Give her some. Lay down the rules of your relationship and make her understand how things will be going forward."

"Starting with keeping your trap shut," Gable added.

"It's going to take her some time to help Elvira straighten up the kitchen. I bet for the rest of that bottle of Fra Angelico you could bribe Elvira to go home early—and you and Alda will have time together."

Luca took in Loretta's advice. He looked toward the barn, where the kitchen lights blazed in beams out onto the snow. "Okay. I'll try."

Gable held out his cone. "One more hit before you go."

Luca doused the cone with booze. He placed the stopper back in the bottle and trudged across the field to the barn.

The crew had mostly gone back inside the inn for their late-night card games. Loretta scooted close to Gable by the fire pit.

"That was pretty good, Gretch," he said, putting his arm around her.

"I'm always better with other people's problems." Loretta always felt warm and safe when Gable had his arms around her.

"You have problems?" Gable teased her.

"None at the moment."

"That's good to know. I wouldn't want be a problem to you."

"You're only a problem when you wrestle me to the ground in that coat."

"You like this coat? Flier Furs. Olympic Boulevard. Los Angeles U.S.A. Made to order."

"Did your wife buy it for you?"

Gable looked around, pulled Loretta close, and squeezed her tight. "Why do you bring her up every chance you get?"

"I'm a smart aleck."

"I'll say. You got crust."

"I'm sorry," she said.

"You mean it?"

"From the bottom of my black heart."

"If you weren't so cute, I'd wring your neck. Tell me something. Why'd you take this movie?"

"The script, of course."

"Just the script?"

"I didn't take it because of you. I didn't know you."

"How am I doing?"

"All right. When it comes to the movies, I try to choose a mystery, a weepie, a family comedy, and one classic every year. Sometimes I hit it, sometimes I don't."

"I do whatever my agent tells me."

"Then you'd better have a brilliant agent," Loretta said.

"Minna's all right."

"I hear she's lovely."

"What's your plan after we wrap?"

"To get off this mountain in one piece and go home where it's warm."

"I meant your career plans."

"Just try to do good work."

"Is there a part you're dying to play?"

"Always. And it usually goes to Bette Davis or Myrna Loy."

"Bette's the gold standard," Gable said.

"I'll say. And Myrna is a treasure. She's like a box of emeralds."

"I like them both. What leading men do you like?"

"I've been lucky."

"Nobody better than Spencer Tracy," Gable admitted. "I'm going to do a picture with him."

"He's good," Loretta said softly.

"I'm not prying."

"I didn't think you were. I figured you meant his acting talent."

"I did. But I'm your friend, if you want to tell me what happened."

"It's pretty simple. It was all feelings, and we didn't act on them."

"No kidding." Gable's black eyebrows shot up. He figured Loretta was more sophisticated than that. A chaste love affair? He'd have to think about that later.

"Spencer is married, and he loves his family. He's a good father."

"When it comes to work, I don't think any of us can touch him."

"You're just as good in a different way."

"What do you mean?"

"Well, you have a very literal approach to the work. You interpret the lines as they are written, no spin on them at all. It's pretty great. Theatrical. It's obvious you come from the stage. You never change a word."

"Why would I? If it's a good script."

"Good point. Beyond the words, I like how you bring them to life. The way you dramatize. You charge into scenes, you take your mark, you perform to the camera, you let the black box have it like it's a lady sitting in the first row of the orchestra. You work efficiently. Clean, I'd call it. Tracy, on the other hand, even though he comes from the theater, goes at it a different way. He keeps his performance intimate. When you're in a scene with him, he pulls you into the material. You really have to listen because he almost doesn't give you the line. Do you know what I mean?"

"He keeps it here." Gable tapped his head.

"Yes, that's it. Neither technique is right or wrong, just different—and both get spectacular results. Look at you—you're a movie star, and Spence is on his way."

"And you?"

"I've been doing this so long, I just hope to get a decent script. That's all. The rest, I feel I can do, given a good director and costars like you—I can make the story happen for the audience."

"You actually consider the audience?"

"What's the point otherwise?" Loretta warmed her hands by the fire.

"I get nervous when I think of the audience."

"You're just telling them a story."

"I guess."

"Just like we're talking. That's the craft. Just make it all seem real."

The fire pit had burned down to a thin layer of glistening orange embers.

"I'm gonna turn in." Loretta stood. "We have an early day tomorrow."

"Thanks, Gretch."

"For what?"

"For talking to me."

"You're a delight, Mr. Gable. Intelligence goes nicely with that handsome mug of yours."

"Hey, kid, I have a question. What happened with Chet and Alda? He wouldn't tell me."

"He's old-fashioned."

"Oh, that."

"Yes, that. Alda had a boyfriend when she was young, and Chet took it as an affront to his manhood and her virtue. He was very rude about it."

"She's a grown woman."

"But grown men can do whatever they please, but turns out they want their women out of a convent."

"How do you feel about the subject?"

"Convents?" she teased him.

"You know what I mean."

"Oh, you mean sex."

"You say it awful plain."

"You asked." She looked at him. "I think it has to matter."

"It?"

"Making love."

"It can work either way, Gretchen."

"And I bet it has for you."

Gable laughed. "I'll see you at breakfast."

"Sweet dreams."

"You can count on 'em." The separation he felt as Loretta left him to go inside the inn sent a chill through him that had nothing to do with the night air.

Gable reached into the pocket of his coat and retrieved a flask of whiskey. He took a swig and looked into the fire. He wondered if his feelings for Loretta were a result of the isolation, the bitter cold, or Wellman's challenge to him not to make a play for her. Gable imagined he cleaved to Loretta because she was confident, and he liked the way she viewed the world. She said what she believed, direct and plain, like a good Ohio woman. Gable was fed up with the southern charm Ria drizzled on him like Tupelo honey. He yearned for a peer, someone who understood his work, and therefore, him. Only a fellow actor could understand the anxiety of performing for the camera, the pressures that came with trying to please a director, and the temptations that were part of being isolated from home life and routine. Gable couldn't be sure that Loretta was his best match—she was so young. But if he were a gambling man, he'd bet she could be someone he could love, a girl he could get serious about.

It seemed everyone in the cast and on the crew of *The Call of the Wild* was weary of the snow, the sub-zero temperatures, and the mountain. But for an outdoorsman like Gable, the delays were an opportunity to challenge himself, to make himself useful and get to know the mountain as he chopped wood, hunted, and hiked. Mount Baker was the perfect place to hide as he sorted out the rest of his life. The last thing he wanted to do was go home to Ria, the pâté on the dainty crackers, and the Aubusson rugs that couldn't take a cigarette ash.

When Gable pictured himself happy and free, he saw the mountaintop in his mind's eye. Snow swirled all around him, a bright sun blinded him, and the only sound he heard was the wind hissing through the canyons. As the picture widened out and took in all of Mount Baker, the fields, cliffs, and ridges, it turned out he was not alone. There was somebody with him. A woman. He could see her as plain as day. He saw a girl named Gretchen by his side, and she was laughing.

———————

"That's it for me, kids," the cook said to Alda as she hung the last copper pot on its hook over the stove.

"Thanks, Elvira," Alda said.

"Lock up on your way out."

"I will." Alda took off her apron and pulled on her coat.

Luca was sitting alone at one of the community tables in the dining room, waiting for her. She passed him on the way to the door.

"You going to lock me in here?"

"Not if you leave now," she said.

"Alda, why won't you talk to me?"

"I don't plan on ever talking to you." She opened the door. A dusting of snow blew in. "I'm locking up."

"Wait a minute," Luca jumped up and closed the door. "At least let me explain." He leaned against the door, blocking her.

"You were perfectly clear that night."

"I thought about it. I was wrong."

"Too late." She was resolute.

"I apologized. I meant it. What kind of person is incapable of forgiveness?"

"I am capable of it."

"But not for me."

"Why are you sorry?"

"I hurt you."

"You should be sorry because you believe the things you said to me, not because you said them."

"I'm sorry for that too. I've had time to think about it. I was out of line. Old-fashioned. You're a working girl. You're independent."

"That has nothing to do with it."

"Then what is it?"

"I don't want to look into the face of a man who judges me, who thinks less of me for decisions I made when I was sixteen years old, who believes he can do or say whatever he pleases because he fell in love with a tramp."

"I never called you that!"

"You called me spoiled. It's the same thing."

"But I don't believe it."

"Why did you say it?"

"I don't know. I got scared. I don't want to be compared to anyone else."

"But it's okay if I am. If I can't live up to the chorus girls, or the background talent or the ingenues, that's fine with you—if I feel badly about myself, that you could live with?"

"It's different for a woman."

"Because we're used to being put-upon."

"No, it's not that."

"Then what is it, Luca? Surely you've been in love before. Surely you weren't using all those women, were you?"

"Of course not. I promise you, I've changed my thinking."

"What assurance do I have that you've changed?"

"I can't give you any. It would take time."

"I have two gifts to give anyone that loves me and that I love in return: the gift of myself, and my time. I already know how you feel about the gift of me, but I'm confused as to why you still want to take my time."

"I'm in love with you."

"That doesn't give you permission to hurt me."

"I understand that. I want to prove my love."

"Well, there's your trouble. You can't prove love. You can only offer it."

"I'm offering! I'm offering!" Luca was vehement.

"Just let me go. You'll fall in love soon enough when we're off this mountain. Once we're back in Hollywood and you're back on the lot, you'll have a bouquet of eager girls to choose from. Let me go. I don't understand you."

"What is there to understand? I need you. You need me. We love each other. It's at the heart of it all very simple."

"Why do you insist on making this hard for me?"

"Because I'm not wrong about us. I said a terrible thing. A terrible thing I didn't mean."

"You might as well have slugged me."

"I understand that now. I come from men who blow hard, say whatever they're thinking, and give very little consideration to what those words can do. I learned my lesson here. But you won't give me another chance. Why?"

"Because I'm happy alone, Luca. Nobody hurts me. Nobody breaks my heart. Nobody makes me feel worthless."

"Who are you if you don't love somebody? What kind of a life is that?"

Alda's eyes filled with tears. "I was going to be a nun because I didn't want to hurt anymore. And for seven years, all I did was work with girls who were hurting—some more than me, and there were days when I didn't think that was possible. I wasn't able to tell you everything about myself, because you judged me before I could. The story gets worse, Luca. I had a baby with Enrico. But the baby was stillborn. My son."

Luca's heart began to race. He wiped his brow and leaned against the door.

"I was a mother. For a flash. For an instant. For a moment, after a very long labor. I made love with a man, and I had his child. And every morning, of every day since, the first thought I have is of my son, the baby I lost. He'd be ten years old, Luca. It's as if he waits for me on the other side of my dreams."

Luca took both of her hands in his. She pulled her hands from his.

"I looked to you as someone who might understand me, who cared about me, who appreciated who I was no matter what I might have done or failed to do in the past. I was hoping for a new life, with the old one as part of the story. I refuse to be ashamed for having feelings and acting on them. I refuse to be ashamed of my son. I don't want to forget him. But you needed me to be your idea of pure, to throw away my past, as though it was worthless. I could have lied to you, but I wouldn't, because I thought that highly of you—I believed you could help me carry my burdens. Do you know how happy I was that this long road had led to you? I believed in everything again. A new start. Love. Redemption! All that suffering led to you. And instead, with your words, you caused more pain. So please, forgive me for praying to God to let me stop loving you. For me, it's the only way forward."

Alda walked out the door and onto the porch. Luca followed her.

"You love me." Luca put his arms around her. "As long as you love me, even a little, we can work this out."

Alda wept because it was true, she loved him, but that didn't mean she had to endure more pain because of it. She didn't want to love him, but she did, and she knew that true love meant forgiveness, not looking the other way but holding him accountable for any pain he caused so he could be better. A good woman makes a man better. She knew the nature of love was connection, but she also knew forgiveness made that bond eternal.

Luca held Alda for a very long time. She wanted to walk away, but she couldn't, which was the great surprise of that night with the sky of pink stars. She thought she was strong and that she could do it. But real strength isn't about being right, it's about being true and letting someone else be strong for you when it's required.

"What was his name, Alda? Your son."

Alda looked into Luca's eyes. He wasn't trying to win her heart. He'd asked the question because he cared, because he loved her. So she told him the name of the secret she had buried so long ago in the hills outside of Padua, in the cemetery by the lake. "His name was Michael."

Without letting Alda go, he pulled her closer and whispered, "I'm sorry about Michael."

Alda didn't feel the wind or the cold, or the desolation that had lived in her heart for all these years. She felt Luca holding her up, and given the true healing power of forgiveness, that night, she let him.

9

Loretta dragged the black rotary phone from her nightstand across the coverlet. She had set her hair in rags, strips of flannel, and rolled them tight to her scalp to curl her hair overnight. Her head looked like the top of a pot of flowers in bloom. The fire she had built was dying down, so she pulled the blankets up to her neck.

Loretta gave the operator the phone number.

"Gretchen, why haven't you called?"

"I'm calling now, Mama."

"Mr. DeMille called—they're delaying *The Crusades* start date. The word around town is that *The Call of the Wild* may never be finished."

"It sure feels like it. Some days it feels like we're buried under an avalanche."

"Are you enjoying the work?"

"It's rugged."

"How's Wellman?"

"Big and mean and adorable as always."

"How's Gable?"

"He's all right."

"Gretchen . . ."

"Mama, don't lecture."

"I'm worried."

"You're always worried."

"Do I need to be, in this situation?"

"No."

"That's what Alda tells me." Gladys exhaled a sigh of relief.

"Believe her. She's my chaperone, and she sees everything."

"Is he persistent?"

"Yes. He is about everything. He is determined to win, whether he's playing cards, chopping wood, or acting."

"But you are steering clear."

"Mama, we're marooned. We are snowed in on a mountain. I can't steer clear of him. We eat all our meals together, and the rest of the time we're working."

"Mrs. Gable will be relieved to know that nothing is going on."

"Is she yakking to Louella Parsons again? Why doesn't she become a reporter? All she wants to do is sniff around stories."

"She does more than that. She investigates. She came to see me."

"What did she want?"

"She wanted me to go up there and set you straight."

"Oh, please."

"Gretchen, you tested my patience with Spencer. Let's not go down this road again."

"I know."

"Promise me."

"I promise. While you're praying for me, say a few for Alda."

"What's wrong with her?"

"She fell in love up here. With our scene painter. He's Italian too. Italian American from Brooklyn."

"I thought something was going on. She was awfully quiet. Do you like the man?"

"He's a fine man."

"Oh, well, then, good for her."

"It had its moments, but they seem good now."

"At first every love affair seems effortless. But once you have opinions, all that lovey-dovey stuff goes out the window."

"I know, Mama."

"You'll find your true love someday."

"I always save my last decade of the rosary for true love. Why not, right?"

"Why not?" Gladys laughed.

"If God can't send me a good fella, who can? I'll holler when the end is in sight up here."

Loretta hung up the phone and leaned back on the pillows. She said a quick Hail Mary; she had lied to her mother. She had fallen for Clark Gable and was now on the other side, the hopeless side, where honoring those feelings would bring them nothing but heartache, but ignoring them would leave her bereft. Gable had Loretta when she started to care so deeply; the pain seemed secondary.

In many ways, Gable was not the man she had expected him to be. She had heard that when it came to the ladies, he was insatiable, and she had certainly seen that with her own eyes, but the gossip had never gotten around to the good stuff. Gable was also down-to-earth and kind. His impeccable manners were not about artifice or position but making everyone around him feel comfortable, including her. If the crew needed a hand, he'd pitch in unasked. How many leading men had she acted with who never lifted a finger to help for fear of ruining a manicure? If a less experienced actor was having trouble with a scene, Gable was patient, taking the brunt of the director's wrath when the clock went into overtime. She had seen directors eviscerate an actor in front of the crew; if Wellman came close, Gable stepped in and defused the situation. Gable had done so for Loretta. Gable was sensitive regarding people's feelings, and, it appeared, he didn't judge them.

Gable had a rule: he didn't work past five o'clock. At first Loretta thought that was ridiculous, but eventually she admired his rule; it benefited the entire company. Crews could get home to their families at a decent hour. In his quiet way, Gable supported working people by demanding fairness on the set. It was something everyone who worked with him noticed and appreciated. In her opinion, his reputation as a lover and romantic idol was overstated; he was mostly a decent man and a fine friend. Loretta, however, at twenty-two, liked the combination of danger and the protection that Gable represented.

Loretta knew she was hooked on Gable when she felt sad on hearing the weather report that the snow had cleared, and they could get back to work. Every frame of film shot was another frame toward the completion of the picture, to the wrap, which meant the end of their time together. Their inevitable return to Los Angeles seemed like a punishment after this long winter. She knew that when the bubble burst, the snow globe would shatter like blown glass, and there would be no putting the picture inside back together. *Not again*, Loretta said to herself. But yes, for certain, it had happened again.

Loretta Young had fallen in love with Clark Gable.

––––––––

Zanuck had secured a large barn in Mount Baker to use as a sound stage. Finally the blizzard blew through, the roads were plowed, and the crew made it to the barn. Industrial heaters were brought up from Bellingham to thaw out the makeshift studio to film the interiors.

The set designer camped out in the barn, overseeing his crew as they built a two-story saloon set, with a Victorian decor, including an ornate banister from which a stunt man would be thrown through the air during a choreographed brawl, a staple of Bill Wellman's pictures.

The set designer's job was to create the place, and it was Luca's job, as the scene painter, to bring the set to life with color that would read in hue and tone on black and white film. Luca had researched the world of turn-of-the-century hucksters, panhandlers, and chiselers and devised a palette that played brightly against the grim background of the Gold Rush's muddy streets, rough-coated horses, and tattered players.

Luca had painted a main street of a mining outpost in four parts, which would serve as a series of murals in a saloon. There was a mountain scene, featuring prospectors combing the creeks for gold, and another of cancan girls dancing on a stage lit by rustic oil lamps as they are cheered on by miners. A third showed a mother tending her children by a hearth, and in the fourth a fundamentalist preacher admonished his frightened flock against the backdrop of a sinful Yukon.

Luca looked to early-twentieth-century French art, the ruffles and flourishes of Degas' dancers, an explosion of color and celebration of the theatrical world to create the American version. Luca's rendering of the times was painted in a fantasia of vivid swirls of green, fuchsia, and deep blue. The contrast would look lively in black and white on camera.

Alda stood against the wall and watched Luca transform the barn into a saloon.

"Alda, honey, lend a hand?" Luca hollered.

Alda went to the set and helped hold up the mural as Luca scaled a ladder to lift the flat into position. While Alda enjoyed being a secretary, she loved being on the set. She found the stagecraft of filmmaking fascinating, though she was pretty sure she was interested in it because of her interest in Luca.

"Hand me that hammer."

Alda gave Luca the hammer.

"Now the nails."

Alda reached for the nails. Before she handed them to him, she said, "*Per favore?*"

"Yeah, yeah, please. All right. Please."

Alda placed the can of nails on the floor and walked away.

"Hey, where are you going?" Luca said from the top rung of the ladder.

Alda went to the far side of the barn and sat on a bench.

"Alda, get over here!"

When Alda didn't move, Luca got off the ladder and went to her. The crew stayed busy on their detail work, but every person in the barn was aware of the brewing argument.

"What's the matter?"

"Nothing."

"Come on, what is it?"

"I'm not your servant."

"Alda, I'm in the middle of working. We're running over time. Don't take it personally. I'm barking orders at everybody."

"That's no excuse. I know you're important. *Grande artista!*"

"I'll watch my tone from now on."

"Thank you."

"But you need to do something for me."

"*Va bene.*"

"Let me in."

Alda was confused.

Luca continued, "Let me into your life. You've given me a second chance, but I'm not feeling the heat—you know what I'm saying?"

"I'm trying."

"Try harder. Marry me."

"Luca." Alda looked around. The sound stage had emptied out, the crew gone on a break, though no one had called for one.

"I mean it. Marry me. The only way in the world to get through to you is complete surrender. Well, here I am, surrendering. If we have a chance, we have to work it out. We just have to live together and work it out."

"Are you ready for that step?" Alda wondered aloud. She was really asking herself the question, but Luca was eager to answer it.

"I'll learn on the job."

Alda thought about it. Isn't every job a process of learning something new, making mistakes and sorting out the rest? Her practical nature took over her emotions. She took Luca's hands in hers and looked him in the eye.

Luca threw his hands in the air. "Damn. I don't have a ring."

"I don't need a ring."

"What do you need?"

"You," Alda cried. She had spent the last seven years of her life trying not to need anyone. She was tired of fighting. If she was honest with herself, she craved connection. She was ready to build a life with someone she loved, and who loved her. Alda wanted the peace that would come from a good marriage, and the stability that would come from a home of her own, with a fence covered in roses.

"Is that a yes?" Luca Chetta said as he covered her in kisses.

———

Reginald Owen, a British actor, played Gable's nemesis in the movie. He would only be with the production for a month, as he would die by drowning in the third reel. His imminent demise did not keep him from beating Gable, Wellman, and Oakie at poker, however. He pulled the chips toward him, then drew out a starched handkerchief to hold the booty.

"Gentlemen, it's been a pleasure." Reginald bowed his head.

"I thought you said you were lousy at poker," Oakie groused.

"I said it with my poker face."

"I don't like my ass handed to me by an Englishman." Wellman puffed on his cigar.

"But we do it with such grace, Mr. Wellman," Reginald said. "I doubt you even felt the pinch."

"I'm feeling it in my wallet," Gable said as he shoved it back into his pocket.

Luca and Alda blew through the door with the crew and a gust of cold wind, which always sent up a round of complaints among those gathered by the fire. Snow blew in with them, showering the floor with a dusting of white. Luca pushed the door closed. He kissed Alda on the cheek, summoned up his courage, and went to Bill Wellman. Alda went up the stairs to wait in her room.

"Sir, I need a favor," Luca began.

"Bad time," Wellman said.

"Reggie just beat him bad at poker," Gable said as a warning.

"What I have to ask is a little more important than your lousy card game."

Wellman sat up in his chair. Gable smirked. Oakie and Reggie looked at one another, gave a signal, and left the table. Actors never want to be part of a fight between the crew and the director.

"What is it, Chet?" Gable asked.

"I'd like to requisition a car for Seattle for the weekend."

"So would I," Wellman joked.

"I'm serious. We have a two-day turnaround, and I'd like to spend mine in church."

"Doing what?" Gable wanted to know.

"Getting married."

"Chet . . ." Wellman sighed. "That can wait until we wrap."

"It can't, sir. I promised my fiancée."

"You never break a promise to a woman?" Wellman shuffled the cards.

"Not yet, sir. And I hope I never do."

"You're a prince among men, Chet," Gable said. "But there isn't a man at this table who will give you the keys to a car to make the rest of us look bad."

"Here's all I know. You may be able to get off this mountain, but I need you back here on Monday morning." Wellman extended his hand to Chet, who shook it.

"Yes, sir."

"There's a food supply truck going to Seattle in the morning. You can hitch a ride on it."

"Thank you, sir."

Luca ran up the stairs to give Alda the news.

"Now that's love," Gable observed. "He'd walk down that mountain to marry his girl if he had to. There's no blizzard, no river, no mountain that will keep him from marrying the woman he loves."

"Until they do." Wellman cut the cards, and Gable picked them up and shuffled them.

Loretta climbed into the empty food truck after Alda. They sat on the jump seat, tucking their suitcases under it. Behind them was the cold steel expanse of the storage area in the back of the truck. The metal shelves that lined the side walls were empty, as were the bins strapped underneath them, held in place by elastic bands.

"This is hardly a fairy-tale coach," Loretta remarked.

"It will get us there."

"It does have wheels and an engine. I would've loved to throw you a wedding by the pool at Sunset House."

"Thank you, but this is fine."

"You say that now, but someday you'll want to look back on this day and have a pretty picture of it."

"Can you take a few at the church?"

"I've packed my camera, and you'll have your memories."

Luca hopped into the passenger seat in the cab of the truck.

"Where's the driver?"

"He'll be here shortly."

"We're bringing food back, right?" Loretta asked.

"I have the requisition right here." Luca patted his pocket.

"They're out of everything in the kitchen," Loretta said. "All she's got left in there is a jar of pickles and a pound of sugar."

The driver's-side door opened, and into the leather seat hopped Clark Gable.

"You're the driver?" Loretta was surprised and immediately pleased.

"I'm the only guy on this mountain who has driven a six-wheeler in snow." He turned to face her.

"How did it get up the mountain?" Loretta teased.

"That's a mystery. My mission is to get these two crazy kids to Seattle and get them hitched. Miss Young, are you with me on this?"

"Yes, sir."

"Then change seats with Chet. He's just the man to keep Alda warm till we get there. It's my policy to never get in the way of true love."

Loretta climbed up to the cab as Luca climbed over her to the back.

"Who's going to keep me warm?" she wanted to know.

"I have a couple of ideas." Gable grinned.

"I'll bet you do."

He took off his fur coat and tucked it around Loretta. As he leaned over her, she saw that he was wearing an elegant navy blue pinstripe suit with a gray-and-blue-striped tie. The collar on his white shirt was starched.

"You brought your Sunday best up the mountain?"

"You never know when you'll need a suit." Gable tucked the fur coat around Loretta's ankles.

"Hey. Keep those hands on the wheel and your eyes on the road, buster."

There was no one like Gable when it came time for a lark. The destination did not have to be exotic; it could be a road trip a few miles from home that would bring out his sense of fun and adventure. He was a man who didn't like to sit still. Loretta marveled at his ability to have fun, no matter what the circumstances. He'd throw a card game together on a whim, take Buck and a posse of pals to hike the woods, or lead the crew in camp songs after dinner. In his own way, he created families wherever he went. She smiled to herself. She could see the headline in *Photoplay*: "Gable . . . He-Man or Family Man?"

Gable's eyes sparkled as he took sharp turns down the icy mountain road, holding the vehicle steady with his massive hands, relishing the opportunity to master in his own small way the terrain that had everyone else in Washington State licked. If someone else had been driving, she would have been nervous, but it was Gable, and she believed, because it had already been proven, that no harm would come to her as long as she was with him.

As Gable drove down the mountain, she took the chance to study him. She understood, sitting close to him, why he drove women wild. He looked like a giant on the silver screen, and he lost none of that stature in life. He was over six feet tall, trim, broad-shouldered, and muscular. His profile was strong and manly, with crinkles around his eyes, deep dimples around his mouth, and a strong, square jaw. His unruly black hair made her crazy; she was always pushing it into place and ruffling it when he teased her. She even loved his ears, knowing that those ears were acts of defiance in and of themselves. They'd almost cost him his career in movies.

Darryl F. Zanuck, who stood to make a big profit on *The Call of the Wild*, had rejected Gable a few years earlier, insisting that no one with ears that large could ever be a movie star. As it goes in show business, first impressions are forgiven and snap judgments forgotten when it came time to tally the grosses. Gable was a star, and no one anywhere on Planet Earth where there was a movie house and patrons to fill it would dispute it.

Loretta liked that he was the biggest star in the world. She thirsted for the challenge to work with the best, and appreciated the wattage his starlight threw on her as his costar. They treated each other as equals, which almost never happened. As a woman who was wholly independent, Loretta didn't need Gable's money; as a fellow actor, she did not need the glow of his fame because she had her own. Together, they were combustible at the box office.

In real life, Loretta was looking for what every young woman her age craved in a romantic relationship: to feel safe and loved. Beneath the charm, Loretta saw the vulnerability of her costar. A man who liked as many women as Gable was rumored to must be afraid of the love of one good woman. Loretta believed Gable could not be tamed, not by her or anyone else. Gable was looking for the perfect woman—as long as he did not have to be the perfect man, and the lady didn't expect him to stick around.

Whenever Loretta found herself imagining something more with Gable, she pictured the hotel maid and the look on his face as he watched her ascend the stairs, and it cured her of the wild crush like a pill for a fever. But in this truck, for as long as it took to get them to Seattle, she had him to herself with a common goal, to get Luca and Alda married. The mission served her romantic nature and filled her longing heart with joy, and it was also the fulfillment of a sacrament: Alda and Luca would be married by a priest in church. For a Catholic, there was no higher honor.

————

Father Glenn Borman, the pastor of the Immaculate Conception Church in Seattle, greeted Alda and Luca at the side entrance. Luca was nervous, and Alda was quiet, so Loretta attempted small talk as she and Clark followed them inside.

The priest looked at Gable, and an expression of wonderment crossed his face,

"Are you Clark Gable?"

"I am, sir. And I can go one better: this is Miss Loretta Young."

"She is indeed." The priest shook her hand.

"It's good to meet you, Father. Alda is my secretary, and Luca is a highly respected scene painter in motion pictures."

"We're making a picture on Mount Baker," Gable added.

"This is a divine church," Alda said, her eyes filled with tears.

"Don't cry," Luca whispered.

"You're not alone, Miss Ducci. Sometimes I come and sit in the church and I'm overwhelmed by the frescoes. They were painted by a group of Jesuit priests. We're proud of them."

"They look like the ones in my church in Italy," Alda said. "I'm from Padua. We have frescoes by the great Renaissance artists, including Tiepolo."

"That's high praise. Thank you."

The priest took Alda and Luca back to the sacristy to prepare them for the sacrament of marriage. Gable took a seat in the front pew, while Loretta knelt before the altar and made the sign of the cross. She stood up and went to the grotto of Lourdes, a replica of the shrine in France where a schoolgirl named Bernadette had seen a vision of the Blessed Mother.

Loretta hoped to visit Lourdes someday. The story of the girl and the blind devotion she had to Mary the Mother of God was something she intimately understood. Loretta's faith was based upon the love of her family, upon their close relationships, and upon the ultimate respect that they had for Gladys. The rosary was said often in the Youngs' home. Perhaps the girls were more at ease appealing to the Blessed Mother, as their fathers on earth didn't do much to look after them.

Loretta knelt down and looked up at the statue of the Blessed Lady nestled in carved stone. There were votive candle holders lit on the cart below it, their blaze so bright that she could make out the beads on the blue marble rosary draped on the statue.

Gable kneeled next to her. "What's this all about, Gretchen?"

"This is a replica of a grotto in France where people who are suffering and dying go for healing, for miracles."

"It's haunting." Gable took in the replica of the cave, the jagged gray stone, the deep crevices lit only by candles.

"A girl in the town would go to this place and pray, and then the Blessed Mother appeared to her. Pretty soon the word spread, and everyone who had an ailment went to the grotto. A spring burst forth nearby in the ground, and they say that the water from that spring will heal anything."

"Why does it have to be so scary-looking?" Gable whispered.

"Maybe the church is trying to make a point." Loretta smiled.

"You believe it?"

She nodded.

"Why do you believe it?"

"If you don't believe in miracles, you might as well not believe in God."

Alda came out of the sacristy and motioned to Loretta and Clark. They joined the priest, Alda, and Luca in the sacristy.

"Both of you are baptized in the Roman Catholic rite?"

"Yes, Father," Gable said.

"Yes, Father," Loretta echoed.

Loretta snapped a few photos of Alda and Luca at the altar. Alda had pinned a small bunch of violets to her caramel wool suit. She had made a hat, and wore gloves to match. Luca wore a charcoal gray suit with a lavender tie.

As Father led Alda and Luca through the vows of the sacrament of marriage, Loretta kept her eyes fixed on the priest. Gable observed Loretta, who listened so intently as each vow was spoken that it was as if Loretta were the one getting married.

Gable felt like a failure as he listened to the priest. He'd had two opportunities thus far in his life to live up to his vows, but he'd failed to do so. He wondered if this stop in Immaculate Conception was a sign, an indicator of a fresh start for him. Alda and Luca had a new life together, and Gable held out hope for his own new beginning. He wanted the chance to try again, to be a good husband, to live with the integrity he admired in others. But to have that fresh start, Gable had some old business to clean up, and it would take time.

Loretta looked at Clark, and he smiled at her. In this light, he noticed a slight bend on the bridge of her perfect nose that he found charming. It wasn't her classic features that held his interest that day; it was her spiritual countenance that gripped Gable by the throat. She was a believer, and that meant when she loved, she surrendered with her whole heart, with a brand of blind faith that gave him the willies. Gable had not hidden his squirrelly past, his lust for women, or his need for solitude from Loretta. He'd shared his yearning to be alone, to disappear in the woods by himself for days at a time, answering to no one, including his wife. No one, including Gable himself, understood why he stayed married to a woman he didn't love, except that it had conveniently prevented him from marrying someone else.

Gable loved all kinds of hunting for sport—everything except trapping, because he was afraid of being trapped. So when it came to women, he pursued them, stayed just long enough to please them, and then moved on.

As Gable stood in church, the particular scents of beeswax and incense brought out his self-doubt, the frescoes made him feel small, and the priest reciting prayers in Latin excluded him. It was then that Loretta laced her arm through his, as if to shore him up, include him, and make him feel part of the sacrament. All his life he would remember this moment, when a woman knew what he was thinking and gave him what he needed without expecting anything in return. For a fleeting second, Clark Gable felt redeemed.

———

Luca assumed that it would be impossible to find a hotel palazzo or anything Italianate in Seattle, Washington, to please his new bride, but he was wrong. After Luca had a long chat with him about the aspects of Italian architecture in the church, the priest placed a call to the Sorrento Hotel in downtown Seattle to see if they had rooms available. The recent blizzard had all but cleared out the city, so there were plenty of vacancies.

Gable valet-parked the food truck at the hotel entrance, which his friends found so hysterical that they tumbled out of it nearly in tears. When Gable went to tip the bellman, he recognized Gable and almost fainted.

"What's the matter, young man?" Gable asked the bellman.

"I thought you drove a Duesenberg, sir. I saw it in *Movie Mirror*."

"I don't like that old car."

"You don't?"

"Nothing drives like a food truck with a stick shift."

As Father Borman had promised, the hotel was practically empty. After Luca had chosen a sunny suite, Loretta gave Alda a hug, and

Gable shook hands with both. They agreed to meet the following morning for the trip back to Mount Baker.

Gable booked two rooms, one for Loretta and another for himself. He inquired about local restaurants, and the clerk recommended the hotel dining room.

"They always do," Gable said under his breath.

"Why don't we go out and have some fun?" Loretta suggested.

"Like what?"

"Let's go to the movies," Loretta suggested.

"Are you kidding?"

"No—I love to go to the movies, don't you?"

"That depends."

"On what?"

"Who's in them."

"Give me your don't-see list."

"Wallace Beery."

"But you did a picture with him."

"That's why."

"Anybody else we should avoid?" Loretta asked as she opened the local newspaper.

"Joan Crawford."

"Are you missing her?" Loretta made a sad face.

"A little."

"No Joan. Norma Shearer?"

"Traveled that long, lonely highway already. And I got slapped for my trouble."

"I see." Loretta's curiosity was piqued. "That long?"

Gable nodded. "And that lonely."

"Are there any of us you haven't sampled?"

"Every day there's a bus from the Midwest with another batch of dancing, singing blondes with ambition."

"And you're at the bus station?"

"If I can help it. Somebody's gotta greet them. Bring them into the Hollywood family, welcome them into the fold."

"I'll bet."

Gable took the newspaper from Loretta and folded it. "The theaters are right around the corner. Let's walk the avenue and see what's playing."

He helped Loretta into her coat, straightened the collar, and kissed her on the nose. "Let's go."

Gable held the door for Loretta. The Seattle air was cold, but there was no wind. "It's actually warmer here than it is on the mountain."

"Are you missing southern California?"

"I'm dreading it," Gable admitted.

"Me too."

"Why are you dreading it?"

"What are you going to do without me?"

"I'll be fine. It's you I'm worried about. You never leave your room. You sit up there and eat chocolates and read fan magazines."

"Who told you?" She punched his arm.

"I guessed."

"Oh, look, Mr. Gable! A whole theater featuring . . . you." Loretta pointed to the marquee. "We can see *Chained* or *It Happened One Night*. Well, we can't see *Chained* because of your Joan problem."

"You mean *your* Joan problem."

Loretta shrugged. "And I've already seen the other one."

"Did you like it?"

"I told you I loved it."

"Right, right. I don't retain positive reviews."

"I saw it with my sisters and Spencer Tracy."

"Oh, so that's whose mail you were looking for."

"Not really."

"Come on, on the level."

"I was waiting for some paperwork. I'm trying to buy a share of the Beverly Hills Hotel."

"No kidding."

"Uh-huh. These looks aren't going to last forever."

"I bet they do."

"Can't count on it."

"I know what you mean. Most actors aren't like us. They think it's going to last forever."

"I thought no one would ever top John Gilbert, and now he's out of the business. Girls would stand in line in the hot sun for hours to see one of his movies, and now nothing."

"You have to plan your exit," Gable said.

"Have you?"

"Working on it."

"Take me with you when you go."

"You're a kid."

"You're not that much older than me."

"I'm a century older, Gretchen."

"In experience maybe."

"I think about us—don't get me wrong."

She ignored the serious tone. "You haven't even bought me a box of popcorn, and we're an us?" Loretta smiled.

"We kissed."

"How did I do?"

"Not bad. At the time I thought, I could go nuts for that girl."

"And have you?"

"I don't know yet."

"Thanks. That makes me feel all gooey inside."

"I'm not saying it couldn't happen."

"So we're leaving it up to fate?"

"Don't you think that's wise?" Gable lit a cigarette and gave it to Loretta. She puffed away happily.

"I think you can have any girl you want, so you don't pick anybody permanently."

"That's your slant." Gable was happy they were outside, because she couldn't see him blush. He had been thinking the same thing in church, but that was one thought he would never share with anybody.

"I think too much selection, and a man loses his appetite altogether."

"You do?"

"Yep, like a Sunday buffet at Pig N Whistle. You go in there starving and you see all that food laid out, and you can't choose."

"You don't know me very well."

"Fair enough."

"You have men chasing you—"

"It's a bore."

"No kidding."

"I'm not looking for just anybody. I want a man I can talk to."

"How am I doing?"

"You're all right."

Gable took Loretta's arm as they walked. "We should pick a movie."

"Have you seen *Cleopatra*?"

"Nope."

"It's one of my favorite stories in history. DeMille directed it. He's after me for a picture called *The Crusades*."

"Are you going to do it?"

"I think so. If we ever get off that mountain."

"I'm doing *China Seas* with Roz Russell next."

"She's a doll."

Gable paid for the tickets. The man in the booth, who was in his seventies, didn't look up as he made the change and put it in the trough. He tore the tickets and handed them to Clark.

"How's the picture?" Gable asked.

"I've seen worse."

"Like what?"

"That movie up the street called *Chained* is a bomb. I like Crawford, but she's nothing but mush in it."

"How about Gable?"

"Somebody needs to take a stick to that fella. He's full of himself."

"I can't stand him myself." Gable winked at Loretta.

The ticket seller sifted through his stubs. "We'd be about the only two people in the world that feel that way. He sells out quicker than the Neccos."

"You don't say. Maybe there's something to that fella."

"Gotta be. How many people could be wrong?" the ticket seller groused.

Loretta and Clark made it inside the glass doors of the theater before they laughed, but once inside, they let loose. Gable bought them popcorn and sodas, and held the door into the theater open for his date.

Gable chose two seats at the top of the balcony. Except for a housewife or two who slipped in after the dinner dishes, the place was empty. Gable laid his fur coat out on the seat and guided Loretta into it. She sank into the soft fur as if it were hot sand. Gable took the aisle seat next to her. He draped one leg over the seat in front of them, and the other he stretched out into the aisle. He put his arm around her; she held his hand, which rested on her shoulder.

Colbert made her entrance as Cleopatra in a risqué gown, part armor and the rest revealing chiffon. "Some gown."

"She wore more clothes in the picture I did with her."

Loretta was riveted by the adaptation of the story. Colbert owned the picture; she was a goddess, yet as vulnerable as a shopgirl hoping for a bigger life.

Gable watched the movie, but only in passing; he was far more interested in the art form sitting next to him. Every once in a while, he was overcome with feelings for her, and he'd kiss her. She'd shush him and push him away, but once, during a long speech delivered by Caesar Augustus, she kissed him back like she meant it, because the truth was, she did.

They were free for one night.

Gable and Young were no longer actors on a set, or charming props for sale at a studio premiere. They were like any Joe and Doris, out on a date at the movies. It was the simple combination of popcorn and a show, an evening most couples took for granted. But Loretta and Clark didn't. They reveled in the privacy of it, the simplicity of it, the chance to talk shop, to laugh, and to share stories and their desires and hopes.

And there were the kisses.

They were equals, and in this regard, Loretta knew a relationship between them could work. Gable wasn't so sure, but it had nothing to do with Loretta, but with his ascendance into the Hollywood pantheon of world-famous leading men. Gable knew his life was about to change again. This time, it would ratchet up on the wings of the blockbuster *It Happened One Night*, which was selling out around the country, with audiences returning to watch it over and over again. That kind of surprise hit was a rarity, Gable knew, and it gave him a foothold at the top that would take years to shake.

With the glory came the sacrifice. Would he ever be able to take a girl to the movies again? He doubted it. But whatever Loretta Young was, that night she would show him that he was still a regular guy, deserving of love not because of what he had achieved but because of who he was, a kid from Ohio who had made good, an ordinary boy who had extraordinary luck. This was how he viewed himself, and it was a relief to be with a woman who saw him for exactly what he was.

———————

Loretta and Clark boarded the lobby elevator at the Sorrento Hotel. He pressed the button and turned to face Loretta. She fumbled to find her hotel key at the Sorrento in her pocket.

"You're in three oh three," he said. "Your suitcase is in your room."

"Thank you. Where are you?"

"Room three oh four."

"That's convenient."

"I hope so," he said, moving closer to her.

"You're getting that wolf look."

Gable laughed. "What are you talking about?"

"Let me show you." Loretta knitted her eyebrows and bared her teeth.

"I don't look like that."

"Yes, you do. It's hungry-wolf-on-the-prowl time, and it's very disconcerting."

"The aim is not to upset you."

"Whatever your aim is, it's having the opposite effect."

"You just shut me right down." Gable turned away from her and leaned against the back wall of the elevator.

"Somebody has to for once."

"Do you say everything that's on your mind?"

"Not always. I try to be tactful."

"Try harder."

"Does every woman in the world go along with your act?"

"Usually. And by the way, Miss Elegant, it's not an act."

"What is it?"

"Technique."

"Ugh!"

"Well, you asked me."

"You didn't have to put it like that. I'm going into my room, and I wish you a lovely evening."

Gable put his room key in his lock as Loretta did the same at her own door.

"Hey, Gretchen?"

"Yes?"

"What if this is our only chance?" Gable said quietly.

Loretta dropped her head against the door.

"You're not praying, are you?"

"No."

"After that kneeling you did at the grotto, and the appearance of your rosary beads, I'm just making sure."

"I'm not praying. I'm trying to resist you."

"Why would you do that?"

"Because of your wife in the purple suit."

"I told you what the situation is."

"I understand the situation. But I'd like to think that I'm smarter than the excuse you're giving me."

Gable grabbed her by the arms. "I have not lied to you. I've told you more about myself than I've told any other woman I have ever known."

"That's a big deal."

"Stop joking. What if this is the beginning of something for us?"

"That's a good point."

"Do you want to turn back, or do you want go forward?"

"If I'm given a choice, I'd like to stay right here with you. Neither forward, nor backward, but right here. With you."

"Then give me your key."

Loretta took her room key out of the door and handed it to Gable. He opened the door to his room. "Make yourself at home."

Gable's was a cheerful yellow room, with wallpaper of a white trellis with scrolling green leaves. It had the feeling of a garden, which soothed her.

Gable appeared in the doorway with her suitcase. "I've fallen for you, Gretchen."

He dropped the suitcase and closed the door behind him. He helped her off with her coat. He hung the coat in his closet.

"When did it happen?" She slipped out of her shoes.

"On the raft. On the river."

"I knew on the train."

"When we met?"

"No. The morning after the first night. I got up early to go to breakfast."

"I was in the dining car," he remembered.

"I thought you had waited up all night for me. At least, that's what I told myself."

"When you walked in, I couldn't believe it."

"I never miss breakfast."

"I couldn't believe I was alone with you. The night before, the car was full of people, and I thought, How will I ever get to her? I was in the front of the car, and you were in the back, and it seemed like a hundred miles. I couldn't figure out how to reach you."

Gable took her face into his hands. He could not look at her enough. Her eyes sparkled with humor, but there was a sadness there that made him want to take care of her.

Clark picked Loretta up in his arms and carried her to a soft reading chair covered in pale green velvet. He sat down, and she made herself comfortable on his lap.

Loretta and Gable were intertwined. This was their way. It was as if she were a trumpet vine that curled up a tree, so close as to become part of it. They had a way of being one with each other that was natural, that neither had experienced with any other person. It had not been awkward between them ever; there was no ceremony to stand on, no odd placement of an arm or a leg or a hand or a foot. They fit. She had scooped her arm behind his neck, his arms were around her, she wrapped one of her legs around his, they were comfortable, connected, as smoothly designed as links in a chain of gold.

Gable kissed her tenderly. "What do you think?"

"I don't think we'll have to tip the maid in three oh three."

Gable laughed. "Whoever said beautiful girls can't be funny are idiots."

"Is Joan Crawford funny?"

"No."

"How about Claudette?"

"About as funny as a mathematician."

"How about Connie Bennett?"

"She's funny."

Loretta pinched him.

"Sorry. But not as funny as you."

"Are you really in love with me?"

"I am."

"Love is everything to me."

"That comes through, Gretchen."

"You know how I seemed a hundred miles away on the train car? I wasn't ever a hundred miles away, I've always been right here."

Gable picked Loretta up and carried her to the bed. As he undressed her, he would stop and hold her for a long time. She helped him with his tie made of the creamiest silk, his vest and jacket made of the softest wool. He wrapped her in the satin blanket. Loretta was enveloped by him. He knew how to touch her without her having to ask. He made her feel treasured, and he meant it. Clark had paid close attention to her, and he believed he knew exactly how to please her. As tall and strong as Gable was, he was delicate with Loretta. Every button, the pull of each sleeve, was a reason to kiss her again, to remind her that she was safe in his arms.

For her part, she wanted to stop time. She didn't want to think about where this romance might go, or write the ending before they had started their journey, so she took her time with every button on his shirt; for every button there was a kiss. She wished for a thousand.

She opened the satin blanket and pulled him toward her. The bed was soft beneath them. For the first time in weeks she felt warm, down to her bones. When his skin touched hers, she felt drenched in velvet. She smiled at the faint scent of bitter orange on his neck. It was as if he had brought the sun inside.

Clark was surprised to find himself full of emotion. It was hard to catch his breath. His heart—something he never offered—belonged to her. It was racing. He wondered if she could hear it, if she knew how much this night meant to him. He wasn't a man who had ever surrendered to any woman. Tonight, Loretta had him.

"What do you remember?" she whispered.

"Everything."

He remembered her lips when she smiled at him for the first time on the train, the arch of her back when she leaned across the table to serve him spaghetti in the kitchen, how her body felt when he pulled her on to his lap the night she made the apple pies, her long legs when she took the stairs two at a time. He remembered the first freezing cold morning on the set when she stood and faced him, reached into his coat pockets, and held his hands to warm them. In honor of that moment, he kissed her hands.

"What will you remember?" she asked.

"Everything."

Now it was Clark who looked around the room for the clock. He wanted more time. He wanted to hold on to the moon and push away the sun. If the sun never came up again, that was fine with him. Clark Gable was in love with Loretta Young. He wondered if she knew.

Loretta draped the blanket around herself like a cloak as Clark pulled her close, enveloping him in the satin. And this is how they stayed until morning.

10

ⵌ

Bill Wellman figured Clark Gable and Loretta Young had shared something more than a pen as they witnessed the wedding of Luca Chetta and Alda Ducci in Seattle. Even though Gable made good on the promise of returning from Seattle with the truck loaded with fresh food and supplies for the hungry cast and crew, Wellman was suspicious.

If Wellman had a hunch his costars had fallen in love, he was right.

Wellman stood behind the camera and watched as the wind whipped up the snow powder on the branches of the cedars.

"No matter what happens, keep rolling," he instructed the cameraman before shouting, "Action!" The echo of Wellman's voice thundered through the white canyons.

Loretta lay in a snowdrift surrounded by wolves (Siberian huskies, standing in for them on camera in fact). She exhaled slowly, then took shallow sips of air, slowing her breath to a stillness that would mimic unconsciousness. Bela Lugosi had taught Loretta to play dead on camera through modulation of her breath. He also showed her how to keep her eyelids closed to prevent fluttering during the close-up: "Keep your eyeballs looking down, even when your eyes are closed." This tip came in handy on Mount Baker that morning.

The camera was placed to film Gable and Oakie wide coming over a mountain pass, riding a dogsled. Oakie commandeered the reins while Gable stood behind, riding the sled blades.

Oakie was a wild man as an actor; he was spontaneous and real. He'd whip the dogs into a frenzy, and drive them fast and furious over the edge of the icy ridge for the sake of authenticity. Gable and Oakie were to spot Loretta in the distance, see the wolves, and react to save her. Gable was to take aim with a gun and shoot the wolves. The camera was over Gable's shoulder, and would cover him as he fired. From this angle Gable would run to Loretta's rescue and hold her in his arms.

The actors took their positions. Wellman shot the scene and called for a second take. Gable and Oakie returned to their starting position behind the cliff. The crew stood by with long-handled brooms to smooth the snow in their path. A third take. The crew swept the snow into position again. A fourth. The crew swept the snow again. A fifth.

"If we go again, I'm jumping off this mountain," Jack Oakie complained.

"Control the dogs, Jack, or you won't have to jump," Gable said. "You'll be eating the bottom of that canyon."

They filmed the scene again. Satisfied, Wellman ordered coverage, and the cameras were moved to film the scene from another angle, from Loretta's point of view in the field.

Gable broke away from the team of experts handling the dogs to catch up with Wellman as he trudged alone across the field.

"What do you need?" Wellman asked Gable.

"I don't like the way you leave Loretta on the ground," Gable complained. "She'll freeze to death."

"I'll take care of it," Wellman grumbled.

"I mean it, Bill."

"I said I'd take care of it."

Gable watched as Wellman caught up to his camera team. Gable turned and went to check on Loretta.

"You okay?" Gable asked her.

"I'm fine."

"You must be freezing."

"I'm okay. The sun is hot."

"I'll come and get you for lunch." He smiled.

"It may be dinner, the way this scene is going."

Alda jumped out of the utility jeep with a thermos of hot coffee for the actors.

"Hey, it's the newlywed," Gable greeted her. "How's it going?"

"Blissful." Alda beamed.

"No dreams of that convent life anymore, eh?"

Loretta slugged Gable's arm. "Clark, what's the matter with you?"

"I thought you'd appreciate my interest. I support true love and marriage, home and hearth—you know, all the stuff they write about in *Movie Mirror*."

Gable joined the dogsled team as Alda poured Loretta a cup of coffee.

"How's Wellman treating you?" Alda said softly.

"He's acting like a spurned lover."

"Are you okay?"

"I'll get through it. I'm doing my job, and the rest is none of his business."

"It's a small company. Word travels fast," Alda said.

"Small town. Small minds. My mother says that about Hollywood, you know. It's a town that runs on gossip. You can't help any of that."

But it isn't gossip, Alda thought. *You're in love with Clark Gable.* Alda knew it for sure. She had fallen in love with Luca on Mount Baker; she understood the kind of temptation Loretta was up against. The bitter cold forced the company to find warmth however they could.

Alda had not seen Loretta this happy since she began working for her. Loretta's friendship with Spencer Tracy had been pure anguish. With Tracy, it was high drama, tearful phone calls, a lot of kneeling in church, and long, soulful conversations in their dressing rooms between takes. There had been very little joy, and almost no fun.

The love affair with Gable was completely different. Loretta was energetic and industrious; she sprang out of bed in the morning looking forward to work. Maybe this particular happiness was a prelude to a whole new life together—but if Loretta and Clark were making plans, they didn't let on. They lived in the moment, savoring their time together. Hollywood and home were forgotten on Mount Baker.

Everyone in the company of *The Call of the Wild* could see the change in Gable and Loretta's friendship after the weekend in Seattle.

During the meal breaks, Gable sat in a folding chair while Loretta faced him in another. He sheltered her, wrapped his legs around hers to keep her warm, and they leaned in, deep in conversation, unaware of the crew around them. If there was a break, or a reset, or a trudge through the snow from one location to another, Loretta and Clark were together. They were better team players now that they were lovers, working as a unit to get the best possible result. United, they were a force. Wellman even upped his game, and so did the crew.

Alda noticed that show people didn't judge one another when it came to affairs on the set. There was an unwritten law: If it's good for the movie, it's good for everybody. After all, they were there to make a romantic adventure story, and if real emotions appeared on film, all the better.

Loretta and Gable were out to beat the clock. They knew their jobs on this film would end, so they took advantage of the time they had together. At night, they sat by the fire in the great room and went over their scenes for the next day. When their work was done, they talked into the night. They were the last to retire, and the first at breakfast.

Gable had moved into Loretta's room. It was so much easier to build one fire than two. Besides, they couldn't get enough of one another's company. Both of them were realistic as they tore scenes out of their scripts once they'd been filmed. When the pages were gone, the shoot of *The Call of the Wild* would end.

Every day Loretta looked forward to the nights, and every night Gable looked forward to the days. They were so in love that the freezing cold did not affect them. They weren't hungry, they barely needed sleep, and they gave each other energy in that way that only love can do. They appeared invincible; it seemed they had all they needed in the company of one another.

Loretta and Clark were living inside the movie, a magical place with its own language, script, and rules, where people meet and fall in love with an intensity of feeling and in physical proximity to one another, without real-life problems or responsibilities to intrude. Onscreen lovers might remain in the scenes long after they are shot, believing they have made a memory instead of a movie. Only the very wise know to trust the words "The End" and leave the feelings on location where they had them.

Loretta knew, as surely as the snow would melt come spring, that the situation between her and Gable would change, but she would not consider it on Mount Baker. She dared not think about the future; it was too complex and layered, forcing her to confront deep feelings of shame at having invited a married man into her heart again. But even her conscience could not keep them apart. She didn't want to waste any time on regret that she could spend with Gable. She prayed for what was best for them, and never specified what the best might be. Staying in the moment is the goal of every actor, and Loretta applied it to her time with Gable. Maybe if she stayed in the moment he would too and they could be together always.

———

Loretta was sitting on her bed, going over the scene to be shot the next morning, making notes to herself.

"You have mail"—Alda handed her a stack of envelopes—"and Georgie sent you another box of See's chocolates."

"Thank God and Georgie!" Loretta opened the box, offering chocolate to Alda, who took a piece. Loretta savored another. "How is Luca?"

"He's still on the set. He's painting the interior of the bank."

"Clark and Oakie shoot that tomorrow."

Alda knew she needed to talk about the return trip home to Los Angeles, but was finding it impossible to bring it up. Alda would be moving out of Sunset House and into Luca's home in the valley, just over the hill from Hollywood. Alda believed her happiness would pain Loretta, who would be returning home alone. Alda had rehearsed a speech several times in front of Luca, but now, face to face with Loretta, she couldn't find the words.

"Is something on your mind, Alda?"

Alda sat down on the edge of the bed. "I'm worried about you."

"Why?"

It was difficult for Alda to broach the subject, even though she, Luca, and Clark had become good friends during the filming.

"Alda, you can ask me anything."

"Is Mr. Gable going to leave his wife?"

"He says he is."

"Do you believe him?"

"Do you?" Loretta asked her.

"He's a good man. But sometimes good men get in difficult situations that they can't get themselves out of."

"You know, it's the strangest thing. Clark and I keep kicking the can down the road, thinking there will be plenty of time to deal with the future once we wrap. But it's hard for me to think about anything beyond this moment. I can't remember home. I don't know if it's this script, or that we've been on location for so long, but I've never felt so removed from my real life as I have on this job. It's almost like what you feel when you go to a movie on a Saturday afternoon and you're swept away by the story, and it ends and you've been in the dark for hours and you walk out of the theater into the sunlight. You can't see and you don't know where you are—you're somehow still back inside, in the world of the movie. I'm in a place where I've never been before, and I don't know what to do."

"Do you love him?"

"Madly."

"What do you love about him?"

"Clark is a good man who has made some bad choices in life. Maybe that's the wrong word, but his choices weren't wise, and they haven't served him. We've talked about it—and it's a lot like the situation when I married Grant Withers. But I had the sense to get out quickly. Mr. Gable has a different view of things. He stays for many reasons that I wouldn't, but that work for him. His father and stepmother live with him, he is ward to Ria's children, he has a life there. But he has another life that he lives, that he's not proud of—but he tells me that would change if he was married to the right woman."

"Are you that woman?"

"I don't know."

"Do you want to be?"

Loretta and Alda sat in silence for a few moments. Alda realized that Loretta's situation with Gable was a lot like her relationship with Spencer Tracy. Both men were married and had complicated personal lives and ambitious professional ones. She wondered if Loretta fell in love with these types because she was as ambitious as the men, and didn't want marriage to interfere with her career. Loretta was also younger, which entitled her to a few callow years of making mistakes before she married and had a family. At least, this was how Alda rationalized the love affair.

"Is there anything I can get for you?" Alda stood.

"I'm all right, Alda. I have everything I need."

Alda went down the hall and back to the room she shared with her husband. She was so worried about Loretta that she felt sick. Alda didn't know how to advise Loretta to separate her real life from her acting. Loretta seemed to believe the lines written for her character in the script were true. She'd almost become Claire to Gable's Jack. They bantered in the same way offscreen as they did when the cameras were rolling.

Alda worried about other aspects of Loretta's career in show business, too.

The attention paid to physical perfection—the hours spent on hair, makeup, and costume fittings—while good for the camera, could not be good for Loretta the woman. Alda had witnessed how Wellman undermined Loretta's confidence to keep her in line. Loretta laughed off the director's comments about her bad angles and scrawny frame. Maybe some of these were motivated by Wellman's envy of Gable, but no matter the reason, it was painful to observe.

Alda hoped that Loretta would come to her own conclusion about Gable and end the relationship. She longed to help Loretta end it. Luca believed Alda should mind her own business, but Loretta Young *was* her business.

Alda heard a knock at the door. "Come in," she called out.

"Alda, I'm sorry," Loretta said, looking down at the floor. "I dragged you up here, and now I'm behaving in a way that offends your moral code. Well, it offends mine too. But I don't know what to do. I love him. Every day we get closer to wrap, and every day I am aware that this time is almost over, and whatever we have together will end. We can't be together when we get home—he has to sort out his life. And I can't help him with that. So you see, I understand how you feel. You can't help me get over him, or put this behind me, because I don't want to."

"I don't care about the sin." Alda looked at her hands. "I care about you and what happens to you."

"I'll handle it, Alda." Loretta turned to go. "I'll get through this. I always do."

Loretta closed the door behind her. Alda sat down on the edge of the bed. How interesting, she thought; Loretta thinks being in love is something a woman has to "get through," as though it's an illness, not something that enriches a life and sustains it over time. Why would Loretta think any differently? Any love she had known with a man had ended badly, beginning with John Earle Young. She was abandoned as a baby by her father and had come to expect that no man would stay beyond his initial obligation. Maybe, when it came to Clark Gable, Loretta knew what she was doing after all.

———

The Seattle Express was loaded with luggage and a weary cast and crew. *The Call of the Wild* had taken its toll. The three-week location shoot had extended to seven weeks, obligations back home being postponed or rolled forward as the studio scrambled to make the delays work to their advantage.

The eager crew that had made the trip up the coast weeks earlier looked as though they had been dredged through the cold ashes of the fire pit on Mount Baker. The boots that had been new going up the mountain were now ravaged from wear, distressed from ice and snow; clothing was faded and worn from days spent hiking through the tundra. Their ambitious hopes were now memories. Their work, recorded on celluloid strips, formed into wheels nestled in thirty-two silver canisters, kept in perfect temperature in refrigerated bins, was the movie—seven weeks of images in pieces, scene by scene, take by take, ready for the cutters poised to begin the process of finishing the picture before Christmas.

There was a lot of affection on this train. The men would miss the brotherly camaraderie, the card games, throwing dice, the whiskey, gin, and bourbon, and the fun. Elvira would miss the jokes about her cooking. The assistant cameraman would miss the hotel maid, who remained on Mount Baker and went on to find happiness with a local. Wellman would say good-bye to the ulcer that began to form when weather delays made it impossible to film.

They carried home a collective narrative, a shared history, stories of daring and danger, of blizzards, avalanches, wild rivers, and near misses, avoiding catastrophe that would be repeated over and over again on sets in the years to come. There was a palpable nostalgia in the air, along with the cigarette smoke that hung over them in one gray cloud in the dining car as the train chugged out of Seattle and headed down the coast for Los Angeles.

Alda fixed her husband's tie.

"None of the other guys are dressing for dinner, Alda."

"I'm not married to them. If they want to look like a bunch of panhandlers, that's their business."

"You're tough."

"When we get off the train in Los Angeles, we are representatives of Loretta Young, the movie star. We have to look better than presentable."

"You're always thinking."

"That's why you married me."

"That and other things." Luca pulled her close and kissed her.

"You've made me happy," Alda told him.

"It wasn't hard. I just have to love you, and that's the easiest job in the world."

A look of concern crossed Alda's face.

"What's the matter? Oh, that." Luca knew what his wife was thinking. "Loretta and Clark."

"It's hopeless."

"Alda, come here." Luca sat next to her on the bed. "I've kept my nose out of your business because it's your business, and I respect what you do. But I've made a few movies with Clark. I don't want to burst your bubble, but he's fallen in love with every leading lady on every movie. Crawford left Fairbanks over him. Norma Shearer almost lost Thalberg over him. They all fall in love with him, and he falls in love with them. Frankly, it makes for a better movie. And that's really what Clark is all about—he's not number one at the box office for nothing. He makes it all look effortless."

"*Sprezzatura*." She sighed.

"Exactly, but it's not. It's not easy. He cares deeply about his work. So he does whatever he has to do to make the movie better."

"You don't think he loves her?"

"Don't count on this thing making it to Easter."

"But Loretta is different."

"And she is also the same. Loretta knows it already. Can't you tell? She's playing out her hand. She's not folding. She's waiting for him to cash in his chips first to end it. She's made fifty movies. Loretta knows the deal. You have to stop romanticizing this. It's not a story in a magazine. It's not a movie. It's not like us. It's not real life. They kiss, they get attached, and when they go home to their wives or husbands, they forget the folly. It's just how it goes."

"But she's better than all that."

"Then she has to say no next time. Otherwise, she has a good time, and that's what she gets out of it."

"I'm heartbroken for her."

"Don't be. She starts a new picture next week, and it will be another whole fan dance with another kickline, and this time, maybe, you hope, you pray, she learned something."

Alda didn't want to believe Luca, but he was right—she didn't need more proof. She had been with Loretta on *Man's Castle* and *The Call of the Wild*, and in both instances, Loretta had fallen for her leading men.

Alda had also observed how strange Hollywood could be. Nothing was as it seemed, including the emotions under the surface. Gorgeous actresses who wore furs and jewels and waved to the crowds at premieres, in private had crushing bouts of self-loathing and engaged in all kinds of self-destructive behavior. Actors who were handsome, strong, athletic, and robust on the set, in private could not stop drinking. Their working world of heightened emotion and perfection was an illusion that fed their unworthiness.

Alda marveled at the content of the fan letters that poured in for Loretta. The audience thought the characters Loretta played were real, that her beauty made her good, and that the snappy lines she delivered made her a bright, inquisitive intellectual. Just as the beam of light from the projector made the image appear on the silver screen, so did the audience project their hopes, fears, dreams, and desires onto the storytellers. For a girl like Alda who had been in the convent, who was trained to look within for all gratification and understanding, Hollywood with its devotion to the veneer was practically a sin.

Alda's job was to care for Loretta. It's how Alda made sense of the mania of show business. To her, it was simply a job where she took care of a young woman who needed her, not that far afield from her work at Saint Elizabeth's.

Alda had grown fond of Loretta, and the entire family. She saw them as seekers, looking to make a better life for themselves and their family. They had made their way, in large part without the assistance and encouragement of the men in their lives. In that way, the Belzer/Young family had a lot in common with the Sisters of Saint Vincent de Paul. They had been poor, and they hadn't forgotten a moment of it. Perhaps that's what made them devout; they had to place their gratitude somewhere. It could not be blind luck that Mrs. Belzer became a force in interior design, and that her children had gotten into movies and done well.

Alda saw what the power of their images did in the world, and how Loretta believed that she must take that audience's affection for her youthful energy and talent and make the world better beyond the borders of the sets that Luca painted so exquisitely. Loretta was more than an actress who wanted glamour and fame; she cared about the content of the stories. It was in this way that Alda saw that Loretta was different from the other actors she had met. Loretta's commitment to quality proved there would be more than movies left behind to remind people of the goodness of Loretta Young. She had a higher goal.

———————

Loretta was in her berth, choosing her ensemble for their triumphant return to the Los Angeles train depot. Unlike the departure, which was orchestrated to throw off the press, the return was staged to promote the movie. This time there would be the hullabaloo of reporters and fans; Mr. Zanuck wanted to kick up as much gold dust in the way of publicity that he could.

Loretta wore a new sky-blue silk suit with a flared skirt. The hat was a gray cloche, with matching gloves and pumps. The outfit would look great in pictures in the newspapers. Zanuck was to present her with a spray of red roses. It was back to business as usual—the movie business.

Gable rapped on Loretta's door.

"Gretch. Come with me." Gable was ebullient. He had spent the first part of the trip in the club car trying to win back the money he lost in a poker game on the night of the wrap.

Clark's mood was something new, shades of which Loretta had not seen before. The movie was over, and he was heading home to the sunshine and a new movie to make on an MGM sound stage, which made for a luxurious schedule after being away on location for so long. Gable was excited about a hunting trip he had planned to Lake Arrowhead. He had a full calendar of golf and sailing planned; he could already feel the healing southern California sun on his face. He longed to jump into his convertible and head to the beach; in a matter of hours he could. "How about dinner?"

"No, thanks."

"Are you okay?" Gable closed the door behind him. "Hey, what's the matter?"

"I'm scared."

"You just tamed a mountain and Bill Wellman—what could you possibly be scared of?"

"I'll never see you again."

"What do you mean? I'm going home, going to finish what I started with Ria, and then we'll be together."

"Together."

"Married."

"Do you mean it?"

"You have to trust me. I made this mess, and I have to fix it. For us. You believe me, don't you?"

"I try."

"All that faith you have when you kneel before statues, throw a little of that my way."

"Okay."

"I mean it."

Gable kissed her. "Now will you come and have dinner with us? The gang wants to say good-bye."

"I'll be right there."

Loretta sat down at the vanity in her berth. She held back tears, promising herself that she wouldn't cry until she was home and in her room at Sunset House. She looked at the clock. They would arrive in Los Angeles in three hours and twenty-three minutes. That's all the time she had left with Clark Gable, as she knew him on Mount Baker when he belonged to her, and she to him. Their conversations by the fire that went long into the night, the teasing when they got ready to go to the set in the morning, the way she would catch him looking at her—it was all in the past. She could not imagine what would come next for them, but she had a pretty good idea.

Loretta wished that the train could keep rolling on forever, past Los Angeles, through Mexico, over oceans and continents, and keep going, never stop, until the end of the world. She wanted to believe Clark's promises, and she hoped he meant them. But she knew better.

In her mind, Loretta had tested her faith and failed. She wasn't even a good Catholic. She dreaded the confessional because she obviously had not learned the lessons from the Tracy affair. She had simply traded one married man for another. For every sin there was a punishment. For every confession there was contrition. She knew she would have to pay for her happiness on Mount Baker. She couldn't say how, and she didn't know when, but the marker would come due; it always did. Something told her to trust her instincts, not Gable's promises and high hopes. No good was to come of this glorious, spectacular, and deliciously tender love affair. Until the train pulled into Los Angeles station, she would pretend otherwise.

Loretta put on her lipstick and went to the dining car for the Last Supper, the *The Call of the Wild* version. She still had a few hours left to laugh, share stories, and delude herself that everything was going to be all right. That much she could do. Beyond that, it was anyone's guess.

———

The starlet Elizabeth Allan was waiting on the train platform for Gable's return from the wilds of Washington State. The press corps was happy to pass the time photographing the British beauty until the big show pulled into the station. They snapped photos of Allan, lovely in a bubble-gum-pink dress and hat. She carried one pink rose, a sign of her devotion to Gable. However, she was not alone. It seemed the entire state had turned out to welcome him home.

The platform was packed with people—press, fans, and studio brass, who stood on the outskirts of the mania like guards surrounding a fort. Zanuck had seen the rushes. Ebullient, he'd called Louella Parsons and Hedda Hopper and spilled competitive snippets of details about the actors' performances, the costumes, and the dangerous terrain. He was thrilled with Wellman's work, and believed Buck would become a bigger star than MGM's Lassie. If there was one thing Zanuck enjoyed more than polo, it was beating Louis B. Mayer at his own game, using his own chess pieces—in this instance, the loan-out of Clark Gable.

The train pulled into the station, and the pack of reporters pushed forward as the Seattle Express came to a stop.

Jack Oakie came off the train first, to a burst of applause and cheers. He held his dilapidated snow boots up in the air for all to see. He hadn't shaved in weeks. His wife pushed through the crowd, embraced him, and then berated him for his shaggy beard as the photographers snapped away.

Buck the dog and his trainer were next. The crowd separated as Buck bounded through the crowd and into a pickup truck with his name painted on the side.

Loretta disembarked the train, posing for pictures on the landing as the crowd whistled and cheered. She was head-to-toe glamorous, in the new suit she had saved for the occasion. She looked elegant, the only member of the *The Call of the Wild* company who didn't seem the worse for wear. She greeted the press corps as though they were long-lost friends. Alda was close behind her, as well as Luca, who was happy to carry their luggage, and happy to be home with his wife.

The press converged on Loretta, barraging her with questions about surviving the blizzard, handling Buck the dog, and her costar, Gable. They pummeled her with queries: "Did you know Gable is number one at the box office?" She answered all the questions graciously, and deflected the ones that implied that she had fallen in love with him. If there was any question that Loretta was a great actress, she proved it whenever she was interviewed.

Luca pushed through the crowd, leading Loretta and Alda to a studio limousine parked just beyond the platform. As Loretta climbed into the car, she heard the roar of the crowd behind her. The mob had swallowed Gable as he came off the train. Flashbulbs popped like bottle caps and girls shrieked at the sight of him, their screams piercing the clatter. Loretta rolled down the window and watched the spectacle for a moment. As Gable was engulfed by the throng, it reminded her of the day they'd almost drowned in the river. But now, instead of rushing water, it was fans pulling him down and under—and this time she was convinced she had lost him.

Loretta was about to roll up the window when the crowd parted on the platform to let Gable through. On his arm was Elizabeth Allan, who next to Gable looked like a pink teacup. He smiled down at the starlet as she skipped to keep up with him.

"Are you ready to go?" Alda asked softly.

"Yes. I've seen enough," Loretta said.

———

Gable lit a cigarette as he leaned against the mantel in his living room, waiting for his wife. He wore a white tie and tails, a dramatic choice for a man who thought he hadn't a prayer of winning at the

Academy Awards that night. He was certain Best Actor would go to William Powell, the most dapper, erudite actor in pictures. But every job in Hollywood is political, and tonight, Gable was showing up to play the game.

Gable had arrived home a few days earlier to the scent of wet paint and wallpaper glue. While Gable was on the mountain working, Ria had been in the flats of Beverly Hills, shopping. She had redecorated the house: every sheer, drapery, and hook was new. His wife had gone French. The furniture was covered in sumptuous ice blue and burnished gold French brocades. The house was padded with wall-to-wall silk wool carpets in buttercup yellow while the walls glittered in the light of crystal sconces and chandeliers.

Ria, petite and compact, descended the stairs in a white duchesse satin gown, appliqued with tiny crystals that fanned out into sequins on a fishtail hem that trailed behind her like the crest of a wave. Ria was sleeved and gloved and cinched as was the imperative of any Hollywood wife over the age of fifty. She could not look younger than the competition, but she could look richer. Her diamond earbobs and thick, matching diamond studded cuff bracelets proved it. If they were not dazzled by Ria's gown, the jewelry would do the heavy lifting on her behalf.

"Clark, darling." She entered the newly refurbished gold living room, looking like a dove as she pulled on her evening gloves.

"Mother, you look splendid."

"We should go, we'll be late."

"Ria, I'm not going to win."

"Oh, who cares about that? We're sitting with the MacArthurs. He's a stitch, and Helen is elegant. This is a swank party."

"I'd like to win."

"Everyone likes to win. Did you ever meet anyone who liked to lose?"

"No, never did." Gable struggled to communicate with his wife. If he was stone-cold sober and honest, he would admit that he was afraid of her, of her volatile Texas temper. A man who is trapped in a marriage by fear has a difficult time explaining how he got there and therefore struggles when it comes time to figure how to get out. "Have you given some thought to what we talked about?"

"Oh, for God sakes, Clark. Look at me. I spent the day baking in black clay. I had my hair done, my nails painted, and a final fitting on this gown. I don't want to talk about anything unpleasant."

"When can we talk?"

"I'll let you know," she said tersely.

"No, I'd like to hash this out."

"I don't hash," she said, ending the conversation. "Choose another moment. This is not it."

"I want out, Ria."

"You listen to *me*. I have no intention of giving you your freedom. For what? That English tart? Elizabeth Allan is not a contender. No one will know that tin horn floozy's name in fifty years."

"This isn't about Elizabeth."

"That Loretta Young? Wake up. She's a bad bet. She was a teen bride, got the marriage annulled, and now she only goes with married men. Something wrong in the head with that one."

"Shut up, Ria."

"I won't 'shut up,' as you put it. I won't stand by and watch you take this golden moment in your career and throw it away as though we haven't both worked hard to get here. This is my moment too, Clark. I am as responsible for your popularity as you are. You may act the parts, but I am here building a life that you can be proud of, that your fans aspire to—that the studio bosses respect. I got you your pay raise, and don't forget it. L. B. Mayer had never seen dinner parties like the ones I threw for you! As for your night crawling, feel free to sneak around town in the shadows with any of the ambitious girls who want a piece of you to further their careers, but they are not entitled to all this, to the pie! You can make love to them by the thousands for all I care, but you will not dictate to me when this marriage ends, or how it will end, or *if* it will end. I am driving this buggy, Mr. Gable."

Ria sashayed out of the living room to the dings of the crystals on the gown and the shimmy of her silk stockings.

Mrs. Gable walked out the front door to the waiting limousine. The night air felt good, and she inhaled it like stiff whiskey. Ria had long believed men were weak and gullible, which made them promiscuous, but she wasn't about to give up her glamorous life over sex, which in her opinion was a lot of nothing.

Gable followed her out the door and into the car. They didn't say another word to one another on the drive to the Biltmore Hotel.

————

Loretta slipped in the back door of Dr. Andrew Berkowitz's office, followed by Alda, who closed the door gently behind her. A nurse appeared and locked the door behind them; not that anyone would have seen them enter. It seemed the entire population of Los Angeles and Beverly Hills was across town at the Biltmore Hotel, where the seventh annual Academy Awards were in full swing, with a dinner dance followed by the awards presentation.

Show business was far from Loretta's mind that evening. Gable had called her, promising her that he was cleaning up his domestic situation. He'd noticed that she was quiet, and worried for her health.

"Loretta, tell me what's going on with you." Dr. Berkowitz sat on a chair, as Loretta sat on the examination table, turning a cotton handkerchief over and over in her hands. Berkowitz had been the Young family doctor for years; he had known Loretta since she began in pictures.

"I'm afraid," she began. "I missed a period."

"Loretta, don't panic. You've been away working on a very difficult job, and that could have something to do with it."

"But I'm never late."

"Let's give you the Friedman test and settle the matter once and for all. It will take a couple of days for the results."

"Can't you get them faster?"

"No, it takes time."

"You'll call me the moment you get the results?"

"I will."

The nurse entered to assist Loretta. Alda waited outside. When Loretta emerged a few minutes later, she was wearing her sunglasses. Alda could see that she had been crying. Alda followed Loretta out to her car. Loretta removed her sunglasses and turned to Alda.

"I took the test. But I didn't need to—I know I'm pregnant." Loretta began to cry. "What am I going to do?"

Alda knew the signs of pregnancy from having worked at Saint Elizabeth's, but even if she hadn't, it was obvious that Loretta was filling out. Her slim frame was curvier, her face fuller, and she couldn't stomach her favorite meal of the day: breakfast.

"You mustn't tell Luca. No one can know." Loretta turned the key in the ignition.

"I won't say a word. I will help you in every way that I can, Gretchen. You are not alone."

Loretta turned to Alda and threw her arms around her. "Thank you. You're a good friend. I am so grateful."

"My mother used to say that there is a solution to every problem. Everything will work out, I promise."

"I don't know how," Loretta cried.

"Are you going to talk to Mr. Gable?"

"I'm going to talk to Mama," Loretta said, and she began to weep.

"Clark has sent notes. Flowers. And he calls at least three times a day. Won't you talk to him?"

"I can't talk to him. Especially not now."

"I believe his feelings are genuine."

"They might be when he's with me. But when he's not, he's married to one woman and distracted by any girl that crosses his path. This isn't a man who is ready to be a father." What Loretta wanted to say, but couldn't, was that Gable wasn't ready to be a husband either.

"He doesn't have a choice now."

"Alda, Clark can do whatever he wants. I'm the one who doesn't have any options."

There was only one comfort for Loretta as she sat in the car with Alda. Loretta thought back to the train, when Gable came to find her for dinner. She knew then that her life as she knew it was over. At that point, she thought it was the end of the romance that was making her sad; she knew she had no hold on Gable, none that could overcome the obstacles before them. At that time, Loretta didn't suspect she was pregnant, but she sensed, and saw in her mind's eye, a fork in the road. Now she had proof that there was a new life ahead, but she was alone in the world and could only rely on herself, her own strength, going forward. She wouldn't count on Gable to love her; that had been a fantasy. Loretta would protect her career, her livelihood, and now her baby, with a vengeance.

Love, the romantic kind, was no longer on her mind.

———————

The ticker from the adding machine hung over the desk in a long white curl speckled with black numbers as Gladys billed her accounts. The ledger was open; Gladys erased a total she had entered incorrectly. She tried very hard not to resent Mutt Belzer for leaving her with this dreaded chore.

"Mama, I need to talk to you," Loretta said softly.

The soft light from Gladys's desk lamp in the study threw ominous shadows against the wall. "Mr. Gable won the Academy Award," Gladys told her without looking up. "It was a sweep for *It Happened One Night*. Didn't you girls tell me you loved that picture?"

"Mama."

"I thought you'd be happy for him. One day it will be you up at that podium. You keep working hard, and you'll win a statue too. Maybe even for *The Call of the Wild*." Gladys looked up at her daughter, who stood in the shadow. "Gretchen, let me see you."

Loretta moved into the light, Gladys could see her daughter was in a state of anguish. Gladys went to Loretta and put her arms around her. Loretta began to cry.

"Tell me what's wrong."

"I'm so ashamed," Loretta said, weeping.

"There is nothing we ever in do this life that cannot be forgiven, if we are truly sorry. Nothing. Now tell me what's the matter."

"Mama, I'm pregnant."

Gladys looked at her daughter and held her face in her hands. "Are you sure?"

"I went to Dr. Berkowitz, he did the test. He said we'd know for sure by the end of the week, but it's no use. It doesn't matter. I know I'm pregnant."

"You're exhausted." Gladys's voice broke. She didn't need the results of the test either; she could see the signs. Loretta had dark circles under her eyes, Gladys's mark of pregnancy.

"What am I going to do?"

"Dry your tears, honey." Gladys handed Loretta a handkerchief.

"But Mama, everything will be over. Our lives. This house. His career. Mine. Clark will be devastated."

Gladys had read the newspapers and seen the fan magazines. She hadn't asked her daughter about her feelings for Gable, because she didn't want to know. She had spent most of the last year working with their priest to guide Loretta away from Spencer Tracy. Gladys liked Tracy, but did not want her daughter to have any part of breaking up a family. Gladys was relieved when she learned that the romance between Loretta and Spencer had been chaste, but it might have been worse than an actual fling or an affair, because real emotions were involved.

Gable was a different story.

Gable was a worldwide sensation. Many careers, including those in the front office and all of those on the lot, profited from his success. No studio was going to lose their top moneymaker on a morals charge if they could help it. The studios worked with the press to control information about their stars. The press could kill a career or rescue one. Given a choice, they would salvage the more important and profitable actor. They'd be happy to kill Loretta's career to keep Gable's afloat.

Men in the press offices manufactured prurient stories about the stars with directives from the studio bosses. A lie would be printed in one fan magazine, then embellished in the next, until it snowballed into a full-tilt scandal. The lives that were ruined in the process provided as much entertainment for a hungry public as the fictional stories shot on film.

The stakes were high for successful actors and actresses. A failure at the box office could do real damage to a studio boss, but they thought nothing of letting talent take a tumble to preserve their jobs. The bosses competed on every level, using scripts, directors, and casting choices as leverage against one another, and while they took umbrage at the Hays Code, they used it to sink projects before they were made and rile the moral arbiters to boycott a movie when it was released.

Publicists and reporters made an industry out of personal weakness and vice as they hunted for stories, followed up innuendoes—anything to find stars in violation of the Hays Code. The chicanery came in handy when they wanted an excuse to get rid of an actor under an expensive contract, or one who had grown old, or an actress who was suddenly box office poison or had lost her allure. A star didn't stay in the heavens in perpetuity. Everything in Hollywood was conditional; roles, fees, contracts, and publicity. When the fans fell away from a star, so did the studio's support. A star's climb to the top was often exhilarating, but the fall was always devastating.

Loretta, as a starlet pregnant with an illegitimate child, was in violation of the contract she'd signed. She would be thrown out of the business. But in this moment she wasn't thinking about her career, but the baby.

"Mama, I have to have the baby," she sobbed.

"You're going to have the baby, honey," Gladys told her.

"You're not angry with me?"

"What good would that do?"

"How could I have done this to you? To my family?"

"You fell in love."

"That's not an excuse."

"But it's what happened, isn't it?"

Loretta nodded. "I'm so afraid."

"You know, when I was pregnant with you, I was so afraid. I went to the priest and told him that I couldn't have another baby. I had Pol and Sally, and your father had disappeared again. And the priest said, 'You have two lovely girls. What if you're lucky, and God sends you another?' And I went home and thought about it, and I couldn't get rid of you. I just couldn't. And look at you. I am so proud of you. You have worked hard all your life, and you've made so many people happy, the least of whom is me. You have no way of knowing what the future holds, or what God has in store for you."

"But Mama, we will lose everything. This doesn't just affect me, it affects you and my sisters and my brother."

"We'll be all right." Gladys sounded confident, but it was an act. She was shaken by the news. Gladys did what any woman of faith did in times of trial; she remembered all she had been through, the loss of two husbands and the fear of being unable to feed her children, reminding herself that she had been through worse. She remembered her strength and turned to it.

"If Paramount finds out—"

"They won't. You'll finish *The Crusades*—you're done in a few weeks—and your contract is fulfilled."

"Mama, how will I keep the baby?"

"We'll find a way. You are not in this alone. You have your family, and frankly, you have Mr. Gable. This is his baby too."

"Oh, Mama, we can never tell him."

"You must tell him. He would want to know. We will figure out how to tell him. Now, go in the kitchen and have some soup. Ruby made a fresh pot of chicken and rice, it's on the stove. I want you to eat something and get a good night's sleep. I promise you, you'll feel stronger in the morning."

"How do you know?"

"I had five babies, Gretchen. My children are the source of everything good in my life. My work, my ambition, my drive—it's all because of you children. And there wasn't one time, in the five times I got the news that I was expecting, that I wasn't afraid. It's part of becoming a mother. You learn to use your fear to stoke your ambition. I wanted to give you children a good and decent life, and the only way I could do that was to work hard and do my best. We are not going to let anything or anybody bring us down."

Gladys dried Gretchen's tears. She stood up and gave her a hug. Loretta went to the kitchen for her dinner, and Gladys went to her desk. She cleared it of the bookkeeping. She brushed away her tears with her handkerchief and returned it to her pocket.

Gladys opened her address book. Her hands shook as she thumbed through it. She found the names of the reporters she had come to trust, and made a list. She also made a list of friends at the studio who would help conceal information from the bosses. She wrote down names in the shape of a family tree, a safety net of people who would help them through Loretta's situation. She also made a note to call her accountant, lawyer, and banker. She would ask them to provide a complete financial picture of all their real estate holdings, cash, and stock. If the worst happened, Gladys would know their net worth down to the penny.

Gladys had many friends in Hollywood, and she knew she could rally them if she needed help to keep the story quiet, or make adjustments in studio commitments and contracts. She knew she would have to call in favors.

There were two issues: the short-term contract commitment Loretta had to Paramount and Cecil B. DeMille and, in the long view, how to keep the secret of the baby without ruining Loretta's long-term career prospects. Gladys jotted some figures down on her scratch pad on the desk. She looked at the calendar. Loretta had made the picture between January 1 and February 15; it was likely the pregnancy was six weeks along. They had time to figure out a plan. In the meantime, she had to keep the romance of Gable and Young out of the papers.

———

Alda was hanging curtains in her kitchen in the bungalow she shared with Luca in the valley when she saw a car pull up in front of the house. Gladys and Loretta got out of the car, carrying a cake plate and a box wrapped in white with silver ribbons.

Loretta stopped to look at the house, the yard, and the street. Just a ten-minute drive over the mountain, the houses went from grand to cozy, from ostentatious to familial. The bungalow, made of pine and fieldstone, was charming. The flagstone walkway was hemmed with daisies. Under the picture window Alda had planted yellow rosebushes. The stoop's wooden canopy was covered in morning glory vines in lush purple, dripping off the simple wooden columns. The house was small, but it was lovely in detail.

Loretta sighed. While she loved Sunset House, she could imagine being happy in a small house that she decorated herself, with a man whom she adored racing home for dinner, a man who couldn't wait to see her at the end of a long day. It was beyond her why the simple joys of being a woman were so far out of reach.

"Come in, come in," Alda said.

Gladys took a look around the charming living room, approving of the decor. Loretta gave Alda a hug and handed her the gift.

"You didn't have to!"

"Housewarming!"

"Alda, darling, can you put on a pot of coffee?"

As Alda made the coffee, Gladys unwrapped a lemon pound cake she had made that morning.

"Alda, open your present!" Loretta said as Alda joined them at the table. She lifted a lovely pale blue ceramic coffee urn out of the box.

"I love it! We'll use it right now." Alda went to the sink and turned to Loretta. "How are you feeling?"

"I'm fine."

"Have you heard from Mr. Gable?"

"Constantly. I won't talk to him. I'm afraid to be seen with him."

"Which is why we're here, Alda."

"What can I do?"

"I'm planning a trip to Europe. We'd like you to come with us. We plan on staying the summer."

"Are you going to have the baby there?"

"No, we figure we'll throw the press off by going to Europe, and we'll say that Gretchen is taking a cure, and then we'll return and she'll have the baby here."

"And then what?"

"We don't know," Loretta said.

"Are you considering giving the baby up for adoption? Saint Elizabeth's works with a Catholic adoption service."

"I don't want to give my baby up."

"And you don't have to," Gladys assured her.

"Saint Elizabeth's was a halfway house. The nuns had a hospital ward right in the building. That's where I worked. The girls would have the babies, and the adoption service would assign the babies and the girls."

"Are you still in touch with the nuns there?" Gladys asked.

"I'm very close to them."

"What are you thinking, Mama? Do you think I should go up there and have the baby?"

"Maybe."

"I don't know, Mama."

"How else will you keep this story private?" Gladys countered.

"The sisters would take good care of you," Alda assured Loretta. "And they would understand your predicament."

"Think about it, Gretchen," her mother said.

"Luca has lunch with Mr. Gable most days at the commissary. Mr. Gable asks my husband a lot of questions. I don't tell Luca anything, so he doesn't have to lie when Mr. Gable presses him. But if you want me to go to Europe with you, I have to tell him everything."

"We can trust Luca," Loretta told her mother.

"Alda, will you speak with the Mother Superior and see if this is a possibility? If they can care for the baby until you can bring him home, it will help us keep the press off the story. By the time you have the baby, believe me, there will be some other headline occupying their minds."

"Where were you thinking of going in Europe?" Alda asked.

"England," Gladys said.

"The press in England is worse than New York or Hollywood. They would badger Loretta."

"So what shall we do?" Gladys was worried.

"I'd like to take Loretta to Padua. Since we'll be there a while, I can see my family, and they'd take good care of us."

"It's a fine idea," Gladys said.

"You'll love Italy. Everywhere you turn, there's a shrine, or a chapel, or a fresco. It will give you peace of mind."

Loretta took Alda's hand and squeezed it. "Whatever luck or providence or answered prayer brought you into my life, I cannot be grateful enough."

"I'm here for you," Alda said.

Alda poured the coffee into the elegant urn. She served the pound cake and the coffee. Despite the plan they had hatched that day, for a moment it was as if no time had passed, and their lives were as simple as they had been the day Alda left Saint Elizabeth's and walked into the house on Sunset.

Loretta told stories about the making of *The Crusades* to keep her mind off her troubles. Gladys laughed, as she hadn't since Loretta came home with the news. It was the last carefree afternoon the women would have. It was time to tell Clark Gable he was going to be a father.

————

Lost in thought, Spencer Tracy was walking across the MGM lot with his hands in his pockets when a chocolate-brown coupe nearly ran him over.

"Get in the car, Spence," the driver said.

Tracy removed his sunglasses. "What the hell, Gable?"

"You should watch where you're going."

"You almost hit me."

"Close, but no cigar."

"Where are you going?"

"I'm running over to Paramount. They want to talk to me about a script. You'd be perfect to costar."

"How's the dough?"

"There'll be plenty."

"If you're in it, the pot goes to you."

"Not if I tell 'em I won't make it without you."

"You'd do that for me?"

"It's true love, buddy."

"I always thought so."

"Get in—let's go turn old Adolph Zukor upside down until his pockets are empty. It worked for me with Zanuck."

"I'm in." Spencer jumped into the car. "I didn't recognize you. How many cars do you have?"

"A few."

"Save some for the rest of us, will ya?"

"You can buy yourself a new car with what you'll be making."

"You'd really slum with me in a picture? I'm touched."

"Don't go all soft on me. I have enough heartache."

"Lady kind?"

"Always lady kind." Gable smiled.

"Who is she?"

"I've been chasing Myrna Loy," Gable admitted.

"Have you caught her?"

"Nope. Have a funny feeling I never will."

"Me too." Tracy looked out the window.

"You're after Myrna?"

"Won't give me a tumble."

"I feel worse." Gable sped across La Brea.

"If this were poker, I'd bail. You'll end up with her eventually. Give it time, Gable. Give it time."

"That's all I've got is time. I'm taking my cues from you. You get the girls. You're the teddy bear."

"That makes me sound fat."

"Sorry, pal."

"How about you?"

"I'm trying to extricate myself, that's what my lawyer calls it, from the most expensive marriage on record. The throw pillows on Mrs. Gable's Louis Quatorze chaise alone are worth a fortune."

"Give her half and get out."

"That's what my lawyer says. Of course he's getting half of my half."

"They always do." Tracy shook his head.

"I have a better use for my money. I'd rather help those in need. I should just empty my bank account and stand on La Brea and hand out ten-dollar bills until every penny I have is gone. Ria would get half of nothing."

"You'd still have to pay the lawyer."

The gates to the Paramount lot opened, and Gable drove through. "Here to see Adolph Zukor," he said to the guard.

"Building C."

"How do I get there?"

"You gotta give it a couple of minutes. There's a parade going through."

"For what?"

"DeMille is filming *The Crusades*."

"Hey, is Loretta Young on the lot?"

"Bungalow seven."

Spencer Tracy shifted uncomfortably in his seat at the mention of Loretta's name. Gable pulled onto the lot and took a back alley behind the parade, peeling through the standing sets.

"Hey, you passed building C."

"We gotta drop in on Gretchen," Gable said breezily.

"I don't know about that, pal." Tracy was nervous. He hadn't spoken to Loretta since she sent him the good-bye letter. He had seen her across the aisle in church at Christmas, but he had to look away because she looked so winsome.

———

Loretta's dressing room was full of bouquets of roses. Her favorite flower was everywhere—long-stemmed red roses in vases, clutches of pink baby roses in small ceramic pots, and a crystal bowl with gardenias floating in white rose petals on the coffee table.

"You know a star by the number of bouquets in her dressing room," David Niven had said.

Loretta stepped into her costume, an emerald green velvet gown trimmed in gold. Alda zipped up the back of the dress. When it still fit, Loretta beamed.

Alda slipped silk shoulder pads into the costume. She placed a flat of padded linen around Loretta's rib cage, which, as she zipped up the dress, made Loretta's waist seem small. Loretta was eight weeks along in her pregnancy, but with Alda's help the actress was still able to hide the truth.

"You're a genius, Alda."

"We're lucky we wrap today. Another week, and there would be no hiding it in these costumes."

Gable and Tracy barged into bungalow 7 like a couple of school-boys. Loretta and Alda were taken aback. Gable was wearing a gray silk suit, while Tracy wore an open collared shirt and chinos. Alda had been in Hollywood long enough not to react to the dynamic presence of a leading man, and here were two, so different, yet each in their way possessing a mesmerizing power over women, especially over her boss.

"Miss Young, you're wanted on the set," Gable said.

"Is it time to burn you at the stake?" Tracy joked.

"Wrong picture." Gable laughed.

Loretta felt her face flush. She did her best acting and joked with the men. "Mr. Tracy, you're a good Jesuit; you should know your Bible stories. I'm not Joan of Arc in this picture. And Mr. Gable, it's well known that you're a lousy Catholic, so you probably think this is a remake of *Polly of the Circus*." Loretta checked her lipstick in the mirror.

"I was good in *Polly*."

"You were terrible," Loretta corrected him.

"The worst. I saw it too. Gretchen is right," Tracy agreed. "Lot of treacle, that one."

"This coming from a man who either plays an angel with cardboard wings or a priest in a cardboard Roman collar."

"I take what I'm offered." Tracy shrugged. "But you're a national treasure. You play those he-man roles, and we need those guys in the movies—right, Gretch?"

"Gives a girl something to dream about."

"What about him?" Gable pointed to Tracy.

"Girls dream about him too," Loretta assured them.

"They dream about me fixing their faucets," Spencer said. "I'm the plumber of American cinema."

Gable laughed. "You sell yourself short, buddy."

"Compared to you, I am." Tracy smiled.

"Let's go, Loretta, or we'll be late," Alda chided her.

"All right, boys, give sister a kiss." Loretta extended her cheek toward Tracy and then Gable, and each gave her a platonic kiss on the cheek. "You're good friends, but I have to go to work."

Loretta and Alda left the men in the bungalow.

"God, she's gorgeous," Tracy said.

"Won't give me a tumble," Gable admitted. "And it's killing me."

"I thought you were after Myrna."

"I'm horsing around," said Gable. "With the idea of Myrna." Gable ducked out the door after Loretta.

Left behind, Spencer looked around the dressing room. Loretta's stock had risen since *Man's Castle*. Back then she had lowly but lovely white carnations in her dressing room; now she had graduated to roses, and lots of them. Her dressing room was bigger, this one the size of a single-story house. There was a living area, a kitchenette, and an elaborate makeup and hair room. He looked at the photographs on the mirror—a series of color shots of Loretta's face, with instructions for makeup beneath them. Tracy looked at them closely and shook his head. Even now, it was hard to look at her. Months had passed; he hoped he was over Loretta, who, it appeared, had moved on. Tracy had too. His home life was solid, and when he fancied it, Louise looked the other way, and he'd take a girl to dinner. The affairs were brief, but they kept his mind off his troubles and off Loretta, the only woman who might have ended his marriage.

Gable caught up with Loretta and Alda on the way to the set. "Miss Young, may I have a moment?"

Loretta looked around. She forced a smile, but was terrified that some press person would walk by, figure out the truth just by looking at her, and plaster it all over the newspapers.

"I'm on my way to the set, Clark," she said breezily. "Call me sometime."

"Sometime? I've been calling you ten times a day. Alda, have you delivered my messages?"

"Don't put her on the spot," Loretta said quietly.

"Alda?" Gable implored.

"I deliver all phone messages."

"Follow me," Loretta said to Gable. She looked around for a private place to talk, and motioned to him. He followed her into the electrics trailer. She pulled the door shut behind them, and Gable put his arms around her.

Loretta wanted to kiss him. But she knew that if he spent any time at all this close to her, he would know the truth, and she couldn't bear the idea of telling him about the baby. Yet.

Gable was direct. "I'm getting a divorce. I want you."

"Myrna told me you chased her around Ciro's."

"I was fooling around. It was nothing serious. I can't stop thinking about you."

"Do you think about me when you're dancing with Elizabeth Allan at the Mocambo?"

"That's nothing."

"It's something to me."

"What am I supposed to do? Elizabeth is strictly a studio setup. It's just business. I'd rather be with you. But you won't see me. I want to be out on the town with you. I want to show you off. I want to drive you over to Santa Monica. We could walk on the beach. I want to take you up to Lake Arrowhead to my cabin. Don't you get it? I'm crazy about you."

Loretta put her hands on his face. Gable had said the words she was longing to hear. In fact, his plea was better than the scene she had imagined. She wanted to trust him.

Alda rapped on the door.

"I have to go," Loretta said softly.

Gable pulled Loretta close and kissed her. When their lips touched, it filled her with the kind of desire that had gotten her into trouble with him in the first place. He kissed her cheek, her neck, and her lips once more. Loretta closed her eyes and remembered how he had kissed her in the snow.

Alda rapped on the door again.

"Don't forget me," Gable said before he opened the door.

As if I ever could, Loretta thought. With the sun behind him, Gable filled the frame of the door, just as he had on Mount Baker the first night when he'd offered her an extra blanket. He'd seemed bigger than the world outside the door that night, and the same was true on this day. How different things would be if she had followed her instincts and never let him in.

"I'm sorry, Miss Young is not in," Alda said firmly into the phone.

Loretta stood in her bedroom between the French doors at Sunset House, looking out over the pool, which was being cleaned by a man in a blue uniform. Loretta watched as he pushed the long silver pole slowly in rows, vacuuming the bottom.

"I understand, Mrs. Gable. I have given her your messages. I'm sure if she needs to speak to you, she will call. . . . No, she is not avoiding you. . . . I will deliver the message when she returns home from work." Alda hung up the phone.

"What is her problem? Besides me, of course." Loretta sat on the bed.

"She wants you to hold a press conference and tell the world— those are her words—that you did not have an affair with Clark Gable on location. She gave me the exact wording for your press conference."

"There's a brilliant use of American journalism. Let me make a list of all the men I'm not in love with. She's out of her mind."

Georgie ran into the room, chased by her new puppy, a brown-and-white mutt named Pickles.

"If that dog goes on my new rug . . ." Loretta smiled.

"Mom will just get you a new one."

"Good point."

"Gretch, are you in love with Clark Gable?"

"Georgie! Who told you such a thing?"

"Lois Patranzino. Her mom reads *Photoplay*. They said you and Mr. Gable had a snowball romance."

"Maybe she meant snowbound," Alda said softly.

"It isn't true."

"I'll tell her. Lois was pretty sure about it, though."

"Don't you girls have better things to do than repeat stories?"

"Not really. Erika Vellucci told me that Jean Harlow is actually bald from the peroxide she puts on her hair, and that she wears a wig."

"That's very rude of Erika."

"Her mother's a hairdresser, and she said that peroxide kills the roots."

"Well, you tell Erika and her mother that Miss Harlow has every hair on her head, and that she brushes it with a horsetail hairbrush from Paris every night. And I know because Miss Harlow gave me the same hairbrush when I admired her hair."

"Okay." Georgie skipped out.

Loretta and Alda heard a whistle from the garden. Loretta went to the French doors.

"Oh, good! You're home for dinner!" David Niven said from the garden.

"You look handsome."

"Goldwyn loaned me out. I have a part in *Barbary Coast*. Don't ask. One line. I play a Cockney. You know I'm not Cockney."

"What are you, David?"

"I'm bangers-and-mash British, of course."

"I'm coming down to dinner. Meet me in the dining room."

"Good girl. I want to catch up with you and the gaggle."

Loretta had hardly seen Niven since she returned from Mount Baker. She heard that he had been dating Merle Oberon, who, she had heard, also had a crush on Gable. Sometimes Hollywood was too small a town, and Loretta wished to break free of it as much as David Niven wished to own it.

Niven took a seat at the head of the table at Gladys's invitation. "Where's Father Pass the Butter?"

"He had a prior engagement."

"Poor him and lucky me," Niven said as he spread the napkin in his lap. "The life of a priest, burying, marrying, and scaring."

"We have to mind our manners when Father is here," Georgie complained. "But not so much when you're here."

"Feel free to be your unfettered self, Georgie." Niv smiled.

"We're always happy when you can make it to dinner," Gladys told him.

"Thank you. I've had such a rigorous filming schedule. You know how it goes when you're a one-line unfeatured player—you arrive at dawn and leave at midnight like a werewolf. Might as well be a piece of scenery."

"One line isn't very much." Georgie crossed her arms.

"How astute. Will you be my agent, Georgiana? I have a feeling you could do a better job than the one I've got."

"I'm only eleven years old."

"It's never too early to get your mitts on raw talent and turn it into a hamburger."

"I don't think you're a star."

Niv laughed. "Are you sure you haven't been talking to my agent?"

"You're being rude, Georgie," Polly chided as she brought a platter of golden fried chicken to the table.

"A real star wouldn't live in our pool house."

Sally placed a basket of hot biscuits on the table. "A lot you know, Georgie. When the Barrymores arrived in Hollywood, they lived in a tent until they could afford a hotel room, and look at them now. They are the greatest actors in the world, and they live in castles in the Hollywood Hills."

"You owe Mr. Niven an apology," Loretta told her.

"Sorry," said Georgie.

"It's quite all right, Georgiana. I'm incapable of holding a grudge. One of the positive side effects of a pickled brain."

Ruby brought a serving dish of okra to the table. "Sally always leaves the okra. Just because you don't have a taste for it doesn't mean the rest of them don't."

"Sorry, Ruby." Sally passed the okra to Niven.

"Thank you, Ruby. Dinner is delicious," Loretta said, and her sisters chimed in.

"Better than any of the restaurants on the strip, Ruby," Niven agreed.

"Why of course, Sir Niv. I know my talent. But the way you people act, you'd think I only serve food out of the can around here." Ruby sniffed as she returned to the kitchen.

"Oh, no, Ruby," Niven called after her, "we don't take you for granted. I know food out of a can. This is gourmet." Niv looked at Georgie. "That's French for homemade."

"Big deal," Georgie said under her breath.

"Have you thawed out yet?" Niven asked Loretta.

"Almost."

"While you were gone, something wonderful happened, Gretch." Polly turned to her sister. "Carter asked me to marry him."

"Polly! How thrilling!" Loretta hugged her sister.

"We're going to be married. Very small. We'll have a mass at church, then a dinner here at home."

"Do I get to be in the wedding?" Georgie asked.

"Of course."

"I'll have to scrounge up a date," Sally said.

"That won't be hard," Niven told her. "There's always me."

"You won't have to go very far." Georgie reached for the chicken.

"That's right, Georgie. I'll roll out of bed and come in my pajamas."

The girls had a good laugh, but Loretta felt tears sting in her eyes. Her oldest sister was getting married. Carter Hermann and Polly Ann Young would have a high mass at the church; their union, a sacrament, would be blessed by the Holy Roman Church. The good news made Loretta feel worse about her own life, but she wouldn't ruin Polly's moment. Loretta would be happy for her. Polly had done everything right.

11

The top was down on Clark Gable's forest-green Jaguar convertible as he sped under the heavy purple blossoms of the jacaranda trees on Doheny before turning onto Sunset. Loretta lived in close proximity to him, yet he saw her so infrequently that she might as well have been on another continent.

Gable didn't spend much time in solitude, healing his romantic bruises or business dustups. Women of late, however, in all corners of his life, were a source of irritation. Loretta had disappeared from his life since the wrap of *The Call of the Wild*. Minna Wallis, his agent, despite his protestations, had stepped aside after he won the Oscar because she felt he could do better, so Gable had signed with a new agent. Ria was dragging out the separation agreement, which attenuated the divorce proceedings to a crawl.

Clark Gable had regrets.

He flicked his hand-rolled cigarette onto Sunset at the stoplight and took a deep breath. As Gable drove up to the portico of Sunset House in his Duesenberg, Alda waved to him from the front steps.

"Is Gretchen here?" Gable asked through the open window.

"No."

"It's just the mother?"

Alda nodded.

"You want to tell me what's going on?"

"I can't."

"All right. Maybe you want to tell me why Gretchen still won't return my phone calls after she said she would."

"I don't know." Alda looked away, uncomfortable.

"She's back with Tracy, isn't she?"

"No, she isn't."

"Then what's this about?"

"Could you park in the back?" Alda motioned to the service drive off the side of the house. "I'll meet you at the kitchen door."

Gable chuckled to himself. He was making his first entrance into the Young house not through the front door but through the kitchen. If that wasn't a message, he didn't know what was. When it came to Loretta Young, he was on par with the gardener.

Gladys Belzer was waiting for Gable at the kitchen table. When he walked into the room, she immediately understood why her daughter had been captivated by him. While Gladys had seen Clark in the movies, she wasn't prepared for the impact of his presence in person. Gable translated from the silver screen to real life in a Panavision all his own. He resembled John Earle Young, Loretta's father and Gladys's ex-husband. Both men had star quality—but Gable had used his allure to worldwide effect, while John Young used his to seduce the laundress.

"Clark, this is Mrs. Belzer, Loretta's mother."

Gable took Mrs. Belzer's hand and smiled. "It's a pleasure, Mrs. Belzer."

Alda excused herself as Gladys poured Gable a glass of ice tea, and one for herself. He toasted her and took a sip. Gable was well mannered and appeared to be a man who would own up to his responsibilities, unlike Loretta's father, who was cowed by any serious demands made upon him.

"Are you southern, Mrs. Belzer?"

"North Carolina."

"I can tell. Sweet tea."

"Are you from the South?"

"Of a fashion. Southern Ohio."

"Large family?"

"I'm an only child. My father and stepmother live with me now."

"That's a hallmark of southern people. We take home with us wherever we go. We live with our families all of our lives. It's a gift to take care of our parents as they get older."

"It's my responsibility."

"There aren't a lot of young people who feel that way."

"Mrs. Belzer, I have no idea why you called me here today, but if I may, I'd like to share something with you. I've tried to communicate with Gretchen, but she ignores me. She doesn't answer my letters or return my calls. I explained that I was separated from my wife, but that the divorce proceedings were slow going. That's not an excuse, it's a fact."

"How do you feel about my daughter?"

"I'm crazy about her."

"Well, we have a dilemma."

"I'll stop badgering her if she doesn't want me. I get it. I make a lot of movies, and an on-set romance rarely sustains itself once everyone is back home. We're all grown-ups, we understand the game."

Gladys realized that Gable must have told Ria that a romance blossomed on Mount Baker, and that's where she'd gotten the information to sic her press pack on Loretta.

"Your wife came to see me while you were on location."

"I had no idea."

"She accused Gretchen of stealing you away. She wanted me to intervene. Since Gretchen came home, she's been calling her incessantly. She wants her to give an interview and tell the world that you and Gretchen are not in love."

"I will speak to Ria about this." Gable thought about it; perhaps this was the reason Gretchen avoided him.

"Gretchen is getting it from all sides, Mr. Gable. We can navigate it on our end but all of this is beside the point."

"If Gretchen is hurt by my actions, or anyone that I'm associated with, I'm sorry."

"I will tell her. Thank you."

"I'd like to tell her myself." Gable was frustrated with Loretta. He hadn't seen her play games, or hard to get, as they shot *The Call of the Wild*; in fact, he believed she was a straight shooter. The current twist in her behavior made him think that he had pegged her wrong. "But there will come a moment, and it's soon, Mrs. Belzer, that I will stop trying."

"Mr. Gable, she has good reason not to contact you. Gretchen is pregnant with your child."

Stunned, Gable sat for a moment, taking in the information. His mind went clinical whenever he was hit with something so deeply emotional that his heart could not withstand the information to process it. He would appear stoic when inside, his emotions raged. He felt many things in that moment. He had clarity about Loretta; he understood why she might not want to contact him or be seen with him, but he was also afraid of what could happen if Ria found out, and he was sad that he could not be happy about the news due to the circumstances. All of these feelings added up to a state of confusion and frustration.

News of out-of-wedlock pregnancies was nothing new to Gable. He'd been hit with paternity suits, which the studio settled quietly and efficiently, the same way he exited most of his love affairs. But this was different; he cared. This should have been joyful news because he loved Loretta.

Gable stood up, went to the sink, and looked out the window. He was a married man with a wife who refused to let him go. He had married a woman beyond her childbearing years; there was no possibility of a baby of his own with her, and he'd known that when he married her. He had three stepchildren with Ria, and was, in his fashion, good with them. Gable had settled on the notion that if there were to be children of his own, they would come in the future, down the line when his career had ebbed, after he had milked Hollywood for all he could, and could leave it altogether with enough cash to last the rest of his life. He had a simple dream. Gable planned to buy a ranch and farm, raise children, love their mother, and be happy. Ria was not a part of his long-term picture.

Gable leaned against the sink. "Gretchen was married. I thought she knew how to protect herself."

"If I had to guess, I would say that neither of you was thinking clearly on Mount Baker. And as for protection, we're Catholic."

"I know all about that, Mrs. Belzer," Gable said wearily. "Where we take our communion doesn't do us much good now."

"No, I suppose it doesn't. What do you propose we do?"

"What can I do? I'm still married to Ria. My lawyer tells me that I have to remain separated from her for a year, and beyond that, the divorce could take another two years."

"So your answer is nothing."

"Mrs. Belzer, you've just hit me with an enormous bit of news. I am trying to figure out what to do—not so much what to say to you, but what to do."

Gladys looked at him. "You agree that we have to keep this situation private."

"Absolutely."

"You must not tell anyone. Your wife calls here constantly, and we ignore her. She must not find out about the baby."

"She won't."

"We have a plan."

"What is it?"

"She'll finish her work on *The Crusades*, and then we'll go to Europe."

"She'll have the baby there?"

"We'll tell the press that she's been working nonstop since she was four years old, and she's exhausted. Our physician will diagnose her with an illness. We'll stay in Europe long enough for any rumors to die down."

Gable was frustrated. He wanted to do something, but he wasn't sure what. Loretta had sidelined him; he felt powerless. "Is there anything I can do?"

"I don't know." Gladys eyes filled with tears. "I would rather that you were my son-in-law and that this had happened within the sacrament of marriage. I want to be happy about this—I want the whole family to be happy."

"I'm sorry, Mrs. Belzer."

"Gretchen has a big heart. I knew it would get her in trouble some-day, but I never thought this would be the trouble."

———————

The blue sky over Bel Air was strewn with wispy clouds that floated overhead like white feathers. The light streamed through the trees behind Sunset House in threads of gold. David Niven sighed as he looked out the window of the pool house, sad to leave the place that had been home as he transitioned from a day-rate extra to an employed actor with an agent and a brand-new studio contract.

David Niven had enjoyed his time in the Belzer/Young compound. He had been comfortable, his laundry washed and pressed, his room kept spotless. Hot meals were on time and delicious, and when he took them in the dining room, Niv was surrounded by gorgeous women. The pool house was his notion of Shangri-la.

As he folded the last of his clothing into his suitcase, Loretta knocked on the door.

"Must you go?" Loretta sat down on the bed, surveying Niv's belongings.

"I must. Merle Oberon has a terrible temper, and she has decided that I can no longer retain my membership in the YB Sorority. She thinks there's a conflict of interest between my friendship with you and her sexual needs. She can't understand how I live here and keep things platonic. And frankly, neither can I."

"You have to go, then."

"Either that or she'll kill my family. My sister Grizel can be a pain in the arse, but death is too steep a punishment for a lousy personality, myopia bordering on blindness, and a congenital neediness."

Loretta laughed. "Poor Grizel."

"Don't worry about her. Worry about Merle. I live in fear of her, you know. She's a pistol, and she owns several. I do what I'm told. She insists I move to the beach and live with the boys—too much temptation at Sunset House for her liking. She'd rather me live with a couple of actors. Thinks I'll be safe."

"Will you?"

"Of a stripe. I'm hoping it will be fun. I'll be pickled by autumn, but I will have a roof over my head."

Loretta began to cry. Niv dropped his pressed shirt and went to her.

"Oh, no, you're not in love with me too?"

Loretta laughed through her tears.

Niv knelt next to her and took her hand. "Is this going to be one of those awful Jeanette MacDonald farewell scenes with all the weeping and none of the screwing? Must I sing my way out of your pain?"

Loretta wiped away her tears. "No, no."

"What can I do for you, my dear girl?"

Loretta laughed.

"Why in God's name is that funny to you?"

"It just is, David. Your eyes. They get like big blue golfballs when you care."

"Big and bulging like a blowfish. Hmm. That's attractive." Niven stood and went back to his packing.

"Will you be my friend always?"

"You don't even have to ask. You have been so kind to me, Gretchen, it's as if I was your long-lost brother. And the irony is: you already have a long-lost brother, that phantom Jackie. So you see, I take my role in your life very seriously."

"I've gotten myself into some trouble."

"Go to confession. It's the only reason to be Catholic. You have the joy of sin and the instant relief of contrition. What a system!"

"I'm serious. I'm in trouble."

"I hope you stole. Stealing is one of the great sins. You get something out of it, and the theft itself is an art form, like a dance. What did you take? You were on loan to Warner's recently. Let me guess. A bracelet from Bette Davis's paste collection? You could have done better. Bette isn't known for her jewelry."

"No, nothing like that. It involves your friend, Mr. Gable."

"What is it?"

"I'm having his baby."

Niven, who could find the humor in any situation, suddenly couldn't. He was speechless, sobered by the news because he knew what this meant to Loretta.

"You must keep this secret until you die," she said softly.

"I will." Niven sat down.

"I trust you because you've been loyal and kept my secrets."

"And you mine."

"And I always will."

"What are you going to do?" Niven need not list the options. Young women in Hollywood terminated their pregnancies, or they hid for the duration, had the baby, and later gave it up for adoption, or they had a shotgun wedding. The choices in an out-of-wedlock pregnancy were very clear-cut; everyone knew them, and every girl had to choose, or the choice was made for her.

"My family keeps asking me what I'm going to do, when in fact it's already done."

"What are you going to do, Gretch?"

"I'm going to have the baby."

"Your sisters?"

"Pol and Sally cried. We won't tell Georgie."

"Does Clark know?"

"My mother told him."

"How did he react?"

"He says he loves me. David, even if he does, he's married. Ria won't let him go."

"She'll have to."

"It won't happen. Besides, he's moved on."

"Elizabeth Allan means nothing to him."

"There are others."

"There will always be others. Hollywood is a candy store, and everybody is wearing a topcoat of powdered sugar. You can't take it personally, Gretchen."

"I want a man who will love me and be true."

"Oh, dear, that only happens in the movies. Wait. I know of one exception. I believe there is one man in Encino who has been faithful to his wife, and he died at the age of twenty-two after six hours of marriage. They consummated their union, he had a massive heart attack, and that was that."

Loretta laughed. "Is it that bad?"

"Worse. I'm a man, so I can vouch for it. So how are you going to do this?"

"I don't know. My sisters will be there for me. Mama. But can I count on you if I need you?"

"For anything. You have my heart and my life. Gable is my good friend."

"He just plays the tough guy. He's really very sweet. He'll need a good friend. Will you look out for him?"

"I can do that."

"You see, I love him, but I can't be with him. It will ruin everything. Our careers would be over. I can't risk it, and neither can he."

"Wait, Gretchen. The studios are powerful. They can get him a quickie divorce."

"We signed morals clauses."

"Oh, you can rip those up."

"Maybe he could—he would be forgiven, but not me. They'd run me out of town. I can't afford to lose my job. I have too many people who rely on me. I have to work. Mama and I will figure out the logistics. Alda will help us."

Niv put his arms around Loretta. "My dear girl, I will keep your secret, if you will do something for me."

Loretta looked at him.

"You mustn't tell anyone I slept with your cook Ruby. It was one of those things. She was lonely. And yes, I was lonely. We could hear the pool filter. It stirred us up. It gurgled, she gurgled, and I gurgled."

"Oh, David." Loretta laughed.

"I have to go, you see. Merle's temper is one thing, but Ruby is worse. She makes a terrible spurned lover. She wants to kill me with saturated fat."

"Well, then, you have no choice."

"Precisely."

———

The *Ile de France* sailed out of New York Harbor, skimming the surface of the Hudson River like a delicate leaf. The art deco ocean liner was the chic cigarette case of transatlantic travel, sleek, simple, and gleaming with accents of gold brass. Painted white, trimmed in navy blue, with vivid red smokestacks, it was not only a celebration of the colors of France but the essence of its style.

Loretta stood on her balcony on the top deck as Alda unpacked inside the suite. Loretta looked back at Manhattan, its skyscrapers glistening in shades of silver against a purple sky. Loretta had dreamed of New York City, and now it was already behind her. Gladys brought Loretta a cup of tea on the balcony.

"Mama, where are we going?"

"We're going to land in Le Havre, and then I'll cross the channel to England and you'll go on to Italy."

Gladys put her arm around Loretta's waist. "You didn't mean the boat, did you?"

Loretta shook her head.

"You take it one day at a time and do your best."

"That's what you told me about acting."

"You took that small piece of advice and turned it into an industry. That's all well and good. Your career is important because you built it. But now you're building something new. This baby will be the greatest love you've ever known."

"But I'm not giving him a father."

"Don't start his life by listing all the things he won't have."

"I can't help it. Why did this happen to me, Mama? There must be a reason. Please don't say it's God's plan."

"But it must be."

"I prayed to fall in love with a good man who would marry me, and we'd have a family."

"A woman is either lucky in love or work."

"But not both. I fell in love with a man just like Daddy."

"Most women do. Why don't you write to Clark? He's made a nuisance of himself trying to see you and talk to you. He told me he was happy when you were together. Were you happy on Mount Baker?"

"Mama, I forgot about everything when I was up there. I couldn't remember home, I didn't want to. I don't know how to describe it. And I was so cold."

Gladys put her arms around her daughter. "That's why there are so many babies in the world. It's called winter."

———

The night before the ship was to land in Le Havre, Loretta couldn't sleep. She left her mother and Alda in the suite and went out onto her balcony. She looked out over the breadth of the black ocean. The lights from the ship threw silver beams of light out on to the water that looked like oars. A full moon, icy white, hung low in the sky. It was as if the ship was heading for it, and would break through it like a stage curtain. The ship could not move fast enough for her as it crossed the Atlantic. Loretta wanted to get there, to someplace new, to see her life from a different perspective. Maybe she would find some wisdom there.

Loretta knew she should answer Clark's letters but she couldn't. It wasn't about whether she loved him or not, as her mother insisted, but whether their lives could ever amount to anything outside the few weeks they spent on Mount Baker. Last winter, she had all of his attention, and he had hers. But as soon as the train pulled into Los Angeles at the end of *The Call of the Wild*, it was clear to her that she had lost him.

A place has as much to do with the choices people make as the people themselves.

Gable behaved a certain way in Los Angeles; he was a movie star, entitled to all the perks that life provides, including willing women. Loretta knew she didn't stand a chance against that mighty system. She had seen great actresses who came before her try and fail.

Loretta believed Clark was persistent because she had rejected him. The moment she pulled him in, held him close, and needed him, he would be gone with the likes of Joan or Jean or Connie. He was a man who loved women, and she knew that always meant more than one.

The night air was cold and salty and clean. Loretta breathed deeply, something Spence had taught her to calm her nerves before a scene. But it worked in life, as it did on the sound stage. It was difficult to leave her work life behind, even for a few months. Loretta longed for it already. It had been her purpose since she was four years old; it wasn't a habit or a way to make a living or even her identity, her work was part of her.

As she filled her lungs with breath, it soothed her anxiety. If she was to be alone on this path, she planned to cleave to her baby, give him a life so rich and full, he wouldn't miss his father. After all, she had done all right without one. Her son would too. Something told her she would have a son. She just knew it.

———

When Loretta saw Italy for the first time, the rolling hills of the Veneto were a soft moss green, tinged gold on the horizon in the late-afternoon light. The Italian sun flickered behind the trees as the sky turned apricot. The train chuffed along over low hills, passing a long, shallow stream that looked like a blue velvet ribbon.

"A few more minutes, and we'll be there," Alda said quietly, looking out the window.

"You're nervous." Loretta reached for Alda's hand. Despite the heat, her hand was cold and clammy.

"I haven't been home in eight years. I was a girl when I left Padua."

"They'll remember you," Loretta teased.

"I hope so."

"Come on. Don't you want to see your father and your mother and your brothers?"

Alda nodded.

"So why aren't you happy?"

Alda searched for her handkerchief.

"Are they tears of joy? Maybe they're tears of joy," Loretta reasoned. "I can't wait to see all the places you told me about. I can't wait to watch your father make grappa. I thought you'd be thrilled to finally get home."

The train pulled into the station in Padua. Alda dropped the window glass and peered out. She found her family on the platform.

"Alda bella!" her mother called to her. Alda's three brothers crossed the platform. They were younger than their sister, but slender and small, like her. Alda's father had a head of thick red hair with touches of gray. He was about five-nine, muscular and trim. He lifted Alda off the steps to the platform, then helped Loretta off the train.

Alda's mother was a birdlike brunette with black eyes. She wept as she held her daughter after so many years. The connection between the two of them made Loretta cry, and think of her own mother.

Soon Alda and her mother were talking over one another, rattling off news in Italian so rapid, it reminded Loretta of Bill Wellman, and how he'd shout "double time" when the actors delivered their lines to make them speak faster.

Loretta heard Luca's name. "He's an outstanding man," Loretta told them. Alda happily translated.

Loretta understood Alda's apprehension now that she observed the reunion of her family. All families are broken to some extent, by grief and time; her own by divorce and abandonment; Alda's by a calling that was wholly spiritual, but had caused hurt to her mother and father. Loretta wondered if anyone got it right. Would she?

Alda gave her brothers a box of Hershey chocolate bars. They hugged their sister, gathered the luggage, and loaded it into a pushcart.

"Do you mind if we walk from here?" Alda asked. "Our house is not very far."

Loretta followed the Ducci family through Padua into the old town. The winding cobblestone streets were lined with stucco houses painted in bright, hard candy colors, topped with clay roofs the color of cinnamon. Signore Ducci led his family under the porticoes festooned with hanging baskets of poppies.

Alda stopped and pointed to the complex of ancient sandstone buildings that housed the University of Padua, where Galileo taught.

As they passed the Basilica of Saint Anthony, Loretta stopped. "May we go in?"

Alda pushed the thick wooden door open. As they entered the church, light streamed into the nave through the stained-glass windows above them. The late-afternoon light danced off the Byzantine mosaics, intricate stonework composed of tiny squares of gold, ruby red, and green that Loretta had only seen in books.

The scent of beeswax and incense had soothed Loretta since she was a small child; she'd always found serenity in church. She genuflected before the altar. No matter the country, the interior of her church was a constant: the tabernacle and altar, the shrines and statuary, were just where they should be. Loretta had a sense of belonging inside a church: it could be incredibly ornate and filled with art, or a chapel with a simple bench and cross, it didn't matter; she was in a place so familiar it was home.

The Duccis lived in an apartment over a leather shop on Via Agostina. The stairs to the second floor were obscured by the waxy green leaves of a lemon tree. Mrs. Ducci had placed a series of terra-cotta pots up the stairs, which spilled over with bright red geraniums and a plant with lacy green leaves. Loretta felt welcome, and the small signs of beauty that she saw everywhere reminded her that she was there to rest and reflect, to seek deeper meaning in her travails.

Loretta was given Alda's bedroom, while Alda moved into her brothers'. The boys were to stay in the apartment behind the leather store. No amount of arguing would convince Mrs. Ducci to change her mind. Loretta would have been fine at a hotel or pensione, but the Duccis would have none of it. Loretta made a final fuss about being a bother, but Mrs. Ducci stood with her hands on her hips and wouldn't budge until Loretta agreed to stay with them. Mrs. Ducci reminded her of DeMille—an implacable leader incapable of executing an alternate plan—so Loretta did what any obedient actress would do: she acquiesced.

The Ducci family wanted to repay her for the kindnesses she had shown their daughter. Loretta soon learned this was the Italian way, to offer the gift of themselves and their home, and in fact, there was no higher honor. Loretta followed Signora Ducci into the room that would be hers for the summer.

A simple bed, nightstand, and chair were the furnishings, so plain they reminded Loretta of a convent cell. Perhaps familiarity was one of the reasons Alda had become a nun. There was a window that, when unlatched, swung out to reveal a side street lined in cobblestone. From Alda's window, Loretta had a spectacular view of the town. She could see the rooftops of Padua, the soft orange tiles softened by the fringes of green of rooftop gardens, smattered with shocks of color from the lemons and blood oranges growing on trees, and grapes nestled in their vines on mottled gray trellises. In the distance Loretta could see the hills of the Veneto rolling out in waves of pale green.

If this window was the only the view Loretta had of Italy, she would be satisfied. It was the change of her view that mattered: she hoped to find a new perspective, one that would help her cope and help her look at the world differently. She wanted to be happy again and to look at the world as she always had, with a sense of wonder. Under the circumstances, this was her most difficult challenge, and it was exhausting. Loretta lay down on the bed and went to sleep. She did not wake until the following morning.

The outdoor market in Padua's grand piazza was a carnival of delicious scents and local delicacies, the harvest of the Italian countryside gathered under sunny yellow awnings by local vendors. Baskets filled with sunflowers tied in massive bouquets were sold next to silver bins of fresh white mozzarella in icy clear water. A white canopy threw shade over a display of freshly caught silver fish with blue eyes, the catch that brought the most haggling from customers, while salami hung from the overhead beam of the portico like stalactites, marked with their prices. There were braids of fresh bread, bright green bouquets of chicory, basil, and parsley, and a slab of *torrone* taffy that looked like a giant square of Italian marble. The purveyor cut off pieces and wrapped them in paper as the children of Padua stood in line. The vegetables were works of art: white mushrooms on nests of green, baskets of tomatoes, white onions that looked like pearls, and fruit, blood oranges and pale green pears, sweet and fragrant. Craving sweets, Loretta bought a bag of blood oranges, and as she walked, she peeled an orange and ate it.

Loretta had avoided the open market in Padua when she first arrived, but a month into their stay in Italy, with her pregnancy over the halfway mark, she was no longer sensitive to the pungent scents of the spices, fruits, vegetables, and flowers as she strolled through with Alda.

Soldiers dressed head to toe in black moved through the crowd. The locals turned away, and kept to their business. Loretta had begun to pick up a few words of Italian, and attempted to read the newspapers. She read about the Blackshirts, volunteer soldiers in the Italian army who backed Mussolini and his Fascists.

Loretta overheard conversations about Il Duce, but typical of Italians, the Duccis cared less for politics than those things that affected *la tavola*, their own kitchen table. Mussolini was a character. The Italians Loretta met through the Ducci family looked upon him as a cartoon, extreme in appearance, dramatic in presentation, and more performer than statesman. Whenever Loretta saw him in the papers, he posed like he was standing for a portrait. Big, big ego like a studio mogul, Loretta thought.

Loretta helped Signora Ducci set the table for dinner. Alda stirred the sauce on the stove. Sweet garlic simmered in butter as Alda squeezed the juice of a lemon into the pan. The lemon danced on the butter. Loretta was always hungry, but the scent of the fresh sauce made her stomach growl.

"I saw the Blackshirts in town today."

"They're everywhere," Alda said as she stirred fresh peas into the sauce.

"What does your family think about Mussolini?"

The mention of Il Duce's name stopped Signora Ducci cold. She looked at Alda, who explained Loretta's question.

"My mother doesn't like him because she thinks he's a braggart and will send her sons to war. No one takes him too seriously."

"They should."

"There's nothing to be afraid of," Alda insisted.

"One time I was at a dinner party in Beverly Hills. I was seated next to Edna Ferber, the novelist."

"I've read her books. What did she look like?"

"You know the ladies that work security at the studios? Like that. She was slim, with gray hair, brushed back simply. She wore a wool suit with a high collar. It was belted. Walking shoes. Everything she wore was expensive, but plain."

"That's exactly how I pictured her."

"She told me something that has stayed with me. Ferber said, 'Beware the clowns.' The leaders who start out as jokes—people make fun of them, they're caricatures, cartoons in newspapers, and people decide they are harmless. Those men are the most dangerous. The day comes when they use their power against their own people."

Alda could sense the changes in Italy. Some were subtle, small freedoms taken away, silly laws enforced, banking hours shortened—the kind of government that affects working people. She did not think much of it that summer, as her thoughts were elsewhere. The mood of Italy, however, one of distrust, made her long for America. Alda was surprised how much she missed it—or maybe it was her longing for Luca.

————

Loretta Young the Movie Star went unrecognized in Padua. She didn't bother to wear lipstick or the new dresses she had packed; instead she blended in as she wore the fashions of the locals, long cotton madras skirts with elastic waists to accommodate the growing baby, flowing blouses, and flat sandals for comfort.

As long as she stayed hidden in Padua, Loretta could protect her image in America while living her life in full in Europe. If she were honest, Loretta would admit that she enjoyed her anonymity in Italy that summer, and didn't. She was an actress who lived for the audience. When she chose roles, she considered them; when she turned a part down, she'd say, "Not for my audience."

Gladys called Loretta to tell her she was hounded everywhere she went in London by press seeking information about Loretta's illness. Gladys spun a tale that Loretta was in an undisclosed location in a hospital, recuperating. If anyone outside of the family and their circle suspected Loretta was hiding in Italy, they didn't let on. The summer of 1935 would be the template for how information about Loretta and Clark's baby would be handled going forward. The Young family would throw off the press by fabricating stories.

Alda stood at the swinging silver scale in the last booth of the open market as the vendor shoveled blackberries into the scoop to weigh them. Loretta sat on a nearby bench with her eyes closed and her face to the sun. Loretta enjoyed the daily ritual of going to market; when their time in Padua was done, she might miss this the most.

———————

Alda looked over at her boss and thought she was at her most alluring. Loretta's skin was tawny from the Italian sun, her full cheeks pink and robust, and her figure had filled out into a soft womanly form. While Loretta's present figure was lovely in life, it wouldn't work on camera, nor would it stand up to the scrutiny, standards, and measurements of Hollywood costumers.

Alda provided the vendor with a starched muslin cloth for the fruit, and the vendor filled it with the berries, twisted it with a top knot, and handed it to her. Alda placed the berries in the basket, and was turning to Loretta to motion to her to move on when she saw a man walking under the portico behind the market, where the sun made shards of gold light through arches striped with dark shadows.

Alda dropped her basket.

"Alda!" Loretta went to help.

When the man under the portico heard the name, he turned to face Alda, who looked away as soon as their eyes met.

Loretta picked up the basket. "The berries are fine. Are you okay?" She handed Alda the basket. "Alda, are you all right?"

"We must go," Alda said.

"Why?"

Alda didn't answer. Loretta looked around and saw the man from the portico—in his late twenties, tall and slim, with sandy curls, brown eyes, and Greco-Italianate features—walking toward them purposefully. A smile broke across his face as he came closer to them. Loretta looked at Alda and then at the young man, back and forth, trying to make sense of the situation.

"Alda?" The man put his arms around her. Alda blushed.

"Enrico. *Come stai?*"

Enrico stood back and took Alda in appreciatively.

Alda had blossomed into a lovely, sophisticated woman since going to work for Loretta. The days of cutting her own hair were over when Loretta pushed Alda into the beauty chair in her dressing room on the studio lot. LaWanda had taught Alda simple makeup. Her thick eyebrows had been arched and shaped and filled in with a waxy charcoal stick. Her lips were lined in soft pink, and a dusting of powder on her cheeks made her brown eyes sparkle. Alda's wardrobe was no longer composed of hand-me-downs from the Young sisters' closets, but custom designed, her suits fitted at the studio. On this day, her trim figure was lovely in a pink gingham skirt and a flowing white blouse, and she wore gold hoop earrings her husband had given her. With the gold band on her hand, that was all she needed to be chic.

"*Ciao, mi chiamo Gretchen*," Loretta said from behind her sunglasses. She extended her hand and they exchanged pleasantries, but Enrico didn't take his eyes off Alda.

"I'm going to take these berries home," Loretta said softly to Alda.

"No, no, I'll go with you."

"No, you stay with your friend. I'll see you later."

Loretta walked through the market. She turned to look back at Alda and Enrico. The cacophony of the market, with its busy proprietors and eager customers, faded away like the words on the pages in a book flipping in a breeze. It seemed that Alda and Enrico were alone in the center of Padua, facing one another in the pink light.

"I thought I'd never see you again," Enrico began. "I spent a lot of time in church on Feast Days when the nuns of Saint Vincent prepared the church. I imagined I'd see you there."

"I didn't become a nun."

"I can see that." He smiled.

"I stayed in America and got a job."

"Where?"

"Hollywood."

"So the cars, the airplanes, the riches, turned your head."

"No, the nuns threw me out."

"That can't be!"

"Oh, it's true." Alda found herself burying her left hand in the pocket of her skirt, hiding her wedding ring. She recalled her nun's habit with the deep pockets, which put her in the frame of mind to confess. "I was a postulant for three years, then a novice, and when it came time to say my final vows, I was let go. Mother Superior didn't think I was suited, so I became a secretary."

"Ah." Enrico smiled at her. "You were busy answering other people's letters; that's why you never answered mine. You forgot about me."

"I couldn't." Alda blushed. "I didn't."

"How long have you been here?"

"Most of the summer."

"Why didn't you come and find me?"

"I'm busy with my family." It was true; she enjoyed spending time with her mother, helping her father in the fields and her brothers in the shop. She looked after Loretta. Alda had returned to the place that defined the perimeter of her heart, which for so long had been filled with love for her family and for Enrico. This was her heart before she left Italy, before she met Luca. She had changed.

The long summer had not been good for her marriage. Every letter from Luca implored her to come home. He had written that he was "no good alone," and she wondered what that meant. His letters were brief and needy. Her husband was an artist, therefore he was impulsive and self-involved. Patience was not Luca Chetta's virtue.

"Alda, I have something that I've longed to ask you."

"All right."

"Why did you run away?"

"There was no place for me here. I couldn't stay. It would hurt my family. My father had just taken over the vineyard."

"I remember." Enrico crossed his arms over his chest. "We made a scandal."

"I had hurt them enough." Alda and Enrico had been brazen. They had stolen away together overnight. When Signora Ducci found her daughter missing, she went to the police, who put out a search party and found her the next afternoon with Enrico. He was ordered home, while she, in shame, returned to her family.

"We all hurt," he said. "I had hoped to marry you."

"Do you believe that we could have made a life together then?"

"My mother was seventeen when she married," he offered.

"Your mother is a better woman than me." Alda smiled.

Enrico grinned at Alda. She had never seen a more appealing smile, not even in Hollywood. Time had no bearing on her heart's desire; she remembered everything about their time together; including the terrible ending, when she disappeared from his life. At the time, she had no choice. Alda would have no part of ruining his life or his good family name, once her own had been compromised. She planned to keep their child together a secret. She bore the grief alone when their son was stillborn.

Enrico still had the carefree countenance of the young man she remembered while she, having suffered the worst grief, did not. Nothing in the world would make her tell him the truth about what really happened; the only gift she had to give him was a clear conscience.

A striking young brunette carrying a newborn in her arms herded three other children under the age of five to the fountain where other children were splashing about. "Enrico!" she hollered. "*Andiamo!*"

"I'm coming, Vera," he said.

"Your wife and children." Alda's hopes sank, and she wasn't sure why. Surely she knew that Enrico would move on, as she had. But it was the children, four of them, who reminded her of all she didn't have.

"You should go."

"I would like to see you. We could make an arrangement." He looked off at his wife, who was busy with the children. "Let's make a plan."

"I can't."

"You don't want to?"

"I'm married to a brilliant Italian American artist named Luca Chetta." Alda's hand with her wedding band found its way out of her pocket. She brushed her hair off her face in the breeze.

"You found an Italian in America."

"It's not so hard to do. There are thousands of them."

"You have children?" Enrico asked.

"Not yet."

"You must have babies. It helps."

Alda said good-bye as Enrico went to his wife, lifting one son on one hip and his daughter on the other. Alda took a final look at her first lover as he kissed his children. She was so pleased for him. That's how Alda knew she really loved Enrico; she wanted his happiness more than her own. As for their son, Michael would remain in her heart and memory; she would bear the burden of his loss alone. It was her gift to her first love.

———————

The Scrovegni Chapel was tucked in a corner of Padua like a forgotten book on a shelf. Loretta pushed the door open and was met with a rush of cool air. The interior shutters were latched closed to protect the paintings and antiquities from the light. Loretta blessed herself with the holy water and knelt in a pew behind a marble pillar, taken in by the fresco before her. In glorious swirls of emerald green, coral, and gold, Giotto had painted scenes from the life of Jesus and Mary as though he were telling the story of any mother and son.

The door creaked behind her, and Loretta turned to see Alda entering the church. Alda did not see Loretta; she walked up the side aisle to the shrine of Mary, knelt, and then buried her face in her hands and wept. Loretta left the pew and joined Alda, kneeling next to her.

"Who was that man?" Loretta whispered.

"I was in love with him."

"Did he break your heart?"

"I broke his."

"Then he should be the one crying."

"I didn't leave Padua to be a nun."

"I don't understand."

"Enrico and I had a baby. He was stillborn. I never told him."

Loretta finally understood Alda's need for solitude and silence. Loretta had mistaken them for vestiges of Alda's life in the convent, but now knew why Alda needed to feel separate from the world from time to time. She assumed that Alda missed her family and Italy. Now she understood the depth of Alda's pain, or at least she could relate to it, now that she was going to be a mother.

"After I had the baby, I couldn't stay here. I was just a girl, and I didn't know what to do. The Sisters of Saint Vincent took me. I wanted to go as far away from Padua as I could. I wanted to forget what happened."

"I'm so sorry about your baby."

"I thought time would heal me, but it can't. Nothing ever will."

"Why didn't you tell me?"

"I couldn't. Especially after Mount Baker."

"And my pregnancy." Loretta patted Alda's hand. "Now I understand why you know so much about having babies. I thought it was your work experience at Saint Elizabeth's that made you so knowledgeable, but the truth is, you lived it."

"You never stop living it."

"Does Luca know?"

"He's been very kind. You know, at first he wasn't, but he's grown up too. I guess we all have."

If Loretta had any lingering doubts about keeping her baby, they were gone by the time she and Alda left the chapel. Perhaps the timing was wrong for her baby, but now that she had seen what happens to a girl who loses a child, Loretta decided to embrace whatever joy she could. Of course, that was easy enough in Italy, where her life was her own. It would be a different story when she returned to California. No matter what, Loretta was determined to control the story. She would write her own happy ending.

———

Lago Maria Lufrano was a pristine navy-blue lake, bordered by soft willows, in the forest near Padua. The road that led to the lake was hemmed on either side by tall reeds of green. Alda juggled the picnic basket as Loretta walked beside her.

"Have you heard from Luca?"

"Long nights of prep for *Mutiny on the Bounty*."

The mention of the movie stung Loretta. She knew Gable was the leading man, though he'd fought the studio not to do the part. They were filming in Monterey—Gable had gotten David Niven a job on the picture as an extra, and he'd sent her a long letter

"Maybe Luca can steal away at the end of the picture."

"Maybe. Have you heard from Mr. Gable?"

"He knows I'm here. Sally included a stack of letters he sent to me in an envelope that arrived a couple days ago."

"Have you read them?"

"They make me sad. I stand in your window, with your view of the world, and I read. The view makes up for the news in the letters. Ria won't give him a divorce, but we knew that would happen. This could go on for years." Loretta pulled a branch off the tree and swung it as they walked, tickling the tops of the wild ferns that grew along the side of the road. "For as many women as Mr. Gable has known in his life, he has learned not one thing about what makes them tick."

"What will you do?"

"What we always do. We figure it out alone. If I wasn't an actress I could hide. But there's something wrong about that. I'm ashamed of myself but proud of this baby—how can that be possible? But it is."

"I understand! It's life. You never thought you could be so happy and so sad at the same time. When I found out I was expecting, my grandmother wanted me to stay in Padua. She said she could help me raise the baby. She'd make me fresh ricotta every morning. She made sure I ate eggs and greens and oranges—all the things that make you grow. And for about a month of my pregnancy, I actually thought, I'll move in with Nonna, and we'll do this. But I couldn't do that to her. Nothing good comes from women who have babies out of wedlock—not in Italy. Not without money and connections. It was impossible."

"May I meet your Nonna?"

"She passed away last year. A few months before I left Saint Elizabeth's."

"I'm sorry."

Loretta and Alda sat on the banks of Lago Maria Lufrano, the lake hidden like a jewel in the deep green forest of the Veneto. Alda slipped into the lake and swam out, barely making a ripple in the water with her even strokes. Alda floated on her back. The blue sky overhead shimmered like lapis. Each morning as the sun rose, she walked over the hill to Michael's grave. It soothed her.

Loretta watched her, dangling her legs off the pier into the cool water. Alda swam over to her.

"You know, Luca is keeping an eye on Mr. Gable. They're on Catalina Island."

"One of my favorite things about Italy is that there are no fan magazines here, not ones I can read anyway."

"Luca says that Mr. Gable goes to bed early every night."

"Alone?"

"Very much so." Alda swam out into the blue.

Alda had a way of making any news from America seem better than it was. The sun was low, like a ripe peach, throwing light on the blue ripples on the surface of the lake. Loretta closed her eyes. She was at peace, and held on to the serenity that was all around her. She liked the idea of Clark Gable longing for her, but she need not travel far to be near him. She placed her hand on her stomach, on their growing baby, and in an instant, he was with her.

———

Franchot Tone, the elegant, well-bred actor with an eager smile and the confidence of an East Coast education, lay on the pier of Catalina Island, the sun turning his skin a golden brown. Gable was fishing off the end of the pier.

"I love a day off," Franchot said.

"Nothing like it."

"What are we doing for dinner?"

"Niven is making plans. And that's a good thing, because I'm not going to catch anything off this pier. This bay might as well be filled with concrete."

David Niven jogged down the pier toward them. He was resplendent in white tennis shorts, a matching pristine polo, and tennis shoes.

"Here he is," Gable said, keeping his eyes on the water. "The white knight."

Niven joined them. "I just got another job on the picture."

"Get you." Franchot Tone sat up and shielded his eyes.

"Not only am I an extra in the torture scenes, thank you Mr. Gable, I am now delivering the mail, which is a torture all its own."

"In this light, you're causing glare," Gable said. "Tennis whites should only be worn on the court."

"I think he looks like an angel," Franchot added.

"You would." Gable chuckled.

Niven handed Gable a letter. "They call me 'Director of Communications.'"

"I bet they do." Gable smiled. "The longer the title, the less you get paid."

"Is it a summons?" Franchot asked.

"You're a card," Gable grumbled. "My luck, I'm getting sued." Gable looked at the return address: Padua, Italia. He stuffed it into his pocket.

"Aren't you going to read it?" Niven asked.

"Not in front of you."

"I don't have x-ray vision," Niven said.

"You never know." Gable yanked on the fishing line.

"If I did, I wouldn't use it to read your mail. I'd find a more pervy purpose for the skill."

"How's Mr. Laughton treating you?" Franchot asked Niven. "Does he bite your hand when you deliver his mail?"

"Well, he doesn't kiss it, if that's what you're asking." Niven shrugged.

"I'd like him to look me in the eye when we're acting in a scene," Gable complained.

"Tell him," Franchot said.

"You tell him," Gable said.

"Gentlemen, this is a dilemma with a very obvious solution. I beg you, let me be of service, because it seems that's all I'm good for in Hollywood," Niven began. "Mr. Laughton is jealous of you, Clark, green-pickle jealous. He looks at you across the deck of the *Bounty* with disdain, not because you're an awful human being, or a great actor . . ."

"Thanks a lot," Gable joked.

" . . . but because you're a handsome man with a trim waist and a fat paycheck, all of which he covets, all of which he can't get because he looks like a potato and can't stop eating them."

"You're a cold Englishman, Niven." Franchot laughed. "Clark looks better in a ponytail. You left that out."

"I hate the ponytail," Gable complained. "And I miss my mustache."

"I found your mustache on a lovely barmaid in Pismo Beach last night."

"I'll bet you did." Gable laughed.

"It barely tickled. Felt like a tease, really."

"Niv has everything figured out, including how not to be lonely on location." Tone was impressed.

"You must become adept at psychology if you're going to survive in pictures. I learned this bitter lesson from Mr. Gable."

"Gable has everybody figured out. Me? Not so much." Franchot flipped his body toward the sun. "Show business is rough."

"Mr. Tone, you are correct. Show business is for swabs. Therefore, I have an announcement to make. I am going back to university to become a doctor, so in the event that I lose my mind in the pursuit of fame and fortune and attractive women, I will have something to fall back on—the ability to give myself my own lobotomy."

Loretta had to stoop to enter the cellar where Signore Ducci made his grappa. The space was so small, only two people could fit. She descended the makeshift ladder down into the dark.

Signore lit a small oil lamp. The scent of dank earth and sweet grapes surrounded them. Loretta could see rows of wooden barrels along the wall, with spigots and stoppers. Signore had written symbols in chalk on the barrels.

"Grappa," Signore said as he swished a sample in a small round glass. "Taste."

Loretta took a small taste of grappa. It was bitter, strong, and left the taste of tobacco. As a smoker, Loretta liked it.

"You're the first woman to like grappa."

"How is it made?"

"It's the skins of the grape, the seeds, and the stems. Any part that is thrown away to make wine, we put aside for the grappa. Grappa is life. You use everything to make it, all the things that no one wants, that no one can use, we use. Everything in life, whether sweet or bitter, ends up in the glass."

When Loretta thought about Italy, she would remember grappa, the drink made from the parts of the grape that no one wanted.

————

Gable undressed to shower before dinner. As he folded his trousers to hang them in the closet, the letter from Padua fell out. It was the first he had received from Loretta, after all the ones he had sent to her, and frankly, he was steamed. He wasn't used to women ignoring him, especially one he had feelings for. He opened the letter, and was surprised when it was from Alda.

> *Dear Mr. Gable,*
>   *I hope you are well. I am writing to tell you that Gretchen is in good health, and blossoming under the Paduan sun. We plan to return home in early September, and hope we will see you then.*
>   *Yours truly,*
>   *Alda*
>   *P.S. Please keep an eye on my Luca and your Chet.*

————

If Luca thought that painting a Yukon gold-rush town in a blizzard was a challenge, the historically accurate English port from *Mutiny on the Bounty* topped it in every way.

Cedric Gibbons had designed an English seaport inspired by the marine paintings of Peter Monamy and the battle scenes of John Wootton. Irving Thalberg had approved of the scope of the set design and wanted the backdrops to be spectacular regardless of the cost. Luca Chetta was responsible for the facades of the shops that lined the pier. He used actual gold leaf on the signage, so it would shimmer on camera, playing off the water in the bay.

Luca was lonely without Alda, and didn't mind filling the long hours with overtime. It kept him out of trouble, though there was plenty to be had on location. Catalina Island and the village of Avalon were enchanted. The company had taken over its charming hotels, bars, and restaurants, which were open around the clock to accommodate them.

Luca was climbing down off the scaffolding to check his work when Clark Gable turned the corner. Luca waved to him.

Gable walked toward Chet with a pretty young blonde wearing a sundress and platform heels. She ran alongside Gable to keep up with him. Around the corner, a petite redhead skipped to catch up.

"How's it going?" Gable asked.

"Most expensive picture in Hollywood history."

"And it's all going for paint," Gable said, surveying the open cans on the pier.

"I like to try things," Chet admitted. "Paint is cheap. My time? Not so much."

"Ladies, this is Luca Chetta, the best scenic artist at MGM. He even painted the lion."

The blonde, shivering in the night wind off the water, latched on to Gable's arm. Gallantly, he put his arm around her waist. The redhead took his other hand.

"I got a letter from Alda," Gable said casually.

"You did?"

"There's probably one waiting for you back at the hotel."

"What did she say?"

"She wanted me to know that her visit was going well."

"That's just like Alda."

"It sure is."

"You know, she has a soft spot for you—you were our best man."

The memory of that day crossed Gable's face like a shadow. "That was a great day," he said. "Hey, we're going to dinner. Going to meet up with Franchot and Niven—and some of the crew."

"Some of my friends will be there too," the young redhead said with a sly smile.

"Come on, Chet. Join us?"

"No, Mr. Gibbons has me on a tight leash over here, but you go and have fun," Luca said.

"I won't hear of it. Meet us in the club room of the Hotel Saint Catherine in an hour. You work hard enough. I'll talk to Irv."

"All right," Luca said.

"Oh, goody," the redhead said, taking Gable's arm again. She turned and winked at Luca as they walked away.

Luca watched Gable walk down the pier with a woman who couldn't keep up with him, and another who couldn't be bothered trying. Chet heard the tap of their platform shoes, hollow on the wooden slats, as they skipped next to Gable.

When the three of them turned to head for the wharf, Luca Chetta exhaled, a long, low whistle.

Luca checked his hair in the mirror of his hotel room. He had planned to turn in early after writing a letter to Alda, but Gable's invitation had changed all that. If Luca were honest, he'd admit that he was miffed that his wife had to spend the summer in Italy with her boss while he stayed behind and worked on location.

Luca noticed a smattering of gold paint on the underside of his hand in the reflection of the mirror. He went to his supply chest, sat down, dipped the rag into a tin of turpentine, and rubbed the paint away. This was a simple chore his wife would have handled for him.

One of the hopes of his young marriage was to have his wife by his side as he worked. He liked Alda's company and her insights—besides loving her, he enjoyed her intellect. Luca was lonely, and because Alda's plans were open-ended, he had no idea when she would be back in his arms. Sometimes he wondered if she ever would. Each day brought more distance and more anger as he resented her absence.

Luca made his way down the avenue to the plush hotel where Gable and the cast were put up for the duration. The crew stayed nearby, but in a decidedly less glamorous hotel. It was clean, that's all that mattered to Luca. He found his mind drifting to the redhead who'd winked at him earlier in the evening. At thirty-five, Luca resisted the temptation to stray with regularity. There were plenty of available women at the studio who longed to get into show business, and that meant befriending any man on the crew who might serve as introduction to the job of her dreams. Since Luca married Alda, he'd found it easy to resist the ladies; he had a home life now, someone he loved waiting for him after the long shifts at the studio. Luca found he liked being married. He wondered why it had taken him so long. Alda provided a closet full of pressed clothing, a cup of black coffee in bed every morning, a hot meal on the table every night, and someone to talk to about his frustrations at work. Alda had made his life better.

When Luca entered the clubroom, he saw David Niven standing by the fireplace, telling a story to a rapt crowd. Gable had the lovely blonde propped on his lap. Luca remembered when Gable had pulled Loretta onto his lap in the same fashion on Mount Baker. This night, the woman wasn't swooning over Gable but toying with him. Gable however, was in on the game.

Franchot was laughing with Frank Lloyd, the director. Lloyd was Scottish and told riveting stories in his native accent, punctuated by his expressive black eyebrows. The actors had learned to look to his eyebrows for approval; if they were arched and open, they knew they were delivering a satisfactory performance.

In his early fifties, Lloyd was at the top of his game. He had the confidence and ease of a man who had nothing to prove, as he had already won an Academy Award. *Mutiny* was a big picture for MGM. Lloyd had a huge budget at his disposal, and the imprimatur of the producer Irving Thalberg, whose fine taste was apparent in every word of the script and every aspect of the production, including historical accuracy. Luca had mixed many samples of paint to get the precise patina of the wood on the prow of the ship. This was a first-class bunch, and Luca felt his work was appreciated.

"Bourbon on the rocks," Luca told the bartender.

A warm pair of hands went up and under Luca's jacket, stroking him from his waist to his chest. A shiver went through him.

"It's me. Red," the woman said.

"I figured." Luca took a sip of his drink. He could feel the full press of the soft curves of her body against his.

"What are you having?"

Luca held up his drink.

"I'll have the same," the woman said to the bartender. "I've had my eye on you for a couple of weeks," she admitted.

"Somebody that spends that much time thinking about me should have a name."

"I'm Peggy."

"Luca Chetta."

"Is that one word or two?"

"Luca is my first name."

"Spanish?"

"Italian."

"Oooh. I love Italians."

"I feel badly for the Spaniards."

Sidling close to him, she said, "Let's get out of here and go for a walk."

"I just got here."

"They're bores."

Luca looked at Peggy. She had lovely green eyes. Her ginger hair was rolled under in smooth waves. She may have been twenty, but not much more. She slipped her hand up his sleeve jacket. Luca remembered what it was like to be a bachelor, happy to go from woman to woman as though he were working his way through a line dance.

"You're persistent." Luca was flattered.

"I'm mesmerized by your work. I watched what you do on the pier, and I can see you're a great painter—not just a scene painter, but a fine artist."

"Now what would you know about art?"

"I'm in school in Santa Barbara."

"Really, what are you studying?"

"Painting."

"You want my job?"

"No." She laughed.

"What do they teach at you at school?"

"All kinds of things. This semester, I'm studying contemporary artists. You know, the Cubist movement that took up much of the first part of this century. Some historians believe that the vivid paint colors and the modern line and sweep are a direct result of the influence of the industrial age. The use of machines, modern equipment, the invention of the automobile and the airplane influenced their style. The art went from realistic to symbolic." Peggy moved in close to Luca's lips and kissed him. The soft touch of her lips against his thrilled him.

When Luca opened his eyes, he felt Gable's gaze. Gable winked at him.

The conspiratorial wink from Gable made Luca's stomach turn. He remembered Gable standing at the altar when he and Alda had been married. The scene was suddenly all too cozy, too much, too cheap. Luca felt trapped.

"Thank you for the art lesson, Peggy, but I have to go."

"Why?"

"I'm married."

"Where is she?"

"She's with her family." Luca felt defensive about his wife and the life they shared.

"Maybe you don't matter to her," Peggy said. "I mean, you kissed me."

"That was a stupid move," Luca said, pulling cash out of his pocket. He paid the bartender. "Won't happen again."

"You're leaving?"

Luca turned to go. He looked back at Gable, who was engrossed in conversation with the woman on his lap. Niven hit a punch line, and the crowd laughed, a long rolling laugh. Franchot was raising a glass as Luca pushed through the door.

Once outside, Luca wiped his mouth with his hand. He wasn't a man to regret his choices, but he was furious. As he walked back to the hotel, his anger toward Alda built to a boiling point. He resented Loretta and her problems and the devotion his wife had for her boss. He wanted his wife home, and he wanted her home *now*.

12

A soft breeze fluttered the new sheer curtains Gladys had hung in Loretta's bedroom in Sunset House. Sally placed small pewter cups filled with the blossoms of pink roses on the mantelpiece. It was early September, but a fire blazed in the hearth. It was late afternoon, and the firelight threw a tangerine glow on the walls.

Loretta paced. She wore a billowing pink organza nightgown with long sleeves and an enormous ruffled bow at the neck, as was the height of fashion in the late summer of 1935. Her chestnut hair hung in loose waves around her shoulders. She wore a touch of loose, pale powder on her face. She had not made up her eyes or her lips, and without the boost of color, she appeared sickly and wan.

Alda and Gladys placed a new lavender satin coverlet over a fluffy duvet on the bed. A series of six large rectangular pillows, covered in matching satin, framed the headboard.

A stack of scripts for Loretta's consideration was strategically placed on the nightstand, with a cup of freshly sharpened pencils next to it. A pale green rotary phone rested on the opposite night-stand, with a cord running under the bed, disconnected. The last thing Loretta needed that afternoon was another abusive phone call from Ria Gable to be overheard by the reporter. The phone would not ring for now.

Ruby entered with a tray of tea, tiny cucumber sandwiches, delicate bite-size scones, clotted cream, and Ruby's homemade raspberry jam. She placed it on the serving table and left.

"Gretch, get into bed," her mother ordered.

Loretta climbed into bed, sitting up, propped on the pillows. Alda and Gladys stood back.

"I have an idea." Alda went to the closet and took two extra feather pillows off the top shelf. She placed them next to Loretta under the covers, which hid Loretta's growing stomach completely.

"Perfect," Gladys said as she stood back. "Your stomach looks flat."

"I can't tell a thing," Sally agreed.

"It's almost time." Loretta bit her lip and looked at the clock.

Alda opened the sheers, leaving the doors onto the balcony open to let the breeze into the room. She lowered the overhead chandelier to dim and flipped the lamps next to the bed on. The soft light illuminated Loretta's pale face.

Gladys did a final check of the details. "Here we go. Good luck, Gretchen." Gladys kissed her daughter before following Alda and Sally out of the room.

Loretta lay in the bed, feeling lucky. According to the doctor, her baby was fine. After she and Alda left Padua, they'd met Gladys in Naples, returned on a different ship line than they used crossing over, dodged the press completely at the docks in New York City, snuck Loretta aboard the Super Chief for the night haul to Chicago, changed trains for Los Angeles, arrived at dawn, and a car waiting at the station in Los Angeles whisked them back to Sunset House. Loretta hadn't believed it was possible to keep a secret in Hollywood, but now she was living proof it could be done.

Dr. Berkowitz stood by the fireplace in the living room across from Gladys's study. As the journalist Dorothy Manners pulled up in her black Ford town car, it was if a director had called "Action." The doctor picked up his black bag and went into the foyer, joining Gladys there.

As Dorothy came into the house with her photographer, a man in his late sixties, in tow, Gladys greeted them warmly.

"So good to see you again, Dorothy." Gladys kissed her on the cheek.

"Happy to set the record straight." Dorothy smiled. "Thank you for choosing me to do the job."

"You're very special to our family. This is Dr. Berkowitz, the physician who has been taking care of Loretta."

"How is she doing, Doctor?"

"It's been a long struggle, but she's showing signs of improvement."

"You can see for yourself. Alda, will you take Dorothy up to Loretta?"

"Right away." Alda emerged from Gladys's office. "Follow me please."

Dorothy and the photographer followed Alda up the stairs.

Dorothy took in the sumptuous mural, deep pile rug, and polished brass banister. She looked up at the crystal chandelier; every dagger, cup, and pedestal gleamed. As she followed Alda down the hallway, the bedroom doors were open, the rooms inside decorated with canopy beds, fireplaces, cozy reading chairs, and ceramic lamps. This was a home, Dorothy decided; it wasn't just for show.

Alda led Dorothy and the photographer into Loretta's room. Loretta leaned back against the pillows weakly. She looked pale, but her eyes had a touch of sparkle; clearly the actress was on the mend.

"Hello, Miss Manners."

"Loretta, darling, how are you?"

"I'm getting better." She forced a smile. "I didn't know you were taking pictures."

Dorothy blushed, embarrassed. "It's for the AP, and they require photographs with the story."

"No problem—anything for you, Dorothy." Loretta knew darn well there was going to be a photographer, and that there would be pictures. By pretending not to know, she shifted the power away from the journalist's pen and back to herself. Now, Dorothy subconsciously owed Loretta a favor, because Loretta had just done one for her.

"Please, let's do the photographs you need first, before I run out of pep," Loretta said softly.

Taken with the sickly Loretta, the photographer began to snap.

"Why don't you get a shot that includes the bed and the fireplace?" Alda asked, afraid that the photographer's proximity might reveal Loretta's real condition.

"Good idea. Readers love to get interior decorating ideas from Gladys Belzer."

The photographer stepped back. Loretta looked like a doll in the bed. She not only didn't look like she was expecting a baby, she looked petite.

"That's good, Tommy. Thank you," Miss Manners said.

Sally stood in the doorway. "Tommy, come with me. Mama made a rum cake, and a big slab of it has your name on it."

"Thank you, Miss Young," Tommy said, following Sally out of the room.

"Do you mind if Alda stays with us?" Loretta asked weakly.

"I'd be happy to pour you tea," Alda said as she served Dorothy.

"Thank you." Dorothy flipped open her notebook. "Loretta, let's get to it. I understand you got sick on *The Crusades*."

"It's my own fault. I had done a series of pictures back to back, and I just wore myself out. Dr. Berkowitz says it's a virus that has affected my muscles."

"Have you been bedridden this whole time?"

"You know my mother—she insisted I see specialists. So we went on a worldwide hunt for doctors to help me."

"Were you in England?"

"She looked in England."

"Germany?"

"We didn't make it to Germany. It turns out our superb general practitioner figured out what was wrong with me and put me on a regimen. It's a lesson for everybody—good nutrition and rest cure just about anything."

"But you did have surgery."

"Minor surgery."

"When can we expect you up and about and back on the set?"

"As you can see, I'd better hurry. This stack of scripts isn't going to sit here forever. I'm hoping to be back in the swing by spring of next year."

"Your fans will be so happy."

"I owe everything to my fans. They have been so kind to me."

"We hear that *The Call of the Wild* will be in theaters this fall."

"Yes, very soon. It's a marvelous picture. Mr. Oakie and Mr. Gable were great friends, and they were kind to me. I am not the outdoorsy type, and it took all their patience to cope with my lack of coordination. I was a mess!"

"Bill Wellman told us that it's going to be a big hit."

"You can take that to the bank. Mr. Wellman is as great as they get in the directing field."

"What did you think of Mr. Gable?"

"He was a good friend to all of us. We all looked up to him. For me, he was a big brother. He actually knows how to trap and fish and hunt and survive in the wild."

"There were rumors of a special relationship between you."

"I'm afraid they're just rumors."

"I had to ask, Loretta."

"I understand." Loretta leaned back on the pillows and sighed. "Is there anything else you need?"

"No, I think I've got it." Dorothy smiled and snapped her notebook shut. "This interview will go a long way to dispel those rumors."

"You understand why I didn't want to talk about my illness."

"Completely, darling. I wish you a full and speedy recovery."

Alda accompanied Dorothy out of the room and back down the hallway. Loretta stayed in the bed, closed her eyes, and waited. She could hear her mother and sister saying good-bye to Dorothy Manners in the foyer.

A few moments later, Sally raced up the front stairs and down the hallway to Loretta's room. "Coast is clear!" she announced.

"Did it work?"

"Are you kidding? Like magic. Miss Manners told Mama that she was embarrassed on behalf of American journalism. Said the fan magazines were ruining everything—printing lies and innuendos. She said her article would syndicate far and wide, to every newspaper in America, and that it would be picked up overseas, and everybody could see for themselves that you've been sick and are on the mend!"

"It's Ria Gable with the pregnancy rumors." Loretta sighed. "Her press agent is out to get me."

"We can't stop her," Gladys said from the doorway. "But we can fight back."

Alda entered the room, followed by Pickles, who jumped up on Loretta's bed and snuggled under the covers. Sally moved the tea tray over to Loretta's bed.

Loretta ate the sandwiches hungrily. "Thank you for doing this."

"You're the actress," Sally said. "Without a great performance, forget it. She bought it."

"Every day we keep the secret is a victory," Gladys said. "So far, so good."

———

Loretta watched Sally's wedding reception through the sheers on the French doors of her bedroom. Her newlywed sister Polly and her husband Carter danced on the lawn as Sally and her new husband sipped champagne with the guests.

Ruby had sent up a tray of food, but Loretta wasn't hungry. She had less than a month before her November due date, and had not left the house for weeks. Loretta had planned to be Sally's maid of honor since they'd been girls. She felt terrible she couldn't be there for her sister. Loretta imagined this would be the first of many sacrifices she would make for her baby.

The article Dorothy Manners wrote had gone a long way to squash the rumors of a love affair with Gable. The article had galvanized Loretta's fan base, who showed their loyalty by admonishing the tabloid press to lay off. Fans wrote, "Let her rest! The sooner she is well, the sooner she will be *back* to work!" Letters of support defending Loretta's virtue poured in. So far, nothing had been proven about Loretta's condition, and it was the Young family's intention to keep it that way.

Loretta watched as outside, under cascades of tiny white lights, toasts were made. She couldn't hear the words, but the guests' laughter was magnified as it sailed over the swimming pool. Loretta wept as she saw Sally, in a fitted lace gown, dancing with her new husband, Norman, to the band's rendition of "When I Grow Too Old to Dream."

Georgie, in a lovely white dress with a blue sash, ran around the pool chasing Pickles. Gladys sat with Sally's new in-laws. Loretta hated to see her mother alone at social functions; she wished for her mother's happiness more than her own. Gladys had not been treated well by the men in her life, and her daughters had done everything they could to fill the void.

As Loretta watched her mother, she saw herself in twenty years, sitting alone at a wedding. Gladys Belzer was a good hostess; she wouldn't let on how miserable she was at a party full of couples. From the look on her face, Loretta knew that her mother would rather be up in her room reading or sketching a new floor plan than socializing by the pool. Men and romance had lost their allure for Gladys Belzer. She was in a new phase of life; never again would she fall in love with a man's charm, mistaking it for goodness.

Loretta had looked up to her mother all of her life, as daughters will. She learned everything from Gladys: how to move through the world, how to dress, how to behave, and how to treat others with kindness. Loretta was afraid that, like her mother, she was also unlucky in love.

Loretta watched as David Niven emerged from the crowd of guests by the pool and went to Gladys, extending his hand to dance with her. Gladys smiled, stood, and accepted Niv's invitation. Loretta beamed as Niv made a fuss over her mother. Good for Niv! Gladys's silk voile dress ruffled as Niv spun her around. The deep shades of green in the layered skirt against the deep blue of the pool reminded Loretta of Italy.

If Loretta could have, she would have gone down the stairs and out into the garden to throw her arms around Niv to thank him. When it came to Gladys and her daughters, David Niven was there when they needed him, and figured out exactly what they needed without having to ask.

The paper shades were pulled down and the raw silk curtains drawn in the house on Rindge Street. Venice was a sleepy beach town, far enough from Hollywood to remain a backwater but close enough to hide a movie star who didn't want to be discovered. Her sister Polly had wanted to be there to help her through labor, but Loretta had declined. Sally offered to return home from her honeymoon early to be with her, but Loretta insisted Sally enjoy her trip; she would need her sister's help later.

Alda sat next to Loretta and gripped her hand, as she had held the hands of so many girls at Saint Elizabeth's as they suffered through labor. Loretta tried not to make a sound through the birthing. Her baby had to be born in secret; it was the only way to protect him and his mother.

Dr. Berkowitz stood by as Loretta entered the final phase of labor and began to push. A milk truck pulled up in front of the house. Loretta could hear the clang of the bottles, the snap of the lid of the storage box, and even the whistle of the driver as he hopped down the walkway in front of the house and back into his truck.

Gladys was on her way to the house when Loretta and Clark's daughter was born at 8:15 in the morning. Dr. Berkowitz handed the baby to Alda, who bathed and swaddled her.

"Are you sure it's a girl?" Loretta asked.

"It's a girl," Alda assured her.

"I thought I was having a boy. But I wanted a girl. I got my wish. Is she healthy?" Loretta asked weakly.

"Perfect," Dr. Berkowitz confirmed.

Alda smiled, and remembered the girls at Saint Elizabeth's who asked the same question after childbirth. All mothers are the same, Alda thought. Even when they're unmarried, and even when they're movie stars, they just hope the baby is healthy.

Dr. Berkowitz filled out the baby's information on the birth certificate. He sat next to Loretta.

"What do you want to name her?" he asked gently.

"Judith."

The doctor wrote the name on the form.

"Loretta, I'm going to ask you to fill out the pertinent information."

The doctor handed Loretta the form. The letters danced on the form in front of her, just as they did when she read a script. Slowly, she filled in the boxes.

Father: Unknown.
Mother: Margret Young.
Age of last birthday: 22 years
Place of birth: Salt Lake City, Utah

Loretta called herself Margret, because it was close to her confirmation name, Michaela. Always a terrible speller, she misspelled it by accident. It didn't matter, as far as she was concerned. This document had to shield her daughter's identity from the world, and she would write whatever she pleased on it.

Occupation: Artist
Industry or business: Motion pictures
Date you were last engaged in this work: June 1935
Total time spent in this work: 10 years

Loretta handed the document back to the doctor. Alda gently placed Judy in her arms. Loretta wept and kissed the baby's head, holding her close. With all the struggle that had paved Judy's path, her mother loved her.

The key clicked in the front door. Loretta covered the baby with the blanket and gasped in fear.

"Don't worry. It's your mother," Alda said.

Gladys came into the room and went to the bedside.

"Mama, meet your granddaughter."

Gladys peeked into the blanket and saw a pink bundle with a shock of gold hair. "My God, we make angels, don't we?"

Loretta handed her the baby.

"How do you feel, honey?" her mother asked.

"She was a trooper. Long labor," Dr. Berkowitz said.

"Thank you for coming out here."

"Anything you need, Gladys."

"Alda was such a help," Loretta told her.

"If you ever want to give up show business, you can come and work for me," the doctor said.

"Thank you, but I think I'll stay with Miss Young."

Dr. Berkowitz left as Gladys handed the baby back to her mother. Gladys looked around the room. All that remained of the birth of Judy Young was a tight bundle of sheets, neatly placed in the corner. The washbasin had been emptied and cleaned; the surface of the desk that Alda had used to clean the baby was cleared.

Alda had cleaned the room, just as the nuns taught her, with efficiency and speed, leaving nothing behind but the mother, freshly bathed in a clean gown, and the newborn, bathed and swaddled. Gladys Belzer breathed a sigh of relief. It turned out her daughter was surrounded by angels.

————

Clark Gable had his feet up on the windowsill of room 867 in the Waldorf Hotel. MGM had sent him east on a publicity tour, which he endured for the sake of his career so his agent might squeeze Mr. Mayer for even more money on the next contract negotiation.

Gable looked down at the scene in front of the hotel: a clutter of cars, fighting to push through the red light at the corner of Park and Sixty-Seventh Street. He shook his head, wondering how anyone could live in this zoo, and took a long, slow drag off his cigarette before putting it out.

He went to the mirror and brushed his hair. He pulled on his socks and his suit trousers, and was buttoning his crisp pale blue dress shirt when the doorbell rang.

Gable went to the door and opened it.

The Western Union delivery boy took one look at the movie star and went slack-jawed. Remembering the telegram he was there to deliver, he managed to stammer out, "D-delivery for Mr. Gable."

"Who did you think Mr. Gable was, son?"

"I—I didn't think it would be you. My mother loves you."

"Tell your mother I love her right back."

"That might kill her, Mr. Gable."

"Then don't bother."

Gable tipped the boy and opened the envelope.

BEAUTIFUL, BLUE-EYED, BLOND BABY GIRL
BORN 8:15 THIS MORNING

Gable sat down on the edge of the bed. At first he reread the telegram over and over again, taking in the news. He was finally a father.

The telegram was unsigned. How he had hoped to hear from Loretta, hoped that having the baby might change her mind about him and their future. Gable went to his wallet on the nightstand and retrieved Gladys's number from the card she had given him the day he went to visit her. He dialed the phone. It rang and rang, with no answer.

He wanted to enjoy this moment, such as it was, but couldn't because he was a married man who was not yet divorced. It added to his frustration that he loved a woman who could give him a child, but as fate would have it, she wasn't married to him.

Gable was also angry at Loretta. She refused to share the burden with him, and therefore he couldn't share the joy. Loretta had pushed him away one time too many. Gable wanted to own up to his responsibilities, but he'd been made to feel superfluous. How dare Loretta send him this joyful announcement when she refused to make him happy!

Gable went to the bathroom and tore up the telegram into tiny bits, then flushed away all evidence of the news that should have changed his life. He went to the phone.

"Eddie, get me out of here. . . . No, no. Next plane. I need to get home to Los Angeles. It's a family matter."

Gable slipped into a phone booth at the airport. He dialed Gladys's number.

"I received your telegram, Mrs. Belzer."

"I didn't send one."

"I have a daughter?"

"Yes, but I was going to call you."

"Somebody sent a telegram."

"I can't imagine who. Now I'm afraid. Who knows about the baby? It must be Carter and Polly. I'll call them."

"My daughter is barely a day old, and already the secret is out? You're not doing a very good job of protecting my daughter, Mrs. Belzer."

"I'll get to the bottom of it."

When Gable landed in Los Angeles, he intended to drive directly to Sunset House, confront Gladys Belzer, and demand to see his daughter and Loretta.

"Where would you like me to drive you, Mr. Gable?" the studio limousine driver asked.

Gable thought it through. If he went to Sunset House, they might not let him in. He could not bear the idea of rejection. He changed his mind. "Take me home. The Beverly Wilshire, please."

Gable decided to spend the evening out on the town. Instead of trying to see the mother of his child and the baby they had made together, he'd drink to forget all about it in the arms of another.

David Niven entered the Cocoanut Grove with two armloads of American beauty, Loretta Young and her sister, Sally Blane Foster. The artificial palm trees had been decorated with Christmas lights; on the floor were giant boxes wrapped as gifts, with oversize bows. A photographer popped out of the faux setting and snapped the trio.

"Merry Christmas to you too, chum," Niv complained to the photographer. "You just hold on to me, Gretch," he said quietly.

"I have to," she said through clenched teeth.

"You look like the Queen's pettipants, pretty and pink. *Relax.*" Niven's teeth gleamed as he smiled at the patrons as they passed.

"Let them see how good you look," Sally said softly through her own version of the forced Hollywood smile.

Niven sashayed through the packed restaurant to whispers and whistles at the sight of the Young sisters.

"I know, my friends, you must be pea-green," Niven announced to the restaurant. "Double trouble. And yes, the answer is: I've earned it."

Niven guided the girls through the restaurant to a private room, where he closed the door behind them. He leaned against it. "If anyone ever doubts I'm a fine actor, I will refer to this glittering, transcendent performance for the rest of my life."

"I think we convinced them," Sally said as she patted her shiny nose in her compact mirror. "Look at me. I'm sweating like a slop bucket."

"Do you think they bought it?" Loretta asked as she looked out the glass insert in the door at the restaurant patrons.

"Eddie Mannix is calling Louella Parsons right now. They're going to put all the horrid rumors about you to rest. You didn't have a love child, you really were sick, and now you're back, better than ever. It will work, Gretchen."

"And if it doesn't, it doesn't." Loretta sat at the table.

Niven sat down and perused the menu. "I have to eat like a horse—in an hour and a half, I've got to do the reverse performance."

"You can handle it," Sally assured him.

"Gretchen, you look awful," Niven said. "You're pale."

"I can't do this."

"You can't hide in your room for the rest of your life," Sally insisted.

"Clark called me this morning."

"Did you take the call?"

"Don't pile on, Niv. Yes, I took the call. I told him to get out of town. He's going to South America on a tour for MGM—and I told him the sooner he left, the better."

"Such loving and kind words."

"What am I supposed to do?"

"You proceed with the plan. Tonight was step one. You go back to work. You make sure you're seen around town doing ordinary things, like buying pearls at Stern's and a Rolls-Royce at O'Gara's and gowns at Jean Louis. You have to blend back into the system, and then all the rumors will die down."

"You have to get control of this, or someone else will write your story," Sally reminded her.

"I know, I know." Loretta lit a cigarette.

"Gable got his legal separation," Niven said. "What is keeping you apart, really?"

"I had a baby out of wedlock with a married man. Louis B. Mayer would cancel his contract, and kill my career. Can I say it any plainer?"

"Let's say we could avoid all that, and that you can be with Clark. Do you want him?"

"I don't know."

Sally and Niv looked at one another.

"There's your trouble, sis."

"Clark wants to see the baby," Niven said softly.

"He can't. They'll find out about her, and I can't risk it!"

"Please, it's all he talks about. You must let him see her. It's his baby—don't you owe him that?"

———

Gable stood on the cliff above Lake Arrowhead and surveyed the position of the sun. The navy-blue lake rippled below, the soft sound of the water against the shore soothing as it lapped against the rocks. The ground was carpeted in orange leaves. He took out his rifle, flipped the gun, and checked the chamber. He heard the flap of geese wings overhead as they circled in the bright blue patch like a ribbon.

He cocked the gun on his shoulder and took a shot. A bird fell out of the sky as the others flapped away, until all that remained was the cloudless sky.

"The master at work," Niven said from behind him.

"When are you going to take a shot?"

"Never."

"Why not?"

"I happen to like birds. My mother had a parakeet, you know. A darling turquoise thing with a pink beak and a yellow ruff. She was Shakespearean. Clever. I taught her to greet all guests with a squawk and a 'Bugger off' in plain English. It was scandalous."

"I'll bet," Gable said.

"I was sent up this ridge to tell you that the bellman at the hotel has loaded the car."

"Good."

"Heading back to Los Angeles."

"Down the mountain and home." Gable checked the gauge on his rifle.

"Might we make a stop?"

"Sure."

"There's a little house in Venice on the beach I'd like to show you."

"Another one of your practical jokes? I get there, and there's an eighty-year-old hooker with less teeth than me?"

"No. Absolutely not."

"Well, what then?"

"Your daughter."

"What are you talking about?"

"Gretchen has the baby in Venice. It's one of Gladys Belzer's rental properties."

"Are you serious?"

"Yes."

"She told me she took the baby away—out of town."

"To be fair to Gretchen, it's not a lie. She is out of town."

"How long have you known this?"

"Not long at all. I took the girls out—Sally and Gretchen—to throw off the hounds."

"And did you?"

"We'll see. How's your divorce coming?"

"I paid my lawyer double to get the separation pushed through—and that wasn't easy. Ria is going to take me for everything I've got. Said she can't put a price on humiliation."

"Does she know about the baby?"

"Suspicious. Ria didn't believe a word of the Manners column in August."

"The public believed the story."

"If the public buys it, so do the bosses. You know what kills me, Niv?" Gable replaced the cartridge in the gun.

"That gun?"

Gable chuckled. "We're in service to the audience, that's it. Forget the bosses, the code, and the church. We could have come out of this."

"She doesn't see a way, Clark."

"Because she's hell-bent to do everything alone. I don't understand it. Let the man take care of it."

"I'm afraid there haven't been many men around the Young family—at least in positions of authority. Darling Gladys runs that show."

"And that's the problem. Whoever those chumps were that Gladys married did a fine job of ruining it for me. Do you have any idea how crazy about Gretchen I have been?"

"I have an idea. Every man that has ever known her has fallen a little bit in love with her."

"You're not helping, Niv."

"Is it over?"

"What do you think?"

"I think as long as there's love and a baby, there's hope."

"Let's get going," Gable grumbled.

"We'll stop in Venice?"

"I want to see my kid, don't I?"

———

Gable and Niv parked his old pickup on the marina in Venice, where it blended in with the trucks parked to haul tuna, swordfish, and sea bass to the local markets.

Niv led the way through the sand-covered streets of Venice to Rindge Street, where a row of simple gray saltbox houses with white trim lined the street. Gable followed his friend up the walk. There was a milk case by the door, and a rocker with cobwebs between the spindles on the porch, but nothing else, not even a house number.

Gable stood back as Niv rapped on the door.

Clark had a sinking feeling, one of dread, but he also held out hope, as that was the kind of man he was. He figured there was a solution to every problem, as long as people wanted to work things out. His midwestern values were ingrained in him, and he applied them to every situation. For most of his life, they had held him in good stead.

He looked at the house and thought it unworthy of his child. It seemed like a shanty, the pinewood exterior faded gray from the sun. There was no landscaping, not a flower; just the low brown brush that grows by the beach. The sand hemmed the street and spilled off onto the sidewalk, which was plain concrete, certainly not the elaborate hand-laid brick of the driveway at Sunset House, or the California red fieldstones at the ranch he had just bought in Encino. His working farm was more elegant than this dump. His daughter had been born in this squalor. It broke his heart.

The door opened from the inside.

Niven walked through the door, followed by Gable.

Loretta stood in the living room of the house in a skirt and blouse. She was barefoot. The shades were pulled down, as though there was something to hide inside, and of course there was—an illegitimate baby.

Judy cooed in her pink blanket.

Gable's heart beat faster when he saw Loretta. She was as radiant as she had been on Mount Baker, but here she was not made up for the camera, with lipstick and mascara; she was natural, just clear skin, sparkling eyes, and a smile that gave him hope.

"Gretchen," he said as he crossed the room to her.

Niv winked at Loretta and slipped out the back door to give the family their privacy.

"Here's your daughter," she said, handing the bundle to Gable.

Loretta stood back and watched as he kissed his girl and gently rocked her in his arms. He pulled her close.

"She's irresistible." Loretta smiled.

"How did you do this?" he said.

"You helped."

"What did you name her?"

"Judith."

"Judy. I like it." Gable kissed his daughter. "Where's the crib?"

"We use a drawer. It's the old-fashioned way. We line it with satin blankets."

"A drawer?"

"She's comfortable and happy. See?"

"How are you doing?"

"I'm all right. Going back to work soon."

"What happens to the baby?"

"You'll go on your trip, and I'll figure it out."

"Why won't you see me?"

"We can't."

"We could get a little place somewhere. I could work the farm. We could have our little family and be happy."

"What about your work?"

"I don't care."

"You're under contract."

"Screw the contract."

"I'm under contract."

"Screw your contract."

Loretta remembered how fired up Gable would get when Wellman tried to control him during a scene. He had the same fire in his eyes, but this was different; the stakes were higher. She could see that she mattered to him, and that the baby did too.

"Let me proceed with my plan. When you get back from South America, we'll talk."

"Will you take my call?"

"I will."

Before Gable handed the baby back to Loretta, he held her close and kissed her.

Loretta had never seen anything quite as moving as Clark holding their daughter. He was gentle and strong, the father she'd longed for in her dreams. She wished that they could find a way to bring up their baby together.

Gable fished in his pockets until he found a wad of bills. He placed them on the table. "Buy our daughter a decent bed, will you?"

The poinsettias on the altar of Saint Paul the Apostle Church were in full bloom two days after Christmas. The dark church was empty, except for the baptismal party of Judith Young that had entered from the back of the church, through the sacristy, past the altar to the baptismal font.

A life-size nativity scene made of hand-painted plaster from Italy was positioned in the side alcove. Loretta held her daughter in her arms as she sat in the first pew of the church. She looked at the baby Jesus in the scene, and then down at her daughter, and said a silent prayer of thanksgiving that her daughter had been born healthy.

Polly, in a blue velvet coat and hat, and her husband Carter, in a black suit, stood next to the font. Loretta rose from the pew and joined them as Gladys and Father Fitzgerald, the pastor at Saint Paul's, joined them. Loretta handed the baby to her sister Polly, the godmother.

As Father blessed Judy and baptized her with holy water, Loretta took a step back and wept. Gladys gripped Loretta's waist and held her tight as Polly and Carter promised to bring her up in the Catholic faith. The priest anointed the baby with oil, protecting her, welcoming her into the faith. When the priest was done, Loretta kissed the baby and her mother. Polly doted over the baby, as Carter stood by, supporting his new bride. He was nervous; as a new member of the family, he had taken on the secret out of respect for his wife's wishes.

Loretta followed Father Fitzgerald to the sacristy. She genuflected before the altar with the priest, then followed him through the door, past the sacristy, and to his office.

Loretta took a seat in front of him at his desk. "Father, thank you for baptizing my baby girl."

"We welcome your baby into the fold. Now I need your help on this paperwork."

"Father, you understand my circumstances. I want to protect my daughter, and in order to do that, I have to change the names on this document."

"I understand, Loretta. I want your word that in the years to come, you will return to Saint Paul's and change this document to reflect the truth and the proper names involved in this baptism."

"I will, Father. Once Judy is settled and we've figured out what to do."

"I'm going to leave this with you. You fill it in, and I will sign it."

"Thank you, Father."

Father Fitzgerald went to the door. She picked up the pen. "Father?

I don't want to put my sister and brother-in-law's names on this document as godparents for now. Can you provide me with a name?"

Father thought for a moment. "When I was a boy, there was a lovely couple who were very devout and couldn't have children. Write down Mr. R. C. Troeger and Mrs. R. C. Troeger." The priest spelled the name for Loretta.

"Thank you."

The priest left Loretta alone as she filled in the rest of the fictional document. She wrote slowly, having thought these names through. Mary Judith Clark was the infant: Mary in honor of the Blessed Mother; Judith as her proper name; and as for the surname, Loretta chose Gable's first name deliberately. She wrote "William Clark" in the space identifying the father. William was Gable's own father's name.

Loretta left the clues for her family and ultimately for Judy, who one day would want to know when and where she was baptized. Loretta would explain why she had to hide the truth on paper. She was protecting her baby, Clark Gable's career, her own livelihood, and the reputation of her family. Loretta made sure Judy was baptized for spiritual reasons; those were more important to her than any of the other reasons for fabricating the names on the baptismal certificate.

Loretta closed the fountain pen and left it next to the document on the pastor's desk. Father Fitzgerald would return, sign it, stamp it, and record it in the permanent ledger of the church. He would make another copy and send it to the prelate at the diocese of Los Angeles.

Loretta was relieved her daughter had received the first sacrament of her spiritual life. She had brought Judy to the church to be blessed, welcomed into the community, and washed in the waters of baptism. Loretta had ensured the salvation of Judy's immortal soul. No matter how Loretta might fail her daughter, on this point she was clear. Loretta's faith brought her comfort. Her church hadn't let her down; it had been there for her in her darkest hours, its prayers had soothed her while the ritual of the mass had given her continuity and grace. Loretta could not give Judy everything, including her father's presence on this special day, but she could give her the gift of everlasting life, even if the certificate that confirmed it was fiction.

———————

The Mayfair Ball at the glamorous Victor Hugo restaurant, with its intimate tables and its indoor garden motif of trellises, lush greens, and exotic flowers, broke up the long winter in late January of 1936.

Carole Lombard, the quirky bombshell actress, hosted, requesting that everyone in attendance wear white. Carole was the highest paid actor in Hollywood at the moment, and she liked to share. She expected opulence, a blizzard of sequins, crystals, and beads hand-sewn on Indian silks, Italian velvets, and French faille, and she got it. The women kept the studio costumers busy up to the final fittings, draping white velvet, cutting white tulle, and hemming white satin until there wasn't a stitch of white thread left in Hollywood.

The men were required to wear white tie and tails. Loretta accepted the invitation of Lydell Peck, a studio executive, a good friend who slipped her the best scripts on the Paramount lot. She decided to go at the last minute, knowing that advance word of her attendance would bring the barrage of questions about Gable. The Mayfair Ball wasn't a night out on the town for Loretta; it wasn't fun, it was strictly business. After nearly a year off for her illness, Loretta had to show she was back in the game.

Loretta entered the restaurant in a white chiffon sheath, anchored with a diamond brooch on her shoulder. Her evening gloves trailed up her arm in sleek satin. As the stars poured into the restaurant, Niv left his date, Merle Oberon, to greet his pal Loretta.

"He's coming," Niv whispered in her ear.

"With whom?"

"Some lounge singer. I think he found her on the MGM extras roster."

"Incorrigible." If Loretta needed proof that Gable was incapable of being faithful, all she need do was check his dinner companions. "I saw Ria Gable at the valet with about a hundred attorneys. I'll have to give her the old dodge."

"I wouldn't worry. She's off your trail and back on Elizabeth Allan's."

"Is he seeing her again?"

"Off and on," Niv admitted.

Loretta turned pale at the thought of Gable juggling so many women. He might claim to be serious about wanting to divorce Ria and marry her, but his actions proved otherwise.

Niven took Loretta's arm. "Are you all right? If you need me to snuff any reporters or steal you away from any dirty old bosses, you just give me the high sign and it's Niv to the rescue."

Niv left Loretta to join Merle Oberon. Loretta took in a long, slow breath to calm her racing heart. She chided herself for having shown up to this party at all, but her agent had convinced her that she needed to be out, to be seen, so that the studio bosses could see for themselves that she was the picture of health. Tonight, even her career seemed too high a price to pay for the humiliation of being part of a circus that included Gable, his wife, and his women. Loretta decided to act her way through the evening, pretend that she was having a nice time, and cut out of the joint as soon as possible, faking a headache to her date.

Carole Lombard had a big raucous laugh that she threw her entire body into. She was wearing satin—a skin-tight bias-cut gown that clung to her as though it were wet, more nightgown than formal wear. Loretta watched Lombard command the room like one of the boys looking like one of the girls. Lombard had style, but very little couth.

"Pretty dress," Gable said from behind Loretta.

The sound of his voice made her heart race. Loretta turned to him, remembering her vow to pretend she wanted to be there. "You look handsome."

"Not handsome enough to keep you."

"Oh, Clark." Loretta let her guard down, and Gable saw through her veneer.

"I miss you," he said.

"Do you mean it?" Loretta was about to invite him to see Judy, to hold her again, to see the crib she had purchased with the money he had given her. As she looked into his eyes, she regretted everything. She wanted him back. She had to talk to him about Judy, and how to have him be a part of their lives. "If you do . . ."

Ria Gable entered the restaurant with more attorneys than the Supreme Court bench. She wore a floor-length white chemise, with enormous puffed sleeves the size of Halloween pumpkins. Ria's dress said *party*, but her face said *execution*.

Sensing the social chopping block, Gable whispered, "I have to skedaddle."

Loretta watched as Gable walked away. He had been sweet to her, a drive-by of warmth, one that any pretty girl in the room would enjoy. Clark joined the MGM studio executives, playing the role of delightful, accessible movie star, artfully working the bosses and their wives with charm. Gable was smooth; whatever he earned, he deserved. Loretta was reminded how hard he had to work to stay at the top. If only she had met him anywhere but Hollywood, they might have had a chance.

An adorable strawberry-blond dancer with a décolleté so deep she could carry Gable's wallet in the abyss hovered beside him as he worked the room.

Loretta's face burned. She knew Gable had girlfriends—after all, she had been one outside of his marriage to Ria—but to see him working the room with yet another girl on his arm humiliated her. Deep down, she had expected him to wait while she sorted out Judy's future, but clearly he wasn't waiting for her, or for anyone. His life had gone on as though Mount Baker never happened.

The wound she felt was as deep as one could go, all the way down to her broken heart. She remembered her father walking out on her mother when she caught him with another woman, the last of a string of others. Whatever else the red-haired laundress was or wasn't, she was Gladys Young's final straw. Loretta did not have the fortitude her mother possessed after having divorced two husbands. Loretta still longed for love.

Loretta saw Ria Gable move her entourage close to Gable, not to greet him with civility but to taunt him. Ria was prepared to fight for every last dime she could wrangle from Gable's current contract, and the word in the papers was that she would be successful. Ria looked like a white spider, creeping up on Gable to make her point. Everyone knew the way to hurt Gable was through his bank account. He had not left his thrifty ways in Ohio.

Where was Loretta in Gable's harem? Loretta was somewhere between the upstart lounge singer and the matron ex-wife. Or was she? Gable still flirted with Loretta as though nothing had happened. But something had, and she was in a crib on Rindge Street.

"Sorry to leave you so long," Lydell said, handing her a glass of champagne.

"No, you go and chat people up. I'm going to say hello to some friends."

"I'll meet you at the table for supper."

"Thank you."

Carole Lombard breezed by with a quick tap on Loretta's shoulder. "Loretta, you look divine!"

"Thank you!" Loretta said as she passed. "So do you."

Lombard made a direct beeline strut toward Gable, who was leaning over Louis B. Mayer's table, where the boss himself, in head-to-toe white, looked like a fat pigeon perched on a fence. Gable was regaling his boss with some story, and whatever it was, Mayer was engaged and amused. There was conviviality and connection between the man who signed the checks and his biggest star, the man who cashed them.

Lombard tapped the dancer on the shoulder and delivered a withering look to her. She got the message and stepped away.

Lombard gave Gable an affectionate pat on the back, and he stood up and greeted her. She ran her hand down Gable's back, teasing him with her long, burgundy fingernails. She excused herself, and he turned back to pick up his conversation with Mayer when Lombard gave him a pat on the backside.

Loretta was shocked by the intimate behavior in public, but Gable, for his part, accepted it and watched Lombard as she walked off, taking her in like a sweet glass of cold champagne. Lombard might as well have been the hotel maid at the Mount Baker Inn.

Lydell Peck dropped Loretta off at the front door of Sunset House. She kissed him on the cheek, and he tapped the horn lightly as he drove down the far side of the driveway and back out onto Sunset. Loretta thought the flat sound of the tin car horn was the perfect ending to a lackluster evening.

Loretta set down her evening bag and removed her earrings as she stood in the foyer. She could hear her mother's voice in the kitchen.

"Mama?"

Gladys, in her nightgown and robe, hung up the phone. "Thank God you're home. It's Alda. She's at Saint Vincent's Hospital."

Loretta changed out of her evening gown and jewels. She threw on a skirt, sweater, and loafers and went to her car.

"Are you sure you don't want me to go with you?"

"Mama, you have to stay with Georgie. I'll be fine."

Saint Vincent's was a small Catholic hospital tucked on a residential street. Loretta pulled up in front on West Third Street, jumped out, and ran into the hospital.

"Chet!" Loretta saw Luca in the waiting area. "What happened?"

"She had terrible pain. I thought maybe her appendix burst."

"Did it?"

He shook his head.

"What is it, Chet?"

"She was pregnant."

"Oh, no."

"She lost the baby, and now they're giving her . . ." Luca began to weep.

"Calm down, Chet. What is happening now?"

"They had to give her a hysterectomy. To save her life. She doesn't know it. They came out and asked me for my permission. I didn't know what to do."

Loretta sat down next to Chet and put her arms around him. "You did the right thing."

"I don't know how I can tell her. It was her dream. She wanted a lot of children. I wanted her to have everything she wanted."

"Oh, Chet."

"I screwed up, Loretta, I screwed up."

"What do you mean?"

"On *Mutiny*. There was a girl."

Loretta felt a punch to her gut. "What happened?"

"I walked away."

"Good."

"But she came to my room. And I was so lonely. I missed Alda. I let her in. I'm being punished for what I did. And now Alda is being punished for what I did."

Loretta went to the water fountain and poured a cup of water. She gave it to Chet and sat down next to him.

"You must never tell Alda about the girl."

"I have to. I have to let her know what I did. I can't live with myself."

"You have to find another way to atone. She can't give you absolution. And if you tell her, you will only hurt her. Especially now. Especially after all she has been through."

"All right."

"Promise me."

"I promise you that I won't say a word about it."

"Forget it," Loretta said. "All that matters is Alda and your life together."

"Mr. Chetta?" A nurse stood before them. "You can see your wife now."

Loretta watched Chet walk through the doors with the nurse. She put her head in her hands and prayed.

"Hey, *piccina*." Chet peeked through the curtain at Alda, who lay in the hospital bed.

"What happened?"

"You're going to be just fine," he said tenderly.

"What happened to me? Tell me," she said softly. "It wasn't my appendix."

"No, no, but you're going to be fine."

"I was pregnant, wasn't I?"

"Yes." Chet's eyes filled with tears.

"I'm sorry." She reached out to him. "I lost the baby."

"I'm sorry."

"For both of us."

"How did it happen?"

"The doctor called it ectopic. You wouldn't have been able to bring the baby to term."

"I can have more children, can't I?" Alda asked him the question even though she already knew the answer. She had seen the truth on the face of the nurse and read it in the countenance of the doctor. Her abdomen was heavily bandaged, which meant she'd had major surgery. The news would be terrible; that much she knew from her days at Saint Elizabeth's.

"The doctor had to save you. He couldn't do that without operating."

"He gave me a hysterectomy."

"I'm sorry, Alda." Luca knelt next to the bed and wept. He felt a deep shame for his behavior, which soon gave way to regret. The dream of their family in the house in the valley was over.

Alda ruffled his thick hair with her fingers. This intimate gesture reassured him but he didn't deserve her affection. Alda didn't cry, which frightened Luca. She seemed to be in a state, with a faraway look in her eye.

"You have to leave me, you know."

Luca lifted his head. "What do you mean?" He was bereft.

"You can't stay with a woman who can't give you a family. There's no purpose in that. I have no purpose."

Luca gripped her hand. "You listen to me. I will never leave you. You will not leave me. We love each other. This is a terrible thing. But you made it through. You're going to be fine. So what? So we don't have kids, we can adopt them, we can do whatever we want. You're here. That's all that matters."

Alda shifted in the hospital bed, making a space for Luca. He carefully slipped into the bed next to her, cradling her.

Alda believed she was paying for her mistake with Enrico, and in that sense, she was relieved that the debt had finally been paid, that she would no longer be haunted, wondering when her punishment would reveal itself and what penance would follow. Now she knew.

What she hoped to salvage from her life of mistakes was a new beginning. When she met Luca, she believed it was a turning point. But it was not to be. She had almost been a mother twice. She had held her son Michael. The baby she lost that night would remain a dream.

"I'm not going to be a mother. You won't have a son who will draw and paint. I won't have a daughter who will learn how to sew."

"I don't care about that, Alda. I have you."

"I'm going to have to be enough."

"You are enough."

Alda drifted off to sleep. Luca lay awake, looking at her. He was certain he was paying for his sins, but he could not understand why Alda had to lose everything to atone for his transgressions. When he closed his eyes to pray, he couldn't. Luca had lost his faith, and he wondered if he would ever find it again.

———

Loretta drove over the canyon to Venice Beach. Her heart raced. She wept at the news of Alda's loss, and it made her frantic. She needed to hold Judy, to be with her baby. She had deep feelings of self-loathing as she sped toward Rindge Street. She hated herself for every decision she had made about her daughter. Hiding her. The secret. The cover-up. It all came down on her at once, crushing her spirit, elevating her anxiety.

How dare she dress up and go out on the town in a gown and jewels when she had a baby to take care of? How dare she work and spend a moment away from her? How dare she hide her? What had Judy done? She was free of sin and entirely innocent. Loretta hid her as though she were ashamed of her. Was she protecting her daughter, or her reputation, or the money she would make as long as Judy's identity remained secret?

Loretta felt sick. She pulled over, got out of the car, and threw up. She was feverish with regret. She pictured the Mayfair Ball, hours earlier, with Gable, the games that were played, the silliness of it all. The gossip, the posturing among the women, and Gable at the center of it, a new father acting like a fool. She observed him as he flirted and joked and felt up every woman in the place. It was too much, and

Loretta was heartily sorry for her part in any of it. That nonsense was beneath her; it was beneath their baby daughter. There were real problems in the world, real pain, the kind of agony that Alda was experiencing that night. Loretta got back into her car.

Loretta wept so much her cheeks began to itch. She rolled down the window and let the night air, cool and light, blow across her face. What good had her earnings been? She had investments, she owned property, and she had the money to pay a nurse to care for Judy, but what good was any of it if she couldn't have her daughter with her? There was something terribly wrong with the way she was living, in fear for her career and reputation, instead of reveling in the days of joy her daughter brought just by having been born.

Loretta parked in front of the house. She didn't care. Usually, she parked around the corner in a carport that Gladys rented so they wouldn't be discovered. She ran up the walkway, fumbled for the key, and entered the house. She called out softly, "Evelyn, it's Loretta."

There was a small bedside lamp on in the back room. The nurse was feeding Judy.

Loretta ran into the room. To see her baby so peaceful soothed her. Loretta inhaled deeply to calm her racing heart.

"May I?" Loretta said.

"Of course."

Evelyn handed the baby to Loretta, who sank down into the rocking chair, holding her daughter. She held the warm glass bottle of milk and fed her baby, beginning to rock in the chair. Baby Judy looked up at her mother, serene and calm. Her downy hair was like spun gold, with waves. Loretta gently touched her daughter's hair. Judy was a perfect baby, pink, robust, sweet, and tranquil. Alda would never know this particular joy. Tears streamed down Loretta's cheeks when she thought about what Alda would miss.

Evelyn, standing by, reached for a handkerchief for Loretta, who took it and dried her tears with one hand while feeding her daughter with the other.

"I missed her," Loretta said, explaining her unannounced visit.

"It's like that," Evelyn said. "You always need them more than they need you."

13

Louis B. Mayer's grand office suite on the Metro-Goldwyn-Mayer lot was decorated with fine English furniture and heavy Scalamandré silk drapes that would have been appropriate decor in a bank president's office. The scent of lemon oil and the mogul's cigar wafted through, carried by the fresh California breeze that blew in from the open windows.

Mr. Mayer set the stage for his omnipotence in the movie business with careful attention to detail. The accents of polished brass, carved walnut, and gleaming crystal were deliberately formal. His mahogany desk was massive. His chair was positioned higher, while visitors' seats were lower, an arrangement that gave the boss leverage. It was easier for Mr. Mayer to say no in an environment that made actors, directors, writers, and agents feel small. In that sense, Louis B. Mayer was the best set decorator in Hollywood.

Ida Koverman, Mayer's eyes, ears, and intellect as well as his private secretary, stirred her tea as she read. Her large walnut desk was polished to a glossy sheen. Her typewriter, a black-and-white Underwood, was positioned on a specially built arm that could swing the typewriter out of the way so Ida might use the broad surface of her desktop to lay out pages of scripts or publicity photographs, or line up the drawers pulled from her card catalog of artisans, producers, actors, and writers her boss wanted her to contact at a moment's notice.

Ida adjusted her eyeglasses, crossed her arms on the desk, kept her head down, and kept reading. She looked like any white-haired grandmother engrossed in a gripping *Saturday Evening Post* short story. In truth, the only trait Ida shared with grandmothers was the jar of hard candy she kept on her desk. Ida was a Hollywood insider, a player who could tip a project into production or kill it.

Anita Loos, the screenwriter—diminutive in height only—paced in front of Ida's desk, hands on hips. She wore a trim navy cotton chemise and matching high-heeled lace-up Mary Janes, tied with large bows of blue velvet laces. Anita's jet-black hair was chopped in a modern pixie cut, with a thick fringe of bangs over her kohl-lined brown eyes. She wore a deliberately *jeune fille* red grosgrain ribbon in her hair.

No one knew how old Anita Loos actually was, but she was closer in age to the sixty-one-year-old matron Ida Koverman than she cared to admit. Anita was funny and bright and eager; she packaged herself with as much zeal as the studio packaged its stars. As a perennial hot writer on the MGM lot, she used her petite figure, courant designer wardrobe, and jet-black hair to sell her pithy scripts, loaded with sex, adventure, and smart social commentary. Anita had been writing scenarios since the silent era. In the front office, whatever age you are when you first make it as a Hollywood writer is the age you remain all of your career, until the bosses change.

Ink doesn't age.

In the mid-1930s studio moguls Mayer, Zukor, Warner, Cohn, and Zanuck were in a death fight to hire the best writers. Loos needn't have worked so hard on her image; her writing talent was more than enough to recommend her. A funny woman adept at writing comedy was pure gold, and she'd earn plenty of it when she put it on the page.

"What do you think?" Anita peeked out through the venetian blinds at the MGM lot. A ground crew of gardeners had parked a golf cart loaded with rakes, clippers, and shovels next to the building as they tended to the boxwood around the Mayer building, giving it a haircut with the same attention to detail as the studio barbers in the MGM makeup department gave the leading men. "Big movie. It's big-ticket, don't you think?"

"I think two million."

"Lot of effects," Anita admitted.

"Yes, but they'll make history. Mr. Mayer wants Academy Awards, and this one would get them."

"You like it." Anita assumed the script would please Ida.

"You can't miss. It's an epic. San Francisco earthquake. Turn of the century." Ida made notes in the margin of the script. "Love story."

"Harlow for the girl?" Anita offered.

"You'd have to make her a dancer. She can't sing."

"Spencer Tracy for the priest?"

"He plays good guys so often, people think he's a saint in real life." Ida chuckled.

"Not if they saw him out last Friday night."

"Always the way. The most angelic are the biggest devils. And the biggest drinkers."

"Gable for Blackie Norton."

"Of course. He can do anything he wants after *Mutiny*," Ida said.

"But will he want to do this?"

"I don't see why not. Let Mr. Mayer sell him if he has doubts."

"*The Call of the Wild* was turn-of-the-century too," Anita reasoned.

"It's doing great business."

"Loretta Young and Gable are marvelous together."

"Too much chemistry." Ida stopped reading and looked over her glasses. "Mr. Mayer would never hire her now."

"*Never* is a long time in Hollywood," Anita said wryly. "About forty-eight hours."

"Do you think it's true?" Ida said without looking up from the script.

"About the baby?"

"They say she gave it up for adoption."

"I doubt that."

"Do you know something?"

"Not really. But I ask you, woman to woman, would you ever give up Clark Gable's baby?" Anita leaned on the desk.

"I guess I couldn't."

"There's your answer. I couldn't either. And I'm about as maternal as that ashtray."

"So where is the baby?"

"I have no idea. Maybe one of her sisters is keeping it, or her mother."

"Good point. But no matter who you are, it's hard to hide a baby."

"I haven't kept up with the latest gossip. I'm up to my ears in *San Francisco*," Anita admitted.

Koverman picked up her phone on the first ring. "Send him in." She winked at Anita. "Mr. Gable is on his way."

"Kismet." Anita smiled.

"I left word for him to come over if he was on the lot."

"Like I said, Kismet by Koverman."

"Nice title." Ida laughed.

Gable pushed through the door to Ida's office. "My favorite writer," he said to Loos, kissing her on the cheek.

"And you know you're my favorite everything else, Mr. Gable," Anita said, flirting. She was forever gulping air around Gable, like a fish he'd caught, as if there wasn't enough oxygen to maintain a steady heart rate. Clark Gable was Anita's idea of male perfection. He was funny. Well-read. Beyond the personality was the sex appeal. Those dimples. The shock of thick black hair. Those gray eyes. And he was tall. Anita liked tall men.

Gable grinned. "What have we got?"

Anita clapped her hands together to sell. "San Francisco earthquake, turn of this century. No ponytails. Keep your mustache. You wear a tuxedo through most of the movie. We want Tracy for your best friend the priest."

"Nice. Who's the girl?"

"We were thinking Harlow," Anita said.

"No Harlow on this one." Louis B. Mayer stood in his office doorway. "I like Jeanette MacDonald."

"Not for me, L. B.," Gable said.

"She's pretty, and she can sing. And most importantly, she is box-office gold."

"With Nelson Eddy," Gable grumbled.

"They're not paying to see him," Mayer huffed. "Jeanette could sing with a moose, and they'd pay for the privilege."

"Not to be a hat pin, but they have," Anita joked. Gable laughed.

"Ganging up on me doesn't work," Mayer assured them.

"Come on, L.B. Spence and I are a pretty good bet on our own," Gable reasoned.

"But you're fighting over this lady in the story."

"We're always fighting over a woman. All I'm asking is, give me one I'd want to take a slug for."

"Let me see what I can do. We have a few scripts for you to look at before this one. *San Francisco* is going to be a megillah in preproduction. Miss Loos brings the entire city down with an earthquake," Mayer complained. "That's going to cost." He grabbed his hat and went out the door.

"Nice to know the San Francisco earthquake was my fault." Anita buried her hands in her pockets.

"No Jeanette MacDonald," Gable said to Anita. "Or I'll take a loan-out to Warner's and do a picture with Bette Davis."

"Oh, no, you won't," Ida assured him.

"Then get me Harlow." Gable kissed Ida's hand. "That's a girl that does it for me." Gable tipped his hand to Anita and left.

"Good to know he chooses his roles based on the script." Anita sighed.

Ida Koverman laughed. Anita Loos couldn't.

———

"You okay over there?" Loretta asked Alda as she drove through the streets of Venice. The Pacific Ocean sparkled bright blue in the morning sun beyond the shoreline cluttered with cottages.

"Yep," Alda said. There was no use explaining that she was depressed. The only reprieve she got from her pain was her work. Saint Patrick's Day was the anniversary of the birth of baby Patricia at Saint Elizabeth's, and every year since, Alda had thought about the baby's mother. She wondered where she was, if she was all right, and how she was coping with the sadness of giving up her baby. She pictured the infant, who would be a toddler now. Thoughts of Patricia made her think of her own losses, of Michael and of the baby she miscarried and never named.

"I'm worried about you, Alda."

"Please don't."

"But I do."

"I'm getting better."

"How's Luca?"

"He can't do enough for me."

"That's what I like to hear." Loretta pulled into the carport and parked next to her mother's car.

Gladys had arrived earlier that morning to relieve the babysitter. Judy was five months old now, her head covered in golden curls. She reached for her mother. Loretta took her daughter into her arms and covered her in kisses.

"Mama, why did you want to see us here?"

"I don't trust the phones. Ria Gable is sparing no expense to find out about Judy."

"She wants to ruin Mr. Gable," Alda said.

"So we need to make some decisions. And fast. Louella Parsons called me. Ria Gable says she has proof that you and Clark had an affair, and she's going public with it. She mentioned rumors of a baby too. She refuses to give Clark a divorce, and is blackmailing him with the baby."

"Let her. I'm tired of all these games, Mama. All that matters is Judy." Loretta fantasized about selling everything and getting out of Hollywood. She was tired of being emotionally blackmailed by the likes of Ria Gable.

"Gretchen, we have to do something."

"Judy can stay with Sally for a while," Loretta offered.

"She can't stay with your sisters."

"I'll take her," Alda said.

"You can't. They know who you are and your relationship with Gretchen. They would find out everything. Ria Gable has detectives."

"So, Mama, what can we do?"

"I don't know." Gladys became emotional.

"What about Saint Elizabeth's?" Alda sat down and outlined a plan. "Mother Superior could take her. Judy would be loved and cared for—you could go up whenever you wished. And Judy would be safe."

"Then how do I get her home?"

"Once Mr. Gable has his divorce, no one will notice," Alda said.

"Oh, they'll notice," Gladys said glumly. "You'll have to invent a story."

"Sally is pregnant—the baby is due in June. Maybe we can bring Judy home when Sally brings home her baby."

"You could pretend that you adopted Judy," Gladys added. "Because you wanted to be a mother like your sister."

"I don't want to do this," Loretta said.

"You have to," Gladys insisted. "Ria Gable wants to blame someone for losing her husband, and she would be thrilled to use you as the excuse."

"Tell our lawyer that Ria Gable's accusations are nothing but petty gossip."

"Gretchen, Clark is a bigger star than you. MGM has all the power in this situation. They're going to protect him. Paramount will do nothing for you."

Loretta turned to Alda. "Will you please call Mother Superior?"

"I'll do whatever you need."

"Are you sure it's a nice place?" Loretta's eyes filled with tears.

"The sisters are kind, and there's a garden," Alda reassured her.

"I trust you with my daughter, Alda," Loretta said as she held Judy tightly.

The Pacific Ocean was silver that morning, the foamy crests of the waves gray under low clouds that speckled the sky in tufts of white. The train sped up the coast at a clickety clip, but not as fast as a story spreads in Hollywood. Alda believed they had gotten Judy out of Rindge House in the nick of time. Neighbors were becoming suspicious of the comings and goings at odd hours. The shades were drawn day and night, causing suspicion. Gladys worried that it wasn't healthy for a newborn to spend so much time indoors, in the dark.

It was time to take Judy to a place where she could grow, in fresh air and sunshine, without the fear of being discovered.

Alda and Luca had been pulled into Loretta's drama from the beginning. Luca showed patience with the situation because of his wife, but it had its limits. Alda had grown to love Loretta and the Young family, and felt useful in her work, but it caused her a great deal of anxiety. Luca could escape to the studio, diverted by long hours in production, but Alda was under pressure to guard Loretta's secret daily. Sometimes Alda thought she would've been better off staying in the convent.

Alda nuzzled baby Judy, who'd slept for most of the trip in her arms. The infant had helped Alda in her own healing process. Alda drove to Venice daily to relieve the babysitter before Loretta arrived. Judy filled a desperate place in Alda's heart now that she would never have children of her own. Alda savored her time with Judy and showered her with attention and love. Even though she knew it was for the best, Alda knew leaving Judy with the nuns would not be easy.

A car met them at the train station. As it careened through downtown San Francisco, Alda felt disconnected from the city where she had lived for seven years. She remembered little of the architecture, and had forgotten the streets. Memories came flooding back, though, as the car pulled up in front of the convent. This time Alda wasn't asking a young mother to give up her baby, to let her leave Saint Elizabeth's; she was bringing a baby to stay.

The entrance foyer had not changed. A bouquet of fresh red roses sat in the gold vase on the table, and the floor tiles gleamed, reminding Alda that life goes on, chores are done, and the nuns that perform those tasks are replaceable, just as she had been. When it comes to the operation of the Holy Roman Catholic Church, the only aspect that ever changes are the altar linens.

"Alda, is that you?" Mother Superior looked up from her desk. "You look terrific."

Alda had changed since she left Saint Elizabeth's. She had blossomed as a young wife, acquiring a simple and elegant style. The girl who had left in a dress from a charity bin had grown up.

Alda curtsied with the baby in her arms. "So do you, Mother."

"Let me see this one. She's precious."

"A good baby too. Hardly cries." Alda handed Judy to Mother Superior.

Mother sat down with the baby. "We'll take good care of her."

"Loretta wants to visit her every weekend."

"She can come as often as she likes. We can put her up in the convent."

"And she has sisters, and her mother Gladys."

"They are all welcome to visit anytime they wish."

"I will let them know."

"Is there any hope the parents will marry?"

"It would be a blessing." Alda held out hope for Loretta and Clark. She believed Gable was a good man, and she was certain that Loretta loved him.

"But it isn't likely?" Mother Superior asked.

"No."

"Tell me about your husband."

"He's a wonderful artist. A good man."

"When will you start your own family?"

"It's not meant to be, Mother." Alda became emotional. She had stepped back into the past in her return to the convent, and while there were happy memories, there was also pain. Whenever Alda thought about the sisters of Saint Elizabeth's, she remembered the son she lost, the loss that had forced her into the convent in the first place. "I can't have children."

"There are many ways to be a mother."

"I tell myself that, but it only reminds me of the one way I can't be."

Alda carried baby Judy to the orphanage, to a separate floor that Mother Superior had made available as the Depression tore families apart, poverty fraying the ties that bonded parents to their children. When parents could no longer feed and clothe their children, they turned to the sisters. Mother Superior had taken in infants and toddlers up to the age of three, some of whom would return to their families; others who went unclaimed would be adopted.

Judy would be safe here. The sisters would take good care of her, and she would have an extended family of temporary siblings around her. Mother Superior had promised to keep an eye on her, and Alda felt confident that she would.

Still, Alda walked out of the convent with a heavy heart. She worried that this arrangement, though temporary, wasn't good for Judy or Loretta. A mother should never be separated from her child. Alda knew all too much about that particular pain.

———————

Loretta stood on her tiptoes to light the torches around the pool at Sunset House. Soon the wicks were blazing in thick orange flames, throwing light on the surface of the water. At night the water looked like blue marble streaked with silver veins. It reminded her of Italy.

The house was lonely now that Sally and Polly were married and Niv had moved out. When Sunset House was full, life had been a carnival; laughter and music poured out of the house, the radio played, and friends came and went. Now the house was quiet for the most part. The only light visible from the back of the house was from her mother's bedroom lamp; the only sound, a distant car horn from Sunset. Georgie was still at home, but she often spent time at her father's in Westwood. It seemed everyone had moved on and started new lives, while Loretta was still negotiating her way out of her old one.

Loretta snapped the chamber on the locket around her neck, which held a curl of Judy's hair. When the enormity of the sacrifice she'd made to keep Judy safe at the convent got to her, Loretta would imagine her baby at home and in her arms. At work, Loretta navigated the guilt she felt about the baby with prayer, reminding herself that it was she alone who had to provide for Judy's future, and that would lessen her anxiety at being away from her daughter.

Loretta lifted her cigarette from the ashtray and took a slow drag.

"May I bum a cigarette?" A man's voice pierced the quiet.

Loretta sat up straight and peered into the darkness toward the house as Clark Gable stepped into the light under the portico. He wore an open-collared white shirt and faded dungarees with a deep fold at the hem. Gable smiled at her, pushing a shock of hair back off his face. Loretta didn't want to be happy to see him, but she was—she always was. She looked down at her chenille robe. She was bare-legged, and her hair was down, a mass of curls. She let it dry naturally when she came out of the shower. Now, she was sorry.

"Who let you in?"

"Evidently Ruby is a Gable fan."

"You're a little late to that party. She's also a David Niven fan."

Gable joined her. "May I?" He gave her a kiss on the cheek and sat down next to her. "I went to the studio, and they said you'd gone home early. I parked in the back by the kitchen so no one will know I'm here. I don't think anyone saw me. Okay, maybe Ria's detectives."

"That's not funny." Loretta handed Gable a cigarette, then her own to light it.

"I remember when everything I said made you laugh."

"That wasn't so long ago," she admitted.

"It seems like yesterday."

"I look like hell," Loretta apologized.

"That's not possible."

"Has there ever been a woman in the history of the world that you didn't find attractive?"

"Yeah."

"I'd like to meet her."

"You rejected me, you know."

"I did, didn't I?"

"Doesn't happen very often."

"Is that why you're here? To make a point?"

Gable didn't want to spar with Loretta. He'd hoped to find her happy to see him. "I wanted to see how our daughter is doing."

"She's still in the convent in San Francisco. I go up every weekend. I'll stay when I have a few days off."

"You could've asked me if I thought the convent was a good idea."

"Do you?"

"I think you know what's best. How is she doing?"

"She's a beauty. She looks like you. Has your ears."

"Oh joy."

"Had to get those ears." Loretta smiled.

"I hope she grows up to look just like you."

"That's very sweet of you."

"I mean it." Gable leaned toward Loretta as if he might kiss her.

"Are you with Carole now?"

"You just come right out with it."

"It's better that way. So are the rumors true?"

"I see her."

"Are you in love with her?"

"I'm here with you. That should tell you."

"How's your divorce coming?"

"Slow."

"Why?"

"She wants to bankrupt me."

"Are you surprised?"

"Ria's from Houston. Everything is bigger in Texas. So she wants a big payout."

"You know, if you gave her everything, you'd be free. You could start over."

"It doesn't work like that. You remember John Gilbert?"

"Of course I do."

"I was there when Gilbert, the biggest star in the world, was canned. They ordered him off the lot after he had made the studio millions. They blamed his voice, said that he couldn't make the leap from the silents to the talkies. But that wasn't it. His voice was all right. The studio bosses lied, made up an excuse to get rid of him. His popularity had begun to slip, and they were done with him.

"One day he was starring with Garbo, and the next he was at a bar in Topanga, wondering where it all went wrong. That's me in a few years. When they're done with me, and they will be, I'll have nothing. Sure, things are going fine now, and I could give Ria everything, but I wouldn't be able to make up for the years I've put in, unless there's some giant blockbuster ahead for me. But I don't want to count on a pipe dream in a business built on them. I'm nobody special, Gretchen. I do romance and adventure pictures. My future prospects are less than spectacular."

"I think you're doing just fine."

"I could be better."

"How so?"

"I'd rather be with you."

"You already have a wife. And I understand that Ria's been helpful to you. She helped build your career."

"The way her lawyers talk, you would think that she did everything but put on the costumes."

"She has a bigger role in your life than that. She keeps you safe from girls like me. As long as you're married to her, you don't have to marry anyone else."

"I'd like to be happily married."

"If Ria ever gives you your freedom, what are you going to do with it?"

"You know what I want."

"You know, you might have to make a real commitment to someone someday."

"Are you talking about yourself?"

"No. I'm talking about our daughter."

"You won't let me see her."

"You came twice, Clark."

"What do you expect me to do?"

Loretta thought about it. When she allowed herself to daydream, she hoped Gable would get a divorce, marry her, and they would raise their daughter together as a family. Beyond that, she had no expectations. She had always made her own way in the world; she didn't need a man for that. But instead of telling him her dream, she lied to him. "Nothing."

"I came over here because I'm worried about you."

"You have a funny way of showing it."

"Why the wisecracks, Gretchen?"

"What exactly are you worried about? You know, when we were on Mount Baker, you looked out for me. You were my protector."

"Those days meant as much to me as they did to you."

"Did they? Every time I see you, you're with a different girl."

"Because you won't have me."

"Because you're married. You act like you have no options. You're the number-one actor in the world. Give Ria whatever she wants and get your life back. Pay for your freedom.

"You've always been cautious with your money. Some even call you a miser. The thought of losing everything makes you feel insecure, and acting, in every sense is an art form of confidence, it requires it. You believe if you lose your money, you'll lose your career. You're convinced you're one divorce settlement away from being back in the theater in Portland auditioning for bit parts. You have no concept of the scope of your power. I understand where you come from and how you feel. I know you would've paid Louis B. Mayer for the privilege of acting. Your film career's an accident. Okay, you've been lucky but that doesn't mean everything you've built will be gone in an instant." Loretta touched his face with her hand. "The problem is, you want to divorce Ria and keep your money. It won't happen, so let it go. Write the check and send her back to Texas."

"Will you wait for me?"

"That's not the question you should be asking me."

"Well, what is it?" Gable was frustrated. It seemed he couldn't give Loretta what she wanted. She was complicated, and he was tired.

"Do you want to be a family?"

"You know I do," Gable said sincerely.

"Then prove it. Fly down to Mexico and get a divorce. Come back here and take me away. You, our daughter, and me."

"Is that what you want?"

"Since the day she was born."

"That's all it would take?"

"That's it."

Gable took Loretta in his arms and kissed her. All the longing and pain left her when he held her again. She didn't want this to be true—she wanted to let go of the idea of Clark Gable in her life, but she couldn't. There was not only love between them, but a child they had made together. Their problems were not of the heart, or their intentions, but of the practical world, which was defined by the wily and improbable laws enforced by the studios that employed them, and by the public, whose ticket dollars gave them the final say. Gable and Young were indentured to the stardom that made their lifestyles possible.

Gable and Young's love affair had suffered from bad timing, and as actors, they knew all about timing. Their baby Judy had arrived at a moment when her birth could not be celebrated in the way she deserved, that any baby deserved. Gable had a wife who wouldn't let him go, and his global popularity made his every move part of a fascinating dance the public relished. Gable believed that it wasn't their indecisiveness about their feelings for one another that was keeping them apart, but the world itself, forces so massive, two people who loved each other didn't stand a chance in the face of them. But when Loretta and Clark were together, even in the dark, for a few fleeting moments, both of them were certain where they belonged.

"I'll call my lawyer in the morning," he said, kissing her good-bye.

"You know where to find me." She took his hands and kissed them.

———

Loretta waited outside Darryl F. Zanuck's office at Twentieth Century-Fox wearing a proper hat, gloves, and a cherry red suit. She wore her highest heels and brightest red lipstick. She was there to be seen and heard.

Myron Selznick, Loretta's talent agent, pushed through the door to join her. Selznick, at thirty-eight, had a full head of wavy brown hair, a dimpled chin, and wore eyeglasses. He looked more professor than agent in his conservative blue serge suit and gray tie.

As the secretary ushered Loretta and Mr. Selznick in, Zanuck putted a golfball across the room into a tin cup. Chewing on the plastic end of a Tiparillo cigarette, Zanuck went to the cup and retrieved the ball with a balletic bow. In her heels, Loretta was two inches taller than the mogul, which made her point. She smiled politely as Zanuck took his seat behind his desk. The office was furnished in hunting-lodge chic, in shades of forest green accented with deep blue on rich leather furniture.

"What's the problem, Myron?" Zanuck squinted at the agent, his blue eyes shining. In robust health, Zanuck was tan from playing polo and had the muscular upper body to prove it.

"The usual. Lousy scripts. You're wasting Miss Young's talent on drivel."

"I won't do *Lloyds of London*," Loretta said quietly.

Zanuck threw his hands in the air. "Why not?"

Loretta kept her voice even, her tone conversational in contrast to her boss. "First of all, you replaced Don Ameche."

"With Tyrone Power. Every woman in Hollywood wants to star in a picture with him."

"Secondly, the script is terrible."

"According to whom? You? You're an actress. What do you know about scripts? We prepare the meal, and you eat it, Loretta. It's a simple process. I produce, you act. It isn't difficult. If it were, Lassie would be out of a job. By the way, he's happy when I throw him a hamburger."

"I don't think you want to compare my client to Lassie," Myron said wearily.

"It's an honor! Lassie is bigger than Bette Davis. And that's saying something. Look at the grosses."

"I have. And if you keep putting my star client in junk, you'll kill her career."

"Maybe she's capable of killing it herself."

"Look, Mr. Zanuck. I'm twenty-three years old. I don't have the luxury of time. I have ten years, tops. If I make lousy pictures now, I won't be offered anything by the time I hit thirty. You understand? I have proved that I can fill seats. But I can't fill them on subpar material, costarring with the latest handsome heartthrob who can't act."

"Tyrone Power can't act?" Zanuck thundered.

"He's a pretty boy."

"Well, Ameche isn't pretty enough."

"And there it is." Loretta looked at Myron. "It isn't about the acting, or the story, it's about sex appeal."

"Now you're getting it! Housewives don't pant over Ameche. They want Ty Power! And you—they want to see you in pretty clothes they can copy on their own sewing machines. Less acting, more clothes, Loretta."

"While they're copying my clothes, they can have their spirits lifted by good writing, directing, and acting. They can have both."

"You're in the picture with Tyrone Power. That's the end of this. Now get out of here, I have work to do."

Loretta looked at Myron.

Myron stood and leaned on Zanuck's desk. "Darryl, look at me. She's not doing the Power picture."

"Then she's on suspension."

The words Loretta had dreaded had been said aloud by her boss. She felt sick in the pit of her stomach. Worries about Judy, mortgages, and loans crowded in. How would she keep her family afloat? Gladys had invested in property with Loretta's approval, but those properties had mortgages that had to be paid.

"We'll live with it." Myron extended his arm to Loretta, and they walked out of the office.

As soon as they were outside, Loretta turned to him. "I'm ruined."

"Naw, you're fine."

"I'm on suspension! Ten weeks to start."

"I have a little something up my sleeve."

"Does it pay?"

"Does it ever."

"What is it?"

"Radio."

Ruby kept a radio on all through her workday. Gladys listened to President Roosevelt's fireside chats. Loretta liked the melodramas, while Georgie enjoyed the comedy shows. Loretta had read that 22 million homes in America had radios and listened regularly. Maybe Selznick was on to something.

"Studios are getting behind their stars acting on the radio. Advertises your movies. Gives you access to a wider fan base. It's all good, Loretta."

"If they can hear me for free, will they pay a quarter to see me?"

"Absolutely. Even the directors are doing radio. Cecil B. DeMille wants you to lead his repertory of actors."

"He was very kind to me on *The Crusades*."

"That's the spirit. You'll be all right. It's not studio money, but it's good dough."

"And then what?"

"Let me worry about that. Zanuck will cool off, and we'll figure out how to get you better scripts so you can be the movie star we know you can be. And then, when we get you to that place, we tell Zanuck what he can do with his studio."

———————

Alda dropped Loretta off at the tent outside the RKO Radio Theater house.

"I'll meet you inside," Alda told her. "I'm going to park."

"See you there." Loretta wore a flowing, cinch-waisted dress of gray organza. On her waist, she had cinched a cluster of violets.

Loretta loved the schedule in radio acting. She rehearsed for a week, arrived at the studio shortly before air on performance days, read the script live, and was out before supper. She didn't miss the "carwash," hours spent in the makeup chair and hair salon. Radio was a whole new way to exploit her acting talent. Convinced by her agent that this would keep her in the public ear, so she could return with a vengeance after her suspension from the public eye, she decided to work hard and forget her ego. Loretta Young was going to prove that she could be popular and a great artist at the same time, no matter the medium.

The assistant director was there to open the car door and welcome Loretta inside Cecil B. DeMille's tent. "Follow me, Miss Young."

A production assistant opened the flap of the large tent. Loretta went inside.

The tent was filled with crew. The grass beneath Loretta's feet was cluttered with wires. She stepped between them carefully. At the far side of the tent was a complex set of black boxes, tended to by a radio crew. Loretta recognized DeMille's bald head from the back. He sat at the center of a collection of canvas director's chairs, facing the equipment, with a headset slung over the back of the chair. His head was bowed as he read the script. Loretta was making her way toward DeMille when she saw a man sitting next to him rise and face her. Clark Gable wore sunglasses, an open-collared shirt, and a sport coat. Loretta's heart sank at the sight of him.

"Loretta, say hello to Clark Gable," DeMille said.

"Hello, Mr. Gable."

"Miss Young."

Loretta couldn't see his eyes, so she was at a disadvantage.

"Clark's going to do a show for me."

"*Hamlet*?" Loretta said innocently.

"I thought I'd try the Henrys," Gable shot back.

"There's a few changes in the script," DeMille said as he handed the binder to Loretta. "You can track the changes during the broadcast. Nothing you can't handle." DeMille had adapted his film version of *Cleopatra* into a radio play. Loretta had been happy to tell DeMille that she'd seen Claudette Colbert in it when it first ran.

"I'll do my best."

"And it's always perfect," DeMille assured her.

"Thank you." Loretta turned to go. She wanted to get out of the tent as quickly as possible.

"I'll take you to your dressing room, Miss Young," the production assistant said to her.

"Thank you."

Loretta followed the young man out of the tent. She practically broke into a run to get inside the theater. When she made it to the backstage dressing room, she sat down and closed the door behind her. Her heart was beating so fast she had to inhale deep breaths of air so she wouldn't faint. She was furious. Gable had promised to get a divorce and return to her. Months had gone by; the year was almost over. She had been duped.

Gable pushed the door open, startling her. "Why did you run off?"

"I don't want to talk to you," she said. "All you do is disappoint me."

Gable was wounded by her admission, but she need not have said anything. He could see the truth on her face.

"The way I see it, Gretchen, you shut me out, and it wasn't just you, it was your mother, your sisters, and your secretary. That army of women over there you call your family."

"It's easy to blame everyone but yourself for not taking responsibility for your daughter."

"What do you know about that? I think about her every day."

"Yeah? Well I'm raising her, hiding her. Pretending she doesn't exist so that her father goes on as though she never happened and her mother lives in fear that she'll lose her livelihood. Is that plain enough for you?"

"Yes, it is."

"It's one thing to make promises. It's another to have me believe them and then humiliate me when you don't come through."

"You're humiliated?"

"I get up every morning sick to my stomach. I want you to leave me alone. I mean it. Don't come around with your lousy plans and half-baked schemes to be together. Obviously you don't want me. Now be man enough to admit it."

"You're making this too easy." Gable walked out the door and closed it behind him.

———

Loretta Young walked out onto the stage of the RKO Radio Theater in downtown Los Angeles to a standing ovation. For her first Lux Theater performance she played Cleopatra. She waved to the crowd and took her seat behind a music stand that held her script. She slipped on her headset. The orchestra behind her began to play, a glorious mélange of strings, woodwinds, and brass, setting the mood. The supporting cast filed out on to the stage and sat in a semicircle around Loretta.

The live audience before them was dressed in their Sunday finest. The ladies sat up straight to see the movie star, and were awed when she made eye contact and smiled at them. The men were smitten; Loretta Young was accessible, it seemed.

The tickets were free, handed out on a first come, first served basis. During the worst and most painful months of the Great Depression, this was a treat for audiences. Loretta was aware of the need for uplifting entertainment in the worst of times, and enjoyed her role in bringing it. The movies might have been the focus of her talent since she was four years old, but at twenty-three, she was looking to expand her abilities and her audience. Loretta Young wasn't a snob, and this would be the cornerstone of her viability and stardom in the years to come. She didn't know it, though, at the time; she was just being her hardworking self.

The live performances transmitted nationwide had caught on with the American public. Radio programming was initially news and sports, strictly informational, but by the fall of 1936, creative storytelling, melodramas, and comedies had become so popular that directors from movies took an interest and began to create programming, enlisting Hollywood screenwriters and playwrights to write material. They had actors perform the original scripts, sometimes adding narration, special musical selections, or performances to freshen the fare. Even the advertisements were entertaining, and they needed to be, as the ads financed the shows and paid the actors.

Advertisers could reach housewives, their husbands, and even their children with programming written, produced, and performed just for them. Radio would bring popular fiction and the classics to life, and offer special programming such as holiday plays and music. It was a new frontier, and while many stars in Hollywood refused to act on radio, the ones who did could sustain themselves through suspensions and career lulls.

Alda raced home after the radio broadcast to pack for Loretta's weekend trip to San Francisco. Usually Loretta took the train, but this weekend she would drive, because she planned to stay an extra day.

Ruby had packed a hamper of food for Loretta to take to San Francisco.

"Your mother made a rum cake for the nuns."

"They look forward to Mama's baking."

"You better know they would. I've yet to meet a minister that didn't like a snort or a soak of booze."

"They're under a lot of pressure," Loretta joked.

"Who isn't?" Ruby snapped.

"Saving souls is backbreaking work, Ruby."

"I wouldn't know. When you gonna bring your baby home?"

"I don't know."

"I don't know how you're holding up."

"Eye on the prize, Ruby. Eye on the prize." Loretta looked out the window. She might act cavalier, but any mention of Judy was like a knife to her heart. Loretta felt that she was failing her daughter every day. Powerless to change the circumstances, she plowed ahead, believing that someday the entire situation would change for the better, for the baby, for all of them.

Alda was typing a response letter when Loretta joined her in the pool house, which had become Alda's office since the suspension. Throwing secretaries off the lot was another way to punish the stars. Alda loaded bags of mail into her car and drove them to Sunset House to answer them.

Loretta's fan mail had doubled since the announcement of the first radio broadcast. Loretta was building a solid fan base beyond the movie crowd, one that she hoped would stick with her in the years to come. As much as she might want to credit her movie career, it was radio that would make her one of the most important young stars of her time.

"You weren't kidding about the mail," Loretta marveled.

"I know movies are big, but they're nothing compared to radio," Alda said as she sorted the mail. "Wait until next week. I won't be able to fit in here for the bags of mail. You know, these letters that your fans send—they're stories."

"What are you thinking?"

"Maybe read them on the radio and answer them."

"I like it. I'll talk to Myron."

"What happened with Mr. Gable?"

"It wasn't good. I threw him out."

"You did?"

"I'm angry."

"It's about time."

"What do you mean?"

"You never get angry at him, even though he's treated you poorly."

"Isn't that love? To endure the worst and love him anyway?"

"He's made you unhappy."

"I've let him."

"Because of Judy."

"I don't need a man to take care of me. But my daughter does. I grew up without a father—I've never felt protected. Sure, I have an agent and lawyers who protect my career, but I'm not talking about business. I'm talking about me. And my heart. My feelings. They need to be honored and protected too. I know I've made it difficult for him, but I haven't done it to be cruel, I've done it because I'm afraid. Afraid for him—for me, for Judy, for my mother. All I wanted was for him to take the fear of it all away—to make me feel that nothing could harm me. But he doesn't understand my fear. He doesn't understand me."

"It's never easy. Not with any man."

"Polly and Sally have good men."

"Yes, but you don't see how much work is going on behind the walls of their homes. Luca and I struggle."

"You do?"

"Sometimes I want to throw him out a window."

"But you're so patient."

"Not really. It looks like patience, but I'm really just slow to react. I take my time before I respond. Nobody has it easy. Nobody."

Loretta felt guilty for having been so hard on Gable. But she didn't believe him anymore. She had bought the promises early on and hoped he was sincere, but he hadn't made any move to indicate he was ready to leave Ria and be with her once and for all. "He's never coming back, Alda."

"You don't know that."

"I know it for sure."

"How?"

"It's the one thing he said to me that he actually meant. He said I made it easy for him to walk out. The only thing I can think of that has ever been easy with Clark is throwing him out for good." Loretta sighed and sat down to autograph a stack of photographs when the phone rang.

"We'll be right there." Alda hung up the phone. "Sally had the baby!"

———

Loretta ran down the hallway of the maternity ward at Saint Vincent's until she found Sally's room. She pushed the door open and peeked inside. Sally was sitting up in bed, holding her baby girl, wrapped in a pink blanket. Carter, her husband, sat on the edge of the bed. Loretta had never seen her sister so blissful.

"Oh, Sal, a baby girl!" Loretta took the infant from Sally and held her close. "She's perfect."

"We're nuts about her." Carter smiled.

"Why wouldn't you be?" Loretta cooed.

"Yep, we are crazy about baby Gretchen."

"Are you serious?"

"We want our daughter to be strong and smart and kind," Carter said.

"She's already got your beauty," Sally said.

Loretta's eyes filled with tears. "I'm honored, but I'm not worthy."

"If she grows up to be half the woman you are, we will be happy," Sally assured her sister.

Loretta was kneeling in Good Shepherd Church in early December when the sun split into rays of bright orange across the altar. Loretta looked into the light, made the sign of the cross, and slipped up onto the pew. The church was empty. It was a Tuesday afternoon, and she was on her way to Sunset House when she decided to stop in to light a candle. Loretta couldn't believe it was almost Christmas, and she still didn't have Judy home. The commute between Los Angeles and San Francisco was difficult, and it was almost impossible for Polly and Sally to travel to see their niece, now that they were busy with households of their own.

Loretta looked to the end of the row and saw Spencer Tracy genuflecting.

"Is this seat taken?" he whispered.

"Yes, but I'll make an exception."

"Mighty big of you."

"I'm known for my largesse."

"I thought it was your legs."

"Those too."

Tracy nodded. "What are you doing here?"

"What do you think?" She smiled. "What are you doing here?"

"I saw your car out front. You still can't park to save your life."

"That's because I'm self-taught," Loretta whispered.

"That's obvious to all. You're hugging that curb with nothing but rubber."

"I'm getting better."

"Tell your mechanic."

"How's Louise?"

"Fine. Fine."

"Johnny and Susie?"

"Both fine. Your mother?"

"She's well. Sally had a baby."

"I heard. Gretchen the Second." Spencer patted her hand.

"And Polly just had a son, James."

"Your mother must be in her glory. Two new rooms to wallpaper."

"She's having a ball decorating the nurseries," Loretta admitted. The Young sisters had always been close, and now that all three had children of their own, it would be a new era in their family.

"And how about you? A place of your own?"

"I'm still at Sunset House."

"I heard you on the radio."

"How did I do?"

"You were swell."

"Thank you, Spence."

"I'm making a picture with your pal Gable. *Test Pilot* with Myrna."

"She's the best."

"Oh, yeah." Spencer picked up a missal and flipped through the pages. "How are you holding up, Gretchen? My buddy Gable treating you okay?"

"Haven't seen him in a while."

"The big vamoose."

"Whatever you want to call it. Said he was getting a divorce, and still hasn't."

"Don't let him break your heart."

"Too late for that."

Spencer took Loretta's hand. "You want me to talk to him?"

"What good would that do?"

"I'd tell him a thing or two. Set him straight."

"I don't think he's the type of man that responds to suggestions. It has to be his idea."

"Sounds like you know this fella pretty well."

"Well enough. He's not like you. One woman isn't enough for him."

"One woman isn't enough for any man—unless, of course, she's the right woman."

Loretta rested her head on Spencer's shoulder, as she had done so often before they ended their strange yet compelling relationship, one that she thought was mysterious and he believed was loving.

They sat for a very long time, without saying a word, as was their way.

The next time Loretta saw Spencer was at midnight mass that Christmas Eve. He and Louise sat on the side aisle, on the end of the pew, close to the communion rail, as was their habit. Spencer would look across the main aisle until he found Loretta. That face always did him good, made him feel better about the world. Spencer wondered if Loretta knew it.

14

Alda savored her early mornings in the bungalow in the valley. The meandering street that she and Luca lived on slowly came to life under the morning fog as a sun the color of a ripe peach burst through the haze. Alda poured a cup of coffee as the screen door snapped shut.

"Get ready for this," Luca said as he handed her the newspaper. Alda's heart sank as she read the headline:

GABLE IN COURT—FATHER OF BABY?

Alda sat down with the newspaper and scanned the words in the article, looking for the name Loretta Young. She went into a state of panic, figuring Ria had somehow figured out that Judy was her husband's daughter and was living in San Francisco.

"It's about another woman entirely," Alda said breathlessly. The article didn't mention Loretta or Judy, but a woman named Violet Norton who had accused Gable of fathering her daughter years earlier. "What is the matter with him?" Alda put the newspaper aside.

"Movie stars."

"I'm tired of looking for excuses for Clark's behavior."

"At least it's not about Loretta." Luca shrugged. "I thought you'd be relieved."

"There's no relief! Ever. I live in fear of the studio finding out. The press. I'm always looking around, afraid to say or do anything that will jeopardize Loretta and the baby."

"Alda, it's not your life. Loretta is tough, and she has Gladys."

"Gladys doesn't know what to do either. None of this has been good for Judy. Loretta is torn. And it isn't right to keep the child from her father."

"Clark hasn't done the right thing from the beginning."

"Will you talk to him?"

"And say what? He doesn't listen to anybody."

"Neither does Loretta."

"So let them work it out."

"I thought I could help her. I can't support the decision she made any longer."

"You moved to Los Angeles because the nuns forced you out. If you haven't noticed, you're not a nun anymore. It's your life, Alda." Luca kissed his wife and went out the door.

Alda heard the engine turn, and the crunch of the car wheels on the gravel as Luca drove off to work. The house was quiet after he left, and she didn't like it. She had made a home for them, but when he was gone, the house was empty, and a still kind of lonesome set in.

Alda believed she hadn't chosen her path in life; events happened to her, and she reacted to them. Her life had been a series of decisions made for her. Her career was decided for her by the Mother Superior and a priest. When she married Luca, it was because he wanted it, and she wanted to please him. Of course she loved him, but he had chosen her first. Alda thought back to her first day at Sunset House. Even her clothes had been selected for her. And yet, even though it appeared that others had control of her life, Alda was entrusted with the most delicate information and the deepest secret Loretta Young would ever keep.

When Alda was on the sound stage and her boss was doing her job, the order of the universe was apparent. There were many planets and moons around the sun, the one who shined brightest, the movie star. Whether they were technical, costume, hair, or makeup, the crew all stood by, waiting to serve the lead actor, who would create the scene that would tell the story of the movie. Every pore, eyelash, and strand of hair was examined and attended to; every line written was rewritten until it could be delivered with ease by the actor. No wonder Loretta thought she could control every corner of her life. She had been doing it since she was four years old.

The aim of the director was perfection, the harmonic orchestration of camera, script, and talent. The actor's job was not to fall short in interpretation of the script and the director's instructions. Alda was sensitive to the position Loretta's choice of career had put her in. The actor was owned outright by the studio for the duration of the contract. When the star made a misstep, a crew of publicists and handlers came along to clean up the problem, rewrite the story, put everything back as it once was, in order to salvage a star's reputation and with it public opinion.

The studio controlled the actors' public and private life. Their personal time was not their own—they were required to make appearances, endorse products, and behave in a manner that reflected well on the product, whether it was lipstick or the movie itself. Movie stars were salesmen, but the profits of their wares went to the studio.

Loretta was asked to sell soap, face cream, and cars. She discovered that her likeness and name had been used on ready-to-wear blouses at major department stores without her permission. When she tried to shut them down, it was discovered that she had signed a release with the studio to use her name and likeness on products, including the blouses, and they need not inform the star when they did.

Alda was growing weary of working within the studio system. The veneer that required constant maintenance was exhausting. The movies, for a paying customer, could be entertaining and uplifting, but for those who worked on the inside, there was a seven-day-a-week grind with little reprieve from impossible schedules and demanding talent. There was rarely a day off, and when Alda had one, she was worried about the workload she would face the next morning. The bags of mail that arrived at the studio for Loretta had multiplied, as had her obligations beyond acting.

At first Alda had been enchanted by the spectacle of movies. She learned to appreciate the work of the artisans who created beauty on the screen. The visions of the costumer, set designer, and cameramen fascinated her. The power of the director intrigued her. She saw directors pull performances from actors using fear and manipulation, and when the scene was right, the director yelled "Cut!" and the actor would be grateful to the director for the abuse, as long as the performance on film was excellent. All that mattered in the movie business was the movie. Life beyond the sound stage was unimportant as long as the cameras were rolling inside capturing brilliant performances. Even Luca's work was an illusion. The false walls, doors, and windows led nowhere and had a view of nothing. Alda wanted the real thing for a change, and she knew she'd have to quit her job to get it.

Alda longed for the simplicity of the life she knew in Italy. She missed the garden, the grape arbors, and the olive trees. She imagined returning to Italy with Luca, leading a good life in the hills of the Veneto by the lake. But she knew that it would never be. Luca Chetta was in demand.

Over the mountain, in Bel Air, Loretta read the same article in the same newspaper with the same wide-eyed disbelief. She looked at a photograph of a smiling Gable in a business suit outside the courtroom as though he were a stranger. A wave of sadness washed over her, his rejection stinging anew, followed by anger. Christmas had come and gone, 1937 rang in, and now it was March, and Clark still didn't have a divorce from Ria. The kicker was a simple sentence that ended the article.

> Clark Gable keeps a suite at the Beverly Wilshire Hotel for appearances only. He lives with Carole Lombard as he awaits his divorce from Ria Langham Gable.

Loretta shouldn't have been surprised about Gable's current living arrangements. He had been married most of his life, and she knew from their time together that he didn't like to be alone. She was disappointed for herself, but the feelings went to her core when it came to their daughter. His serious love affair with Carole Lombard was a rejection of Judy.

Loretta knew instinctively, after she professed her love for him, that Gable would put distance between them. He had gotten what he wanted, an admission of her feelings for him. Once Gable knew he had Loretta's heart, he could put her in line with all the other women who were crazy about him. Gable was her true love, but he was also a first-class cad.

Loretta picked up the phone and called Alda. "Did you see the paper?"

"I did."

"I'm done. I'm done with him."

"It's about time, Loretta," Alda said.

"I'm bringing Judy home. I don't care what anyone thinks or what anyone says, I want my baby with me."

"I'll make the arrangements."

The moment Alda had waited for had finally come. Loretta Young was standing up for herself, choosing her daughter over the hopes of a life with Gable and the distant dream that they would ever be a family.

Alda would put her own needs aside until she returned Judy safely home to Sunset House. Once Judy was settled in with her family, Alda would leave Loretta and the Young family for good.

Alda Ducci Chetta was done with Hollywood.

The director Jack Conway had just turned fifty when he took on MGM's hottest script, *Saratoga*, and its two biggest stars, Gable and Harlow. Anita Loos had lost the battle to use Harlow in *San Francisco*, and she didn't forget that Louis B. Mayer owed her a favor when he greenlit *Saratoga*. Anita got her Harlow.

Conway was striking, tall and dapper; he had been a successful actor in the silents, a matinee idol. Actors loved him because he understood their process, while the studio bosses loved him because he didn't go over budget. Conway thought it was impossible to make a good movie from a lousy script, so he steered clear of stunt movies, conceived in the publicists' office and cast off the popular covers of the fan magazines. Conway relied on good actors who happened to be stars for his project, and would accept nothing less.

Hattie McDaniel checked her costume in the set mirror. She liked the cut of the dress, with a slight dropped waist, which made her round frame appear long. The black actress, singer, and dancer, a veteran of vaudeville and the theater, put her hands in the pockets of her maid's costume. She slipped off the diamond pinky ring she had forgotten to leave in the dressing room. She motioned for her dresser to fetch the ring.

"I can't serve Miss Harlow oatmeal wearing a diamond ring."

"No, you can't," her dresser, a wizened white woman of sixty, replied.

"That'd switch up the plot." Hattie chuckled.

"I'll put it in the safe." The dresser slipped it onto her own finger before giving Hattie's crisp black uniform a once-over with the lint brush. "May I get you anything, Miss McDaniel?"

"I'm all right."

Hattie stood quietly off-camera as Clark Gable took his mark. The cinematographer checked Gable's light in the gauge. If MGM was a museum, Hattie looked at Gable like the statue of David. Whatever he had, she liked it. And while Hattie enjoyed her work, she looked forward to working with Gable because they had as much fun between takes as they did when acting.

"Hattie, five-card stud?"

"I'll beat you like eggs and sugar, Mr. Gable. And when I'm done, there'll be a pie on the table, and you'll be under it crying."

"Meet me in my dressing room."

"We'll have to keep the door open."

"And two feet on the floor," Gable teased.

"I have control of my impulses," Hattie said.

The crew erupted in laughter.

"Well, I don't," Gable said, and got an even bigger rolling laugh from the crew.

"That's what I heard, King. That's what I heard." Hattie chuckled.

Gable's costar, Jean Harlow, lean, small, and shaped like a violin, wore a fitted gingham day dress and gloves as she sauntered into the scene. Her trademark platinum blonde hair looked like tufts of white cotton candy. Harlow was a glamorous shopgirl type. Her features were ordinary—small lips and eyes, and a nose that was neither retroussé like Myrna Loy's nor razor-straight like Joan Crawford's. But it was Harlow's imperfections that made her a beauty; she had a wide-open face, and she sparkled. She used her soft body like a prop, wrapping it around furniture and men.

Harlow was trailed by an entourage of hair, makeup, and costume assistants, who checked every seam so the satin lay flat against her body without a wrinkle. "Are you two at it again?" She grinned at Gable and then Hattie.

"We'll cut you in, sis," Gable assured her.

Jean pointed her thumb at Gable. "I'm his sis when he wants to bankrupt me at cards."

"You can take him," Hattie said to Jean. "You're a killer card sharp. You'll pluck him clean."

"Then she's out," Gable joked. "I don't like to lose."

"You know how to play Gable, right in the wallet." Harlow winked at Hattie.

"I'd give everything I had to you ladies."

"Too late for that. Wife number two already has her mitts on your stash," Harlow joked.

"Jean, take your mark. You look marvelous," Jack Conway said from behind the camera.

"Just so you know, I won't make another movie without these two. Jack, did you hear that? Call L. B. and tell him."

"Running a rehearsal," the first assistant director announced.

———

Saratoga was a dream shoot: a strong script, a cast filled with old friends, and a sage director who enjoyed his work. The players looked forward to coming to the studio, and Hattie and Gable took turns hosting lunch in their dressing rooms. Jean took the company out to dinner at the Mocambo. Most shoots weren't this much fun, but *Saratoga* made up for them. It helped that the movie they were making was a good one. Conway ran a smooth ship, and the company was right on schedule.

"Oh, you big bear of a thing." Hattie looked down at her cards and up at Gable, trying to read him. "You don't let on."

"Poker face," Gable said, making one.

Hattie laughed. "Here's mine." Hattie made a face.

Gable laughed. "Nobody makes me laugh like you."

"You need to find a woman that cracks you up." Hattie shuffled the cards.

"I have one."

"I'll bet you have twelve."

"I don't like to bore anybody, Hattie. A little of me goes a long way, so I have to spread it around."

"You don't think very highly of yourself."

"I know my limits, let's put it that way." Gable picked up a card.

"How's your divorce coming?"

"How's yours?"

"Husband number three packed his bags a week ago last Friday. I should be ashamed."

"Are you?"

"Not really. I learn a little something with each husband. Not enough to fill a book, but enough not to feel guilty when I move on."

"That's a good way to look at it. But I don't learn anything, I just get mad."

"That's bad for your heart." Hattie studied her cards. "Don't let love make you angry. It'll kill you. You gonna marry Miss Lombard?"

"Why do you ask?"

"I just did a picture with her. She sure as hell wants to marry you."

Gable laughed. "She does, does she?"

"You better dust off the old top hat. She's gonna want a white-tie-and-tails situation."

"Well, she won't get it."

"How is it I know more about what makes you happy than the woman you're in love with?"

"You pay attention, Hattie. You're observant."

"I'd go for you, but you're the wrong shade."

"I'd go for you, but you'd grow tired of me, Hattie."

"How so?"

"I'm not one for church."

"You have to go to church if you want to be with me. And if you wanna make me real happy, you have to sing in the choir."

"I figured as much."

"But I'm not for you either. I don't go for hunting and fishing and farming. You need a girl who can handle a rifle. I've never held a gun in my life. And I'm from Kansas City."

"I could teach you."

"Don't bother. I don't want to learn. I am not the outdoor type."

"Maybe you'd like it. Nothing like the woods."

"I want my mink from the store. Not from some trap I set myself."

Gable laughed. "All right, Hattie. We'll stay indoors."

"I don't do Westerns, if you've noticed. Of course, there's not a lot of call for black people in Westerns."

"We take the roles they give us, whether they are written in your color or my color."

"The best ones are written in your color, but that's show business."

"Yes, it is."

"Jean is on the set," Jack Conway said as he passed. "Let's go, kids."

"I haven't been called a kid since vaudeville," Hattie said as she folded her cards.

"Me either," Gable said.

Conway was blocking the scene with Harlow on the set. Hattie joined them, standing off to the side, awaiting her turn while Gable sat in the makeup chair and was powdered down.

"Looking good, Gable," Luca said as he wiped his hands on a rag.

"Chet, where have you been?"

"I'm working nights. Mr. Mayer has added two movies to the schedule. I'm doing a ballroom for Gibbons besides the hotel for *Saratoga*."

"Don't they know you're an artiste?"

"They do, and they don't care."

"How's Alda?"

"She's just fine." Chet looked at the makeup artist and hairstylist. "Might I speak with Mr. Gable alone?"

"I think we're done, ladies. This is about as good as this mug gets."
Gable's makeup artist and hairstylist left for the set.

"They're bringing the baby home," Luca said quietly.

"Okay."

"She'll be at Sunset House."

"I'm not welcome there."

"She's your kid."

"Chet, you don't know what's going on."

"If you've moved on, just tell her."

"I can't do anything definite because of Ria."

"She won't be an excuse forever."

Luca was right. Gable didn't know what to say. Carole Lombard
was direct and persistent and didn't care about Ria. Carole gave him
confidence. She made him feel that if he lost all his money and property in the divorce, he'd still be rich. Carole was carefree, and Loretta
was not; she was an anchor. Gable had been moored in a bad marriage long enough. He didn't want more responsibilities and obligations. He wanted a romantic relationship that was light and full of
laughter—the one he had with Lombard.

"Mr. Gable, we need you on the set," the first assistant director
called out.

"They're leaving in the morning," Luca said softly. "Taking the train."

"I'll take a drive up," Gable promised. "I like the drive up the coast."

"I'll let Alda know."

Luca smiled and patted his friend on the back. It was almost like
old times. He couldn't wait to tell Alda the good news.

———

Loretta had taken the express train to San Francisco so many times
over the past year to see her daughter that she swore she knew every
bridge, rock, and tree along the tracks heading north. Gladys pulled
the shade down on the window to block the hot California sun.

"I'm glad you could come with me, Mama."

"My first grandchild is very special to me."

"Clark won't believe how big she got." Loretta was pleased that
Judy's father was going to make the trip. She wanted him to be there

more than anything. Alda had sent directions to Saint Elizabeth's through Luca, including the Mother Superior's instructions to enter through the back of the convent where no one would see him.

Gladys had hoped that by the time they arranged Judy's adoption, Gable would have accepted his responsibility as the baby's father and been on the train with Loretta.

For her part, Gladys had tried to include Gable. Without Loretta's knowledge, Gladys had set up a secret bank account for Judy in San Francisco. She'd called Gable and gave him the account information. He was polite, inquired about her health, the baby's health, and Loretta's, and hung up quickly. Gable had not made a deposit in the account. It wasn't that the Youngs needed the money to care for the girl; Gladys wanted Gable to do something for his daughter, so one day she could tell Judy that her father had made an effort on her behalf from the start.

Loretta folded the newspaper and handed it to her mother.

Loretta Young is set to adopt twins from a San Francisco foundling hospital. The girls, named Jane and Judy, are robust and healthy at 23 months. The single Young couldn't bear to wait for motherhood, as sisters Sally and Polly are new mothers. Loretta wanted children of her own, so the star decided to adopt. Further information will be kept private, due to the nature of the adoption.

"What are you going to do about the twin?" Gladys asked.

"When the time comes, I'll say the birth mother wanted to keep her. That's one smokescreen. The other is Judy's age. She's only twenty months old. If we admitted her real age, they would do the math, and then it would be all over. Louella promised she'd run photos when we were ready," Loretta said. "But I don't want to show photos of Judy to the public."

"She doesn't have to be a secret any longer."

"Not to us. But to the world . . . yes, we have to keep her a secret. Clark is still a married man."

"What are you going to tell Judy?"

"I don't have to worry about that for a long time."

"Just because he's with another woman doesn't mean that he can't be a part of Judy's life."

A look of pain crossed Loretta's face.

Gladys took her daughter's hand. "I'm sorry. That was inconsiderate of me. You still have feelings for him, don't you?"

"I know. Thick as plank, that's me. I can't get it through my head that he has moved on—I don't want to believe it. But he has, and I can't count on anything. I've learned not to—"

"From me."

"Mama, it's not your fault."

"I chose men that made beautiful babies and not much else."

"Well, I could say the same."

"You know, when Clark came to see me, I could see that he loved you. Now, I'm not saying that he knows how to love you, but just that he does."

"Doesn't that come naturally? Loving someone?"

"No. You can have all the feelings in the world for someone, and you may not know how to make them happy."

"Is there a man in this world who could be faithful?"

"Sure."

"It hurts me that he wants Carole."

"It shouldn't. That won't last either."

"How do you know?"

"He goes out with so many girls because he's looking for something he lacks. He wants to have fun. Eventually that too will bore him. Once a man goes down the path that he is on, it's very hard to love one woman. It's a rush to be in love, then once that glow is gone, he's gone. He's chasing the glow."

"I thought we had it."

"You did. And now you have Judy. But she's innocent. And she has to stay that way. She will be loved by our family, no matter what you decide."

"I did all right without Pa."

"You did. But you've always had a purpose. You aspired to a life. You meant to go to the top. That's always been the way with you. Your daughter will appreciate that about you someday."

Loretta and Gladys walked into Saint Elizabeth's, this time, with joy and a purpose. On Loretta's prior visits, she'd been sad the moment she entered, anticipating the time when she would have to leave Judy. Not this time. This was it. Loretta was there to claim Judy, and there was no reason to arrive at night and leave in the darkness.

Mother Superior led Judy by the hand out of her office.

"My baby!" Loretta exclaimed as Judy ran toward her and into her arms. Loretta showered Judy with kisses. Her blond curls tumbled in spirals, and her smile was pure Loretta.

"Here's Grandma," Loretta said, introducing Gladys officially for the first time.

"I can't thank you enough for all you've done, Sister."

"Well, if you don't mind, I might think of one or two. I hear you've raised some money for the Los Angeles diocese. We could use your help up here."

Loretta and Gladys laughed.

"Whatever you need, Mother," Loretta assured her.

Loretta smoothed her daughter's hair over her ears. She had her father's ears, and they were so obvious, there was no way to hide them, except with a bonnet. Loretta anchored the bonnet on her daughter's head and tied the ribbon under her chin.

"Judy, honey, we're going home. Can you say train?"

"Train," Judy repeated.

Mother Superior and Loretta applauded.

"There's a birthday party for one of our little girls who's leaving today. Is it all right with you if Judy attends?"

"Absolutely."

Loretta and Gladys followed Mother Superior outside into the garden. The place was just as Alda had described. Loretta even remembered the bench where Alda sat as a novice when Mother Superior told her that she would never become a nun.

"This is lovely." Gladys took in the statuary and the fountain. "So peaceful."

A small group of children was gathered in the center of the garden. A nun passed out cardboard party hats, while novices in their habits juggled the children on their laps as they ate birthday cake. Loretta stood back with Gladys as Judy joined in, climbing up on a postulant's lap to claim her slice of cake.

"Do you think Judy will remember Saint Elizabeth's?" Loretta asked Gladys.

"They say you don't remember anything before the age of three."

"I'll never forget it. I hope we've done the right thing, Mama."

"We had no choice."

"The problem with a secret is that it requires maintenance. It's a job to keep one."

"There will come a day when it won't be a secret any longer. You'll be able to tell Judy everything."

"I hope so, Mama."

"Right now you can't think about that. We have to get her home. Think about all she has waiting for her. Aunts and uncles who love her already. And think of her cousins her own age! She has a ready-made family. If you ask me, she's a lucky girl."

Loretta wanted to believe her mother, but she knew better. Luck would have been if her father had decided to stay.

A postulant pushed through the garden gate, carrying a folded piece of paper. She gave the paper to Mother Superior, who read it and then brought it to Loretta.

"A message from Alda."

Loretta unfolded the paper: "C.G. unable to make trip to S.F. Has reshoots."

Loretta put the note in her pocket. She went to her daughter and joined in a party game of hot potato. She wouldn't let Judy's father ruin the party.

———

Jack Conway stood in a horse barn built in the middle of the MGM sound stage. As they loaded the horses into their stalls, Gable stopped to pat a palomino, who nuzzled her nose into Gable's neck.

"I sure wish that was me," Hattie said to her makeup artist as she stood in her reclining chair, getting a touch-up of powder.

"We all do," the young woman said to Hattie.

Jean Harlow passed them in a riding costume. "Good morning, ladies."

Hattie watched Harlow as she joined Gable on the set. "Those two are like dynamite. Tick. Tick. And. Boom."

"Chemistry is everything."

"You know it. Without it, we'd all be out of a job."

Hattie was still watching Gable and Harlow when she saw Harlow's knees buckle as she fainted. Gable caught her and looked around for a place to set her down, as the makeup team came running.

"We need a doctor!" Gable shouted. He picked Harlow up in his arms. Harlow's head fell limply against his arm. "Come on, sis," Gable said in Harlow's ear.

Hattie kept her eyes on Harlow. Sometimes Hattie got a feeling, an inkling of something to come, a voice that whispered softly in her ear; sometimes she even dreamed it. This morning, something told her that they would never finish *Saratoga*.

———

Loretta carried Judy as she and Gladys followed Mother Superior into her office. Mother had the paperwork to release Judy ready on her desk. The radio played softly in the background—a baseball game out of Sacramento with DiMaggio at bat—as Mother Superior handed Loretta a pen. Just then the programming was interrupted.

From Hollywood, an Associated Press report has been filed from Metro Goldwyn Mayer studios; Jean Harlow collapsed in the arms of Clark Gable on the set of Saratoga *earlier this morning. No word on Harlow's condition.*

Mother Superior, who knew Judy's history, placed her hand on the document. "Would you like to take a moment, Loretta?"

"No, I'm fine," she said as she signed the paper. "Pray for Jean, will you, Sister?"

———

Alda was waiting at Sunset House when Loretta, Gladys, and Judy arrived home. Judy was fast asleep in Loretta's arms as Alda followed them up the stairs to the new nursery.

Gladys had set up a room for Judy, decorated with wallpaper that featured dancing elephants, leaping zebras, and acrobats. She'd had a cheerful bright yellow satin coverlet made for the bed. There were books and toys on the shelves, and, in the window, a collection of small clay pots with green sprouts.

"Might as well get used to the Hollywood circus right away," Loretta said as she tucked the blankets around her sleeping daughter.

"It's a high-wire act," Alda agreed.

Alda followed Loretta down to the kitchen. As soon as they were out of earshot of the baby's room, Alda confided, "I spoke with Mr. Gable."

"And what did he have to say?"

"He said he'd come and see Judy here at home."

"Well, he hasn't honored any of his previous promises, so let's not count on this one."

"I thought for sure he'd make the drive up to San Francisco. I'm sorry."

"Alda, it isn't you. I don't know what I would do without you."

"I wanted to talk to you about that. Now that Judy is home, I think it's time for me to move on."

"Oh, Alda, you can't." Loretta began to cry. "I'm sorry, of course you can. It's your decision. I just don't know what I would do. You save my life every day in a hundred little ways."

"And you took me on, out of the convent. I didn't even own a pair of decent shoes. You have provided a life for me that was beyond my imagination. I met Luca through you—had I not been on that train, I doubt I would have ever met him and fallen in love with the finest man I know. I owe you everything. But it's a heavy load to carry a secret. I worry for Judy's future, and yours."

"You've been through so much, Alda. If this is hard for you, to be around Judy, I understand." Loretta was sensitive to the fact that Alda couldn't have children of her own.

"It's not that. I love her. All the trips, watching her grow. I would miss her terribly."

"Then stay. Is there some way I could make the job better for you? Thanks to you, Judy was safe for a very long time. And now she's home. Now we can plan the rest of our lives—and you can plan yours. The gossip has died down. There are always rumors in Hollywood, and a new scandal is right around the corner. We won't be bothered, I promise you. I want you to travel home to Italy again—to do things you want to do. But I'm also selfish—I don't want to lose you. How about we trade more time off for you to stay? And a raise too!"

Alda laughed. "I'm well paid."

"Not enough. I don't want you to be tempted by anyone else stealing you away."

———

As Alda got into her car that night to make the drive over the mountain, home to Luca, she thought about her conversation with Loretta, the raise and the time off. It would go a long way to give her the new perspective she needed in her life. She and Luca had put off making a decision about adopting children of their own. He had immersed himself in projects at the studio, and she was busy with Loretta's obligations. Alda would always have to work; why not stay with people she cared about?

Loretta didn't want anyone to steal Alda away, Alda thought, the way Gable had been stolen away by Lombard. It was so odd how their lives intersected, with neither Alda or Loretta getting exactly what they hoped for, and yet they had everything because they trusted each other.

———

Loretta tiptoed into Judy's room and kissed her. She placed her hand on Judy's heart and said a Hail Mary. After months of heartache, Loretta felt redeemed. She had her baby home.

In her room, Loretta opened the French doors and the windows. She drew a bath, and was about to sink into the bubbles when the phone rang.

"Can you come to Good Samaritan?"

"Myrna?"

"Loretta, can you come to the hospital?" Myrna Loy was a sensible woman. She delivered the best of news and the worst with the same solid midwestern cadence.

"What's wrong? Are you all right?"

"Not me, hon. Jean Harlow is gone."

"What do you mean?"

"She died tonight."

"Poor Jean."

"They didn't see it coming. It was a bad infection. It took her."

"Myrna, is Clark there?"

"He's a mess. That's why I called. He could use a friend. Hurry."

Loretta pulled on a skirt, sweater, and loafers. Clark Gable had confided his feelings about Loretta to Myrna, who had always been a good friend. Myrna let Loretta know Clark's feelings, and without prying, let Loretta know that she was always available to talk. Loretta believed that Myrna was her most trustworthy friend. Myrna knew about Judy, and never engaged in any gossip about her. She kept an eye on Gable for Loretta, because she believed they belonged together.

"Mama, I'm going to the hospital. Will you look in on Judy?"

"What happened?"

"Jean Harlow died."

Jean Harlow was only a few years older than Loretta, at twenty-six—too young to die. On the way to the hospital, scenarios ran through Loretta's head, but mostly she was worried about Gable. He'd been with Jean when she collapsed; he had to be devastated. All of Loretta's thoughts went to Gable—how she would comfort him through this terrible time.

Loretta pushed through the doors of Good Samaritan Hospital. She never used her name to get results, but tonight was different. She knew there would be security around Jean's room, so she marched up and told them that Myrna Loy was expecting her. A security guard escorted her to the fourth floor. When they got off the elevator, Loretta could see a crowd outside Jean's room. She broke into a run when she saw the back of Gable's head. When she got closer, she stopped.

Gable was holding Carole Lombard, who was weeping. The sight of him comforting her made her stomach turn. Where had he been in her dark hours of despair? Where was his heart when his daughter was in the convent in San Francisco, hidden away because he wouldn't get a divorce? Loretta felt rage rise within her. It wasn't that Gable had chosen another; it was that he refused to acknowledge that he had chosen at all.

Loretta found herself turning so that Gable would not catch a glimpse of her. She pushed through the door and ran down the stairs and back out to her car. She would call Myrna and apologize in the morning, but she couldn't face Gable that night. She saw with her own eyes that Gable had moved on. The days of deluding herself that he loved her were over. Carole Lombard was going to be the next Mrs. Gable, and Loretta wouldn't have to read it in *Photoplay* to believe it.

————

Luca threw his car keys down on the kitchen table. Alda was stirring sauce on the stove, waiting for the pot of water to boil to make her husband his favorite spaghetti. Luca put his arms around his wife.

"I called the studio—they said you had to drive for supplies."

"I feel like a traitor," he said.

"Why?"

"Because of you."

"What did I do?"

"Nothing, honey. It's about your boss. I didn't drive to Arizona for paint. I drove Clark and Carole to get married. It was Otto Winkler's car, so no one would recognize them."

"Why didn't you tell me?"

"I didn't want you to be compromised. It'll be in the papers tonight. All over the radio by morning. They had Gable's houseman drive his Packard out there, and I turned around and came home. Can you forgive me?"

"Clark is your friend—you did him a favor."

"But I didn't tell you about it."

The lies, half truths, and stories that had formed a wall between Loretta and Clark had not only shut them out of each other's lives but compromised their relationships with their family and friends. Alda and Luca were part of their world, and had accommodated their view of it since Mount Baker. Alda was still surprised how easily they manufactured alibis and stories for their friends in the movie business.

"How about this? I forgive you."

"I'd feel better if you yelled at me."

"I don't want to yell. I love you."

Luca took his wife in his arms and kissed her.

Alda pulled out a chair and invited her husband to sit as she finished preparing their dinner. "The code we live by cannot be found in Hollywood." Alda stirred the sauce on the stove. "As long as we know this, and we live our lives truthfully, we'll be all right. The minute we start to think anything that happens on the other side of this mountain is acceptable, we're over."

"I don't want to be over. Not ever."

"You know, all of us that work on the crews, in the offices, deliver the mail, sew the costumes, and paint the sets, we all work for our families. We take care of each other. The stars are different. Do you ever notice how strange nice, decent people act when they meet a movie star? They act like some deity came off the mountaintop to greet them. The stars are separate from us. And maybe that's why people pay to see them. They know there's something about them that they can never be."

"Or maybe," Luca ventured, "they make them feel something."

"Tell me about the wedding."

"We got to Kingman, and everything was arranged. They had a justice of the peace. There was a lawyer there with all the paperwork. By the time they were married, the press had figured it out, so some local stringers showed up. They take a couple of snaps, and pretty soon, the news is on the radio."

"What's she like?"

"Carole Lombard? She's silly. She's a nice enough girl, and she's lots of fun, but she tries too hard with him. She tries to make him laugh all the time. It's too much. You know, when we were in Seattle, I was so happy for Clark. He told me when he met Gretchen, he'd finally found a girl he could talk to—this one, I don't know. She doesn't take anything seriously."

"Not even the wedding vows?"

"Giggled through the whole thing."

"And what did Clark do?"

"He went along with it. It's as if he lets the woman lead on the dance floor, you know?"

———

Myrna Loy had been called to sound stage A on the MGM lot. As she turned the corner to enter, she ran into Clark Gable.

"This is all Spencer Tracy's fault," Gable grumbled.

"Be a good sport," Myrna chided him.

Ed Sullivan, a young reporter from the Associated Press, had set up a table for a press conference. A scrum of photographers and reporters stood behind a red rope, which was suspended in front of them mainly for looks. As Gable and Loy joined Ed Sullivan, the photographers began to snap photos.

"We're here today to crown the king and queen of Hollywood," Ed began. "Miss Loy, we have a crown for you, and one for you, Mr. Gable. Would you like to say anything to the fans?"

"Thank you. It's a big honor."

"I feel the same as Mr. Gable—it's a big honor, and we hope we live up to your high expectations."

"Congratulations, Queen Myrna and King Clark!"

Gable took Myrna's arm and led her off the sound stage. "Did you ever?" Gable laughed. "Humiliating," he said.

"Horrifying! They should've given it to someone who wants a crown, like, say, Norma Shearer."

"Myrna, they picked you because you're down-to-earth."

"And you?"

"I'm going to kill Spence. That's all there is to it. He started this king stuff, and he's going to end it."

"Before you do, can we finish the picture?"

"Sure, sure."

"I like this one. You made an honest woman out of me."

"It's about time," Gable joked.

"How's it going with you and your new bride?"

"We're very happy."

"Now you have everything a man needs. A good wife, a big career, and a crown. You're the king of Hollywood. "

"The crown is made of paper, Myrna. Trust me. I get too close to a lit match, and I'm John Gilbert."

Loretta slipped into the nursery at Sunset House and tucked the blanket around Judy. Moonlight shimmered through the trees. Loretta kissed her daughter and went outside.

Hiking up her skirt, she sat and lowered her legs into the pool. The cool water sent a chill through her. The cold moonlight made her shiver.

Judy was beginning to ask questions about her daddy, and there was a sadness in the four-year-old when fathers showed up at school and carried their children home on their shoulders. Now that Gable had married Lombard, Judy wouldn't have those ordinary moments with her birth father.

Loretta remembered filming *The Primrose Ring*, almost every detail of it. Going forward, Judy would remember everything that happened to her, and she would believe everything Loretta told her. Loretta still could not come to terms with how to tell her about her father. Worse than that, she didn't know how to tell the child that she was her real mother; inevitably, the questions would lead back to the identity of her father.

Carole issued a statement that said she wanted ten children with Gable, and that their ranch in Encino could grow with as many rooms as she could fill. Loretta felt as if the message was directed at her—Judy, just one child, wouldn't matter as much as a baseball team of them.

Loretta decided to stop pining for Gable. She knew it would take work, but discipline and focus were her best attributes. It was time for Loretta to get serious about creating a home with a proper husband for her daughter. No more dinner dates set up by the studio; no more favors to moguls or photo opportunities with available young male stars to promote movies. She would find a way to give Judy a father—but this time, it had to be a man who would stay.

Darryl Zanuck loved a historical epic. He had a crazy idea to put the Young sisters and Georgiana in a movie together, playing sisters. Zanuck remembered that Loretta enjoyed working with Don Ameche, so he cast him as the lead in *The Alexander Graham Bell Story.*

Polly and Sally had decided that this movie would be the end of their movie careers. They'd never had much interest in acting, and now that they were young mothers, their ambition lay elsewhere. For Loretta, the Bell story would be a farewell too; she wanted to leave Darryl Zanuck for good. She was burning up the last weeks of her contract so she could leave Twentieth Century-Fox, a free agent again.

Loretta stepped into her gown as the costumer fastened the buttons up the back.

"Stay still, Miss Young," the costumer warned.

"I swear Mr. Zanuck chose this time period just so I'd be tortured with buttons and bustles."

The costumer shrugged. "He likes historical accuracy."

Myron Selznick pushed the door open. "Loretta, I got someone here for you to meet."

"I have to get Miss Young to the set," the costumer groused.

"This will take a second," Myron promised.

"Keep buttoning," Loretta joked. "The buttons buy you time."

Tom Lewis appeared in the doorway. He had a thick head of hair and a big smile. He also towered over Loretta, who hadn't put on her shoes. "Hi, I'm Tom Lewis from New York."

"I'm Loretta Young."

"I know. I'm here because I have a part for you."

"What sort of part?" Loretta was intrigued.

"On the radio. We're going to do a show for the Motion Picture Relief Fund. Jack Benny and Judy Garland did the last one, and we'd love to have you on our next show."

"Yes, I'll do it."

"Tom, I'm taking you everywhere I go from now on." Myron turned to Loretta. "What gives? You haven't said yes that quickly in all the time we've been working together."

Loretta smiled at Tom. "That's because he's the one asking."

Tom Lewis laughed. "I'll get you the script."

"You do that." Loretta slipped into her shoes.

Myron waited until Tom Lewis was out of earshot. "He's Catholic."

"He's also tall," Loretta observed.

"And he's very very single. Now, which of those attributes is the most important to you?"

"The height," Loretta joked. "I like to wear a heel instead of date one."

"I'll make the deal," Myron promised.

"Please don't call it a deal. I'm a romantic, remember?"

Tom Lewis had a different energy from the men Loretta had met since Judy was born. He was a businessman, there was none of the Hollywood spit shine on him. She didn't feel manipulated by his charm, but energized by it. It was a brief introduction, but Loretta had seen all she needed to see, and was intrigued to find out more. Perhaps it was time to stop looking for a fellow actor, or anyone in her line of work, to get serious about. Maybe it was time for a more traditional fellow, a man who could be the head of a household, a good father and mate. Loretta craved stability and security in a man, and she had yet to find it. Perhaps that man had just walked through her door, just as everything was changing in her life for the better.

Judy was about to turn five when her play pal Cammie King invited her to her fifth birthday party.

The Kings lived in the flats of Beverly Hills, wide, winding streets dotted with a mix of architectural styles—Tudor, Cape Cod, Georgian. Somehow, just like the back lots, where Western saloons were built next to a replica of the Parthenon, the crazy quilt of mixed styles worked.

Judy was dressed as Bo Peep for the costume birthday party. Irene the costumer had made Judy a blue satin dress, pantaloons, and, by request of Loretta, a matching bonnet. Loretta had tied the bow under Judy's chin and said, "Remember, Little Bo Peep wears her bonnet at all times."

Judy ran up the walk of her friend's house and into the party ahead of Loretta. Cammie's mother, Pamela, a trim California blonde, greeted her at the door.

"I'm so glad you could make it, Loretta."

"Wouldn't have missed it."

"I'm up to my ears," Pamela said.

"Let me help."

Loretta followed Pamela into the kitchen, modern and white. The table was filled with trays of food, miniature hot dogs, cups of chili with faces made of cheese strips, and stalks of celery filled with peanut butter and studded with raisins.

Beyond the kitchen, Loretta could see the backyard, where the children were playing in a pint-size circus, with clowns helping them play games.

"Can you clean the strawberries?" Pamela asked.

"Happy to."

"Loretta, I wanted to talk you. You were a child actress."

"I was four when I was in my first picture."

"Cammie just wrapped on *Gone with the Wind*."

"Did she enjoy it?"

"Loved it. Mr. Gable was so kind to her—and evidently Vivien Leigh is lovely. We're going to show some rushes later—Mr. Selznick is sending his man over here."

"How nice." Loretta got a knot in her stomach. She'd been out to dinner a few times with Tom Lewis, and was having a wonderful time, looking to the future, but nothing stopped her heart like the mention of Clark Gable.

"Do you think it's all right for Cammie to continue acting?"

"Pamela, the business was so new then. It was a lark. All my sisters were extras—we did it for fun. I think once it isn't fun, you pull her out of it."

Loretta helped Pamela bring the platters outside, and the children came running for the goodies. Judy saw her mother and ran for her.

"Mama!" she called.

The children gathered around the platters, grabbing whatever was closest to them.

"Judy, you can take your bonnet off. It's hot out here," Pamela said as she turned to hand out bottles of soda to the children.

Judy looked at her mother. Loretta gave her daughter a look, which Judy obeyed. The bonnet stayed on.

"Judy has big ears!" a little boy in a cowboy hat announced.

"Elephant ears!" another boy taunted her.

Mrs. King went over to the boys. "That is not nice. You apologize to Judy, or there will be no cake for you two."

"Sorry," the boys chimed to Judy.

Loretta was devastated for her daughter but made light of it, by joining in a game of Pin the Tail on the Donkey.

As the sun went down, the flats of Beverly Hills were covered in a soft lavender haze. The children gathered inside to open presents. Cammie was a sweet girl, and tore into each gift with relish.

Loretta stood back against the wall with the other mothers as Pamela orchestrated the opening of the gifts.

"Wanna see me in the movie?" Cammie said, standing up.

The children cheered, Judy Young the loudest.

As the lights went down, the familiar *whap* of the projector began. The children settled down, and the mothers were giddy.

"I heard this movie is spectacular," one mother said.

The images jumped on the screen, first with the scrawl bits between the scenes. Cammie jumped up. "There I am!"

Pamela played a scene where Cammie as Bonnie Blue Butler was riding a pony, dressed in ruffles from head to toe.

Judy was mesmerized by the image.

Gable stood up and cheered his daughter on as Vivien Leigh sat primly in a chair. The camera went in close on Gable, and Loretta couldn't breathe.

Her daughter was watching her father. This was more than Loretta could stand. The best actress in the world wouldn't get through the pain of this, and she could not fake it. She felt like someone was choking her, or not someone but something—the memory of a love that she could not shake, no matter how hard she tried.

All Loretta had left from the glorious days when she had Gable all to herself was Judy. And she couldn't share the truth with her daughter. How could she ever ask an innocent child to keep a secret that carried such shame?

Loretta knelt down and reached for Judy, who crawled to her mother. "Honey, let's go home," Loretta whispered in her daughter's ear.

"But Mama, the cake."

"I'll make you a cake."

"Okay!" Judy was happy.

Loretta and Judy snuck out of the previews and out of the house. Once outside, they ran to Loretta's car to head for home.

15

All of southern California, it seems, had turned out for Loretta's wedding to Tom Lewis at the chapel of Saint Paul's Church in Westwood. The intimate ceremony had turned into a premiere, with fans lining the streets and sitting on their cars to get a better look. Tom's relatives came from the East, while folks who loved a Hollywood extravaganza had come from as far away as Carmel, packing picnic lunches to sustain them as they waited outside for a glimpse of the bride and groom following their nuptial mass.

The costume designer Irene had made Loretta a wedding gown in shades of blue, using layers of tulle netting that rolled like the waves of a lake in the sun as she walked down the aisle. With each step Loretta took, she was more confident that this was a solid decision. It was time. Her sisters were in stable marriages. Georgiana was growing up. Gladys Belzer's interior design firm was solid and prospering. And everyone around Loretta had married, including Mr. Gable. At twenty-seven, Loretta felt like the last single woman standing in Hollywood.

Every aspect of Loretta's decision to marry Tom Lewis made sense to her. Judy would finally have a father. Loretta would create a family of her own, with a fine man. Her career would move forward; Tom was fully supportive of his movie star wife.

But first, Tom Lewis had work to do. He had to take control of Loretta Young Enterprises.

Gladys Belzer had been an accidental visionary, putting any spare money into real estate in Beverly Hills and the surrounding communities. She had superb taste and a thriving interior design studio, but she was a lousy bookkeeper. She had collected so much real estate over the years, she wasn't certain how much land she actually owned. Tom, a crack businessman, buried himself in the deeds and paperwork and sorted out the complex system Gladys had created.

Lewis negotiated deals to sell property, refinanced mortgages, opened accounts, closed others, and cleaned up their taxes. He took the burden of the accounting off his new mother-in-law, who didn't enjoy numbers or keeping the books. Loretta, for her part, welcomed the input. She craved the order and management that Tom brought to the marriage and to the family business interests. She let him do whatever he wished with her money, trusting him implicitly.

While the wedding reception was winding down, Alda had slipped away to organize and display the wedding gifts in the living room of Sunset House. Loretta's honeymoon trousseau was packed. All Loretta had to do was change into her going-away outfit.

"I've never seen so many boxes!" Loretta said, peeling off her picture hat.

"It was a lovely mass. Everyone enjoyed the reception," Alda said as she tied a ribbon around a stack of unopened cards and telegrams.

"What a mob scene."

"That's what happens when a movie star gets married."

"That's why they elope." Loretta smiled. "I'm going up to kiss Judy good night. She seemed to have a good time at the wedding."

"She's happy whenever you're with her."

"I was that way with my mother." Loretta turned to go up the stairs.

"Loretta?"

"Yes, Alda?"

"Does he know?"

"Does he know what?"

"Have you told Tom that Judy is your daughter?"

"He hasn't asked."

"Loretta"—Alda deliberately called her boss by her screen name whenever she wanted to make a serious point—"he knows how much money you have, and he knows how much property you own, but he has no idea that Judy is your daughter."

Loretta snapped, "Alda, I know what I'm doing."

"I don't think you do. You have to tell your daughter the truth. And you have to tell Tom the truth."

"It's none of your concern."

"I've been with you for eight years. Eight volatile years in your life. I've watched you navigate some painful situations with grace. I'm your friend, which is why I can tell you the truth. You have to tell your daughter that you're her mother and Clark Gable is her father. And then you have to sit Tom Lewis down and tell him the truth. He has cornered me several times with questions. He thinks Judy is Sally's baby—"

"That's ridiculous. I asked him if there was anything about me he wanted to know, and he told me he knew everything he needed to know."

"You're the only person who can tell him the truth."

"I can't."

"You won't."

"I can't. He'll leave me."

"You're married all of six hours. I don't think he'll leave you."

Alda followed Loretta up the stairs to her bedroom suite. In her opinion, Loretta at twenty-seven was still young enough to chart a new course, yet old enough to have acquired some wisdom. Alda saw hard edges developing around the tender girl she'd met when she moved to Los Angeles, and she didn't like them. She didn't think they were natural, or true to Loretta's nature. Alda figured that losing Gable to Lombard had left Loretta resentful of what she would never have.

Alda closed the bedroom door behind her. She helped Loretta into her going-away suit, a blue silk suit with a cargo jacket and big pockets piped in white.

"I'll deal with this when I get home," Loretta said quietly.

Tom Lewis poked his head through the bedroom door. "Is everything all right, darling?"

Loretta beamed. "Fine, just fine."

"I'll be downstairs."

Tom Lewis stopped in his stepdaughter's room. She was sleeping soundly in the moonlight. Tom smiled. She was a cute kid, quiet and well-mannered. He was lucky that he wasn't walking into a situation where he had to navigate parenthood with a spoiled Hollywood brat. He had enough on his plate, with his wife's convoluted finances and real estate holdings. Tom tiptoed across the room and left a note for Judy, with a small box. He had bought her a charm bracelet filled with tiny crystal stars. Tom wanted Judy to know she was important to him, and that he would take good care of her. The wedding day had gotten away from him—with the crowds, guests, and hoopla, he had hardly seen his new stepdaughter.

Alda handed Loretta her purse.

"I put your retainer in its case. It's in your purse. Don't lose it."

"Thank you. I haven't told Tom about the retainer yet."

"He'll get used to it," Alda reassured her.

Loretta turned to Alda and gave her a big hug. "Trust me."

"It's not about trust. It's about peace of mind. You finally have the opportunity to have it. Please take it. Own it. It's yours. You deserve it."

Loretta nodded. "Take these gifts to the Camden House, would you?" she asked. "And stay on top of Mother. I want Tom to carry me across the threshold of the new house when we get back. Please make it happen."

"I'll do my best."

Loretta stopped to kiss sleeping Judy good-bye. She tiptoed across the room, gave her daughter several kisses, and stepped back to look at her. Her eye caught the envelope and box on the nightstand. It was addressed, "To Judy from Daddy."

If Loretta had had any doubts about her decision to marry Tom Lewis, they were gone now. She had made the right decision. She would have everything she'd dreamed of, and everything she had wanted for Judy, including the fence with the roses.

Loretta was lying in the hotel bed with a stack of fan magazines when Tom came through the door. "Feel like going to the pool?"

"Of course, darling."

Loretta and Tom had driven for their honeymoon to Mexico, where Tom had made arrangements at the Del Sol, an exclusive resort just over the border.

"I spoke with the hotel management, they're setting up a cabana for us."

"Good idea." Loretta could see that Tom was frustrated. "You did a splendid job planning the honeymoon. I love it. And I'm sorry that there's so much interest in us."

To Loretta's surprise, fans had figured out the location, and had been waiting outside the hotel for them. If there was one thing fans loved more than a good movie, it was a real life wedding. At first Tom was patient, but as the honeymoon went on, he began to lose it. If one more person shouted "Mr. Young!" at him, he'd let them know how he felt.

"I wanted to be alone with you."

"We will. When we get home, life will get back to normal. In Los Angeles, I'm one of the crowd."

"I wanted this to be special."

"It is! Now, go and change and I'll meet you at the pool."

Tom kissed Loretta. "More mail," he said, handing her a stack of envelopes.

Loretta rifled through the stack. Her eye caught the name NIVEN on a telegram. She ripped into it.

GRETCH, YOU ARE NOT THE ONLY ONE MARRIED THIS WEEK. PRIMMIE AND I LOCKED. LOVE TO YOU AND TAD. NIV.

Loretta hid the telegram at the bottom of the stack as Tom grabbed a towel and headed out to the pool. As soon as he was gone, she tore up the telegram and threw it in the sink. She lit a match and burned it until it was nothing but black char. It seemed the moment the priest pronounced them married, Tom changed. His strength, which she admired, became controlling; his worldiness now appeared as arrogance. Loretta learned that every woman compromised when it came to marriage. No one person could possibly make her happy in all the ways she hoped a husband might. Tom was responsible and solid. He was not an actor. She reminded herself that she chose a civilian because she wanted a stable life with a man who would be faithful to her.

Loretta already understood Tom Lewis's vulnerabilities. He couldn't understand Niv calling him Tad, and he didn't find it funny. In fact, Loretta didn't think the two men would get along at all. Different senses of humor, opposite approaches to life. Loretta was going to make this marriage work, and in order to do so, she would manage everything she said and did. She was determined to have a happy marriage and a father for Judy. She would play the part of dutiful wife and compromise to make Tom happy. It also meant building a wall between her life and friendships before Tom and her marriage after. Loretta was used to sorting her relationships into compartments, and so it would go as Mrs. Tom Lewis.

———

The August sun burned through the palm trees on Sunset as Alda drove to the Camden House, Loretta's new home with Tom Lewis, which was under renovation and refurbishment by Gladys Belzer. While Loretta and Tom were off on their honeymoon, Alda and Gladys were hastily preparing the home for the newlyweds. New appliances had been installed, floors refinished, and finally the walls were being painted in preparation for the hanging of the draperies.

Alda pulled up in front of the elegant cottage, obscured by trees with low, lush green branches. A white fence surrounded the property. It was covered in red roses, just as Loretta had imagined.

"Yoohoo!" Gladys called through the window.

Much work had been done, but there was a lot to finish before Loretta and Tom returned. Alda had goosed Gladys as much as she could. Nevertheless, the house was a jewel box. Gladys had painted the walls in shades of blue, and the living room wall was covered in a mural of a fairy-tale castle. This was an ideal place for a newlywed couple, but for sure, Gladys hadn't forgotten her granddaughter.

"What do you think?"

"Gretchen will love it."

Without taking her eyes off the mural, Gladys asked, "Do you think Gretchen is happy?"

"I hope so."

"She called to speak to Judy. She said it was a madhouse in Mexico. Fans found out where they were staying. Well, you could imagine. She seemed preoccupied."

"Mr. Lewis seems like a practical man. He had to understand how popular Gretchen is with the public. Especially since radio. Radio reaches millions of people."

"Good point."

"I'm worried that Mr. Lewis believes Loretta is going to retire. I don't think he has any idea how much she loves her work."

"How would he know? He flew in and out from New York, he'd see her for dinner, and he'd fly out again. He has no idea how hard she works."

"He saw a bit when she was working with him on the radio play," Alda reasoned.

"Has Tom asked you any questions about Judy?"

"He asked me where she came from, did we know anything about her original family."

"What did you tell him?"

"Nothing."

"Good."

"It isn't good, Mrs. Belzer. I think Mr. Lewis's imagination runs wild. I don't think that's good for Judy or their marriage. Loretta tells me she has it under control, but I don't believe it. Judy needs a safe place where she can know the truth, and it should include her stepfather."

"Everything will be better when they have a baby together."

"Better for whom?"

"For everyone. Judy will have a sibling. No one will care where Judy is from once they have a baby."

"But Judy will."

"I don't think so. We love her to pieces. She is loved, Alda. That's all that matters."

Gladys, like her daughter Loretta, had a way of ending a conversation that made it clear that the subject was closed. Alda knew that Loretta was making a terrible mistake, but she would have a hard time convincing her if Gladys Belzer wasn't on board. Maybe Loretta would come to her own conclusion in the matter and do the right thing by Judy, but Alda doubted it.

After a few months of living with Gladys at Sunset House, Tom and Loretta finally moved into Camden House—"their little blue heaven," as Gladys called it. Tom was annoyed that the house wasn't ready when they returned from their honeymoon, and decided one day that whether the house was finished or not, he was moving. Loretta could not convince him to wait, so they moved over, living in rooms with paint fumes and empty of furniture.

Tom handled conflict by pushing through it to get his own way. If Loretta was late, he'd sit in the car and steam, laying on the horn until she joined him. If she was telling a story at a party and got a detail wrong, he'd correct her in front of the company. He was subtle but controlling.

Alda's inability to push Gladys to finish the house put her in dutch with Tom Lewis. He pushed Alda aside and took on more of the responsibilities of Loretta's work, reading scripts, prioritizing appearances, and dealing with the agent. Alda had more time to answer fan mail, which was now out of control because of Loretta's reach in radio. The pool house at Sunset House was filled with sacks of mail.

"You need some help, Alda." Loretta took in the volume of the mail that had arrived.

"I'll get some. I put a query letter up at Saint Paul's. I'll bring some ladies in to help."

"Good idea. I'm taking Judy to the hospital today."

"Today is the day? Do you need me?"

"I can manage. Mama is going to come with me, and Mr. Lewis is going to stay in New York for a few more days, so I figured this was a good time for Judy's surgery."

"Whatever you say."

"Alda, do you have a problem with Judy's operation?"

"Forgive me. I think what you're doing is wrong."

"We have an exceptional doctor. Judy will be safe." Loretta's eyes filled with tears.

"I'm sure she'll be fine, but that's not the point. Look at my nose, Loretta. It's an Italian nose. When I was a girl, I hated it, I thought it was too large. Then I went in the convent and I didn't care about my nose at all. Didn't give it a thought. Then I met Luca Chetta and he liked my nose. So I thought about my nose again. Now, when I look in the mirror I see my mother and father, who are far away, but I'm reminded of them."

"What are you saying to me?"

"You shouldn't change Judy's ears."

"She's being teased at school."

"Teach her to handle the bullies. That builds character. Mr. Gable is part of who she is. If you change her ears, you're taking away an aspect of him."

"She's getting braces for the buckteeth that she inherited from me."

"It's not the same thing. She knows you're her mother."

"Her father doesn't have any interest in her."

"It doesn't matter. That's between them. But there should be nothing but truth shared between you and Judy. Loretta, you have to believe me, no good will come of this secret."

"Her father is dead."

"That's a story you've made up. The problem is, he's very much alive."

"I agonize about it constantly. I pray about it."

"I'm not saying you tell the world. But in the world that your daughter lives in, her aunts and cousins know the truth; the children at school, their parents know the truth, though it's really none of their business. They're just guessing, and even that, I'll give you. But you cannot continue this charade. She will grow up and hate you for it."

"She'll understand someday."

Alda's eyes filled with tears.. "You need someone in your life that tells you the truth. But I understand why people don't. There is no getting through to you."

Loretta walked out of the pool house. Alda didn't understand the pressure she was under. Loretta's marriage was already in trouble, even though she was determined to make it work. She missed living at Sunset House with her mother and Judy. It had been a peaceful life, and now she had to deal with her husband's needs and moods.

Her husband tried to be a good stepfather, but Loretta disagreed with his parenting style. She was afraid she had married Tom because Gable married Lombard, Sally married Norman, and Polly married Carter. She'd felt left behind, and she'd desperately wanted Judy to have a stable home life.

Judy's operation to pin back her ears was as much for Tom Lewis as it was for Judy. Tom hadn't asked Loretta direct questions about Judy's background. He'd eventually assumed she'd been adopted anonymously, and that was that. Loretta dismissed any of Tom's queries as gossip. She told him the story of Saint Elizabeth's and finding Judy there, the same story she had concocted for the newspapers. Loretta had taken the lie into her new marriage, but only because Gable had rejected her and Judy.

———————

The first face Judy Lewis saw when she opened her eyes at the hospital was her mother's. She would remember the soft pink lipstick, her mother's loving gray eyes, and her encouraging smile.

"How are you feeling, my baby girl?"

Judy was eight years old, and she didn't like being called a baby. But when her mother scooped her up in her arms and held her, she didn't mind.

Judy felt pain behind her ears. She reached up and touched the bandage that encircled her head.

"Try not to touch the bandage, Judy."

"Mama, it hurts."

Loretta rang for the nurse, who came quickly. "My daughter is in pain."

"I'll take care of it," the nurse, dressed head to toe in white, said.

"She looks like a bride," Judy said.

"She does, doesn't she?" Loretta smiled.

"Mama, did it work?"

"The doctor said your operation went perfectly."

"I won't get teased anymore?"

"I don't think so."

"Mama, will you stay with me?"

"Forever. There's no place I'd rather be."

"And no daddy?"

"He's in New York. Judy, is he nice to you?"

"Sometimes."

"Do you like him?"

"No."

"Oh, Judy, he's your daddy now."

"Will my ears be better by the time he gets home?"

"Oh, yes."

"Good. I don't want him to see the bandages."

"Why?" Loretta's voice caught.

"He doesn't like me to cry."

"Judy, it's all right to cry. Sometimes we need to."

"Do you?"

"Sure."

"Daddy doesn't like it."

"I'll talk to him." This innocent statement became the words that Judy would hear her mother say through the years. For Judy, there would be no talking to Tom Lewis, no reasoning with him. Judy was adopted, and therefore she was not his. There was distance, and that meant there could only be affection, not love. And sometimes even affection was too much of a chore.

"Mama, do you have to go back to work?" Judy didn't like that her mother worked, and that people she didn't know knew who her mother was. Shy and discerning, Judy saw through everything, and now that she was eight, she saw more.

"No, I'm here every day and every night. I will not leave you."

Judy felt relief. This was a moment she would return to in the years to come. The memory of her mother, steadfast by her side through the long days and nights of her recuperation, would never leave her consciousness. Her mother read to her, they played games, and when Judy was well enough to get out of bed, they went up and down the halls and read to the other children.

Judy watched her mother's generosity and kindness, and she became proud of her. It wasn't like the movie premieres, where people applauded and hollered and made noise and wanted to touch her mother. It wasn't like her mother's wedding, which had lasted all day and was hot, and people rushed the doors of the church to see her. This was pure. Loretta was just another mother, Judy's mother. It was just the two of them, healing. The world outside didn't matter, only their relationship. And nowhere in that memory was her stepfather. That Judy would remember too.

––––––––

The cars were double-parked on Wilshire, but the cops issued no tickets. Outside the Hollywood Canteen, local girls gathered to present socks they had knitted for the soldiers before they were deployed to Europe. Frank Sinatra crooned on the radio in the parked cars, underscoring the excitement. Inside, Hollywood's most glamorous stars were working, serving the soldiers as an act of support and gratitude before they shipped out.

Loretta poured hot coffee for the midshipmen while her friends Roz Russell and Irene Dunne passed out doughnuts. Roz was a tall, athletic brunette with flushed, rosy cheeks, while Irene was a strawberry blonde, slim and elegant, with a regal bearing.

"Dance with me, Miss Young?" a shiny eighteen-year-old recruit asked.

"They never ask me to dance—I'm taller than they are," Roz whispered to Irene.

"It's because you're married," Irene reassured her.

"So's Loretta."

Loretta came from behind the bar and joined the soldier on the dance floor. As Loretta and the young man in uniform took a spin, the floor cleared. The men were enraptured, watching their favorite movie star dance with their fellow recruit.

"We have an announcement. Ladies and gentlemen, an announcement." Throughout the evening, announcements had been made. The music would stop, the dancing would cease, and everyone in the canteen paid attention.

"Sad news. Our good friend and supporter Carole Lombard has been killed in a plane crash while on a bond tour. The plane went down on a mountaintop in Nevada. Miss Lombard had raised more than two million dollars in bond rallies around the country."

Loretta was stunned. Roz and Irene ran to her. They knew what this meant to Loretta, though they never spoke of it in detail.

Loretta's first instinct was to go to Clark, to find him, hold and comfort him. She remembered Tom Lewis, and knew she couldn't.

"Should we drive out to the ranch?" Roz wondered. She had made two movies with Gable and adored him.

"Let's call first," Irene said.

"No, there's nothing we can do for her now. We need to take care of these men," Loretta said. "We made a promise."

Irene and Roz looked at one another.

"I guess that's what Carole would do," Irene said.

"I'll call my husband. Freddie will go over to be with Clark," Roz said.

Loretta took the stage and made an announcement, "Gentlemen, I'd like us to pray for Carole Lombard. She was grand, talented, and an excellent wife to our good friend Clark Gable. She was also a great American. She served her country splendidly."

The entire canteen cheered for Carole Lombard.

Loretta's rival Carole really hadn't been one. Lombard had grabbed Gable as she had grabbed everything in her life—with joy, relish, and determination. Beyond that, Loretta didn't know what to feel.

Roz Russell went onstage and took the microphone. "She was a great girl. No one liked to laugh and dance more than Carole. So please, let's enjoy the band for the rest of the night—let's celebrate in honor of Carole Lombard."

The band began to play, and Loretta remembered her promise to dance with the soldier. She took him by the hand, and they went back to the dance floor.

Spencer Tracy requisitioned a car to drive him to Las Vegas to be with his friend Gable. As he climbed into the sedan, he was trailed by a group of studio executives, grousing that he was holding up production, but he was intent on his mission.

He sank low in the back seat, pulled the brim of his fedora over his eyes, and went to sleep.

At the Las Vegas airport, Spencer climbed out of the car. It was a simple hangar, one that he was familiar with, as they had run drills there for *Test Pilot*, a film he had made with his friend. There were murmurs and whispers from bystanders as Spence pushed his way through the crowd and into the waiting room before a policeman stopped him.

"Sir, I have to ask you to wait outside."

"Like hell. Tell Gable Spence is here."

The cop recognized the actor and let him past the ropes. Tracy took a deep breath as he turned the corner. Gable was standing, looking out the window, his back to the studio flacks who had shown up as soon as word of the plane crash was out. Tracy went to him and put his hand on Gable's shoulder.

"Buddy," Tracy said softly.

"I told her to wait," Gable whispered. "But she wanted to get home."

"It was an accident."

"Her mother was with her. And about twenty-five soldiers."

"Oh, God," Tracy muttered.

"Otto was with them too."

Tracy put his arm around Gable. Otto Winker was Gable's publicist, but he was also his friend.

"They won't let me up the mountain."

"You shouldn't go."

"But I want to see, with my own eyes. I want to see if they're telling me the truth."

"I'm sorry."

"She was a good girl."

"The best."

"Never gave me any trouble. She was my life. We laughed all the time."

"She loved you."

"I don't know what to do."

"We wait." Tracy didn't have a plan for his friend. That night, all he could do was stand with him. When the park rangers rescue unit arrived, Gable insisted on going with them. Spence felt that Gable should not be alone, so he accompanied him. They loaded into an army jeep and drove up the mountain, as far as they could go, until the snow and rain made it impossible for them to see.

Gable sat in the front seat and did not say a word as the driver navigated the rough road. Spencer tried to keep the chatter up with the rangers, if only to take pressure off Gable.

Gable had finally found happiness. He had pursued it ardently, as men do. He was satisfied with Carole; they loved all the same things, and she spun a dream of home life that he had found irresistible. Gable wanted a simple, comfortable, agreeable life. The woman who had provided that lovely life, who had waited for him, suffered through the years of Ria's waffling, the girl who had made him laugh when he was at his lowest, had left him, having suffered a brutal death, the picture of which he would have to live with for the rest of his life. Carole Lombard, who had brought the light, was now responsible for Clark Gable's deepest despair.

Tracy was unable to provide any comfort that night to Gable. He stood by his friend through the worst of it, unable to say or do anything to assuage his grief. Gable would remember little of that night, but when he thought of it, he would remember Spence, who stood by him like the brother he never had. Whatever warmth there was, Tracy provided it, but Gable couldn't feel it. He watched Gable's spirit die that night. His soul left him, and behind it was only darkness, and a kind of quiet fury that would mark Gable for the rest of his life.

———

Loretta spun around in the chair at the beauty parlor in the Waldorf Astoria and faced her friend Myrna Loy.

"Hair looks good," Loretta told Myrna. "You look like a movie star."

"Good, maybe I can rattle some of these New York society types to plunk down some money for the boys. How are those nails?"

"Short. I spent too much time in the garden before we got here." Loretta looked at her hands. "What time are we due at the Stork Club?"

"Eight."

"It's gonna be a late night."

"Live a little. Your husband's in California, right?"

"Yep."

"So it's just us girls."

"That's how I like it, Myrna. Safer that way."

"I hope you don't mind, I invited Mr. Gable up to my suite for drinks."

"What's he doing here?"

"He joined the army."

"You mean it?"

"Yep. Enlisted. Said that's what Carole would have wanted."

"But he's forty-two years old."

"They took him." Myrna looked at her friend. "If it's too much, if you can't handle it, I can cancel the drinks."

"Don't do that."

"You know, I understand." Myrna sat down next to Loretta. "You'll never get over him."

"I'm married now," Loretta said firmly.

"Marriage is one thing, love is another." Myrna sighed. "I'm taking my third shot at it, so I should know."

"Experience counts." Loretta smiled.

"Let me ask you something. Are you over him?"

"What do you mean?"

"Is Gable out of your blood?"

"I don't know how to answer that."

"I knew it. He isn't."

"We have a long history, Myrna."

"Those are the stories that get you. In real life and the movies."

"It hasn't been anything like a movie. It's been all too real. Too much pain and compromise and longing, frankly. All of it rolled into one. And I haven't handled it very well. I tried, but I couldn't. If you don't mind, I'll skip the drinks and meet you at the club."

"I'm sorry." Myrna gave Loretta a hug. "He asked to see you. But I can make up an excuse."

"He asked for me?" Loretta's heart filled with sadness.

"Yes, he did."

"Don't cancel the drinks."

"Whatever you say."

Myrna only ever had one side in a fight. She was on the side of love. She knew it would do Gable good to see Loretta, and she already knew what it meant to Loretta to have been invited.

Myrna's suite at the Waldorf was decorated in peach, a perfect back-drop for a classic redhead. There were several flower arrangements set around the room, filled with calla lilies, daisies, and peach roses.

Loretta knocked on the door. Myrna opened the door and whistled.

"Sister, you know how to work a pencil skirt."

Loretta wore a black velvet skirt and a white silk blouse with bil-lowing sleeves. Her hair was down and loose, as were the strings of pearls she had thrown casually around her neck.

"Follow me. Captain Gable is here."

"Captain? How quickly he went up the ladder!"

Gable stood in his uniform by the bay window that overlooked Park Avenue. There was white hair at his temples, and the lines on his face, once lightly etched by the sun, were now deep. There was no other way to describe it; he was a man consumed by grief.

Loretta went to Gable and embraced him. His uniform was made of thick wool, the buttons polished, strictly utilitarian, the opposite of the fine silk suits that were custom made for him at the studio.

"I'm gonna leave you two kids alone—I got an interview to do."

Loretta looked at Myrna, who winked at her and left.

"I'm so sorry about Carole."

"Don't know how to go on." Gable looked out the window at noth-ing in particular.

"Hey. It's me. You can talk to me." Loretta led him to the sofa.

They sat down. She put her arms around him, and he rested his head on her shoulder.

"I was afraid you'd throw me out the window after the last argument we had."

"That was on me, Gretchen. I handled everything wrong."

"Let's split the agony. It's better for both of us that way. Now, tell me about Carole."

"It's my fault. I told I missed her and wanted her home. So she arranged the plane. When I heard about the weather, I told her to take the train, but she wanted to get home."

"She wanted to get home to you. That's love."

"She lost her life over it."

"She didn't know that was going to happen, and neither did you. Besides, circumstances don't matter. She loved you."

"And I loved her. We had so many plans."

"Why did you sign up?"

"I can't go back to the life I had before. I hope they get me, Gretchen."

"Don't say that. You're still a young man."

"Older than you."

"I'm an old married lady now."

"Still my girl."

"I will always be your girl. And you should see Judy. She's a delight."

"When I get back, I'll come and see her."

"I hope so."

They sat in silence for a long while, until he began to weep.

Loretta held him tight. It was as if she was holding on to him for dear life, to save him. She laced her fingers through his, and he held on. They were forever intertwined, connected, wedded to one another in some deep way that was instantly familiar and somehow impossible.

In what seemed like a lifetime ago, she remembered a conversation she had with Spencer Tracy. When the worst happens, he'd said, there is nothing you can say, nothing you can do, except show up. Loretta caressed her old lover's face with the tenderness of a mother. Even that wasn't enough; all she could do was hold him and wait for the darkness to pass.

What she felt for Gable wasn't youthful passion, or the longing within the lonely moments of a good marriage for something out-side it, something a woman imagines to be better; what Loretta felt was something completely new to her. Loretta had a deep and abid-ing love for Gable that was deeper than romance, more lasting than physical passion. It was history. It was love over the expanse of many years. It had grace and meaning. It was spiritual, and it mattered to both of them. They shared equally in their mistakes and missteps, but underneath their shortcomings was always an understanding that the other had the capacity to forgive. Loretta felt gratitude that she could be there for him, and Gable, for that day, felt less alone.

Loretta never made it to the fund-raiser, and neither did Gable. Loretta found a blanket in the closet, draped it over Gable, and curled up next to him on the sofa. They went to sleep holding one another. And this is how they stayed until morning.

———————

Gable was strapped into the B-17 fighter-bomber. The whirl of the engine was deafening. Gable adjusted his goggles, which had steamed up from the sweat on his brow. Looking out the tiny sliver of Plexiglas, his only portal to the sky and the ground below, he saw black clouds of smoke and streaks of orange where the shells had detonated on the fringe of Berlin. He held the jammer control on his gun and waited for his instructions to fire.

Gable hoped the war would put distance between him and his grief. He'd joined up because Lombard made him promise he would, but that was just to appease her. If he ever served, he figured he would wind up in a special unit, making movies for the cause. Instead, he re-quested active combat, and after training, he got his wish. He hoped to be hit in midair, explode into a million pieces, and join Carole on the other side, where he believed she was waiting for him. It was the only way he could make sense of losing her so young, before they had a chance to enjoy their marriage, their new home, and the wealth that came after *Gone with the Wind*. How profoundly his views on money had changed when he lost her! The jewels, cars, and homes meant nothing without her. He attached to her the meaning of his own life. While Gable thought about death and dying, he didn't want to do anything that would prevent a reunion in the afterlife. That message of religion had gotten through to him loud and clear.

The commanding officer shouted out a code, and Gable gripped his machine gun as the gunner dived close to the rooftops of Berlin. Shells popping around them, the pilot navigated through black smoke, using only his instruments. For a split second Gable was sure they would crash. He thought of his wife and how she must have known before the plane hit the Nevada mountain, how those moments of pitch-black either lead you out into the blue or hurl you into the mountainside in an instant fireball.

Gable steadied the machine gun and peered through the slit. The gunner climbed heavenward. Gable looked down and saw Berlin burning. Turning in his jump seat, the officer gave the crew the thumbs-up, and Gable felt a wave of relief. Perhaps he was ready to live again. This was the first moment since Carole had died that he wanted to; in that sense, it was the start of something new.

———

Primula Niven, David's wife, held their son in her arms in the garden of their English cottage on the outskirts of London. She was an English beauty, with a lovely complexion and clear blue eyes.

There was a one-day ceasefire for Christmas Day, which had everyone outdoors, without fear of grenades, bombs, and gunfire. Primmie reveled in the peace. Clark Gable, in full uniform, unlatched the garden gate.

"What'd you make for me, Primmie?"

"Your favorite chicken pot pie, Captain."

Gable kissed her on the cheek. "Where's your husband?"

"He went for flour."

"Do you think he'll find some?"

"He's a charmer. I only worry what he'll have to do to get it."

"Let's not imagine the worst."

"Let's not," she said as she placed her son in the pram. "It's his naptime—he's out. Here, sit. Make yourself comfortable."

Gable sat down under an old elm tree. He fished in his pocket for his cigarettes and lit one. He looked at the cottage, with its thatched roof, and thought about trying to re-create it on his ranch when he returned. Primmie had hung red velvet ribbons in the window for Christmas decorations. The simple adornment made him smile as Primmie returned with a tray of tea and biscuits for her guest.

"How are you?" Primmie asked.

"I'm beat."

"You know, you'll feel better as time goes on."

"Will I?"

"Grief is never as bad as it is when you first feel it. The trick is to walk with it. Make it a part of who you are. Don't rail against it."

"Accept it."

"When you can."

Gable's eyes filled with tears. "I miss her."

Primmie put down her tea, went to Gable, and put her arms around him.

"Take your hands off my wife, you horny Yankee!" Niv thundered from the gate. Niv too was in uniform, his officer's cap pushed back on his head like a newsboy's.

"You'll wake the baby."

"Better it be the father waking the baby than the lovemaking sounds of his wife's affair."

"David, you're uncouth."

Niv swept his wife into his arms. "Oh, Primula. I hope you like it."

"I don't."

"Here's your flour. I have returned from France, and all I have to show is a bag of flour."

"You've been home for a week now, darling. Let's stop talking about France. Keep an eye on the boy, will you?"

Primmie went inside to make dinner.

"Old boy, you look a fright."

"I'm finally fit to be Marie Dressler's love interest."

"She wouldn't have you."

Gable laughed. "Probably not."

"It's almost over."

"Yep."

"What's the matter?"

"The usual." Gable offered Niv a cigarette.

"There's a lovely lady in Bath who has a spectacular view of Cordel Lake . . ."

"I don't need a diversion."

"Seriously?"

"Nope."

"But I thought . . ."

"Doesn't help. Funny. It doesn't help," Gable said.

"Well, that's going to put a dent in the old girls' business. And during the holidays? You cheap Scrooge."

Niven shook his head. Gable laughed. Soon, Niven joined him. They hadn't laughed this hard since their days on the boat. Before the war, before Carole. Before Gretchen. Before Primmie and the boy.

———

Loretta's dressing room for *The Bishop's Wife* was crowded with hair and makeup artists, the costumer, and a shoemaker, Signore Stanziani from New York City, on his knees, who was outfitting her for ice skates.

"They feel tight," Loretta told him.

"I make skates for the Olympics. You leave it to me."

David Niven came in wearing his minister costume. He tugged at the white Roman collar.

"Niv, you look like you're about to choke to death."

"There's good reason. I wanted to play the angel."

"Cary got there first."

"That's the trouble. Cary always gets everywhere first."

A playpen and a crib stood empty in the center of the room. "Where are the little brats?"

"Christopher and Peter went home with my mother."

"About time. Louella Parsons was going to tell the world that you're running a home for unwed mothers out of here."

"Okay, everybody. Beat it," Loretta said. "I look as good as I'm gonna get. "

The team that made Loretta sparkle dispersed like bubbles down a drain. "Done with the carwash for now."

"You do realize that I have one makeup man, and only one, to prepare me for the cameras? You know the bloke, he buffs pancake into my face like car wax."

"It takes an army for me. And every day past thirty, add in the Navy, the Air Force and the Marines."

"You and Cary Grant. He has a team that plucks, massages, and brushes him down like he's prepping for the Preakness. He's outside getting a golden glow between scenes with some foil contraption they used to shoot down fighter planes over Berlin. Of course, all he's getting out of it is a suntan. I told him that no one in New England has a tan this time of year. He said he was playing an angel, and angels live close to the sun, ergo the tan."

"You're just jealous."

"Probably. He is so handsome, next to him I look like a wall-eyed pug."

"My character wouldn't be married to a pug."

"Fair enough. We all know how picky you are."

"Watch it, Niv."

"Gretch, I need your help with something."

"That was your windup to ask for a favor?"

"Pathetic, isn't it?"

"What do you need?"

"We have to find something for Clark. A part in a movie. Mayer is putting him in real junk, so he's sitting out a lot. Our old friend is not the same. He needs work. He got back from the service, and he's out there on that ranch all by himself."

"You're going through your own terrible grief, and you're worried about him."

"I have the boys. Gable has nothing."

"Clark needs a job." Loretta knew what she was talking about. She had pushed for Niven to be cast in *The Bishop's Wife* shortly after Primmie died in an accident. It was a silly accident, a fall down a flight of stairs during a party game, but Primmie never recovered. Niv had been inconsolable, but Loretta knew that work would help him heal. Any heartache or disappointment or grief Loretta had lived through was eased by having something to do. Work was not a balm or a distraction, but salvation to the broken-hearted.

"I'll figure something out," Loretta promised him.

"He needs his friends, but he doesn't know how to ask for help," Niven explained. "You know, I'm different. I want to burden my friends. For some reason, Clark can't do it. He doesn't want to be a bother." Niven's eyes filled with tears. "I believe in running from it, to a point. But the truth is, you don't get over it."

"Let me see what I can do."

"You have a very big heart, Gretchen. I know he broke yours, so it's an act of compassion to even think about helping him."

"You only want someone to hurt because you want them to understand the pain you're in. The nature of revenge is to prove you're right. I didn't have to be right about Clark, I just wanted him to be happy. Whatever that meant. Whatever that means."

"How's that husband, Tad?"

"Tom."

"Right, right. Tom Thumb, except he's tall."

"You are evil!" Loretta laughed.

"Let's get the old gang together. That might help. And if you get Gable cast and you come up with a tasty little part for me in the proceedings, I'll be eternally yours."

"We already made that picture, Niv."

"Right, right. That's the one that turned me into Limburger cheese at the box office."

"Don't blame me for your fickle public."

———

Alda sat on the floor of Loretta's bedroom, stitching the hem of the evening gown Loretta would wear to the Academy Awards. The emerald-green taffeta confection, designed by Loretta's pal Jean Louis, had a series of dramatic ruffles on a full skirt, anchored by a matching satin medallion. The top featured a tight bodice and delicate straps. Jean Louis had designed a matching opera coat that was pure whimsy, with cascading ruffles that trailed behind her like waves.

"You could've been a professional seamstress, Alda."

"Too late for that."

"Why? Helen Rose, Edith Head, Irene—none of them are babies."

"They're designers. Big picture. I'm good at the details. Beadwork? Embroidery, I'm your girl."

Alda helped Loretta as she slipped into her gown.

"You know I'm going to lose. This is Roz's year."

"It's an honor to be nominated."

"That's what they say."

Loretta was thirty-four years old and could feel the ground shifting beneath her. The starring roles were going to the younger girls, the movie business was changing, and she was determined not to settle for parts in movies she didn't believe in. She was too young to use the word *retirement*, but she was too old not to see that her world was changing. She had just a few years left in pictures. She could not compete with her younger self, when she was nineteen, nubile, and fresh. Loretta was a different kind of beauty now; she had lived, borne three children, and married a second time. She had a bit of wisdom, and that cannot be concealed from the camera.

Judy slipped in and watched her mother dress.

"What do you think, Jude?"

"I like it."

Loretta sat down beside her twelve-year-old daughter, who had grown a foot in the last year. Her blue eyes sparkled; her heart-shaped face, in Loretta's eyes, was a work of art.

"Do you like the green?"

"It's nice."

"It's symbolic. See, when I was a girl, the first movie I ever made was called *The Primrose Ring*. I played a fairy."

"Did you fly?"

"Like a bird. In a leather harness. Anyway, the costumer put me in this beige shirt and stockings, and then she took emerald-green satin and tied it as a skirt around my waist and sprinkled glitter all over me."

"You sparkled."

"Exactly! Aunt Carlene played a fairy too—but she hated it. But I knew that was the job for me."

"Mama, what if you lose?"

"Losing is easy."

"It is?"

"All I have to be is gracious."

"What if you win?"

"That's easy too."

"Why?"

"All I have to be is gracious."

"Judy, don't let the boys stay up late," Tom said from the doorway.

"Yes, sir." Judy looked at her mother.

"No monkey business," her stepfather said firmly.

"I'll do my best," Judy said glumly.

"Watch your tone, Judy," Tom Lewis said as he left. "I'll be outside, Loretta."

"He's not very gracious," Judy said softly.

"No, he isn't. I'll talk to him."

"It's all right, Mom. Sister Karol says everybody's got a cross. He's my cross."

"That's a good way to look at it, but I won't tell him."

"Please don't. He'll have me washing his car in the morning." Judy rolled her eyes.

"Remember what Grandma says. No cross, no crown."

Loretta entered the Dorothy Chandler Pavilion on the arm of Tom Lewis. He was proud of his wife, but the scene, an industry hive, wasn't for him. He was raised to believe that a man led the household; if there was spotlight on the family, it should shine on him.

The cracks in the marriage were getting deeper. Tom had a terrible time with Judy. He questioned her, challenged her, and demanded perfection in her grades and deportment. Loretta didn't know how a father should behave with a daughter, since her own father had left when she was young, so she went along with Tom's approach to discipline. She didn't like it, but she acquiesced to keep Tom happy.

Loretta hadn't brought Judy to the Academy Awards that night because she thought she would lose. When her name was announced, Tom Lewis had to pull her out of her seat and push her toward the stage.

In what Loretta would call an underwater moment, sound went away and the world went blurry when her name was called as Best Actress for *The Farmer's Daughter*. Loretta looked back in the theater and saw her sister Georgie jumping up and down in slow motion. Her sisters and their husbands were all there, in the audience. They stood and cheered.

Judy sat by the radio and listened as her mother's name was announced. She jumped on the bed, the sofa, the chair, and the table, elated. The audience laughed when Loretta said she was glad she'd overdressed. Judy beamed with pride.

Later, when Judy went off to sleep, she dreamed of her mother, but she wasn't an Academy Award winner. She was a fairy, sprinkled in glitter, flying through a silent movie in black and white.

———

Loretta stood on the set of *The Key to the City*. Luca hollered at her from the grid above.

"Loretta! I just put the final touches on San Francisco!"

She looked up at a series of flats hanging from the ceiling.

"It's like the old days," she hollered.

"I like old days," Gable said from behind her.

"Me too." Loretta gave her costar a warm hug.

"You think we still got it?"

"We got something. I don't know if it's an 'it,' but it's something."

Gable laughed. "You mind if Sylvia hangs around? She wants to paint us in action."

Lady Sylvia Ashley, the ex-wife of Douglas Fairbanks and prior to him some nobleman in England, had married Gable hastily, in a way that worried his friends. She had already transformed the Encino home from an early American ranch to a chintz palace with a faux view of the Thames, a lot like one of Luca Chetta's backdrops.

Loretta got the feeling Gable was scared of Sylvia. She smiled at his wife. "Paint whatever you like, Sylvia."

Sylvia nodded. Gable smiled and waved to her before she went outside.

"Yes, my current wife is a painter and a ballbuster."

"Is she better at one than the other?"

"Hard to say." Gable laughed. "Same old Gretchen."

"Old. Hmm. I'm still younger than you."

"You always will be. It's funny, isn't it?"

"The script, I hope."

He laughed. "No, our lives. How they've worked out. Are you happy?"

"We have a job in a good picture. I'm happy."

"With Tom."

"Marriage is hard."

"You're telling me. Would it have been hard for us?"

"Absolutely." Loretta smiled.

"I don't think so."

"I've grown up, you know."

"I can see that. How's your girl?"

"Our girl is fine. She's fifteen."

"Where did the time go?"

"Up in smoke."

"What's she like?"

"Very sweet. Has a temper. She's pretty."

"Like her mother."

"Like her father." Loretta blushed. "Would you like to see your daughter?"

"I remember holding her in that fleabag your mother owned in Venice."

"It wasn't that bad."

"It was not fitting for our child."

Loretta blushed, remembering the moment she handed Judy to Clark the first time. "She had a humble start."

"The best people do." Gable shrugged.

"I guess."

"Do you ever wonder about us?"

"Are you unhappy with Lady Ashley?"

"She's stealth."

"What do you mean?"

"Changes things, one teacup at a time. I turn my back, and where there was wool, there's now a ruffle."

"One of those."

"Oh, brother, one of those."

"Do you think it will last?"

"Until she finds a pack of matches with a phone number, or lipstick on my collar."

"How long will that take?"

"That depends," he said, flirting.

"Oh, no. No. No. No."

"Not even a little?"

"The problem is, there's no 'little' with us. It's all out or all in, for better or worse. It's just the way it went."

"It's never over, Gretchen."

Luca watched Loretta and Gable from the catwalk. The two stars stood together, having a deep conversation in the middle of the production circus as the crew rushed around, carpenters built the set, and costume racks careened through. Luca remembered how Loretta and Clark had stood in the middle of a blizzard on Mount Baker and had a similar conversation, as though they were the only two people on the mountain. Luca couldn't wait to get home and tell Alda what he had witnessed. It was exactly as Luca remembered, two lovers with so much to say that there wasn't enough time, so they took their portion, knowing it too wouldn't be enough. Nothing had changed. It was all there, everything but the snow.

Gable knocked on Loretta's dressing room door. When she hollered for him to enter, she was sitting cross-legged on her sofa, reading her script. He opened the door and found her in corduroy overalls and a turtleneck.

"You look like a kid."

"I'm not." She patted the seat next to her on the sofa. "Mother of three."

Gable sat, and she offered him a cigarette. He took it. She handed him her cigarette, and he lit his own.

The years had given Gable gray hair at his temples. He was thicker through the middle, and his hands, once so genteel, were rough and spotted with age. Loretta liked Gable older, though when she looked at him, it was so easy to recall him in detail in his prime. He had grown into himself. The tiny flutter of lines around his eyes had deepened, as had his dimples. In his countenance he bore the scars of the losses in his life, and it pained her to think that she was one of them.

"Looking at this scene for tomorrow," she said.

"The new one?"

"Yep. It's all right, don't you think?"

"It's fine. Fine."

"Any way to beg Anita Loos to come and give it a rewrite?"

"She's long gone, Gretchen. She went to New York. She's in Paris with her books. I don't think we could lure her back with a sack of gold."

"Good for her. See how obsessed I get over the script?"

"It's why you have a great career."

"I'm in there slugging."

"Would you like to go to dinner?"

"Where's Sylvia?"

"I thought I'd bring her. You bring Tom."

"Let me call and see if he's free."

Loretta reached for the phone, and stopped herself.

"There's something I want to talk to you about."

"Sure."

"I want you to get to know Judy."

"Has she been asking questions?"

"All the time. I'm evasive."

"Is Tom a good father to her?"

"They don't get along."

"Why not?"

"At first, when she was little, he was very sweet with her. But she's willful, and he doesn't appreciate that. But I raised a willful child on purpose. I want her to be able to take care of herself."

"Like her mother."

"Like my mother." Loretta put out her cigarette and turned to him. "Judy is a responsible older sister. She's good with the boys. You would be so proud of her."

"I'm sure you raised a great girl."

"Maybe when you've become friends, we can gently tell her the truth."

"Is she happy?"

"Seems to be."

"Why would we ruin it? You know, you've done a great job with her, she has friends, she has a stepfather, she's well adjusted. Why would we tell her now?"

"Because I've worried about this every day since she was born. I have wrestled with it, prayed about it, wondered how her life would go if she never knew, told myself over and over again that she would be fine if she never knew the truth. But what is there besides the truth? What could possibly be more important to Judy?"

"You did the best you could, Gretchen. All by yourself. I was useless."

"I didn't bring this up to make you feel bad, I really didn't."

"I have my own way of dealing with my mistakes. I don't know if it would be good for her to learn about me now. She has a good life. If we tell her, she may react badly, run away—you don't know."

"No, we don't."

"I wanted a relationship with her, but it was such a mess back then, I didn't know what to do. You had so much pressure on you at the time."

"I was afraid I'd lose my job. That you would lose yours."

"I think we did what we could do, Gretchen."

"If we had been in any other profession, I wonder if we couldn't have done better. Look at us. We're still acting."

"It's so much easier to act out the feelings than to have them." Gable put his arm around Loretta. "Maybe that's why we're still at it."

"We haven't cracked it."

"We haven't figured anything out."

"How sad is that?" Loretta wondered.

"Look, Judy has you, your mother, your sisters, the cousins, her brothers. You've given her everything important."

Loretta smiled. "Everything but you."

"I wanted to be a father, you know. Had big dreams and plans. Wanted a houseful. And here we are. Sylvia's a little long in the tooth to engage me on that subject. I'm not going to have children. We had Judy, but it didn't work out—I couldn't be her father. I think there's something phony about trying now."

"I understand." Loretta summoned everything within her not to cry in front of Clark. She had cried so many nights over him, over Judy, over the loss of the family that could have been. She could not let him know the depth of her pain because there was nothing to be done about it now.

"I hope you do." Gable went to the door.

"Clark?"

"Yes, Gretchen?"

"You know I love you."

Gable stood for a moment, his hand on the door. "I've known it all along. But I wasn't worthy of it."

"That's not what you're supposed to say when a woman tells you that she loves you."

"Give me the line." He turned to face her and grinned. It might as well have been 1935 on Mount Baker.

"You're supposed to tell the girl that you love her too."

"That's too easy," Gable said. "Come here." Gable extended his hands to Loretta and lifted her up to face him. She stood before him as she had fifteen years earlier, when she challenged him on Mount Baker. This time she looked deep into his eyes and saw more than the years; she saw what those years had meant to him too. Loretta had spent so many nights wondering, when she needn't have.

"I'm going to do something that I've never done before with any woman. And that includes Carole. And the reason I grieved so deeply for her, and always will, is because I never told her how I felt about her. We were too busy laughing to get down to the business of true love."

"Carole knows you loved her."

"We said the words, but we didn't have the years, the history over time, that defines love—do you understand what I mean?

"We have that. You and me. We met when we were young—well, you were very young—and that counts for something. Time invested counts for something. I know I made you cry and I brought you pain, and for that, I hope you can find it in your heart to forgive me, even at this late date. I'm a louse sometimes, and I can't help myself. I react in the moment—whatever is front of me is what I eat, drink, smoke, or hunt. What I pursue. I don't examine my conscience, or the past, and I don't even make plans too far into the future. You get me as I am, or you don't get me at all.

"I want to tell you what you mean to me because I never have, and not because I didn't want to, but because I didn't want to hurt you anymore. After we came home from Bellingham and Ria was on the warpath, you were pregnant with Judy and pushed me away. And rightly so. After that, after the baby was born, when I saw you out on the town, you looked like you had moved on. But I was happy for you—when you were happy, I was too.

"But I never moved on from you. I've spent the last fifteen years running from my feelings for you, and sometimes I thought I outran them. You made it easy for me to let you go, and that was an act of kindness on your part. You loved me, and you didn't make any demands on me. Now I'm almost fifty years old, and I have learned very little on this hayride, but you taught me what love really is. It's letting the person you love be who they are, faults and all, failures and all. It's letting go when you would really rather hold on. So you see, I love you, Gretchen. But I never said those three words to you because they weren't enough. And they still aren't."

Loretta put her arms around Clark. She had been reminded of him every day of Judy's life. She had resisted calling him when their daughter did or said something extraordinary or needed his counsel when she fell short. Loretta felt she had half-parented Judy—cheated her in a sense, though that would have meant she deliberately rejected Gable, when it seemed to Loretta he had been the one to move on.

Loretta buried her face in Gable's neck; the scent of bitter orange and pine reminded her of when they were young. It hadn't been a dream. It hadn't been a scene in a movie, shot on location and forgotten. They had loved each other, always would. It was a bit of a miracle to Loretta, but then again, it always had been.

———

Judy threw her schoolbooks down on the stairs and was on her way to the kitchen when she noticed a man standing in the living room. He turned to face her and smiled.

"Mr. Gable?"

"You must be Judy."

"I am. Are you looking for Mom?"

"She's taking a call."

"Are you having fun making a movie together?"

"Your mother is a lot of fun."

"She can be. And she can be a drag, but don't tell her."

"I won't." Gable tried not to laugh. He invited Judy to sit with him. "Tell me about yourself."

"I'm learning to sew."

"That's a good talent to have."

"It's practical, I guess."

"Any idea what you want to be when you grow up?"

"Maybe an actress, like Mom."

"Have you been in any plays?"

"At school."

"You know, I've been friends with your mom for years."

"I know. Since *The Call of the Wild.*"

"You know about that movie?"

"I've seen it. Mom's seen it about a million times. It's her favorite movie."

"It is?" Gable was pleased.

"We watch it a lot on movie night."

"A lot?"

"Are you kidding? She'd watch it every time if she could. But sometimes I just feel like Jerry Lewis, you know?"

"I know."

"Sometimes she cries when she watches it. I think she's sad for those guys that go down in the creek."

"That must be it."

"What's your favorite movie? Let me guess. *Gone with the Wind.*"

"I'm afraid everybody likes that picture but me."

"You were good in it. It's long, though."

"You ever see *Night Nurse*?"

"Nah. Mom doesn't have it."

"I think she burned the print."

"She's like that. If she hates something, look out."

"I'm kind of like that too."

"Mom says it means you're made of something. You know, when you have an opinion."

"I agree with that."

"I guess."

"Well, Judy, it was good to meet you."

"You want to wait for my mom?"

"I'd be waiting forever." Gable smiled.

"No kidding. She takes hours no matter where she's going, even if it's just to Delaney's."

Judy walked Gable to the door.

"You be a good kid, okay?" He extended his hand, and she shook it.

She looked up into his eyes. Like all old people's, his eyes were watering. She wondered if he used drops. "Well, see ya, Mr. Gable."

"Good-bye, Judy." Gable kissed her on the forehead. Judy did not think much of it, but it was all Gable could do not to embrace her. He saw grace notes of Gretchen in Judy, but he also saw aspects of his mother in their daughter—the wide-set eyes, the fine bone structure, and the sweet smile.

Gable walked down the sidewalk. He turned back to look at Judy, who stood on the portico, waving. He waved back. He got into his car and turned the key. He put his hands on the steering wheel and realized they were shaking. He clasped his hands together to stop the tremors.

Gable wondered if he would ever have the chance to tell Judy the truth: that he was her father, and even though he hadn't been there for her, she would always be his. He wouldn't have found the words to explain his absence, the Hays Code, the way the world was in the 1930s, and he doubted that she'd understand even if he could. He drove out of the driveway and onto the street.

Despite the deep well of regret that anchored the soul of Clark Gable, there was joy for him that day. He was able to connect himself to his past and to understand that all he was would go forward in Judy. Perhaps he was simplifying it, but that's how it went in Hollywood. A story was told in scenes, and usually there was one moment that turned the key, that sent the characters in the direction that would lead to their happiness or their demise.

But this wasn't a script, it wasn't a movie; it was his life, and the life of his daughter. Maybe he was wrong to tell Loretta that they shouldn't share the truth with Judy. Maybe the truth would serve their daughter. He was confused about that, and would have to give it more thought.

For a split second he thought about turning the car around and going back to Judy, but something told him a better time would come for them. When that time came, he would be ready to tell Judy the truth—*his* truth, as he remembered it and lived it. He only hoped that when the time came, she would be ready to listen.

∽◯∾

16

Loretta Young sat at the head of the table at Lewislor Productions at the NBC studios in Burbank. Floor-to-ceiling glass windows offered a view of the sound stages, and the glass-topped table in the conference room reflected the morning light.

Tom Lewis was meeting next door with the network executives to determine a license fee for the anthology show they had pitched and NBC had bought. In 1953, there would surely be product endorsements to defray the cost of production, but Loretta didn't mind. She was enthralled to be in control of the storytelling, taking her years of movie experience with scripts and applying it to television. Alda sat next to her boss, taking notes.

"Did you ever think all that mail you answered would become a television show?"

Alda laughed. "I used to call them 'Letters to Loretta.' "

"And that's what Tom is calling the show."

Just as Loretta had rushed headfirst into radio when Darryl Zanuck put her on suspension, she was charging into the new medium of television. Movies had taken a hit as the public's tastes changed. Louis B. Mayer had just been fired as the chairman of the MGM board, marking the official end of the studio system that had thrived during the golden age.

Loretta's movie-star friends would have no part of television; she argued with Roz Russell, reasoned with Irene Dunne, even had lunch with Joan Crawford, who said she would die on a sound stage in front of one camera before she would act on "the little box." Only Loretta, who played her career with élan, with a sense that she had nothing to lose, had figured out that she could work on her own terms to offer great stories to her audience on television.

Unlike many of her friends in the movies, Loretta never lost sight of the audience.

No leading actress on camera in Loretta's memory, except for Marie Dressler in the 1930s, had worked much past the age of thirty-five. That might not be fair, but Loretta was not about to wage war against a system that had been in place since the turn of the century. Instead she decided she would go where she was wanted. As she neared the age of forty, she still had her beauty, her intellect, and her charm, not to mention her acting ability. She would work harder, longer hours, produce, sit in on rewrites, and arc the narrative of her series. She would be responsible for the content and the message. At long last her audience would get the full range of her gifts. Like her mother before her, Loretta's work would fill her up where her marriage could not.

"What time are you leaving tonight?" Loretta asked Alda.

"We're flying to Chicago, spending the night, and then on to New York."

"Are you packed?"

"All set."

"What are you going to do in Brooklyn?"

"Eat."

"What's it like?"

"We stay in the basement of the family brownstone. Three generations of Chettas live in that house. Breakfast is continental. His sister makes espresso, and we steam milk and dip the heels of day-old bread into it, and I'm in heaven. Dinner is at six in the family kitchen. Monday nights are soup, Tuesday night macaroni. You get the gist. Sundays are the best. The entire family, all the cousins, aunts, and uncles, come for Sunday dinner. I make stuffed artichokes. Luca's family rolls up the garage door and they scrub it down, set up tables, and everyone comes over to eat. If it's hot, the men will open the fire hydrants for the kids to run through. If not, they play ball in the street. Luca will play with the kids, and we'll have a great time."

"Sounds heavenly."

"You wouldn't last five minutes. The streets of Brooklyn are packed with people. They sit on the stoops and holler from the windows. It's big and loud and noisy and I wouldn't trade it for anything. It's a life closer to Padua than Hollywood."

"Alda, have I ever thanked you properly? For Padua. For everything."

"So many times."

"You've been as close to me as my mother and my sisters."

"I never had a sister."

"I hope I've been a good one."

"You have, Loretta. And I hope I haven't been too hard on you."

"You're always honest."

"That's the first time those words have been uttered in Hollywood."

Loretta laughed. "I think you're right. While you're being honest, tell me what you think of this television racket."

"Well, it's something new. I've never seen you fail. You've never turned away from a challenge. You embrace them. I think you will succeed. You always do."

"Can you believe we're starting over again?"

Alda was amazed by Loretta Young. She was tireless in her pursuit of quality projects. Loretta turned down more movies than she had made over the course of her career, and she had made over a hundred. Loretta had always wanted control over the kind of stories she wanted to tell, and with the blockbuster *Come to the Stable*, she'd proved she still had great instincts when it came to choosing stories.

Tom Lewis joined them in the conference room. "We got the licensing fee." He beamed. "They've ordered twenty-two episodes."

"I can do my work and be home for dinner every night." Loretta applauded.

"That's the idea. You in the kitchen," Tom agreed. "Are you ready to pitch the storylines?"

"We are." Loretta looked at Alda. "Send them in."

Tom went to gather the network executives as Loretta took one last look at her notes.

"I haven't seen Tom so happy in a long time," Loretta said softly.

"This was a great decision," Alda said.

"I have to do something to bring us together. This is the happiest he's been since we married."

"Sometimes you have do things to make your husband happy. There's nothing wrong with that," Alda assured her.

"I have to try. No matter what it takes." Marriage to Tom had been such a struggle of wills that Loretta was happy to try anything to make her home life better. But she wondered if stardom of another sort would only antagonize Tom further. He had grown more territorial and less enthusiastic about her work life over time. The only solution, in her mind, was to include him and let him run the show. Always practical when it came to her acting life, Loretta gave Tom power on the production side, hoping they might share in the success of the new business. She would share her work life, he would have the prestige, and hopefully both of them would be happy with the deal.

———

Alda sat on the stoop of Luca's family homestead on Avenue U in Brooklyn. The entire neighborhood had come out to watch the softball game. Luca insisted on playing. At fifty-one, he was fit and trim, though his black hair was now gray.

Luca's sisters had the garage ready for the Sunday meal. Alda had hand-rolled manicotti, while they simmered meatballs and gravy in a pot that Luca's mother had brought from Italy. With fresh bread, a big salad of fresh greens and sweet onions, and the Chetta family's homemade wine, it would be all they needed for a perfect Sunday-afternoon meal.

The sisters had made cannoli and cookies, knowing that the family would talk long into the night. Whenever Luca and Alda visited, it seemed there wasn't enough time.

Luca hit the ball, and it sailed over parked cars and headed for the cross street. As he rounded the bases, the family cheered. His nephews shouted for him to head for home, so Luca took the bases at a clip. As he rounded third base, he stopped and put his hands on his knees.

"Uncle Luca, what's the matter?" His nephew Anthony dropped his glove and ran for his uncle. Clutching his chest, he looked up, saw his wife, and called out, "Alda!" before he collapsed onto the street.

Alda ran to his side while his sister Elena ran for the phone to call the ambulance. Soon every window and stoop was filled with neighbors, come to see if there was anything they could do to help.

———————

Alda raced alongside the gurney as Luca was brought into Mother Cabrini Hospital. Luca was rushed into the ER, and Alda followed.

"You have to stay in the waiting area," the nurse told her.

"No, I have to go with him. He doesn't speak English," Alda lied off the top of her head.

"All right, follow him in," the nurse said.

Luca was placed in an examining room. The nurse quickly attached oxygen to a tank and laced the tubes over to the gurney, where she placed a mask on Luca's face. Alda stood beside him, trying not to cry. Luca was very pale, and she felt a sense of doom, time slipping away from them.

"We're going to get you fixed up."

Luca tried to smile. He tapped the cup over his nose and mouth. Alda lifted it.

"I wasn't perfect."

"Neither was I, honey."

"You deserved it," he whispered. "I want to tell you something."

"Do I look like a priest?"

Luca smiled. "No."

"So save your confession."

A look of peace crossed Luca's face. Alda placed the oxygen on his face.

"You listen to me. I don't care about perfect. I wanted a real husband. I have one. I love your temper and your cursing and your impatience. I love the way you love me, and I don't care about anything else. I have been so proud to be your wife. And you're stuck with me for another fifty years."

Luca made the *mezzo mezzo* hand signal, which meant fifty more years was a stretch.

Luca closed his eyes. Alda knelt beside his bed and prayed, but she knew not to ask for more time, but for the salvation of Luca's soul. When she rose to her feet to kiss him good-bye, Luca Chetta was already gone.

———

Alda was numb as she made Luca's funeral arrangements in Brooklyn. She spoke with the priest and bought the grave site for her husband, next to his parents, purchasing two so she could be buried with him when her time came.

Loretta and Tom Lewis sent a glorious arrangement of flowers that were crowded next to sprays from MGM, Mr. Gable, his union, and his friends. Everyone who had worked with Luca remembered him.

Alda's sister-in-law Elena brought an envelope full of mass cards to Alda as she was packing.

"We want you to stay, Alda. You don't have anyone in California."

"I have my job. And the house. I'll have to do something about the house," Alda said, weeping. "I thought about going home to Padua. But it's not where I belong. I want to be with the people who knew Luca, who worked with him. I think it will help me."

"Is there anything I can do for you?" Elena asked.

"I don't want my husband to be forgotten."

"We'll never forget him."

"No, his art. He was a great painter. No one knew, because he painted sets, that he was also a fine artist. I have his sketches and paintings, all his supplies. Someday I'd like to send them to you, so you can choose one of the nieces or nephews who loves art, and give them their uncle's work and his tools."

"I'll do that." Elena patted her sister-in-law's hand. "You know, we all thought he was crazy when he went to Hollywood. But he was hooked. We went to Palisades Park, the whole family, and we each had a nickel. Some of us bought candy, others went on rides, but he spent his money at the Nickelodeon. After he saw those images, he was never the same. He wanted to be in that black box."

"That's what it is, Elena. It's an obsession. It's a calling."

"Like becoming a nun."

"I can't imagine Luca without a paintbrush in his hand. He taught me about form and line and light and shadow. I looked at the position of the sun differently, the way the moon moved, how it left a trail in the sky, if you knew how to look for it between the shadows."

"What an Italian way to live, to see the world and the sky that way."

"We were all we had. Each other. We had time to look at things, to take them in."

"An artist's life. You had it too."

"Because of him. Your brother was an artist down to his bones, and it was my privilege to observe him at work. It's what made me fall in love with him in the first place."

Polly draped her leg over the side of Loretta's canvas chair, taking a bite of Loretta's sandwich. Sally stood close by with her hands on her hips, holding a Brownie camera to get a shot of Loretta as she came out of the doors used on her television show.

"Cue Loretta," the stage manager hollered. The lights on the set poured on, streams of pink and white bathed the stage. Loretta opened a set of French doors trimmed with brass details and walked through to center stage. She wore a yellow organza cocktail dress embroidered with black velvet sunflowers. Her hair was cropped in the Italian style; her lips, a bright magenta, were courant.

Every week, Loretta opened her show by going through the French doors on her soundstage, dressed in a glamorous dress designed by Jean Louis and greeting her audience at home.

"Cut!" the stage manager called out.

"Is that it?" Polly asked.

"For Loretta."

"When do they need us?"

"In a minute."

"Over here, Georgie!" Sally called out to their baby sister.

Georgiana, now a mother, smiled and made her way over to her sisters, skipping over the wires. Georgie was a homemaker who had left show business to raise her family, but you couldn't tell from her movie star looks. She was as lovely as any ingénue working.

"Come on, girls, let's go." Loretta motioned to her sisters.

Sally, Polly, and Georgie gathered around Loretta to have their picture snapped by the show photographer.

"Mama will love this," Loretta said.

"Who are you kidding? You're just superstitious. You want to win another Emmy."

"Well, we did have our picture made before the first one," Loretta demurred.

"That's all right. We want you to win, sis." Polly smiled.

Loretta's sisters were proud of her. She was the first woman to star in and produce her own television show, which caused Joan Crawford to call her old friend and tell her that for the first time in her life, she had been wrong. Joan promised to come off her high horse about the movies, and down to earth where television was king. From now on, she was going to listen to Loretta.

———

The attention had shifted from the Young sisters to the new generation. At twenty-three years old, Judy Lewis was engaged to be married to a young television director named Joe, who had worked on *The Loretta Young Show*.

Alda sorted through the response cards. She pulled a regret card from the pile: "Mr. and Mrs. Clark Gable will be unable to attend." A couple of years before, after his short, unhappy marriage to Lady Sylvia Ashley, Gable had married Kay Spreckles, who had two children. It was an old friendship; Gable had known Kay when she was a young starlet in Hollywood in the 1940s. Just as in any small town, eventually the eligible bachelors and single ladies cycle through, and re-meet, and sometimes sparks fly anew. They did for Gable and Kay.

Alda was troubled by the regret. Gable and Loretta had been on friendly terms since they made *Key to the City* eight years earlier.

"Alda, have you seen my mom?" Judy asked.

"She's at the studio."

"How are the invites coming?"

"You're going to have a standing-room-only crowd."

"Anybody say no?"

"Here's the regret pile."

Alda handed the cards to Judy. She shuffled through them and stopped to look at the Gables'.

"I remember meeting Mr. Gable."

"You do?"

"He came to see me when I was still in high school."

"Your mom and he are old friends."

"I think she dated him. You were there. Did she?"

"Your mother had so many beaus."

"No one could keep up. I know, I know. But wasn't Mr. Gable a special one?"

"Why would you think that?"

"She can't talk about him."

"Your mom dated Spencer Tracy," Alda offered, getting the conversation off Gable.

"I know. I can't see that one, though. Not her type. Mom is strictly the tall, dark, handsome type."

"Like you." Alda smiled.

"I am my mother's daughter." Judy laughed.

Alda watched Judy walk out of the office and jump into her car. She wanted to tell Judy the truth, but it was not her place. It was time to confront Loretta one final time, to do what Alda thought was the only thing to do—the right thing—to tell Judy the story of how she came to be.

———

Gable skippered the sleek white speedboat from Naples to Capri over the turquoise waves of the Tyrrhenian Sea. The sun glittered on the surface like speckles of diamond dust. Kay Gable held onto the rig, the wind blowing in her platinum hair as they hit waves in the open sea. Gable smiled at his wife before he turned to guide the boat into the Marina Grande at the foothills of Capri.

Gable was fifty-eight years old, hired to play a lover to the starlet Sophia Loren in *It Started In Naples.* He laughed when he got the offer; he couldn't believe anyone would still pay him to star in a romantic movie and give him the most popular actress in the world as his costar, an international sex symbol who happened to be thirty years younger than he.

"Where are we going?" Gable turned to his wife.

"Up the mountain." Kay, a petite blonde in her early forties, had vowed to go anywhere in the world Gable wanted to go, and promised to be with him on location. Gable had finally found the woman whose sole purpose in life was to take care of him. Kay adored him, and he was crazy about her.

Kay had been to Capri, and she wanted her husband to see it, but she also had a mission in mind. As they jumped into the caravan jeep that would take them to the top of the mountain, Kay kissed her husband.

"What's the big treat here?"

Once on the mountaintop, Gable helped Kay out of the jeep and onto the glorious town square that overlooked the Mediterranean. Bougainvillea draped the limestone walls in bursts of purple and hot pink, while beach roses in shades of magenta covered the sandstone walls.

Kay took Gable by the hand to a small shop, Da Costanzo's, off the town square. Gable had to duck to enter the tiny shop, filled with shoes. Kay rang the bell on the desk.

"Costanzo!" she shrieked, throwing her arms around the young proprietor. Costanzo was compact and small, his black hair receding, though he was still in his thirties.

"Clark, this is Constanzo. I knew his father years ago when I was a girl—my parents brought me here, and he made me sandals. They were the most comfortable shoes I ever owned. Costanzo, my husband's feet hurt. Make him shoes. I'll be back in two hours."

"Where are you going?" Gable asked.

"To get my hair done."

Gable sat down with Costanzo and looked around the shop.

"Is something wrong with your feet?"

"I'm old."

"That's not a problem."

"Not for you."

"I'm going to make you a pair of slip-on loafers. You like suede or leather?"

"Suede."

"Blue, brown, or black?"

"Black."

"You like brass bar or no brass bar?"

"No brass bar."

"Follow me."

Gable followed Costanzo to the garden behind the shop. He pulled up a seat for Gable and then poured Gable a glass of limoncello.

"What's this?" Gable sniffed the glass.

"I make it myself. It's booze."

"Now you've made me a happy man."

Gable sat back, lit a cigarette, and sipped the limoncello as Costanzo measured his feet.

"*Kay e bellissima!*"

"Thank you. She's wife number five."

"Five? You're crazy!"

"No kidding. Let me tell you about divorce. I've had three of them. It's like a twenty-dollar bill. You keep tearing off a piece, a piece for this one, a piece for that one, and pretty soon you're broke."

"That's why I only married one woman."

"Do you like her?"

"She's my life."

"You're lucky."

"No, no, she's lucky. Look what she got."

"I've used that strategy and it got me nowhere."

"Who did you love the most? Out of the five."

"The current one, of course. Kay. Your friend."

"Good answer."

"I'm very grateful. I'm almost sixty, and I have some wonderful memories."

"You're going to have a baby."

"What are you talking about?"

"Kay is going to have a baby."

"How do you know?"

"I have a feeling."

"Are you a shoemaker or a fortune-teller?"

"Both."

"I'm going to come back to this island some day with my baby."

"I'll make the baby shoes."

"I'm going to hold you to it."

Loretta cut the rose deep at the stem. The petals were closed tight. She added the flower to her cutting basket. She planned to make a large bouquet to bring to Judy at the hospital where she had just given birth to her first baby.

Loretta thought about calling Clark when Judy gave birth to their first grandchild, Maria, on November 16, 1959. She was a perfect baby, and Loretta would have loved to share the news, but she couldn't. Gable was on location in Arizona shooting *The Misfits*, his wife Kay was with him, and after they sent their regrets to Judy's wedding, Loretta had given up any hope of bringing their families together. Kay made it perfectly clear when she didn't send a gift that any further contact was not welcome. This was nothing new in Hollywood. The new wives always set the social agendas. Any small acknowledgement of Judy would have been welcome, but it was not to be. Loretta felt better about never having shared the truth with her daughter. Perhaps Clark had been right so many years ago when he said that the truth would only make Judy unhappy. Judy had her own family now; what good could possibly come from opening old wounds? Loretta surveyed her rose garden. She had cut at least two dozen roses from the patch, but the garden was so lush, it was as if she hadn't taken any.

Kay Gable was around five months pregnant when she called the ambulance to come to the ranch in Encino. Gable could not sleep.

He had pain in his arm, he was feverish, and he refused to go to the hospital. Kay forced him to go anyway.

Kay stood in the hallway outside her husband's room.

"How bad is it?" she asked the doctor.

"He had a massive heart attack. But he's very strong. We think we can help him."

Kay's eyes filled with tears. "You have to. He has to help me raise our baby."

"Don't lose faith. You got him here in time."

Kay went into Gable's room and sat by the bed. Gable opened his eyes, and when he saw his wife, he smiled.

"Ma, I want to get up," he said.

"You stay in that bed, or I'll kill you," Kay teased. She ran her fingers through his thick gray hair.

"How's our baby?"

"Growing." Kay placed Clark's hand on her stomach.

"I got to get out of here and build the crib."

"You've got plenty of time, Pa. Don't worry about your chores."

Gable took Kay's hand and kissed it. "You've made me happy."

"We have years ahead of us," Kay promised.

"You more than me."

"I don't want years without you in them."

"You need your rest. Go and lie down."

"I don't want to leave you."

"Doc says I'm fine. I'm checking out in the morning. Now go."

Kay kissed him tenderly. "Are you sure?"

"Yes. Look. I got a stack of magazines here with photos of me looking jowly and fat."

"But they ran the Rhett Butler."

"Him. Pain in my ass."

Kay laughed. "Honey, I'm making a blanket for the baby."

"Pink or blue?"

"Yellow, to be safe. I want to name the baby John Clark Gable."

"I like it. But what if it's a girl?"

"I've always loved the name Gretchen."

"Gretchen?" Gable's eyebrows arched.

"It's my middle name. Do you like it?"

"I like it just fine."

Clark kissed his wife and sent her to rest. He flipped on the television set. The program was about paintings in the White House. Gable remembered his friend Luca Chetta, the great scene painter. He had a feeling of doom as he remembered how Chet had died suddenly of a heart attack.

The noise of the television bothered him, so Gable turned it off. He had a funny feeling in his head. He was dizzy, but he figured that was the inactivity, lying in the bed all day. He couldn't wait to get out of this hospital.

Gable opened up the newspaper. He closed it. He leaned back on the pillow and thought about his wife, and the baby on the way.

Gretchen.

He remembered a raft on a river, and saving a girl with gray eyes, who had his baby. He remembered the years. Carole. The war. A royal flush with Hattie. The chocolate brown hood of a new Packard. A blue sky. A silver marlin.

The dizzy feeling turned to a throbbing pain in his head and spread through his body. He felt as though he were falling through space and time. He tried to speak, but no words would come. He opened his fist to reach, but he could not hang on. He let go.

A nurse passed the open door to Gable's room. She took one look at him and knew something was wrong. She rushed to his side. She took his pulse. He was gone.

Alda slipped into the back pew of the Church of the Recessional at Forest Lawn. Clark Gable's casket was covered in a sheath of red roses, with a small crown of burgundy roses anchored in the center. Gable's favorite Strauss waltzes were played as the mourners took their seats.

Kay Gable walked down the aisle in a black suit, hat, and veil. Alda recognized a lot of the old faces from MGM, men who had worked with her husband and Clark. As the pallbearers filed in, she felt a hand on her shoulder.

"Alda," Spencer Tracy said. "I got old."

"We are all getting old."

"Not you. Never the Italians," he whispered. "How's Gretch?"

"Come see us."

Tracy nodded and joined Robert Taylor, Jimmy Stewart, Howard Strickling, Eddie Mannix, Ray Hommes, and Eric Dunliner by the casket. As they lifted Gable's casket, even the men wept. When a man's man dies, it brings out the deepest feelings in everyone, especially the stoic men. Kay Gable rose to kiss the casket a final time. Alda remembered when Gable stood up for her and Luca when they got married. Clark Gable had been their best man. It was an appropriate title for him. It would be how Alda would remember him.

———

Loretta picked up the paper in her office at NBC. She was scanning the news when her eyes fell on an item in Louella Parson's column.

Kay Gable gave birth to John Clark Gable on March 20, 1961, in Beverly Hills. Mother and son are well. Gable predeceased his only child by a few months. His final movie, The Misfits, *was released on February 1, in honor of Gable's 60th birthday.*

No, it wasn't in honor of his birthday, Loretta thought; it was in pursuit of big box office. Loretta shook her head, remembering how, when Jean Harlow died, MGM had rushed to release *Saratoga* seven weeks after she died to capitalize on the grief of her fans. Twenty years later, and the studio bosses were still up to their old tricks, profit over decorum.

Loretta got in her car to drive home for dinner with Tom. Instead of going over the hill, she found herself driving to Forest Lawn Cemetery.

Every night before sleep, she remembered her conversation with Clark in her dressing room when he gave her his advice about Judy. She remembered how his hands felt in hers when he said he loved her.

Loretta parked behind the Great Mausoleum. She went inside. The cool chamber had the scent of carnations as she made her way through the crypts. She read the names as though she were searching the stacks in a library. When she found Carole Lombard, she found Clark. The finality of his passing became real to her. She knelt before his crypt, bowed her head, and as she had done every day of her life since falling in love with him, she said ten Hail Marys for the repose of his sweet soul. When she rose to her feet, Loretta took a moment to place both hands on his crypt. To his right was Carole; to his left, Kay's crypt was already marked.

"I never really had you," Loretta whispered, "but none of us did."

It bothered her that Kay's son was listed as Gable's only child; it wasn't true. But she still had no idea how to set the record straight, or if she ever would.

The mass at Good Shepherd during Lent in February 1965 was standing room only. Judy sat with her mother and took her hand after communion. Loretta looked over at her daughter and marveled at what a beauty she had become, inside and out, as a mother, as a daughter, and now as her friend. Judy would turn thirty that November, and it seemed as though it couldn't be possible.

As the members of the congregation filed out, Loretta fished for change in her purse.

"You want to light a candle, Mom?"

"Sure. Do you?"

Judy nodded. "How about at the shrine of the Blessed Lady?"

Loretta snapped her purse shut and rose from her seat. She followed her daughter out of the pew. Judy genuflected, and Loretta did the same. When Loretta rose from the kneeling position, she was face to face with a lovely blonde in a blue pillbox hat and matching bouclé suit. Her eyes were sky blue. Loretta knew instantly it was Kay Gable.

"Hello, Kay." Loretta smiled.

"Hello, Loretta." Kay smiled back at her, but it was a polite greeting, not particularly warm. "This is my son, John Clark Gable." An adorable boy, around five years old, in a navy suit with short pants and white oxfords, was busy staring off at the statues. Kay tugged her son's arm, and the boy looked at Loretta and nodded.

"This is my daughter, Judy," Loretta said to Kay.

Kay nodded and walked out of the church with her son.

"Mrs. Gable is too old to have a boy that small," Judy whispered.

"She's a few years younger than me." Loretta bit her lip. She knew more about Kay than she'd admit. She remembered that there was a three-year age difference between them: Kay was forty-nine, Loretta fifty-two.

"You're a grandmother."

"Anytime is always a good time to have a baby—old or young."

"I guess." Judy shrugged.

Loretta drove Judy back to her house, where Gladys had made brunch after mass. She turned to Judy. "I'll meet up with you later. I have an errand to run." Loretta watched as she walked to the front door. She turned and looked at her mother and waved before going inside.

As Loretta drove off, she thought it was odd that Kay Gable was attending mass at Good Shepherd. She was a member of Saint Cyril's; everyone knew she had baptized her son there.

Had she come to Good Shepherd to show Loretta her son with Clark, or was it just an accident, one of those strange show business coincidences? Either way, Judy wasn't wise to Kay, and surely did not suspect that John Clark Gable was her half brother.

No matter how many times over the years Loretta revisited Judy's paternity in the confessional, there was no epiphany on the subject, no resolution. It remained a dreary, dark corner in her subconscious and a heavy burden on her soul. She dreamed about Gable, and the dreams were always chaotic. Once he held her hands as they navigated the river at Mount Baker on a raft; in another, he called to her in an empty mansion, and she searched for him room to room and couldn't find him, only her baby sleeping in a dresser drawer. Loretta had consulted so many priests on the subject that she couldn't count them. It was an ongoing source of frustration for her, but no one in her life knew it.

Polly and Sally and Georgiana knew the truth, but it had been so long since it was discussed it seemed that they too had almost forgotten the story. They were busy in their lives and marriages, with children of their own. The fear that Loretta had instilled in them on the subject of secrecy was so deep that it stayed buried next to the truth of their father John Young, or with the divorce decree rendered to their stepfather Belzer.

Her husband still did not know the truth. Tom had heard the rumors too, but chose to ignore them. When he married Loretta, he learned not to press her. He figured she was entitled to her privacy. If she wanted him to know something, he was certain she would tell him.

Loretta had successfully built a wall around the truth, sealed the windows, latched the door, and dug a moat. No one, if she remained vigilant, would ever get near it. She was determined to leave the story in the past—it could not possibly do anyone any good now. Besides, Gable was gone. All that was left behind was the legacy of his career, his fifth wife, and their only son.

Judy couldn't have a relationship with her father now; he was gone. No attempts that Loretta had made, or that Clark had initiated, had taken with their daughter. Gable's own words rang in Loretta's ears. *Judy is a great girl. Why upset her? Let it go.* As for her half brother, Judy had a daughter his age. John Clark Gable could hardly be a brother to her now. At every turn the situation seemed impossible, but then again, the truth deferred always is. With a revelation, an unveiling, an exposure, comes the regret, the wild river of emotions, for which there are no explanations or solutions that make sense, only more questions, only more bad dreams, worse nightmares and sadness. And of course, in the face of the truth, there would be accountability. Loretta, for all the energy she had expended on the matter, could not see what good would come by owning her mistakes to the world, her family, and Judy, when she had already sought and received forgiveness from her God.

Loretta thought about the gift of her daughter, who initially had been a challenge, but luckily grew out of her teenage years to become a practical and intelligent woman with a keen mind and a good heart. Could Loretta have wished for more for her? Loretta saw aspects of all the women in the Young family in Judy. Her daughter had inherited Loretta's sisters' creamy skin and her grandmother Gladys's dazzling eyes, like agates really, which sparkled when Judy spoke and disappeared when she laughed. Loretta worried whether Judy loved her. She loved her daughter for sure, but she was a young mother, and young mothers have neither the benefit of experience nor the knowledge that a career, personal goals, and private dreams can wait. Loretta didn't know any of that at the time. All she knew for certain was that she had done her best, without the benefit of a husband, a true partner, and the father of her daughter, helping her navigate the perils of parenthood. She had longed for that and hoped for it with Tom Lewis, but the marriage had stayed on a plateau; there had been no deepening of trust to make her feel secure enough to reveal her deepest secret to him. It was his pain, and her loss. Maybe the truth would have made a difference in their marriage.

The secret had become a member of the family. It had its own space; each person bore a responsibility to it in their fashion. No one other than her sisters, her mother, and her secretary could ever know the truth. But the problem with any lie is that it is as transparent as the truth. Loretta had denied it for so long that she made the mistake of thinking it dead. But it wasn't.

As Loretta drove, she made a list of all the things she had given her daughter, starting with a close family: a loving grandmother, a slew of aunts and their wonderful husbands, and two younger brothers. Judy had grown up with a fine education, good friends, and a loving circle, an upbringing made complete by opportunities to travel and see the world in ways that Loretta had only dreamed of. Now that Judy was a mother herself, surely she understood the sacrifices Loretta had made—and even if she didn't, Loretta was confident that her daughter would understand them in time. Maybe everything would be made right by Maria, Loretta's granddaughter, who at six already had Judy's keen mind and curiosity.

Loretta had always worked, and when she thought about the past, it was to retrieve a memory about something that had happened on a movie set—whether it was being berated by the director George FitzMorris, or laughing so hard with Jean Harlow that the director had to yell "Cut!" until the girls "got it out of their system," or kissing Spencer Tracy for the first time on the set of *Man's Castle*, the first kiss of her life that had meant something.

It was work that she thought about when she let her mind wander. Her children sustained her; they were the essence of her, as she and her brother and sisters had been for Gladys. Loretta did not question her devotion or the depth of her love for her children. It was the mighty river under the indestructible ship she had built by the labor of her own hands. Both the river and the ship belonged to her, and she to it. Her convictions about that were as deep as her faith.

Loretta ranked her achievements when she examined her conscience. The children were always first, then her career. Family and career, in that order, she believed. She had gotten into the movies to help her mother—but found bliss and challenge and artistic freedom and the integrity that comes from using one's gifts. She had done her best, but believed most of the time that she had not measured up to her own high standards. That, Loretta decided, was the Catholic in her.

Loretta drove and drove that morning, off the freeway and into Woodland Hills, a sweet village in the San Fernando Valley. She rolled down the window, took off her hat, and leaned back in the seat. She would drive slowly, and then speed up, and when a gentleman passed in a blue Pontiac and shot her a look that said, *You can't drive, lady*, she smiled back at him. He almost drove off the road when he realized who the bad driver was.

Loretta pulled off the road to a flower stand and purchased an enormous bouquet of gardenias and tuberoses. Somewhere in the fog of her deep memory, she recalled that Mae loved this combination. The woman who ran the stand recognized Loretta, and offered the flowers for free. Loretta paid anyway, and left her autograph on the canopy of the roadside stand.

Loretta drove past a manicured acreage, the sod was green and lush, hemmed by a fence. The entry drive revealed the Motion Picture Country House, a sprawling single-story Spanish-style building with a terra-cotta roof and a wide entrance, canopied from the sun.

It looked like a place that could easily accommodate a premiere, and the party that follows, but in fact this was a hospital and rest home for the folks who had worked in the movies—in front of the camera and behind it—during the silents, and then the talkies that gave birth to the golden age of Hollywood. For every senior citizen gaffer and electrician, there was a screenwriter and a leading lady or man, sharing a room, side by side. It was as if the artistic collaboration had not ended but instead was slowly seeping away in a swirl of glorious memories that abide old age. The facade of the home had just enough swank to remind the tenants of the glamorous industry they had built with their talents.

Loretta put on her hat before getting out of the car. She pulled on her gloves. She checked her lipstick in the mirror, and, satisfied, got out of the car with the bouquet of flowers.

Loretta entered the lobby of the Motion Picture Country House. The walls were lined with residents in wheelchairs, chatting with one another, reading the newspaper, or doing nothing at all, just sitting. But they weren't alone; they were in the company of their peers. This comforted Loretta as she checked in.

As Loretta passed the old folks, one looked up and remembered her. She stopped and took the man's hand when he reached for hers, and spent a moment talking with him. She pulled a rose out of the bouquet, snapped the stem off, and placed the flower in the man's lapel. He beamed as he watched her go on her way.

She stopped at room 110 and peeked in. Sitting high in the bed, propped by pillows, was Mae Murray. Mae rested her hands on the half-moon hospital table that stretched across her bed. Her hair was white, as were the sheets, the blanket, and her simple dressing gown. Mae was almost eighty years old. She was completely made up, her bee-stung lips drawn on with orange pencil and filled in with pale coral lipstick. Her eyes were rimmed in the black kohl powder they used in the silents. Mae still possessed a version of that "it" quality. Loretta wanted to feast her eyes upon Mae and keep watching forever. Mae Murray was still a star.

Mae studied a yellow bird outside her window, fascinated.

"Mate-zee?" Loretta said softly.

Mae turned and looked at Loretta. She squinted, put on her thick eyeglasses, and studied her guest. "Gretchen?"

"It's me!" Loretta went to her and put her arms around her.

"Are those for me?" Mae asked.

Loretta handed her the flowers.

Mae inhaled the scent. "Jesse Lasky used to send me a bouquet every Monday when I was shooting. Wasn't that nice?"

"He was one of the good ones."

"I'll say." Mae handed the flowers back to Loretta. "Please put them in water."

Loretta went into the bathroom to look for a vase. There were few personal effects there, just towels stenciled with the regulation MPH and a toothbrush. She opened the cabinet over the sink. It was empty.

"There's a vase in the closet there," Mae said.

Loretta opened the closet. There were two cotton dressing gowns on hangers and a pair of foam bedroom slippers on the floor. Mae Murray didn't even own a sweater. Loretta remembered a different closet, the one in Mae's Beverly Hills mansion. It was deep, shelves on either side, drawers with crystal pulls, dresses hung in a row on velour hangers, arranged by color. Hooks draped with beads, satin shoes displayed on raked shelves, gowns made of tulle, and coats made of sable and fox. There was a carpeted runway made of plush silk wool in Mae's signature lavender, at the end of it, a full-length mirror with three panels and a velvet stool, overhead a skylight that beamed a funnel of light where Mae would stand after dressing and check her outfit from every angle.

It was bliss to play dress-up in Mae's closet at the height of her fame as a movie star. Carlene and Loretta would write plays, then choose their costumes from Mae's wardrobe. They wore gowns trimmed in marabou feathers, delighting Mae as they dragged the trains of the skirts behind them while teetering on sequin-covered high heels.

Loretta recalled pulling on Mae's evening gloves, which smelled as sweet as fresh gardenias. She used to snoop through Mae's evening bags after a night on the town. Loretta would find a small mirror, a pack of Camels, and matchbooks from all the glamorous places that Mae would frequent: Ciro's, Mocambo, Romanoff's. The boxes of matches were as artful as any memento from any fancy place, and sometimes Mae wrote on them—a phone number, the title of a script going around town that she might consider, or the name of a new hairdresser, fresh from Paris, who was making the studio rounds to find a job.

Loretta remembered the opulence. She could picture Mae's bedroom suite, the satin bedspread with ruffles of palest lilac, so pale it was almost silver. She and Carlene had played hide-and-seek in the matching draperies and danced on the plush carpet dyed to match the spread and the curtains. She remembered Mae's organza dressing gowns in the same shade, and entering the bedroom to greet Mae in the morning, thinking she looked like a cream puff in the window of Gladman's Bakery in Beverly Hills.

Loretta was devastated for Mae, but did not show it. She found a thick, plain glass vase on the shelf and went to the bathroom to fill it.

"They're my absolute favorite flowers, Gretchen. Thank you." Mae smiled.

Loretta took a seat next to Mae.

"Are you still dancing?" Mae asked.

"Not so much."

"I believe in dance. It's the foundation for everything. If you can't move, you can't act, you know."

"That's true."

"Do you mind that I still call you Gretchen?"

"Oh, no. I love it. It reminds me of the days when we were girls."

"I named you Loretta, you know."

Loretta nodded. The actress Colleen Moore had actually given Loretta her new name, in a scheme hatched with the director Mervyn LeRoy. But if Mae wanted to take credit, that was fine with Loretta. She smiled, thinking success had many mothers in Hollywood, and credit was always there for the taking, even now. Still, Loretta was grateful to her benefactor. She took Mae's hand. "There would have been no Loretta Young without you. You gave me music lessons, dance classes. Carlene and I loved to stay with you at the house in Bel Air."

"It was grand. You should bring Carlene by sometime."

"I will."

"Remember the swing?" Mae smiled.

"You had the only house in Bel Air with a swing in the front yard."

"Why hide it in the back? We were players, weren't we? We knew how to play."

"You taught me where to look when the camera was rolling."

"Oh, you came by that naturally."

"No, everything took practice."

"Practice over time becomes skill, dear. That's why, as soon as I'm feeling up to it, I'm going to give Lew Wasserman a call. He's the cheese now, isn't he?"

"A very powerful talent agent."

"I'm in the mood to work again. He'd be the man to call."

"Absolutely."

"My third husband, what a dreadful man, really scotched everything for me. Threatened L. B. Mayer. Can you imagine that?"

Loretta shook her head. No one had ever sued Louis B. Mayer and won.

"But that wasn't the worst of it. He's still an oozing sore. Took my boy. I only had the one child, you know. Imagine, after trying so hard for so many years, I lose him because of that thug. The court gave him to a foster family. Did you read about it?"

Loretta shook her head—but in fact, she knew all about it. "Matezee, we can't do everything right."

"We don't. I haven't. But what would I do—given all that time, and all those choices once again, what would I do with it?"

"Everything, right?"

"I would have held on to my work. It came easily to me, and I figured it would last—that I would last. You know? It was a gift, that talent. We don't treasure the skills and the breaks and the good things that come naturally. At least, I didn't."

"Look at all the great things you did. You helped build this hospital. Your name is on the plaque with the original trustees."

"Fire insurance, baby. Fire insurance."

"What do you mean?"

"You Catholics invented it. It's called an indulgence. You do all the good you can to make up for the sin."

"But all sins are forgiven when the sinner is contrite."

"Sure. But that doesn't mean the sinner feels the redemption. Sometimes the sin overpowers the forgiveness. That's why we build hospitals. We don't feel clean."

Loretta wanted to go back in time with Mae. She didn't like this conversation; it reminded her that sometimes the story of a life doesn't end as it might in the movies, in one happy frame, sealed with one glorious kiss. Sometimes it ends like this, in a room with one gown and a spare. At least the window was big, and beyond it a view of a green field and a blue California sky.

Loretta wanted to cheer Mae up, so she asked, "Do you remember *The Primrose Ring*?"

"No."

"Nineteen seventeen."

"Oh, honey, that was almost century ago." Mae laughed.

"You played a nurse. I was four years old and played a fairy. My first job in show business."

"You remember that?"

"Every moment. In my four-year-old way. I flew from the grid in a harness. It was cinched so tight, it left a mark. But Mama rubbed coconut oil on my stomach for six months afterwards until it faded. But I didn't care. When I was on the sound stage, I was flying."

"You never feel pain when the camera is rolling. Why is that?"

"Never figured it out." Loretta patted Mae's hand. "Bobby Leonard was a good director. Taught me how to play checkers."

"A fine man and a good husband."

"You started Tiffany Pictures with him."

"And I should've stayed there. And I should've stayed with him. But he really wanted a child. Well, I went on to have one—with the wrong man. And I heard he had children. Why do we let the good ones go?"

"I don't know, Mae. That's one of those questions I plan on asking God when I see Him." Loretta's eyes filled with tears. She remembered Spence and Clark—both gone, and neither knew the depth of her feelings. She might have shown her feelings on the screen, but in life she kept them hidden. Safer that way, or so she thought at the time.

"Oh, let's not go down that road. It's got a terrible view," Mae joked.

Loretta took Mae's hand. It was as soft as it had been decades ago. Actresses never go in the sun, if they're wise. They preserve the skin, and when they preserve the skin, they lengthen the career.

They sat in silence for a few moments. Mae looked out on the fields behind the actors' home. There was a lemon grove. The manicured trees were full of ripe fruit, the bright yellow bursting through the green like canary diamonds on a velvet evening glove.

"Bobby used to say, Don't act, Mae. Just be. And that's all I tried to do all my life, just be. But staying in the moment, it has its price. You're sewing the days and years together, and when there's no plan, you drop stitches here and there."

"Not many. You changed my life, Mae."

"Oh, honey, I wish I would've steered you to a different racket. Pictures are for suckers, and movies, what are they really? It's art you can put your hand through. It's just light and air and silver. It'll dissolve in those canisters and turn to dust. Just like us. Well, me a helluva sooner than you."

"Along the way, you make people laugh and cry and think."

"They'd do that anyway, honey." Mae closed her eyes. "Can you come and see me again sometime?"

"I will."

"It took you a long time to get here."

"It did. Too long."

"Well, we fixed that up, didn't we?"

"You rest, Mate-zee. And I'll see you soon."

Mae closed her eyes and went off to sleep as though the ability were on tap. Loretta walked down the hallway. She would remind herself to visit Mae, and to buy her a proper robe and slippers, something in velour, something in a shade of lilac.

———

A bright red bird landed on the windowsill. Loretta sipped her coffee and watched the bird through the glass. The bird looked her straight in the eye, which sent a chill through her.

Loretta went outside and picked up the newspaper on the driveway.

The paperboy had missed the entrance, and the roll had landed on the lawn. She tiptoed through the wet grass and picked it up. She unrolled it and began reading as she walked back to the house. It was March 24. The night before, Mae Murray had died in her sleep.

Loretta sighed as she read the litany of bankruptcies, lawsuits, and failed projects that had dogged Mae, and for a moment wished for the days of the powerful studios, when an obituary was a love letter and not a police blotter. Eddie Mannix, or any of the boys in the front office who controlled the flow of information, would never have allowed this—it reflected poorly on everyone.

Loretta stopped and took a deep breath. She sat down on the front step of the porch and wept. She decided to put a swing on the branch of the oak tree in her front yard. Her granddaughter Maria would enjoy it, and it would be a fitting tribute to Mae Murray, who taught her that to play was to live.

17

Loretta waited in the baggage area of LAX for Judy. Occasionally someone would see Loretta Young out running an errand and figure she was *somebody*, but at this stage of her life, so long away from pictures and television, they couldn't figure out who she might be. She carried herself like a star; maybe age had brought a different kind of sophistication and beauty, but the elegance that had made her special was still there.

When Loretta saw her daughter come down the escalator, she was thrilled to see her.

"Mom, this car is crazy."

"It's a brand-new nineteen sixty-six Rolls-Royce."

"And you're still a bad driver."

"No, the man who sold it to me assured me that if I bought it I would instantly be a better driver."

"Money talks. Or should I say, money lies."

"No kidding."

"Should we go out tonight?" Judy asked.

"I called your brothers—they've got plans, but if you stay through the weekend, they'll come over for supper on Sunday. We'll get all the aunts together, Mama. The whole shebang."

"Where's my stepfather?"

"He's around." Loretta and Tom were living apart. Once she decided to retire from acting, and the boys were grown, there was little to hold them together.

"I don't want to see him, if that's all right with you. I'm old enough now to choose how I want to spend time."

"That's fine."

"I wish you would have put him in his place when I was a girl."

"That's in the past."

"I still think about it. He resented me. I'm a mother, and I can't understand how he could look at me at five years old and consider me a rival."

"I didn't see it then."

"You couldn't. You never had a father, and you had no idea how good fathers treat their children. Well, I can tell you this. A good father doesn't make a child feel unsafe, unworthy, and unwanted, and your husband made me feel all those things and still does."

"When I met Tom I thought he was a good man. I thought he was strong and principled."

"I didn't spend much time with him before the wedding."

"Judy, that's not how it was done back then. Children and parents were separate."

"I know, the old children-should-be-seen-and-not-heard. But the problem with that is that children grow up and they find their voices, and by then, we can't be silenced. So look out."

"No kidding." Loretta drove onto the freeway to a cacophony of car horns. Judy's stomach turned, and she gripped the leather handle on the door. "Careful, Mom."

"I'm always careful."

Judy believed that her mother was incapable of being cautious; Loretta Young was ruled by her emotions. She had never been careful. She was so lax, she'd had an affair with a married man and became pregnant. Judy knew this for sure because she was the product of that carelessness. She had enough proof of her paternity: the time line, her aunts' whispers, the open secret in Hollywood finally revealed to her, and of course the surgery on her ears to remove the last obvious detail of her connection to Clark Gable. Loretta had spun a Hollywood melodrama, and Judy felt that she was placed in the center of it against her will. And now, finally, after years of trying, Judy had flown to California to confront her mother and demand the truth.

Loretta pulled into the driveway. Judy grabbed her overnight bag from the back seat and climbed up the stairs behind her mother.

Judy marveled at her mother's physical countenance. She floated into a room, and on the stairs that night her feet barely brushed the steps. She made Hollywood entrances and exits in her real life, using all the tools of the great stars—costumes, makeup, even the right vehicle, the brand-new Rolls-Royce befitting a star who'd shone most brightly during Hollywood's golden age.

Judy caught her mother up on the details of her and Maria's lives, including her divorce, whose details Loretta listened to carefully. Loretta might not have been a good example for Judy when it came to marriage, but she had taught her daughter well about divorce. Divorce was as big a business as the movies, the accompanying paperwork and contracts sealed and signed as if Louis B. Mayer himself were pushing the paper across a polished desk.

For all their differences, Judy was her mother's daughter: she was charming, intelligent, and unlucky in love. Evidently the Gladys Belzer strain of bad romantic luck had been passed along through Loretta's line down to Judy.

Judy threw on her pajamas and went across the hall to her mother's room.

"You know, it's always strange when it's just the two of us."

"Are you going to complain about all the time you gave up babysitting your brothers?"

"No, I had fun with Peter and Chris. I love them."

"You were lucky—you got two brothers."

"You had Uncle Jackie."

"He was not built to live in a house of women." Loretta laughed.

"He didn't have a father, and that's tough. Peter and Chris had Dad, so they had a better time of it."

"They had an ally, for sure," Loretta said. "I always worried he was spoiling them."

"He spoiled them, because I got the opposite," Judy said.

"I don't feel well," Loretta said. She was queasy; she had gotten shots to travel abroad, so her arm was sore and her stomach was upset. She went into her bathroom and closed the door. Soon, she was throwing up.

Judy rapped on the door gently. "Mom, do you need help?" She sighed. Every time she tried to have a serious conversation with her mother about her father—not her stepdad, but her real father—something derailed it. Judy hadn't persisted because she didn't want to hurt Loretta—but the truth was, she was past worrying about everyone else's feelings. Judy Lewis wanted the truth. She wanted to know who she was and where she came from. For years she'd believed it wasn't in her mother's sphere of knowledge, but now she knew that wasn't true.

Judy had enough pieces of the puzzle. She knew who she was, but she wanted her mother to corroborate what she believed. Judy believed that if Loretta would acknowledge the truth, it would allow Judy to move through the rest of her life in the light, instead of the constant emotional fumbling she had known since she was a girl. Judy wanted her place at the Young/Belzer table as a Gable.

Judy pushed the door open. Her mother was at the sink, washing her face.

"I think it's the shots for my trip," Loretta said.

"I'm sorry."

"Can't travel without them, I guess."

"Mom, I just turned thirty-one."

"I know how old you are, honey. I'm your mother."

Judy smiled. "I need your help. I want to know about my father."

"Why do you bring this up now?"

"Mom, I have a knowingness that I've had since I was a girl. I began to figure it out—your sisters would say things, the kids at school would make comments."

"Judy, what would they know?"

"More than me. Evidently everybody knew but me. On my wedding day I got sick not because I was nervous, but because I was getting married and I didn't know who I was. I'm not blaming you—I assume you have your reasons—but I want to understand who I am from your perspective."

"You're my daughter."

"And I have a father. Is Clark Gable my father?"

Loretta put her hand on her heart, and felt it racing. She was at long last tired of the secret; she could no longer keep it. It didn't matter what was for the best, or what Loretta's intentions might have been. It was time to tell the truth. It was as if a storm had blown through the house, shattered the windows, blown down the doors, and crumbled the bricks. The secret that had taken her energy and her focus and her determination as it lay dormant and hidden had finally defeated her. The world had changed—not the one outside her home, the one within it. There was no reason to hide Judy's father from her any longer. It was just the two of them, mother and daughter. Loretta knew she might lose Judy when she confirmed the truth, but it was too late now. What was hidden had to be revealed.

"Mom, I'm going to ask you again. Is Clark Gable my father?"

"Yes."

"Why didn't you tell me?"

Loretta sat down on the edge of the bed. Judy knelt before her. "Your father was married, and it was awful. I got pregnant, and I was supporting our family, and our faith—well, I would never have an abortion, so I had to have you, wanted to have you, but I couldn't marry your father." The facts tumbled out at a rate that made Judy's head spin. Loretta had never pictured this scene the way it was playing out in real life. "I couldn't marry him!"

"Did you want to?"

"Yes. And he wanted to marry me. But there was no way to make it work. You have to understand the time. We lived in fear of all of this"—Loretta motioned around the room—"going away. We'd lose our jobs, our livelihood."

"Your fans."

"That was secondary. It was our way of life. We had built up our family from nothing, without the help of a man, without the help of our fathers, they were gone. We had to take care of ourselves."

"How did I become a secret?"

"Out of necessity. For you. For your safety. You see, your father's wife would call me, and I wouldn't answer the phone. Alda figured out how to handle her, but we had to take pains never to run into her. She wanted to ruin me, hoping that would keep your father in the marriage. Your father called me and called me, and I was so afraid someone would figure it out. It would have ruined his career and mine, and so I pushed him away."

"Did you love him?"

"Madly."

"Did he ever come to see me?"

"He came to the Venice house, and he was wild about you. Couldn't put you down. You were perfect, a little angel that fell out of the sky. You had gold hair in ringlets, and he was besotted."

Judy held back her tears. "Why didn't you tell me?"

"Do you remember when your father came to visit you at the house on Camden?"

"Yes, I thought it was strange."

"We were trying to have you spend time together. I wanted to tell you then, but you weren't interested. And your father said, 'Leave it alone. She's beautiful and smart and well-adjusted.' Remember when I begged you to come to the set when we were making a movie? You were fifteen, a teenager, and I didn't want to force the issue."

"Mom, you should have made me go to the set. That's no excuse."

"Your father thought it would devastate you at that point in your life."

"That's the moment you let him make decisions about my future? How could you let me get married without knowing who my father was?"

"I invited him to your wedding, he and Kay, thinking that might be a fresh start."

"But he didn't come to my wedding."

"So then I thought I didn't want anyone or anything to hurt you. So I let it go."

"Mom, everybody in the world knew but me."

"Everything I did was because I loved you. And the problem with a secret is that it lives, and as it lives, it gains power, and it got too big for me. And I thought it would be too big for you. After Clark died, I thought about telling you, and I was afraid you'd hate me for it."

"Mom, you understand why I'm struggling. I struggle with everything. On the surface, my life is like one of Grandma's rooms. Every aspect appears perfect, every chair is placed just so, the draperies hang without a wrinkle, and there's a fire in the hearth, just as there should be in any home. I look fine. I look like you and my father. I appear to have everything I needed. I was loved by my aunts and uncles and cousins. I have two half brothers who love me, and I love them. I had a stepfather who didn't care for me, but that was okay, I had you and Alda and Luca, and LaWanda at the studio, and your friends, who were so kind to me. And I was almost content to live the rest of my life with my daughter in the bubble, with the truth banging on the glass and me inside with no way to let it in. But I can't do that to myself anymore, I can't do it to Maria, and I won't do it to you. You should know me as a person who owns her truth. If I was born of a mistake, I forgive it. And if I was born of love, I have a right to revel in it, to share it with my daughter, and someday for her to share it with her children. That's what family is, that's what history means, and that's all we have to offer each other going forward, our mutual truth."

"It's true," Loretta said softly. But the truth brought neither the mother nor the daughter the joy they had dreamed of—the admission only confirmed the sadness of all that had been lost.

Loretta folded down the coverlet on her bed. She kissed her daughter.

"Will you stay with me?" Loretta asked Judy.

"Of course, Mom."

Judy got into bed next to Loretta. She reached across and embraced her mother, who began to weep.

"It's all right, Mom." Judy cried too, not for her mother's sadness, though it hurt her—she cried for the father she'd never know, the father who lived only in her imagination, in her dreams, and when she wanted to visit him there, on the silver screen.

———

Loretta and Tom's attenuated divorce settlement was nearing an end. She had longed for her freedom and looked forward to making her own decisions again. The process of divorcing Tom Lewis was illuminating for Loretta. If she had it to do over again, she never would have become Tom's business partner. She had seen it so many times in Hollywood. A star would turn over her financial interests to a husband who was a successful businessman in his own right, and hope that he would take as good care of her business as he had of his own before entering into a marriage with her. But for some reason, it never worked out that way in show business. Show business, it turned out, engaged more than goods, services, and the manufacturing and distribution of products, it also peddled egos, and those, it turns out, are priceless.

"Your lawyer sent the last of the divorce papers for you to sign."

"I'll take care of it."

"You tried to make it work."

"I suppose I could have tried harder. Tom is still making me feel like I can't do anything right."

"It wasn't to be."

"This leaves me time to take care of Mama, to give her the attention she deserves."

"You could be happily married and still look out for your mother."

"That's true. The children are on their own now. It's funny, Alda, nobody ever told me motherhood was temporary. You think you have years and years with them, but the truth is, you don't. Had I known that, I might have handled things differently. I would have done everything differently with Judy. She really suffered."

"She was loved. That saved her. It saves all of us."

"But it can't make up for what she missed. I will carry that always. Alda, I have always wanted to ask you something. Why didn't you and Luca ever adopt a child?

"I lost a baby boy, and then another, and by the time I learned to move with my grief, the years of motherhood were over for me. It's just the way it went. I remembered the parents at Saint Elizabeth's, their joy when the baby was placed in their arms, and somehow I knew that joy would never be mine. I would have other kinds of happiness and plenty of it. We all get some, we have to be satisfied with our portion."

"That's the key, isn't it? To be grateful," Loretta said.

"I guess so."

"You've been a good friend to me, Alda."

"I had hoped to. You've been everything to me. Boss. Sister. Friend. Confidante." Alda patted Loretta's hand.

"What did I ever do?"

"You were my maid of honor. You were my witness on the happiest day of my life."

"And on my wedding day, you told me to run for the hills," Loretta joked. "I should have listened."

A petite lady around forty years old stood under the portico. "Miss Young?"

"May I help you?" Alda asked.

"I'm Susie Tracy."

Loretta sat up. "Spencer and Louise's daughter?"

"Their one and only."

"I'm going to make a tray for us," Alda said, rising slowly from her chaise.

"Please don't—I can't stay."

Loretta winked at Alda, who went to make tea anyway.

"I have something for you, Miss Young." Susie handed Loretta an envelope.

"What is this?" Loretta opened the letter and remembered. She recognized the handwriting: it was her own. The drafts of the letter came flooding back to her, along with the feelings she'd had at the time. She had been so madly in love with Spencer Tracy, and it was high drama—swings of desire and despair, craving something they couldn't have, wishing they had met at a different time, under different circumstances, all the puffery of young love and dreams.

"My mother said there were two women in my father's life. One was her, and the other was you."

"Your father was a remarkable man."

"Mom was always grateful that you sent the priest to see him when he was dying. She wasn't Catholic, and even though she went to church with him, she didn't think of it."

"Your father believed in a good confession."

She nodded. "He did. But you thought to send the priest. And I wanted to thank you for that."

"Your mother was the most important woman in your father's

life. I saw a lot of marriages come and go in Hollywood, including my own, but your parents were the real deal."

Susie's eyes stung with tears. "I read so much junk about my parents. I remember one article said they had an arrangement."

"Every marriage is an arrangement. It's a construct of two lives, and the two people in it have to work it out. No matter what you hear about your parents, you cling to what you knew about them, and that's the truth. All the rest of it is chatter."

"Thank you for that."

"I know people have said things about your dad and me, and we were good friends. Every woman that met him adored him, but none rivaled your mother. That's why they stayed married. They were devoted to you and John completely."

"I know that."

"You hold on to what you know. Don't let anyone tell you who your parents were. You know your family. You know who you are. This is a town that thrives on made-up stories—if we aren't telling them, we're filming them. Don't take any of it too seriously."

"I won't." Susie gave Loretta a kiss on the cheek. By the time Alda had made it outside with the tea, Susie had left.

"What was that all about?" Alda asked.

Loretta handed her the letter.

"What do you think, Alda?"

"Never put anything in writing."

Loretta chuckled. Alda remembered the drafts of the letter, and how she had burned them. She hadn't worked in Hollywood much more than a week, and she had already learned how to torch evidence.

"Nobody thinks about the children," Alda said. "I know they're matinee idols, but they're real and they have lives, and their children have feelings."

"We trade all that in when we become famous. It's what I love the most about being retired. I don't have to think how my actions that day will affect my audience or my ability to do my work. It's a ridiculous burden."

"That brought you a great life."

"No question. But was I any happier than you were with Luca in that house in the valley? I don't think so."

"Do you think Mr. Tracy was happy?"

"He had a wanderlust. Not physically, not as a traveler, but in his heart. He wanted to see and know everything he could. He had a worldview from that Irish heart."

"And Katharine Hepburn?"

"She took care of him. And I don't know if any other woman would have put up with his drinking. I'm afraid she got the worst of him."

"Do you ever think about Mr. Gable?"

"I pray the last decade of the rosary for him every night. When I was a girl, I prayed to find true love with that last decade, and now I pray for his soul."

"What was it about him?"

"Oh, if I knew that, I'd have a movie studio or we would have been together. He was the one that got away, though if he were here right now, he'd tell you I pushed him. I guess I always knew he was a man you couldn't own, and in my way, I kept myself separate from him because I knew if I ever had him, I wouldn't be able to make him stay. That would have been a fate worse than never having him at all. I had his baby, and I couldn't keep him. I know he loved me, but he didn't know *how* to love me. And that's the difference between a love that lasts and all the rest."

Loretta tucked a pillow behind her mother's head on the sofa. Just as it had been in the beginning, when Sally and Polly married and Georgiana was out of the house and husbands had left her life, Loretta and Gladys were back together again, the two of them, living happily in one house, decorated by Mrs. Belzer herself.

"Mama, I don't want to talk about your estate."

"We must. I'm ninety-two years old," Gladys said. "How long am I going to last?"

"You're still working."

"What's your point?"

"You're not going anywhere."

"You don't know that."

"No, but you're in good shape."

"Here." Gladys handed her an envelope "This is everything we own."

Loretta looked through the real estate portfolio. Gladys still owned the house on Rindge Street where Judy was born. "Mama, this is the story of our lives . . . in houses."

"I feel like a movie. Let's run a print tonight."

No matter how many times Loretta tried to explain VHS tapes, Gladys still called movies that they watched at home "prints."

"What do you want to watch?"

"Something with Myrna."

"*Thin Man*?"

"No, I just watched all of them. They're good but something else."

"*Test Pilot*?"

"I watched that one too. That's a favorite. Has your old beau Spencer Tracy in it."

"He was a good one. But a lost lamb."

"The good ones always are." Gladys nodded.

"How about *Too Hot to Handle*? Mama, that's got Gable."

"And Myrna."

"We can watch something else." Gladys still worried that Loretta was sad about Clark Gable.

"Nope. We're watching Gable and Loy."

Loretta curled up on the sofa next to her mother. They watched the black-and-white film as Gable performed daring stunts in an airplane, Myrna, practical and wise on the ground, pointing out his flaws, all in all a good story.

Soon Gladys was fast asleep. Loretta flipped through her address book and dialed New York.

"Myrna? It's Loretta."

"What's doing, sis?"

"We just watched *Too Hot to Handle*. Mama and me. Well, I watched. Mama slept."

"Did it hold up?"

"They should put your nose on Mount Rushmore."

"I think they have. Lincoln has my nose."

"Retroussé? Don't think so. Mama's asleep, or she'd say hello."

"How is she?"

"She's ninety-two and kicking. Went through her real estate portfolio. She still owns the land on our first boarding house."

"Why didn't Gladys Belzer pull me aside and tell me to buy something?"

"You had those husbands handling your money."

"Every time you get a divorce, you cut your money in two. And I had four divorces. Do the math. I'm sitting here drinking half a cup of coffee."

Loretta laughed. "I was always afraid we'd be in the poorhouse."

"And look at you. I have to work, and you're a lady of leisure."

"But you're a better actress. Nobody misses me."

"Did you hear about our dear Niv? He's in a bad way. Can hardly speak. He has ALS."

"Where is he?"

"In Switzerland. With that wife. A ladies' man always ends up with a mean wife. She's dreadful, Loretta."

"Niv was my best friend. I could tell him anything. And I told him everything. He deserved an angel."

"He could keep a secret," Myrna said. "You know, he told me something once about you. Said when Judy was born, he sent Clark a telegram."

"That was Niv?" Loretta was astonished. "Of course it was. I should have known."

"Yep. He spent a lot of time trying to get you and Clark back together."

Loretta hung up the phone. She draped an afghan over her mother and tucked a pillow under her neck.

Loretta popped the cartridge out of the VHS. She looked on the shelf and found *The Call of the Wild*. She put the movie in the recorder and hit play.

Alda came through and watched the front roller as she stood behind the sofa.

"Come and watch."

"Thanks, but not tonight. I'm going to bed."

"I'll put Mama in bed when the movie's over."

Alda had sold the house she and Luca shared in the valley. At

Loretta's insistence, she had moved in with Gladys and Loretta. As Alda climbed the steps, she remembered the first time she met Loretta. That was so long ago, before she met Luca, and before she lost their baby. This wasn't the old age that Alda had planned for herself. She was sixty-three years old, and she was back where she started. She believed Luca would have approved. After all, Loretta, Judy, and Gladys were family. Alda could hear the overture of *The Call of the Wild* as she closed the door to her bedroom.

Loretta stretched her legs out in front of her as Gable filled the screen, hat cocked on his head, holster and belt, a natty tie and a scruff of day-old beard. She leaned back on the sofa and watched as the man she once loved dazzled and delighted with his confident swagger and his down-home charm. She liked the scenes best before she entered the picture. Loretta knew how the story went once she was onscreen, and for the first few minutes, she could rewrite what might have been. When Gable found her in the snow, she could feel the cold. When he held her, it was never long enough, never tightly enough, never enough.

Loretta couldn't get enough of him, and she hadn't.

If Gretchen Young had one regret in her life, it was that she never married Clark Gable.

EPILOGUE

∽◯

OCTOBER 2000

Roxanne Chetta waited for her family at the entrance of Moreau Hall at Saint Mary's under a banner that announced "The Mary Ethel Meeks deWolfe Art Show." She wore a tuxedo jacket she had bogarted from the theater costume shop over a Ziggy Stardust T-shirt and a floor-length skirt made of tulle, in layers of blue, that rolled wide and fierce like ocean waves. Her hair was piled on her head in a mass of dark curls, and she wore the brightest red lipstick Urban Decay offered at the CVS.

The world would see Roxanne's painting for the first time that evening, and the thought of it made her feel nervous and vulnerable. If there was a form of stage fright for painters, Roxanne was sure she had it. She was shivering as she looked out into the blue darkness, broken open by wide beams of yellow light from the streetlamps in the parking lot, when she heard her mother call her name.

Roxanne waved to her mother, who moved toward her in the midst of a clump of relatives. Joe, Roxanne's father, her two brothers, and her three sisters had made the trip from Brooklyn, along with a face Roxanne could not make out in the dark.

The Chetta family traveled in a pack, a small army of Italian Americans who never missed any event involving one of its members. It didn't matter if it was an art opening, a school play, or a neighborhood basketball game, if you were a Chetta and you were in the spotlight, you could count on a cheering section.

Roxanne's mother embraced her daughter and sniffed her neck. "Are you still smoking?"

"Nah, that's old smoke. I quit this morning."

"We have a surprise for you!"

There was always a surprise on a Chetta family road trip. Usually it was food—fresh mozzarella, salami, and prosciutto transported in coolers or boxes of pastries from D'Italia's Bakery, which her mother would hold on her lap for hours on the interstate so the *sfogliatella* wouldn't arrive smashed or the shells on the cannolis shattered before reaching their destination.

Her brothers parted to reveal their great-aunt.

"Aunt Alda!" Roxanne put her arms around her.

"I didn't want to miss your art show," Alda said. Her white hair was pulled back in a simple chignon. She wore a black dress coat made of silk wool, gloves, and black leather flats. Her square pocketbook was vintage, but so well cared for that the patent leather looked new.

"Best surprise ever!" Roxanne kissed her on the cheek. Alda's skin was cool, like a seashell. Roxanne's eyes filled with tears.

"Oh, don't cry."

"I can't help it. I wish Uncle Luca were here. But I'm so happy you are."

The Moreau art gallery was filled with student artists and their families and friends. A group of nuns from Augusta Hall milled about with art patrons from the city of South Bend. There was a table of college-style hors d'oeuvres, silver trays filled with blocks of cheddar cheese that had been picked over until they looked like Roman ruins. Members of the senior class served empty-bodied white wine in plastic cups as the guests took in the art show. Roxanne led her family to her painting.

"Oh, Roxanne, it's magnificent," her mother said.

"It's huge," her father said approvingly. Whether it was art, houses, or cars, for Joe Chetta, bigger was always better.

Aunt Alda took a step back to take it in. The expanse of white, the dots of silver, and the strokes of blue brought her back to Mount Baker in 1935. She opened her purse, found her handkerchief, and dried a tear from her cheek.

"What do you think, Auntie?" Roxanne put her arm around Alda.

"My husband would be so proud. You're a fine painter. When you wrote me and told me the inspiration behind the painting, I couldn't believe it. Mount Baker had meaning for us for many reasons, but you've made it come alive here. I have something for you." Alda gave Roxanne a wooden box with a handle. "L. Chetta" was engraved on a small brass name plaque. "Your uncle would want you to have this."

Roxanne opened the box. It was Luca's paint kit, his brushes, palette, and knives, stored neatly in flannel sleeves as though they had been used that day. A black-and-white photograph was tucked in an elastic band under the lid.

"Oh, Auntie." Roxanne studied the photograph of Clark Gable and Loretta Young and the film crew, between takes on the snow-covered mountain as they made *The Call of the Wild.* "I don't know what to say. With this kit, it's like I'm a real painter now. And the photograph, it's a treasure."

Sister Agnes pushed through the crowd to get to Roxanne. "I just endured the fibers exhibit. Don't get the dangling threads at all."

"Sister Agnes Eugenia, this my great-aunt Alda. Her husband was the scene painter in Hollywood I told you about."

Sister Agnes shook Alda's hand. "I was a big Loretta Young fan."

"Did you ever write her a letter?"

"I might have. I loved her in *The Call of the Wild.*"

"Then I probably read it. I read all her mail."

"What a career—such an exciting life," Sister said with a tinge of envy. "For her and for you."

"I was lucky. It started as a job, and then, as things go, it became a calling. I worked for Loretta until the end. We lost her on August twelfth."

"Heart attack?"

"Loretta had cancer."

"Terrible."

"She had a very happy last few years. Did you know she had married again? Jean Louis, her good friend, the costume designer, was widowed, and they married after Mr. Lewis died. She divorced him but waited until he passed away to remarry."

"A dyed-in-the-wool Catholic, as we say." Sister chuckled.

"Oh yes." Alda smiled. "Loretta was staying with her sister Georgie at the end. She adored her sons with Mr. Lewis, and she and Judy—her daughter by Mr. Gable—had worked through their problems."

"Oh, good. I heard that her daughter had written a book about their relationship."

"Loretta loved Judy dearly. Judy needed to write that book. Loretta eventually accepted it, and they reconciled and had some good years at the end of Loretta's life."

"That's wonderful."

"They were lucky. You know, Sister, we think we have the luxury of time. We figure that there will always be a moment to have the conversation that we meant to have, and then the moment passes and it's too late. I learned so much working in Hollywood, working for Loretta—but the most important thing I learned was to say what you mean when you have the moment to say it. It works in life, it works in the movies. Don't wait, because the time may not come again."

Sister Agnes took Alda's hand. "She had a good, long life. Did she have her faith at the end?"

"She did."

"That's a blessing," Sister Agnes said.

"I knew you two would hit off." Roxanne put her arm around her aunt. "Sister Agnes is a big fan of the movies of the 1930s and '40s," Roxanne said.

"I love the old ones the best. I marked important events in my life with movies," Sister admitted. "The last movie I saw before I entered the novitiate was *Top Hat*, with Fred Astaire and Ginger Rogers. I went into the convent on a toe-tapping high."

"The old movies take me right back," Alda admitted. "Not everyone has a movie to mark the moment their lives changed or they fell in love."

"We were married in Brooklyn the summer of *Saturday Night Fever*. Our wedding song was 'How Deep Is Your Love,' " Roxanne's mother said wistfully.

"Every once in a while, my parents disco dance for us. It makes us throw up." Roxanne laughed.

"Yeah, well, be grateful. You exist because of the Bee Gees," her father commented.

"Are you going back to California after the show?" Sister Agnes asked.

"No, no, it's time for a change. It's time to be with family again."
Alda smiled.

"Auntie just turned ninety," Roxanne's father said proudly. With
his thick gray hair brushed back off his face, Joe Chetta resembled
his uncle Luca. "We finally convinced her to give up the bright lights
of Hollywood for the police sirens of Brooklyn."

"That's marvelous! I was going to offer you a room in Augusta
Hall with the retired nuns."

"Thank you, Sister. But I think I'll try Brooklyn." Alda chuckled to
herself. How funny that she might end up back in the convent, where
she began. Alda wanted to be buried next to Luca when her time
came. She would have no assurance of that unless she left California
and returned to Brooklyn for good.

"Look!" Roxanne said, pointing outside through the glass doors of
Moreau Hall.

The Chetta family and Sister Agnes moved to the doors and
peered out. Beyond the glass, the first snow of the season fell in pin-
wheels of silver through the blue night.

After a moment, Alda pushed through the glass door and walked
outside. Joe called out to her, but she didn't hear him.

"She'll catch her death out there," Roxanne's mother said, following her out.

Roxanne stopped her. "She needs a moment, Ma."

"Don't worry. Auntie is a tough cookie," Joe assured them. "Northern Italians. They're part goat."

Outside, Alda took a deep breath as the snowflakes touched her
face in small, icy bursts.

The cold, dark night brought back the warmest of memories.

Alda remembered her first dive into the pool at Sunset House,
and how the water felt like satin against her skin. She remembered
her feet and how they felt the first time she slipped them into proper
leather after having worn work boots all of her life. She remembered
her infant son Michael in Padua, baby Patricia in her swaddling, and
holding Judy on the train. She remembered Luca's promise that he
would never leave her after he found out she couldn't have his children. She pictured her garden in the valley where she grew lush red

tomatoes in the California sun. But of all her memories, of all the flickers of the past that popped like camera flashes in the dark, most of all she remembered snow.

Alda recalled the majestic beauty of Washington State, the train station in Bellingham, the peaks of Mount Baker, and the broken-down old inn on the mountain. She saw Loretta laughing there in the barn as she made spaghetti, and Clark Gable in the drifts, wearing his ridiculous fur coat. She smiled when she recalled the dyspeptic look on Gable's face when she and Luca made their wedding vows.

Soon the Indiana sky opened up, and white glitter blew through the night and dusted the fields. Each dizzy snowflake found its way to the ground, where it rested and waited for the others. The world in Alda's sightline was pristine, wrapped in white velvet as if to hold it all together, to make it whole, maybe even perfect.

For the first time since he'd died, Alda felt her husband beside her. She missed Luca's kisses and the security she felt whenever he took her hand. She felt the anguish she'd experienced when they first fell in love, and the healing that would come later, when they were ready for it. She remembered the relief he felt when she forgave him, and the peace she knew when he forgave her. She recalled the scent of the fire pit on Mount Baker and how sweet the waffles and snow cream tasted when they were hungry. She would have paid attention to the sounds, the colors, and the light, if she had known that what once was so vivid would fade with time. If only she had known that those moments might last her whole life long, that they would live in her as surely as her own breath, she might have savored them, she might have tried to stop time.

Alda was certain that Luca had sent the snow and painted the world just for her.

She was grateful.

The flurry was a reminder of the love Luca and she had shared, the friendships they had made, and the work that had given their lives purpose and meaning. And when Alda was sad and she longed for Luca, she would remember the joy that filled their days, the serenity that filled their nights, in a place that belonged to them, and only to them, on a mountaintop covered in snow, in a time known as the golden age of Hollywood.

ACKNOWLEDGMENTS

This novel is dedicated to Mary J. Farino an Italian-American girl, (1905–1985), my great aunt, a wonderful single mother of two sons, a machine operator in a blouse mill, an exceptional Italian cook, and a fan of movies made during the golden age of Hollywood. I wish I could take you back to her home on Garibaldi Avenue in Roseto, Pennsylvania. It was a work of art. She lived in the family homestead all of her life, a two-family red-brick house with a striped awning over a long front porch. When you entered, there was a hallway back to a bright kitchen where you would find Aunt Mary at the stove. The house was always pristine, every surface gleamed, and no matter how busy she might be, she found time to sit down for a cup of coffee and a chat on her sunporch.

Mary Farino was a small-town girl, but she liked to travel and she often took trips with my grandmother, Viola. She had a wicked sense of humor and an unflinching view of people and the world. Her manner of speaking came straight out of an Anita Loos script. She'd call a particular kind of a lady a *jezebel*, another a *dame*, a certain kind of gentleman a *duke* or a different type a *chiseler* and when I'd ask what those words meant, I'd get a lesson in the movies directed by Frank Capra or George Stevens or Preston Sturges. When I was a girl in the 1970s, we'd watch black-and-white movies on television that she had seen in the theater when they first ran in the 1930s and '40s. From her living room, Aunt Mary introduced me to the work of the players in this novel and set me on a path to aspire to write their style of snappy dialogue. Her passion for movies made during the golden age became mine. I thank her with great love.

Many minds, hearts, and hard work go into the publication of a novel.

I am deeply grateful to the brilliant team at HarperCollins, led by

Brian Murray and Michael Morrison, who support our efforts with gusto.

Jonathan Burnham, my editor and publisher, is the best in the business. He edits as he publishes, with wisdom, restraint, and humor. I adore him. Maya Ziv, Jonathan's excellent right arm, is magnificent. Thank you Jennifer Civiletto and Gina Forsythe for making all the necessary connections and quickly.

Our marketing and publicity teams are inventive, energetic, and tireless. Thank you Kathy Schneider, Tina Andreadis, Kate D'Esmond, Leah Wasielewski, Renata Marchione, Katie O'Callaghan, Jennifer Murphy, Mary Ann Petyak, and Tom Hopke Jr. Virginia Stanley is a treasure; she brings authors and libraries together like matches and firecrackers and has for over twenty years. Viva Virginia! Her superb team includes: Annie Mazes, Amanda Rountree, Louisa Hager.

The glorious artists who create the cover and interior art are Robin Bilardello, Joanne O'Neill, and Gregg Kulick. I am crazy for the gold stars on the cover art that look like the pastina my mother made for us when we were kids.

Our hardworking and delightful sales force includes Doug Jones, Mary Beth Thomas, Andrea Rosen, Kathryn Walker, Michael Morris, Kristin Bowers, Austin Tripp, Christy Johnson, Brian Grogan, Tobly McSmith, Lillie Walsh, Rachel Levenberg, Frank Albanese, David Wolfson, and Samantha Hagerbaumer. The great ladies of paperbacks are Amy Baker, Mary Sasso, and Kathryn Ratcliffe-Lee. We are grateful to our bookstores, online vendors, and libraries everywhere.

Our superb production team is Cindy Achar, John Jusino, Miranda Ottewell, Leah Carlson-Stanisic, and William Ruoto. In the audio department, Katie Ostrowka and Blair Brown delivered the stars in these particular heavens with audible dazzle.

At William Morris Endeavor, I am grateful to a team that works on two coasts with the precision of the gears of a Swiss watch—though I think not one is of Swiss descent, but many have visited—my thanks and love to the dynamic beauty Suzanne Gluck, Clio Seraphim, Kitty Dulin, Eve Attermann, Alicia Gordon, Sasha Elkin, Joey Brown, Tracy Fisher, Alli Dyer, Cathryn Summerhayes, and Siobhan O'Neill. In film and television, I am represented by my lifelong beautiful sister Nancy Josephson, her trusty Ellen Sushko, and the great minds of the film department led by Graham Taylor and including Michelle Bohan, Joanna Korshak,

Chris Slager, Liesl Copland, Alli Mcardle; when it comes to putting it all to music, Amos Newman and Lauren Danielak do the job. Thank you all.

At The Glory of Everything Company, my love and evermore thanks to the brilliant, beautiful, and forward-thinking Sarah Choi. Donielle Muransky stepped in between her own writing projects and jobs, saving the day and my sanity. Our interns and researchers were smart, funny, and hardworking, and are all on their way to superstardom: thank you Claire Zajdel, Hannah Drinkall, Annella Kaine, Maggie Kane, Sarabeth Bukowski, Lauren Weiger, Erin Cassidy, Olivia Olson, Arden Bastia, Elizabeth Kenney, Claire Bleecker, Monica Murphy, Michelle March, Jamise Stidham, Adeline Wilson, Jennifer Vosters, Daniela Cardinale, Samantha Rowe, and Jillian Fata.

Nancy Bolmeier Fisher is the executive director of The Origin Project, our in-school writing program in southwest Virginia that brings authors into the classroom to work with and inspire students to write their stories. In two years, Nancy has taken our program and grown it, serving hundreds of students with her energy, drive, and open heart. She's a miracle and I'm proud to be her sidekick.

In Movieland, my thanks and love to Donna Gigliotti, Richard Thompson, Bryna Melnick, Helen Rosenberg, Jean Morrissey, Wade Bradley, and the team at Altar Identity Studios who brought you *Big Stone Gap*; Matthew T. Weiner, Darren Bartlett, Antony Platt, Reynaldo Villalobos, Don Bixby, Christopher Passig, Ben Bolling, Andrew J.D. Hauser, and Joe Rudge.

I have engaged the infinite resources of the brilliant mind of Larry Sanitsky of the Sanitsky Company too many times to count; consider me grateful and greedy.

At Picturehouse, my gratitude to Jeanne and Bob Berney, Marlee Chizari and their excellent team, and to Brian McNelis and Lakeshore Entertainment.

John Leventhal is a dream to work with and a brother in all other ways. Thank you Laura Bermudez, Joseph Craig, Rita McClenny, Andy Edmunds, Reuben Rios, and Michael Pitt. The *Big Stone Gap* team at Random House includes the hardworking and fabulous Libby McGuire, Kim Hovey, Anne Speyer, Paolo Pepe, and Beth Pearson.

At Simon & Schuster UK, I am proud to be published by Ian Chapman and edited by Suzanne Baboneau.

Gina Casella of AT Escapes at Adriana Trigiani Tours is a force of nature who continues to bring the novels to life around the world with magnificent tours in Italy, the UK and beyond, and here in New York City. Thank you Frank Dabell, Maria Perla, Emilia Grassi, Leonardo Marra, Ottavio Amendola, and Gabriele Massa; the memory of Costanzo Ruocco burns bright at Da Costanzo on Capri, now in Antonio's and Alvina's excellent care. Antonia Trigiani does a fabulous job with our merchandise, and Mary Trigiani of Spada Inc. is our brilliant media advisor.

My evermore gratitude and love to Chris and Ed Muransky, Hoda Kotb, Jennifer Miller, Kathie Lee Gifford, Christine Gardner, Kathy Ryan, Tony Krantz and Kristen Dornig, Jan Allison, Brian Balthazar, Julie Durk, Nigel Stoneman, Charles Fotheringham, Christine Onorati, Dona DeSanctis, Monique Gibson, Bunny Grossinger, Kathy McElyea, Mary Murphy and Bob Minzenmeizer, Liza Persky, Lou and Berta Pitt, Doris Gluck, Mary Pipino, Tom Dyja, Liz Travis, Eamonn McChrystal, Diane and Dr. Armand Rigaux, Dagmara Domincyzk and Patrick Wilson, Dan and Robin Napoli, Louise and Len Riggio, Sharon Ewing, Robin Kall, Eugenie Furniss, Jane Krakowski, Philip Grenz, Christina Geist, Joyce Sharkey, Jack Hodgins, Jake Morrissey, Gail Berman, Debra McGuire, Cate Magennis Wyatt, Ian and Ryan Fisher, Carol and Dominic Vechiarelli, Jim and Mary Deese Hampton, Jackie and Paul Wilson, Greg D'Alessandro, Mark Amato, Meryl Poster, Sister Robbie Pentecost.

Heather and Peter Rooney, Aaron Hill and Susan Fales-Hill, Mary K. and John Wilson, Jim and Kate Benton Doughan, Ruth Pomerance, Joanna Patton and Bill Persky, Angelina Fiordellisi and Matt Williams, Michael La Hart and F. Todd Johnson, Richard and Dana Kirshenbaum, Marisa Acocella Marchetto, Violetta Acocella, and Emma and Tony Cowell.

Hugh and Jody Friedman O 'Neill, Nelle Fortenberry, Cara Stein, Whoopi Goldberg, Tom Leonardis, Laura Monardo and Mario Natarelli, Rosalie Ciardullo, Dolores and Dr. Emil Pascarelli, Eleanor "Fitz" King and daughters Eileen, Ellen, and Patti, Sharon Hall and Todd Kessler, Aimee Bell, Rosanne Cash, Liz Welch Tirrell, Charles Randolph Wright, Constance Marks, Jasmine Guy, Mario Cantone and Jerry Dixon, Lee Boudreaux, Judy Rutledge, Greg and Tracy Kress, Father John Rausch, Judith Ivey, John Benjamin Hickey, Mary Ellen Keating.

Nancy Ringham Smith, Sharon Watroba Burns, Dee Emmerson, Elaine Martinelli, Kitty Martinelli (Vi and the girls), Sally Davies, Sister Karol Jackowski, Jane Cline Higgins, Betty Cline, Beth Vechiarelli

Cooper (my Youngstown boss), Max and Robyn Westler, Gina Vechi-arelli (my Brooklyn boss), Barbara and Tom Sullivan, Brownie and Connie Polly, Silas House and Jason Howard.

Catherine Brennan, Karen Fink, Beáta and Steven (the Warrior) Baker, Todd Doughty and Randy Losapio, Craig Fissé, Anemone and Steve Kaplan, Christina Avis Krauss and her Sonny, Veronica Kilcullen, Lisa Rykoski, Tara Fogarty, Eleanor Jones, Mary Ellinger, and Iva Lou Johnson.

Thank you Michael Patrick King. I hope everyone has a friend like you whom they can call any hour of the day or night and read aloud any lousy paragraph, relay any wild scheme, pitch any insane idea, and have it received with the support, grace, and love you have shown to me over these many years. When the call goes to voicemail, I will know the jig is up.

Cynthia Rutledge Olson, Mary Testa, Wendy Luck, Elena Nachman-off, and Dianne Festa, there aren't enough purses, jewels, or fancy shoes to fill your closets to express quite what you mean to me, but knowing you girls, you wouldn't want the stuff anyway, so thank you.

We remember Ray Oleson (Kathy's beloved) and J.T. Caruso (Barbara's beloved), and Edward Feeley (my sister-in-law Tina's father) fine fathers, good men, terribly missed.

Thank you Ann Godoff for opening the door to my literary career and a life in the world of books.

I remember my aunt and godmother Geraldine Beaumont Bonicelli. She was a gorgeous and elegant lady who will live in my heart always, as will my aunt Irma Bonicelli Godfrey, who was beautiful and kind, and my mother's most excellent sister.

Thank you Tim and Lucia, and our families, for everything.

There is no way to ever properly thank my mother Ida Bonicelli Tri-giani for everything she is, for everything she has done, and for what she means to me. I am lucky to be her daughter.

If I may, one last story before you go. When I was a student at Saint Mary's College in South Bend, Indiana in 1981, Sister Agnes Eugenia, a nun in full habit paid me a visit. She handed me an envelope; inside was an eight by ten photograph of a boy in a straw hat. The inscription read: *Dear Sister Agnes Eugenia, Here I am, 4 years old. Mother said to please continue praying for us and our "Pa." Big hugs.* It was signed by his mother for him, *John Clark*, and dated *1965*.

Sister Agnes had read a poem I had written about Clark Gable published in the school literary magazine and had sent it to Kay Gable, Mr. Gable's widow and the mother of his son, John. Sister told me that Mrs. Gable had chuckled at the poem and was pleased that someone so young remembered her husband (not every girl had an Aunt Mary Farino!). Sister Agnes was getting on in years and wanted me to have the photograph. (No, I never asked Sister Agnes how she knew Mrs. Gable—the ignorance of youth!) I intended to meet Mrs. Gable some-day, and promised Sister Agnes I would, but Mrs. Gable passed away in 1983 before we could meet. The photograph set me on the path to find out about the boy in the hat, his mother, and his father, which led me to the story you read herein, the stars I saw in these heavens, in my own particular way, out my own little window. This is the photograph that lit the spark that became this novel. Thank you, Sister Agnes Eugenia.

ABOUT THE AUTHOR

ADRIANA TRIGIANI is the author of fifteen bestsellers, including the blockbuster epic *The Shoemaker's Wife*; the Big Stone Gap series; *Lucia, Lucia*; the Valentine series; the Viola series for young adults; and the bestselling memoir *Don't Sing at the Table*. She is also the award-winning filmmaker of the documentary *Queens of the Big Time*. Trigiani wrote and directed the major motion picture *Big Stone Gap*, based on her debut novel. It was filmed entirely on location in her Virginia hometown, and was released in 2015. She lives in Greenwich Village with her family.